The Big Rock Candy Mountain

WALLACE STEGNER

The Big Rock Candy Mountain

American Century Series
HILL AND WANG · NEW YORK

Library of Congress Catalog Card Number: 57-12439

Reprinted by special arrangement with
Duell, Sloan & Pearce, Inc.
Manufactured in the United States of America

The Big Rock Candy Mountain

I

The train was rocking through wide open country before Elsa was able to put off the misery of leaving and reach out for the freedom and release that were hers now. She tucked her handkerchief away, leaned her shoulder against the dirty pane and watched the telegraph wires dip, and dip, and dip from pole to pole, watched the trees and scattered farms, endless variations of white house, red barn, tufted cornfield, slide smoothly backward. Every mile meant that she was freer.

The car was hot; opened windows along the coach let in an acrid smell of smoke, and as the wind flawed, the trailing plume swept down past her eyes, fogging the trackside. Two men up ahead rose and took off their coats and came back toward the smoker. One of them wore flaming striped suspenders and stared at her. She turned her face to the window. The wires dipped, lifted, dipped, in swift curves like the flight of a swallow. She felt her stomach dipping and lifting with them. The tiny thick locket watch that had been her mother's said eleven o'clock. They must be about thirty miles from home. Except for one visit to relatives in Iowa she had never been so far from home in her life.

By eleven thirty the rocking of the car, the bite of the smoke-smell, had begun to make her sick. Forlornly she tried to brighten herself, sat straighter and stared harder, with a sick simulation of interest, at the country outside. But the wires dipped and lifted; her stomach lifted with every swoop of the wires, and she had to shut her eyes. Her face began to feel stiff, and there was a briny taste in her mouth. She swallowed.

A preliminary spasm made her stand up desperately, her throat locked against the surge of nausea. Staggering, clinging to the seats, she made her way back through the car, looking neither right nor left. There were toilets on trains, she knew, but she had no idea where. At the end of the car, seeing a man come out of a small side door, she made for it. Her hand was on the knob when she read the sign: MEN. Sick shame gripped her. There were separate toilets, then, and she had almost walked into the men's room. The women's must be at the other end. She would have to walk the whole way back past all those people. . . .

A lurch of the car threw her sideways, and her throat muscles locked. In desperate haste she went back between the plush seats, head down, burning with forlorn and miserable shame, the vomit in her very mouth. In the women's room she retched, rose, tidied herself shakily before the smeared mirror, started to go out, and returned to retch again. It was so hot in the little cubicle that perspiration burst through her skin and left her sticky all over. Bathing her face in cold water helped, but then she discovered that there was no towel except a blackened rag. Her handkerchief was back in the seat. All she could do was to wait till her wet face dried.

But the closet was too smothering. Instead of drying, she grew wetter. It was all she could do to stand. In a moment she was on her knees again, her lips wet with bitter gall.

In despair, fearing that at this rate she never would get back to her seat, she washed again and dried her face on the lifted edge of her petticoat. Then back to the middle of the car, past passengers who looked at her, she was sure, with disgust or lurking smiles, until she fell into her seat with a half sob and closed her eyes, feeling defiled and dirty and weak.

People the length of the car were eating. Papers rattled, tin tinkled, and into the stuffy heat came the strong smell of peanut butter. Elsa's stomach rolled, and she gritted her teeth. She was resolving to do a half dozen desperate things rather than go back in that women's room when the train began to slow, the wheels pounded in a gradually lessening tempo, and the conductor poked his head in the door. "Sioux Falls," he said.

Her lunch box under her arm and her telescope in her hand, Elsa followed the crowding passengers out to the step. Her stomach was still queasy, she felt that her face must be green with nausea, and the station platform was strange and busy, but she clinched her mind around the thought of a rest, a stop. On a bench up under the protecting eaves of the station she sat the full hour of the stop-over, letting her stomach gradually settle and her muscles relax. After a long time she opened her shoebox and tentatively nibbled a sandwich. It made her feel better, and she ate another, then a little square of cheese, then a piece of cake. By the time her train was ready she could face the prospect of another three hundred miles.

Afterward she found that the train no longer made her ill. Through the long hot afternoon she sat and watched the immediate trackside flowing straight as a river backward, the horizon revolving in a slow circle. There were few trees now. Somewhere, while she had been sick, they had come to some sort of dividing line. Farms were more scattered, the buildings unpainted, and either ramshackle or staringly new. There were no hills, only a wide bare green-gold plain, pasture and unthrifty-looking cornfields. Once in a while they came to creeks or rivers flowing turgidly in sandy beds between strips of dusty cottonwoods. Mile after mile, hour after hour, past sod shanties with weeds growing green on their roofs, past unpainted shacks and ragged sheds, past windmills and discouraged plantings of saplings, past fields of wheat still meadow-green in the heat, past flocks of crows that flapped heavily off the wires as the train roared by, past herds of nondescript cattle with cowbirds sitting on their hipbones.

The sun went down redly behind a ridge of scattered buttes, throwing into black relief the broken skyline and flushing a low range of hills beyond. Elsa ate from her lunch box, watching the light die and the dark come up out of the ground. When they stopped at a town the elevators loomed high and angular against the darkening sky, and the spout of a watertank outside the window was like the upraised trunk of a huge elephant. A little later, when it was black as a wall outside, the porter came in and lighted the kerosene lamps at the ends of the car. The girl leaned her head against the dark reflecting glass and watched the strange, unknown, lonely country flow past like a banner of darkness starred with tiny ephemeral lights. After a while she slept, and when she woke they were in Fargo.

There was a half hour stop, and she got up to walk on the platform. On her second round through the group of workmen and trucks and strolling passengers, a man lifted his straw hat and smiled, and she stopped in surprise, thinking he must be someone she knew. But he was a total stranger, and the half-bow he made, the uplifted hat, the smirk on his face, put her to flight. She went in and sat down in the station restaurant and ordered a cup of coffee.

After the momentary glad shock of thinking she had met an acquaintance the depression of utter strangeness was on her again, accentuated by the flaring yellow lamps, the tired movements of the waitress, the midnight lackluster actions of the people sitting there, the dusty last-year's calendar on the side wall telling her that it was December 24, 1904. She looked at the smoke-grimed hands and faces of the trainmen eating at the counter, the withered pies and bare hard stools, and through the door at the yellow benches of the waiting room, and the sense of being alone, friendless in a desolate land, rose in her like a sickness, so that she gulped her coffee and went out to the friendlier activity of the platform.

The oppressive darkness crowded in from the far side of the tracks, pushing against the platform lights and the clustered yellow panes of the town. When at last the train started again she sat for a long time staring blankly into the solid black outside, looking past her faintly-mirrored image and thinking of her father and Sarah and home. Her home seemed now very dear, her rebellion childish and petulant; oppressed by her own loneliness, she could understand Sarah's now.

Then she slept again, waking fitfully through an interminable drowsy discomfort until the world outside lightened into color, emerging in flat lines of cloud and horizon and field. At five thirty the conductor came through and shook her, thinking her still asleep. The next stop was Hardanger. She did not remember until she stepped off the train that she had entirely forgotten her uncle's instructions to wire him when she would arrive. And she had forgotten to tip the porter. Hurriedly she felt for her purse and started back, but the train was already moving. The conductor waved from the step and she was alone, with the helpless feeling that everything she had done in getting there had been done wrong.

The country about her was flat as a floor and absolutely treeless. On both sides of the tracks the town sprawled, new, temporary-looking, cut by rutted streets whose borders were a jungle of sweet clover and weeds. Across the roofs of two cottages Elsa could see the square high fronts of stores on what seemed to be the main street. Toward them she started, pulled off balance by the weight of her telescope. As she passed the first cottage a man in his undershirt threw open the door and stood in the sun yawning and stretching and staring at her.

The main street was a river of fine powder between the raised plank sidewalks. On both sides a row of hitching posts stood in vanishing perspective down to the end of the street, which trailed off weakly into open country. As she walked, looking for her uncle's store, Elsa saw with sick certitude that Hardanger was ugly. Frame buildings, false fronts, gaping vacant lots piled with old barrels, boxes, blowing newspapers, ashes. Dust-choked streets and sidewalks that were treacherous to walk on because sometimes the ends of the boards were loose. A general store whose windows were crammed with overalls, pitchforks, gloves, monkey wrenches, spools of barbed wire, guns, boxes of ammunition, ladies' hats. A butcher shop and bakery under the same roof, the windows of both opaque with fly specks. On the first corner a two-story frame hotel, its windows giving her a momentary glimpse of leather chairs and a disconsolate potted palm. A drug store across the street, its sides plastered with advertisements for medicines. Next to that a vacant lot, then a pensioned railroad car set end-to to the street and wearing on its front the legend "Furs bought for cash." Another vacant lot, a store labeled "Gents and Ladies Haberdashery," a billiard hall and bowling alley, and then her uncle's store: "Karl Norgaard, Plain and Fancy Groceries."

But the store was closed. It was only, Elsa discovered by a look at her watch, twenty minutes past six. There was not a soul in the street. She was standing on the sidewalk, clasping and unclasping her fingers to restore the circulation after the weight of the telescope, when a young man came out of the pool hall. He was tall, slim, but heavy in the shoulders. His black hair was parted in the middle and pomaded flat over a forehead dark as an Indian's from the sun. His sleeves were rolled up to expose powerful arms, thick in the wrists and roundly muscled.

"Hello!" he said, staring at her. Elsa flushed. The man had a merry and speculative glint in his eye; his stare bothered her as the smirk of the man at the station in Fargo had.

"You looking for somebody?"

Elsa stooped and picked up the telescope, some notion in her mind that that showed she was leaving in a minute. "I was looking for my uncle, Mr. Norgaard. You don't know where he lives, do you?"

"Sure. Just down around the next corner. You can see it from here." He came toward her with a slightly lurching stride, his shoulders swinging, and pointed to a gray frame house on the first cross street.

"Thank you," Elsa said, and started away.

He followed her. "You his niece? I could tell, though, by that hair."

Her hot, suspicious look made him laugh. "No need to get mad. We all been expecting you."

"I was supposed to wire him," she said. "He didn't know when. . . . Well, thank you for . . ."

"Can I lug that satchel for you?" He kept pace with her, watching her, talking with a hidden burble of laughter in his voice.

"No thanks. I can carry it."

She hurried faster, and he stopped, but all the way to her uncle's house she could feel him watching her, and her mind's eye could see him standing in his shirt sleeves on the sidewalk with the sun on his dark face. It irritated her. There was something fresh about him.

Karl Norgaard was not yet dressed when she knocked. After a moment his red head appeared in an upstairs window.

"Hello, Elsa! I thought you were going to wire me."

She tilted back her head to smile at him, feeling suddenly very tired and hungry and soiled. "I forgot, Uncle Karl. Can I come in anyway?"

"You bet you," he said. "Be down in a minute."

In a minute the door opened and he was grinning at her, his pink round face so full of welcome that she found herself laughing weakly aloud. *"Velkommen!"* he said. *"Velkommen,* Elsa."

Elsa unwound her scarf from her hat and said, "Thanks, Uncle Karl. It's nice to be here at last."

"You came in a hurry," Karl said. He stood in his felt pantofles and regarded her with shrewd eyes. "How's everybody at home?"

"Fine. Everybody's fine. But I had to come in a hurry, Uncle Karl. I couldn't stay there a minute longer."

Karl rubbed one apple cheek. "Well, you're young. *Herregud,* the fool things you do when you're young." He grabbed her by the arm. "Well, come in, come in. Come on upstairs. Want to wash your face? Take a bath? There's a tub in the cellarway. I'll heat some water."

"Let me get my breath first," she said. "Can I put this bag somewhere?"

He showed her her room, led her into the other two upstairs rooms, one his own bedroom, one his office. "You might as well learn right away to leave the office alone," he said. "I can't find anything as it is."

"How about your bedroom? Can you sleep if I take off those dirty old sheets and put some clean ones on?"

"It was changed two weeks ago," Karl said. "That's pretty good for an old batch." He frowned. "Maybe I made a mistake letting you come. You get so neat a man can't stand you and I'll send you home."

"I'll be good," she said. "I'll be as sloppy as you want, but don't send me home." She took off her hat and lifted her hair with her fingers to ease its weight. "You go get a fire going and I'll get your breakfast."

After breakfast he went off to the store. In spite of his instructions to go to bed, she tidied up, swept, changed the beds and laid out a washing for the next day, cleaned up the sardine cans and cracker boxes and cheese rinds from the kitchen. The curtains, she decided, had not been washed since the flood, and took them down to add them to the washing. Then she went up to her room and unpacked. By the time she had things put away, the telescope stuck into the attic, and the daguerreotype of her mother set up on the dresser, she began to feel settled and permanent. The mere fact of working in this house made it her own, her clothes hanging in the wardrobe gave her proprietorship.

But when she sat on the bed and looked at the dark, thin-faced woman who had been her mother, she felt herself go slowly, weakly sick with the old anger. Staring at the picture, rubbing her knuckles back and forth across her lips and teeth, she thought how her mother too had run away from home, younger than Elsa herself, no more than seventeen, and after three days let her parents know that she had married the carpenter on their place at Voss, in Norway. She risked everything for him, and got only him: he was below her, they never took her back. Within six months she was on her way to America, where for a life she had the backbreaking work of a Minnesota farm—she who had never been used to working at all. It was a short life; Elsa was fifteen when her mother died worn out at thirty-four, and it was Elsa who took up the work her mother had let go. She had father, sister, brother, to take care of; the school she had dropped out of at fourteen to nurse her mother saw her no more. And then less than three years after that lingering death they had all had to watch too closely, Nels Norgaard announced he . . .

Elsa shut her eyes down hard on the smart of tears. It isn't only that Sarah is twenty years younger than he is, she said silently to the empty, strange room. It's that she was supposed to be my best friend.

Counting up what she had left behind her forever, she saw them all as if their faces were propped on the dresser beside her mother's daguerreotype: her father's stern long-cheeked face slashed across by the guardsman's mustache, his eyes merely veiled, unreadable; Sarah in the posture she had been reduced to by Elsa's anger and scorn—stooped over, weeping, with a slack mouth and flooded gray eyes that said pity me, pity me; Erling's corkscrew red curls and red farm-boy's face emerging from the blackened towel by the kitchen cistern pump; Kristin's awed, aghast, pretty face in the bedroom when she found Elsa packing, the affected pompadour and the vain ribbons, and the whispering voice full of love, kinder than spoiled little sister had ever sounded: "Won't you take that hat I made last week? You could wear it on the train. It'd look lovely with your hair—it's green,"—and then the tempest of tears.

She knew already that she would miss them more than she had ever thought possible; she ached for them this minute, she could even have been respectful to her father and pleasant to Sarah. Maybe . . . and yet what else could she have done?

From the dresser the daguerreotype looked back at her calmly, the lips compressed. It was not a good likeness, and like all pictures of the dead it had petrified the memory of the living, so that every recollection Elsa had of her mother was now limited by this stern and pinched expression. Her mother had been ill when the picture was taken. Perhaps for that reason, perhaps because of the narrowing of memory to fit the one picture she had, Elsa had always felt the daguerreotype to be a portrait of martyrdom.

"Mor," she said in Norwegian, groping for some contact or reassurance. "Mom . . ."

Out the window she saw a summer whirlwind spinning across the level fields beyond the flanks of the town. The funnel of dust lifted, dropped again, whirled forward across a road, stopped and spun, moved off in jerky rushes like a top spinning on an irregular surface. It hit a mound of dumped refuse, and tin cans rolled, papers sailed flatly, slid back groundward. Beyond the whirlwind was the prairie running smoothly, the planed horizon broken by two far homesteads, ships on the calm green-bronze sea; and far beyond, the glitter from the moving blades of a windmill.

It was very big; she felt she could see a long way, even into the future, and she felt how the world rolled under her. After she had watched the summer plains for a long time, and the smarting under her lids had passed, a meadowlark sang sharp and pure from a fencepost, and she began to think that the future into which this new world of her choosing moved with her could hardly be unfriendly, could hardly be anything but good.

2

"Elsa," Karl Norgaard said, "how'd you like to go to a ballgame?"

He was sitting at the kitchen table opening a jar of *gamelost* with a screwdriver. Elsa turned from the stove.

"Are you going?"

"They couldn't play without me," Karl said. "I've closed the store for every ballgame in fifteen years."

"Sure," she said. "I'd love to."

He bore down with the screwdriver, prying at the lid. The blade slipped, and he leaped up with a startled howl. *"Fand slyta!"* he said. He shook his fingers, and the blood welling from his gouged palm spattered on the floor. *"Heste lort!"* Karl said, almost jumping up and down. For a full minute he swore savagely in Norwegian, looked at Elsa, bent his lips into a baffled, half-humorous smirk, and looked back at his hand.

She came running with the iodine bottle and soused the wound. Karl swore again. "Shame on you," she said.

"Well, hell," Karl said. He looked at the deep gouge in his palm and shook his head incredulously. "You haven't got any business knowing what I said," he said. "That's the trouble, having a Norske girl around."

Elsa giggled. "Anyway you sounded good and mad," she said. "Norwegian swearing sounds ten times worse than English, somehow. It's just like ripping canvas."

"I guess you'd swear too," he said. "Dug my whole damn hand out."

"If there was any of that smelly old cheese on the screwdriver you'll be infected sure," Elsa said. She tore a strip off a clean cloth and started bandaging.

"You mean you don't like *gamelost?*"

Elsa made a face. "Erling put some on my knife once, just stuck the knife in the jar and then laid it beside my plate, and I was sick for two hours."

"You're a traitor," Karl said. "You don't like *ludefisk* either."

"No, nor herrings."

He shook his pink head over her. "But you like ballgames?"

"Ballgames are all right."

"Vell, you batter like dem," Karl said. "You yoost batter like dem."

He went out to the store muttering, shouting back that she yoost batter be raddy at two o'clock, or a little before, and she saw him stomping through the sweet clover crosslots to the store, holding his gouged hand tenderly against his stomach.

It was a blistering day. The ground, when they walked out at two o'clock, was dry and baked, with cracks splitting through the yellow grass of the yard. What had once been a mud puddle in the road was caked into a hundred cupped plates laid together like a Chinese puzzle. Elsa picked one up; it took all the strength of her fingers to break it. Around them the sweet clover, just drying into clusters of seeds, was bone-stiff and dusty. West of the town three whirlwinds raced and dipped and lifted over the flats.

They walked past the two grain elevators, across the cindery, fire-bitten tracks. On the other side a tier of crude seats was already well filled. Buggies lined the edge of the field, crowded with women under big parasols of fringed canvas faded from the fierce sun. There was a persistent flash of paper fans. A booth wound with red, white, and blue bunting was doing a land-office business in lemonade and pop and ice cream. There were bottles and papers littered along the weedy edge of the diamond.

Standing below the plank seats, Elsa felt people's eyes on her. Men spoke to Karl, and he grinned, squinting up into the sun, saying, "Hello Gus, hello George, hello. Ought to be a hot game."

"We got it on ice," somebody said, and there was a laugh.

Feeling conspicuous, Elsa stood silently under her big hat while her uncle picked out a place in the stands. Then someone was calling from a buggy over on the first base line: "Come on over here. You'll melt down to grease in that stand."

"Ah," Karl said. "There's Helm. That'll be better."

The woman who had called beckoned. Elsa saw a broad, dark face, a wide hat, a shapeless body in a loud, intolerably hot-looking dress, a cluster of children. Then they were at the wheel of the buggy, and Karl was saying, "This is Helm, Elsa. Never call her Mrs. Helm or she'll burst a blood vessel."

Grinning with bad teeth, Helm stuck down a broad hand, her dark eyes running over every detail of the girl's hair, dress, face. At the first clutch of her hand Elsa thought her knuckles would crumble. She flushed, grew angry, and squeezed back with all her strength until she felt her knuckles slip back into line and the broad palm in hers begin to give. For an instant more they gripped each other, until Helm opened eyes and mouth in astonishment.

"My God!" she said loudly. "You're strong as a horse. Where'd you get it?"

"Milking cows," Elsa said sweetly. Give me another chance and I'll squeeze your fingernails off, she thought. She wished Karl hadn't brought her over here.

"Come on up," Helm said. She stuck down her hand again, and in one mighty heave hauled the girl up beside her, where she inspected her again, closely, with brown shining eyes.

"You ain't so light, either. How much do you weigh?"

"I don't know. A hundred and thirty or thirty-five."

"I got you by a hundred pounds, honey," Helm said. She rumbled with laughter, and her thick fingers pinched experimentally at Elsa's arm. "You don't dint easy, either. First off, I had you pegged for one of these *ladies* with fainting spells and weak chests."

Jammed uncomfortably close to Helm's radiating bulk, Elsa looked around into the box of the democrat, at the clot of children there. Helm caught her looking. "Ain't that a brood for you? They all look like their granpa. He was a Sioux Indian."

"Are you?" Elsa said.

"Half," Helm said. "The best half, if there's any choice." She picked at a tooth with her fingernail, her eyes warm behind the broad hand. "Their old man was a good-for-nothing," she said. "After he got all these he run off and left me with a shape like a bale-a hay. Good riddance to bad rubbish." She got whatever she was digging for and took her hand away. "You like baseball?"

"Very much," Elsa said stiffly. She didn't know what to make of this great vulgar woman, but Karl, sprawling on the grass beside the buggy, must have thought she was all right or he wouldn't have come to sit with her.

"This ought-a be a good game," Helm said. "We got a team, last few years. Got a catcher used to play in the Three-Eye League."

"Oh?"

"You watch him. He's a one. Bo Mason's his name."

"He runs the bowling alley next to my store," Karl said. "If he didn't have a trick knee he'd be in the big leagues."

"Oh!" Elsa said. "I think I met him the morning I came. Is he dark, sort of slim—looks slimmer than he really is?"

"That's him," Helm said. "Parts his hair in the middle and a hide like shoe leather."

A minute later she pointed. "In the blue shirt," she said. Elsa looked, and saw the young man of that first morning. As he said something to a companion his teeth were very white in his almost negroid face. She wondered how he got so dark running a bowling alley. That would keep him inside, out of the sun, she would think. And she didn't know whether she liked his looks or not. There was a kind of rolling swagger in his walk, and as the home team pegged the ball around the infield he kept making bright remarks. A little of the smart alec in him.

But he was as good as they said he was. In the very first inning he caught an Oasis man trying to steal second, caught him by three feet with a perfect ankle-high peg. After that the opposing baserunners took short leads and went down only with the crack of the bat. When he came up to bat the first time, Mason was out on a screaming grass-cutter that the first baseman tried in vain to get out of the way of, but in the fifth he drove in two runs with a thunderous triple that chased the centerfielder far back in the wild mustard. Helm, pounding Elsa on the back, announced three times that it would have been a homer sure except for that trick knee.

In the seventh inning the score was tied, eight to eight. The first two Oasis hitters were easy outs. The next one was a slugger. The stocky youngster on the mound took his time, mopping his neck with a bandanna between pitches. Squatting on his hams behind the plate, Bo Mason talked it up. Easy out, easy out! Give him the old dark one.

The pitcher wound up and threw. Strike! The hitter swung so

hard he had to put the end of his bat down to keep from falling. "You need a little oil on your hinges, son," Mason told him, and the stands hooted. Next pitch, ball. Next one, ball again. Mason's soothing voice went out over the infield. "All right, boy. Can't hit what he can't see. Right down the old alley. Let him swing like a shutter in a cyclone. Feed it to him, he's got a glass eye."

The next pitch was grooved, and the Oasis slugger rode it deep into left field. The fielder lost it in the sun, and the runner went down to second, his feet pumping quick explosions in the dust. A strained look showed him the fielder still chasing the rolling ball, and he legged it for third, where the players on the sidelines waved him frantically home.

Mason, his teeth showing in his dark face, waited spraddle-legged in front of home plate. The relay from the short stop reached him two steps ahead of the runner, who swerved, skidded, and scrambled back for third. He was in the box. The crowd was on its feet, yelling, as Mason chased him carefully back, holding the throw. He faked, then threw, and the runner reversed and tore for home again. But the ball was there before him, and the catcher blocked the baseline. The Oasis man put his head down and butted through under Mason's ribs, and Mason, as he was plowed out of the path, lifted the ball and tagged him, hard, on the top of his bare head.

The sound of ball on skull cracked in the heat, and the grandstand let go a long, shivering "Ahhhhhhhhhh!" This might mean a fight. They stood higher in the stands, eyes joyful and faces expectant. "Atta boy, Bo!" they said. "Atsy old way to slow him down!"

Karl Norgaard was standing by the buggy wheel, his pinkish hair damp. He was concentrating on the figure of the Oasis man, slowly pushing himself up from the dust with his flat palms. Karl's voice rose with him in the expectant hush, thin, tremulous, singsong: "Batter we gat a doctor. Ay tank he ban sunstruck."

The stands exploded in mirth that rode the thick hot air and echoed off the elevators. The Oasis man scowled, looking at Mason, standing just off the baseline with the ball in his hand. Contemptuously Mason pulled off his mitt and turned his back, walking over to the Hardanger bench. With his head down the Oasis man started after him, pursued by the hoots of the spectators, who began to jump down from the lower tiers to get in on the scrap. But other Oasis players grabbed their fellow's elbows and held him while he stood in the clover, fists balled, swearing. Then abruptly he jerked himself loose and ran back into centerfield, and the crowd settled back.

After that there wasn't much to the game. Hardanger batted

around in the eighth; the final score was sixteen to nine. After the game Helm yelled until Bo Mason came over, and as he stood talking at the buggy wheel Elsa forgot her dislike for his smart alec streak. He was the best player there, there was no question. But his grin embarrassed her when they were introduced, and she sat back in the hot sweaty alley between Helm and the rail and let the others talk.

"What were you trying to do, kill that guy?" Karl said.

Mason laughed. "He ran me down, didn't he? He wants to play rough I can play rough too."

"I bet he can't get his hat on for a week," Helm said. "How about some beer? You look hot, Bo."

"You could fry eggs on me," Mason said. "Sure. Over at your place?"

Elsa, sitting uncertainly beside Helm, caught her uncle's grin. "You want to come along, Elsa?"

The girl flushed and laughed. "I don't drink beer," she said, and was furious at how squeaky her voice sounded. They laughed at her, and Helm patted her on the back with a hand like a leg of lamb. "You don't have to, honey," she said. "We c'n take care of that."

3

In the hot morning hush Elsa walked down the plank sidewalk toward her uncle's store. There wasn't enough housework to keep her busy more than a few hours a day, even on Mondays, when she washed, and Saturdays, when she baked. It was a problem to know what to do with her time. Unlike her father, Karl did not have many books around, and though he had given her money to subscribe to the *Ladies' Home Journal,* the first number hadn't come yet.

She could have called on Helm, but the prospect was still a little terrifying. As she thought over that afternoon with the beer drinkers she felt a little weak. They had all got a little tipsy, they had laughed uproariously, they had told jokes that she knew weren't quite clean, and she had just pretended not to hear. Before long, if she didn't watch out, she wouldn't know what was respectable and what wasn't. Fiddlesticks, she said. What was wrong about it? But she didn't quite dare call on Helm.

In the window of the hotel she caught sight of her reflection, and was pleased. The white dress, perfectly ironed, not yet wilted by the heat; the red hair puffed like a crown in front; the round, erect figure, slim in the waist, full breasted. When she walked past three young men lounging on the sidewalk she stepped self-consciously. Feeling their eyes on her, she hurried a little in spite of herself. She was ten steps past when she heard the low whistle and the voice: "Oh you kid!"

She remembered the time she had bloodied George Moe's nose for him when he got smart about her hair. Men were just the same. They'd say smart alec things and if you turned on them, even if you bloodied their noses, they'd laugh even more. But she would have liked to say something sharp to that loafer. Oh you kid! The smart alecs.

But anyway, the next window told her, she looked nice, cool as a cloud.

In front of her uncle's store she almost ran into Bo Mason, bareheaded, his pomaded hair sleek as a blackbird's breast. As he looked at her his eyes were sleepy, the full upper lids making them narrower than they really were. His voice was slow and warm. "Hellooo!"

"Hello."

"Going somewhere?"

"No. Just looking around."

"Seeing the city?" He lifted his head to laugh, and she saw the corded strength of his neck. He pointed down the street to the weed-grown flats dwindling off into dump ground and summer fallow. "You must take a stroll in the park," he said. "Five thousand acres of cool greenery. This is one of the show towns of Dakota. Prosperous! Did you see that magnificent hotel on the corner as you came by? Gilded luxury, every chamber in it, the fulfilled dream of one of Hardanger's most public-spirited citizens."

Elsa was a little astonished. She said demurely, "Very imposing. Bath in every room?"

"Some rooms two, so a man and his wife can both be clean same time."

"Must take a lot of water."

"Oh, they've got water to burn. Gigantic well just outside, clean pure alkali water, no more than seven dead cats in it at any time."

"You don't sound as if you liked the hotel much."

"I love it," he said. "I love it so much I live there. I love this whole town. Just the spot for an ambitious young man to make his fortune."

Curiosity uncoiled itself and stretched. She took a peek at the swinging doors behind him. Maybe he wasn't doing so well in his place. Bowling alley, was it? All she could see was a dark stretch of bar and two dim yellow lamps in wall brackets. Into the bright hot sunlight came the jaded click of pool balls.

"What're you doing, really?" Bo said.

"Nothing. I thought I might help Uncle Karl in the store."

"Let's go have a soda."

Elsa hesitated, her eyes on the darkly polished bar inside. It looked almost like a saloon, but she knew saloons were prohibited in North Dakota. Her curiosity rose on tiptoe, peering. "Why, that'd be nice," she said.

Instead of turning into his own place, he took her arm and led her down to the corner. "Why can't we have it in your place?" she said. "Then you wouldn't have to pay for it."

His look was amused. "You want to go in my place?"

"Why not?"

"Naw," he said, and moved her along. "My place is a billiard hell. It's a man's joint. You'd scare away my two customers."

"But you sell drinks, though, soft drinks?"

"Soft enough. But Joe down here makes better sodas."

She wondered if he might be running an illegal saloon. That ought, according to what the Reverend Jacobsen had always said, to make him one of the undesirable element. Looking at him again, curiously, she saw only that he looked clean, brown, athletic. She didn't ever recall seeing a man who looked so clean. Either the respectability she had been brought up in was narrow, or Bo Mason wasn't one of the bad element. But he drank beer, and told stories that weren't always quite nice. But so did her uncle, and he was respectable. And so did Helm, and Helm was a woman.

Sitting at the sticky marble slab of counter sipping sodas, they laughed a great deal and gurgled through the newfangled straws. By the time she had left him to go home she had decided that he couldn't possibly be one of the bad element, in spite of his billiard hell. The bad element were distinguishable by their evil faces, their foul mouths, their desire to trample everything decent and clean underfoot. Bo Mason wasn't anything like that. He was cleaner than anything. Even while he stood on the sidewalk just before she left he was trimming his nails with his pocket knife. She noticed too how cleanly the blade cut the thick soft nail, and she was enough a farm girl to respect a man who kept his tools sharp. Moreover, he had been all over, worked at a dozen different things, talked easily about Chicago and Milwaukee and Minneapolis, the places that had been golden towers on her horizons for eighteen years.

The thought of what her father might say if he knew she had had a soda with a man who ran a pool hall made her almost laugh aloud. Even if he ran an undercover saloon, blind pigs they called them, it didn't make any difference. She was a grown woman, and could have sodas with anyone she chose. If she found a saloon-keeper who was clean, and interesting, and pleasant, she would have a soda with him any time she pleased. The sidewalk ended and she jolted herself stepping unexpectedly down.

As she passed Helm's yard she heard the racket, the shrill, snapping snarl of a dog, Helm's voice swearing, the sudden yipe of a mongrel hurt. "Now, God damn it, will you lay still?" she heard Helm say. The dog yiped again, and as Elsa stopped at the gate its voice went up in a high wail.

She must be killing it, Elsa thought. She found herself at the side of the house, looked around the corner. In the corner of the fence Helm was kneeling. Her wide stern loomed like the gable of a barn. Then she rose, grabbed a handful of dry grass, stood back. The moment the pressure was off him the dog tucked his tail and hiked. Helm, starting back toward the kitchen, saw Elsa and scowled, red-faced. "Those sonabitching kids!" she said.

The Reverend Jacobsen, Elsa's mind said, would have told anyone to walk away from language like that. But she stayed where she was. "What was the matter?" she said.

"They're allus doing something like that," Helm said. "Tying cans to dogs' tails, or tying cats' tails together and throwing them over a clothesline, or catching frogs and blowing them so full of air they can't swim. I catch any of them I'll lay into 'em, I don't care who they are."

"What did they do?" Elsa said.

"First time I ever see this one," Helm said. "It's a dirty damn trick, even on a cur dog. They fed this mutt a ball of string, wrapped up in meat or something, I guess, and before he knows it he's trailing yards of it out behind, and ever'body stepping on it fit to pull his guts out. Ain't that a dirty trick, now?"

Elsa tried to keep her eyes up. She felt the slow red coming into her face. She ought to have gone right on by, then she wouldn't have got trapped like this. Helm, watching her with shining eyes, began to smile.

"Why honey, I believe that shocked you!"

"I . . . think it's an awful dirty trick," Elsa said.

"I forgot you was a lady," Helm said. "I didn't aim to shock you. First minute I talked to you I knew you was a lady, a natural-born lady, not one of these dames with studhorse airs. I wouldn't want to shock you any time. But I couldn't let that hound run around that way, could I?"

"No," Elsa said. "I think . . . you're very kind . . ." She escaped, feeling almost as if she were going to cry, because Helm was kind, that was a kindhearted thing to do, and all the bad language and vulgarity that went with it couldn't make it any less kind. She went about getting lunch feeling as if a bed were unmade in her mind.

Not all the people she met were as hard to assimilate as Helm and Bo Mason. Most of them she met at Helm's house, and most of them were commonplace enough. Gus Sprague, a little bandy-legged carpenter, was ordinary and pleasant; so was his wife, as little and henlike and bandy-legged as Gus. And the elevator man, Bill Conzett, was nice too. Bill's belt cut so low under his pendant stomach that small boys were always following him around waiting for his pants to fall off. There was a little group of Norwegians who sometimes came around, but they stuck together and were more pious than the rest, a little more like Indian Falls. Karl was the only Norske who seemed to have left the old country completely behind.

None of those people was disturbingly new. But Jud Chain and Eva Alsop were.

Jud Chain was a professional gambler and Bo Mason's partner. Knowing that before she met him, Elsa expected almost anything—a sinister, pale, diabolic creature with burning night-time eyes was what her anticipation finally resolved itself into. But the man she met one afternoon in Helm's cluttered parlor was a handsome blond giant, six feet three or four inches tall, abnormally wide in the shoulders. The only part of him that matched her imaginings was his pallor, and even that was not the evil midnight thing she had expected. She shook his hand in confusion, this beautifully groomed, sleek, white-handed gentleman. His smile was friendly, his eyes gentle, his manners impeccable. When he moved around bringing her a cup of coffee or pulling up a chair so that they could talk more comfortably, he moved with easy grace, and when he bent over to listen to something she was saying she smelled the bay rum on his pocket handkerchief.

He was, like Bo Mason, fascinating in a way no man in her life had ever been fascinating before. He had travelled around even more than Bo, even to Cuba and South America. He said he had been working with Bo for three years now, and when she said she hadn't seen him around town his eyes smiled. His work, he explained, kept him up all night sometimes. He was generally asleep in the daytime.

So there he was, her amazed mind said. A card sharp, another, like Bo, from the class of people all the good people of Indian Falls would consider outside the pale. Yet he was handsome, almost as imposing physically as Bo, though more willowy and fragile-looking in spite of his wide shoulders. His hands were immense, flat, slabby, with wide palms and long fingers, the nails trimmed round. She could imagine how deftly he could handle cards. A gambler, a sharper, yet more gentlemanly, deferential, polite, than anybody she had ever met. She spilled coffee on her dress at the thought of herself sitting next to this dangerous man and talking as if she had known him forever. Instantly the bay rum scented handkerchief was out, his languid ease galvanized into careful helpfulness. If she had spilled anything at home, among the men she knew, they would have stared at her with their hands on their knees and done nothing. Jud Chain could make any woman think she was both fragile and charming.

A few days later she met Eva Alsop, and that was another sort of experience. Small, doll-like, blonde, she looked the part of the Bad Woman. Her laugh was too loud, and when she was serious her mouth had a weary and petulant droop. Once in a while she placed her hand on her side, and if anyone caught her doing it she looked up with a wan, brave smile.

To her Jud Chain was as deferential as he was to Elsa, but even Elsa's inexperience detected a difference, a certain familiarity, a subtle knowingness in the way Eva looked at him, and when Jud rose to go that afternoon, saying he had business to attend to, Elsa saw the wizened petulance on Eva's mouth—a very red mouth, redder than she had ever seen a mouth before. Jud bent elegantly over her, said something the others could not hear, but Eva's eyes, as she watched him take his hat and leave, were cold.

Helm talked about her afterward. Eva Milksop, she called her. "She's a little snivelling cheap slut," Helm said. "Common as manure, making out she's the grandest lady you ever seen. Paints her face and bleaches her hair and dolls herself up like Mrs. Astor's plush horse. She makes my belly ache, her and her pains."

"Well, maybe she is sick," Elsa said.

"How would you act if you had a pain?" Helm said. "Would you go around whining and holding your belly and making ever'body feel like a sonofabitch if he didn't run right out for the hot water bottle?"

"I guess. . ."

"You damn betcha you wouldn't. You'd try to grin if you had the God-awfulest belly ache in the world. You're two different kinds of people, honey. Don't go wasting sympathy on that canary-legged little slut."

"There must be some good in her," Elsa said. "Anybody's got some good in him."

"There's about as much good in her as there is in my backside," Helm said. "And that's mainly lard. You see her shrivel up and get mean when Jud had to go?"
"Yes. I wondered."
"I wouldn't bother even to wonder, honey," Helm said. "She ain't worth it."
"Is she in love with him?"
Stacking the coffee cups, Helen made a prissy face. "If she ever decides to hook up with Jud she'll decide it when Jud makes a killing. She ain't going into no nest without a lot of feathers in it."
"Well," Elsa said. "Live and learn. I never knew there were so many kinds of people."
Helm stood with her legs planted, as if she were going to give a lecture. She was. "If you're the right kind yourself, you'll find the right kind," she said. "There's not many people'll do anything for you but kick you when you're down. I aim to save my kicks for the butter-butts and give anybody that's down a hand instead of a foot."
"Maybe Eva's down."
"She's one of the butter-butts," Helm said. "I like the kind of people that don't play they're something they ain't. I'm a sucker, honey. Don't try to learn anything from me. A fella that's down on his luck, or some simple guy that the world is kicking around, or somebody that's straight-out what he is so I don't have to keep jumping around to know what I'm dealing with, those are my kind of folks. Every hobo that ever hit this town was on my back step in half an hour." She snorted, folding freshly ironed clothes into a basket. "Jus' a softy!" she said.
She looked up under her eyebrows, still stooping. "You lonesome for home, honey?"
"Sometimes," Elsa said. "I miss the kids. They were a pest when I had to take care of them, but I miss them just the same. I miss Pa too, I guess, only he's married again, and everything."
"Married a girl a lot younger, didn't he?"
"My best friend," Elsa said. She couldn't even yet mention that without being angry and hurt.
"Yeah," Helm said. "It's funny. When you're a kid something like that can smell like a carcass, and after you get older it don't seem so bad. You liked your ma a lot, didn't you?"
"I took care of her a long time," Elsa said. "That was what made me so mad. I don't think he ever went to her grave, even. I went just before I left and it was all overgrown with weeds, right when he was going around with Sarah."
Helm sighed wheezily, stuck a thumb down inside the chafing

edge of her corset and wriggled a fold of skin into place. "You're all right, honey," she said. "You stick by the things you love. Nobody can hurt you if you stick with what you know is right. They can't hurt what's inside you."

4

"That Bo Mason gets away with murder," Elsa said. "Why don't people tell him where to head in at?"

"Oh, that's just Bo," Karl said. "If it was anybody else you'd knock his head off."

"That doesn't excuse him," she said. "He was just plain mean to Eva."

"I guess Eva sort of has it coming," he said, and steered his way up the stairs to bed.

Elsa tidied up the downstairs, thinking of the way Bo had acted. The way he'd said to Eva, "For God's sake come down off your high horse and quit acting like the Duchess of Dakota. Can't you walk without looking like Dan Patch in hobbles?" The way he caught up everything anyone said all evening and turned it back, with a sting in it. The way he had sat, while Helm and Eva and Karl and Jud were playing whist, and bullied her for an hour and a half because she didn't even know how to play casino. How would she know how to play casino, when her father had never even allowed a deck of cards in the house?

She had seen him that way once before, over at Helm's, and she suspected that he was mad about the way his bowling alley was doing. Sometimes he seemed restless and dissatisfied. When he got to thinking about that too long, she supposed, it brought on one of these black and contrary moods. Or maybe it might have been only something someone had said, something he took it into his head to be mad about. He was as vain as a boastful little boy. But that didn't excuse his going through a whole evening the way he had, smiling as if he had a knife ready to stab somebody, jumping from bald insults to compliments as suave as butter that were more insulting than the insults.

He was a hard man to understand, she thought as she went upstairs with the lamp. You never knew how you'd find him. But why should she worry herself about the way he acted? Let him go on being moody and sardonic and insulting.

Yet she found herself, later, asking people about him—Karl, Helm, even Jud Chain. How could a man be so many contrary things at once? How, for instance, could anyone have grown up and never even been inside a church? He said he hadn't. Yet in a good mood he could be so very pleasant and thoughtful. There was a kind of warmth that radiated from him when he wanted to let it. And how had he come to be so good at everything he did? He was the best ball player in town. Helm assured her that he was also the best shot, the best bowler, the best pool player, and one of the two best skaters.

"But where did he come from?" Elsa asked. "What's he doing out here?"

"He's from Illinois," Helm said. "Rock River. His old man wasn't much good, I guess. Just let his family run loose. I've heard him talk about it once or twice, just odds and ends of things."

That was all Elsa got, odds and ends, scraps that could be pieced together into a skeleton biography. She did not admit to herself, did not even think about, the unusual eagerness she had to reconstruct that biography. She did not say to herself that he was the most masterful, dominating, contradictory, and unusual man she had ever met, but she picked up everything she heard, nevertheless, and she pumped Bo himself when he came over in the evening to sit on the steps and talk.

When Fred Mason came home to Illinois from the war in 1865 he had left an arm somewhere in a field hospital near Vicksburg, and most of his disposition in the Andersonville prison. In the ten years after his arrival he successively married a Pennsylvania Dutch girl of broad dimensions, begot seven children, and became the nucleus and chief yarn-spinner of the livery stable crowd.

For money he depended on his pension and a few scattered odd jobs. Working for anyone else tired him; orders were more than his irascible individualism would stand. "Nobody in my family ever took orders from anybody," he used to say. "My pap come into this state when she was nothin' but oak and Indians, and he never took no orders from any man. Neither did his pap, or his pap's pap. I'm the on'y one ever did, and I on'y did in the army. And I don't take no more."

He spent his days lounging at the stable talking bird dogs and battles. Once in a while he took over a job in a burst of ambition to augment his pension, because, though he was not especially a drinking man, he loved to eat, and his shapeless and rather sullen hausfrau couldn't make the pension stretch to cover much more than sowbelly and eggs. Often, too, he sat in the sun with the fecund stable smell about him and a coach dog dozing among the flies, and generated great schemes. He invented, on paper or in drawings sketched in the dust with a twig, all sorts of gadgets: revolvers with twelve chambers, a telescopic ramrod that could be carried in the vest pocket, a folding bootjack, an artificial arm that could be moved by a complicated system of wires and pulleys, with a miniature ice tongs for a hand. He even went to work and whittled out the arm, laboriously fitted it with pulleys and strung the wires, but when he had a fellow-loafer strap it on him, and tried it out before the eyes of his crowd, he got tangled up and bit himself in the ribs with the ice tongs. In a fury he threw the whole contraption in the Rock River.

His six boys and one girl grew up untended in the shambling old frame house his wife had brought him as dowry. The children learned early to avoid their father, for his one hand was quick at back-handed slaps, and his temper was hair-trigger. A crying or teasing or noisy child set him mad with irritation; he was fond of telling what a damned pest kids were—his especially, the damnedest pack of mongrels ever whelped.

But if they were mongrels, they had the mongrel's knack of making his own way. Any one of them above the age of six could have lived on what he could catch or steal. They grew like savages, black-haired, husky, broad-faced children with their mother's German features and their father's long bones. Most of their time in summer they spent roaming the wilderness of brushy woods along the Rock River, fishing, robbing garden patches, shooting rabbits and grouse with slingshots or whatever weapon they could lay hands on.

By the time the youngest boy, Harry, was eight years old, they all had guns. One by one, mysteriously, the firearms came. Fred Mason swore they had been stolen, and stamped around the house whenever a new gun appeared, but he could never beat a confession out of any of the boys. Elmer had worked for a farmer and made the money for his. George had found his lying right out in the open on a bridge rail, and had waited all day to see if anyone would come and claim it, but nobody did. Harry had been given his by a woodchopper up along the river. And so on.

Probably the boys felt that guns were a necessity, in order to provide food. The chances were two to one that any time they came home for a meal they would be cornered and whipped for something, if not by their father then by their mother, who sometimes flew into insane rages and drove even her hair-trigger husband from the house. So the boys stayed away, at least in summer, and lived on the fish and rabbits and corn and vegetables and watermelons of their expeditions. Sometimes they stayed out in the woods for days at a time.

In winter there was nothing much to do except go to school. It was a way of avoiding the domestic uproar, and it was a fairly painless way of satisfying parental demands. "My kids gonna have an eddication," Fred Mason was fond of saying. "They're gonna learn to read and write and figger if I have to beat it into them with a wagon tongue."

But one by one the boys dropped out, found jobs, wandered away. None of them, except Harry, remained in school beyond the fifth grade. Harry stayed till the eighth, partly because he was less indocile than his brothers, partly because he was brighter.

He was an intractable enough pupil, and the cause of much academic grief, but his intelligence and his sense of self-preservation were sharp enough to tell him when to stop, and once in a while he got a chance to outface his teacher with some monumental feat of brains.

His teacher quit picking on him, and gave him his unruly head, when Harry was in the sixth grade. From that day on she looked upon him with something like awe, tinctured with mild horror. They were reading McGuffey's Second Reader. For three or four weeks Harry slaved like a malicious little demon, reading every selection, prose and poetry, over and over until he knew almost the whole book by heart. The class, meanwhile, had spelled its way through sixty or seventy pages. Harry had ceased utterly to pay attention in reading class, loafed ostentatiously at his bench, whittled his initials, honked weirdly when the teacher's back was turned and then played he had been blowing his nose, pulled the girls' braids, pinked his fellows with a peashooter, and raised so much uproar that he was hauled up into the corner and a dunce cap set on his head. From there he grinned and made faces and commented audibly on the reading performances of the others.

The teacher was in a tooth-gnashing fury. She had tried whipping before: he was too tough to hurt. Sending him home would just be giving him a chance to go out in the woods and have some fun. So now, smelling a way of humiliating him (the only way he could be hurt), she slapped her ruler down on the desk and walked over to him with a wicked and wintry smile. "Of course, Harry," she said, "you're too brilliant to need any training in reading. But suppose—just suppose, now—you take your book and read to us for the rest of the afternoon, *pronouncing every word!* We'll let geography go, just for the pleasure of listening to you. Go on down to your desk and get your reader."

The class snickered. Harry grinned, shaking his head. "I don't need any book," he said.

"I suppose you know it all by heart!"

"I've read it over. When you're smart that's all it takes."

"All *right!*" she squealed, so outraged at his impudence that her voice cracked. "You can start right at the beginning." With her back stiff and her face tomato red, she marched back to her desk and sat down, her book open before her, ready to pounce on his slightest mistake.

At four o'clock she reluctantly turned him and the rest of the class loose. He had reached page ninety-two with only a few minor errors.

Harry Mason had good reason to hate his father, and he took advantage of his reasons. By the time the boy was fourteen he was big for his age and hard as flint from an active life of hunting and sports. Yet the beatings that had soured his childhood went on as if he were still a child. All the boys except Elmer had left, George to Chicago, Oscar and Bill to nearby farms, Dave to drive a dray in Davenport. As a result, whenever a neighbor missed a chicken, or complained of kids in his melon patch, or had his buggy wheels taken off and hung on the ridge of his barn on Hallowe'en, or found some youth toying with his daughter in the haymow, Harry had to look sharp if he wanted to avoid a tanning for it. Sometimes he was guilty, sometimes not. Sometimes he got beaten for Elmer's misdeeds because Elmer was too big at sixteen to be handled.

The procedure was monotonously reiterative. Fred Mason would lay for his one punishable son whenever he heard of a prank or theft. If he caught him (as he seldom did, and the infrequency of his success only whetted his wrath) he would take him out on the porch in full view of the offended public and administer punishment there. Because of his missing arm, he couldn't both hold and whip the boy, and so he held him by the collar and kicked his backside with brutal shoes, or hammered his head against a porch pillar. The more he kicked and hammered, the madder he got, and the more stubborn the boy's grim silence became. He never cried for pain, but sometimes after a thumping he would go off in the woods and throw himself on the ground and weep with rage and hatred. Once or twice he ran away, to be gone for two or three weeks, but he always came back, until one day in the summer of his fourteenth year.

In that July Fred Mason had had one of his occasional spells of ambition, had got together a couple of scythes, and had contracted to cut off the hay in the river meadow west of town. Elmer and Harry were impressed as free labor. They went unwillingly enough, but before they had been working half an hour they got into a race to see who could mow the greatest swath by noon. They shucked their shirts and slaved mightily in the early heat, while their father sat with his back against a tree, smoking his corncob.

Heads down, elbows bent, arms and shoulders swinging, the boys went down the field of damp grass close together, mowing almost in unison. At the fence along the road they turned and started back, still together. Then Elmer, two years older and a little bigger, began to inch ahead, and Harry strained to catch him, reaching for the exact cutting power of the scythe.

Harry never knew quite how it happened. His head was down, his eyes on the next semicircle of long wild grass that the scythe would reach. Either Elmer moved a little closer, or Harry in his hurry reached out too far, but in the warm hay-smelling quiet Elmer suddenly yelped, just as Harry, having felt the sudden solid obstruction to the blade, stood up.

Elmer sat down and rolled up his pants leg. Jets of blood pumped from a long deep gash in his inner calf. "Oh my gosh!" Harry said. He dropped on hands and knees and tried to stop the bleeding with his hands, but it burst out of the red lips of the wound and flooded his wrists. Their father came running, swearing at every step. For once Harry saw him move quickly and efficiently.

"Get me your shirt!" he said. Harry raced for it, came back on the dead run. His father had already laid Elmer on his back, found the artery above the cut, and was pressing deep with his thumb into the brown flesh. The bleeding lessened, came in feeble, choked spurts. Mason jerked his head at the twist of black eating tobacco in his shirt pocket. "Chew that up, a big hunk of it."

Harry stuffed the end in his mouth, bit off a great mouthful, and chewed desperately. Some of the juice ran down his throat; he choked, gagged, felt his bowels heave in nauseated protest, but he chewed on.

"C'mere!"

Harry knelt, helped his father fit a stone into a strip of cloth and press it against the spot where his thumb had been. A burst of blood shot from the wound, was choked down again. "Tie that around his leg," Mason said. "Tight as you can tie it."

His cheeks bulged with the evil wad, Harry tied, pulling until Elmer snapped at him. His father, kneeling on the ripped shirt, was tearing off another strip with his good hand. "All right, lessee that tobacco."

Harry spat it into the outstretched palm, watched it smeared on the wound, rubbed in with dirty fingers. Elmer winced, his eyebrows drew down, his lips pulled away from his teeth. "Gosh I'm sorry, Elmer," Harry said. "I must-a reached out too far."

"Tie that!" his father said harshly. The boy tied the strip of sweaty shirt over the daubed wound. For a moment he remained squatting beside his brother, contrite and sympathetic, and in that moment his father's anger, restrained till now by the immediacies of first aid, blew out of him like an explosion.

"*God* damn you!" he howled. The boy saw the blow coming, but couldn't duck. The back of his father's hard hand hit him across the mouth, bowled him over on his back. He arose slowly, watchfully, his sullen face sallow, his eyes burning with hatred. "I didn't go to do it," he said.

The hand hauled back again, and Harry backed away slowly. "Give me your lip!" the old man shouted. "God damn it, ain't I got enough worries without you cuttin' Elmer all to hell and bringin' on doctor bills? Who's gonna cut this hay now?"

Harry had backed away to a safe distance. "Well, I'm not, by God!" he blazed. "That's the last time you ever hit me!"

He turned and ran across the mown edge of the meadow, climbed the fence, went into town and hunted up the doctor and directed him to the place where Elmer lay, and started west out of town. He never came back.

In Davenport, three days later, he found his brother Dave. "You did just right," Dave said. "The hell with the old bastard."

"Only thing I feel mean about is running out on El," Harry said. "That was a bad cut."

Dave, while driving his dray, had learned to talk tough and smoke stogies, and he wore leather wrist protectors studded with brass nails. "Hell," he said, "what's a cut on the leg? He'll be all right. Anyway, you can write him a letter."

So Harry wrote a letter, and in a week got a scrawl back from Elmer saying that the leg was healing and itched like hell, and as soon as it was well he was going to pull out too. He was getting sick of hearing the old man moan about his hay. Maybe he'd come to Davenport himself. He'd see how things looked.

"This town ain't what it used to be when the arsenal was booming," Dave said to Harry later, "but there's a lot of building going on. Why'n't you learn a trade? That's where the wages is. Learn a trade and you're set. I haul for two-three lumber yards. Maybe I can get you on with some carpenter. Want to be a carpenter?"

"I don't care," Harry said. "That's all right."

A week later he was apprenticed to a carpenter, working for board and room and clothes. He stayed at it two years, and when he quit he was good. Even his crabbed old boss admitted it; he had never seen a kid pick up a trade any faster. He had a knack with tools; they cut straight for him, and he didn't cripple himself or them by their misuse. There was also something stubborn and persistent in him under the veneer of toughness he borrowed from Dave. He double-checked measurements, calculated angles two or three times, drew out a job till he knew what was what. Experienced carpenters seemed to go out of their way to teach him the tricks, and he was earning two dollars a day when he was sixteen.

In the evenings he hung around the fringes of Dave's crowd, learning to drink beer, sitting in now and then on a cheap poker game. From those men, teamsters and roustabouts and left-overs from the almost-vanished river traffic, he heard stories that put an itch in his feet. They knew Iowa and Illinois and Wisconsin, "Chi" and Milwaukee. One or two of them had rafted timber all the way down the Wisconsin from Wausau and down the Mississippi from Prairie du Chien to St. Louis. The life they had lived and the places they had seen and spoke of had space in them. So when the master carpenter on a big mansion job snarled at Harry for taking time off to smoke a stogie, he picked up his coat, went home to the room, shook hands with Dave, stuffed into his pocket the few dollars he had saved, and caught a ride on a shanty boat down the river.

For six months he was on the bum, sleeping in jungles and knowledge boxes, picking up scraps of useful knowledge from hoboes and transient laborers moving with the crops. He visited Chicago, and the sight of that city roaring into incredible size and impressiveness on the shore of Lake Michigan left his mind dazed with grandiose visions. Here was really the big town, here were the gangs of men creating a city out of a windswept slough, here were freight engines, passenger engines, lake boats, nosing in smoking and triumphant from every direction, here was money by the millions, a future as big as the sky. But two weeks in the big town convinced him that the days when you started with nothing and got to the top were gone as far as Chicago was concerned. All the big money was already well grabbed. And when, nosing around the freight yards, he almost got picked up by a cinder dick, he did the most direct and logical thing. He ducked between two moving trains and swung aboard the outside one.

His wanderings took him out through the canal to the Mississippi, and down the river to Natchez on a coal barge. Then he worked north again, picking up a few weeks' work here and there on building jobs, getting offers of steady work but turning them down to hit the road again. By the end of six months he had a belly full for the time being, an ingrained and educated contempt for the law and law-abiding people, a handiness at making himself liked by hardboiled and suspicious men, and an ambition to get somewhere where the cream hadn't been skimmed off, get in on the ground floor somewhere and make his pile. And he had the nickname of Bo.

He took the first job that offered, driving spikes in the new spur of the Illinois Central working westward through Illinois and Iowa. The heavy labor developed him into a man, sheathed his chest and shoulders with muscle, left him hard as a hound. But it brought him again into conflict with authority, with the voice of the boss. The Irish foremen on the line were drivers, loud mouthed and quick with their fists, and Bo was anything but docile. He talked back, sneered at the section boss, made no effort to keep his voice down when he beefed. That came to a climax on the graded roadbed just at the end of the steel.

The crew was bending rails for a gentle curve, locking them in the heavy vises and heaving against them with a surge of muscle. It was hot, back-breaking work in a sun over a hundred degrees. Stripped to the waist, the men launched themselves against the springy steel, relaxed, strained again. McCarthy, the foreman, stood at the end cocking his eye, estimating the curve. He had a hangover, and apparently his cigar was nasty in his mouth, because he threw it away.

"Come on!" he roared suddenly. "Get some beef into it. You ain't bending a willow switch."

Bo wiped the sweat out of his eyes with his forearm. "I can think of a place I'd like to bend a willow switch," he said. He heaved with the rest, rocking against the rail. McCarthy stepped three paces closer, dropping his head between his shoulders.

"Where would that be, Squarehead?"

Bo heaved, grunting. "Right across your ass, Shanty-Irish," he said pleasantly.

As if at an order the men were back from the rail and dropping into a half circle. Bo and the foreman faced each other on the banked gravel, their feet shuffling lightly, their eyes sparring, their hands up.

The foreman lashed out, caught Bo beside the head, took a stiff right cross to the face in return. Like stiff-legged dogs they circled. The foreman dropped his head and rushed, swinging. For a full minute they stood and slugged it out, neither giving an inch. Then McCarthy stumbled and fell on hands and knees, his mouth hanging and his eyes amazed. The watching men howled as Bo, fighting as he had learned to fight on the road, gave him the boots. McCarthy covered up with his arms and started to roll away, and Bo, tiptoeing like a dancer, followed to crash a kick into the foreman's ribs that shocked him shudderingly still.

There was not a sound as he walked away. The men parted and let him by, and wiping his bloody nose as he went, he walked over to the bunkhouse, his head still singing with the power of McCarthy's fists, his ear swelling, but his blood pounding with a triumph so high and savage that he wanted to yell. The picture of McCarthy lying back there with his ribs caved in was raw alcohol to his soul. He was drunk on it; the toughest Irishman on the crew was back there cold as a clam.

The next day he was on his way to Wisconsin, bound for a logging camp where another section hand had worked the winter before. The food, he said, was good, the work hard but agreeable, the wages fair. They would just about be getting crews ready for the winter's cutting.

Two winters in Wisconsin gave him many skills. Either with rifle or shotgun he was the best shot in camp, so that frequently he got laid off the saw to go hunting for the cook. Those days of prowling the timber with a gun only deepened the wild streak in him as the work on the crosscut deepened his chest. He took to skis and snowshoes as if he had known them all his life, and he went out of his way to make friends.

He was genial, a good story-teller, a hearty drinker and a ribald companion in the towns where the rafts and the wanigan tied up and the men swarmed ashore for a bender. On winter evenings, when there was nothing doing in the bunkhouse steaming with the thick smell of drying socks and scorched leather and mutton tallow, he often lay on his bunk reading the one book he had found, a volume of Burns, and before the first winter was up he had added the whole volume to his fantastic collection of memorized McGuffey. He learned Paul Bunyan yarns, or invented them himself, and when half tight would sometimes take off on an extemporaneous ballad or poem that lasted half an hour. And he played poker, for higher stakes.

Those two summers, when the camps were shut down, he worked on a farm out of Portage, simply because he liked being outside better than he would have liked a carpenter's job in town. The Portage baseball team discovered him, and in the end of his second summer he leaped into local notoriety by getting a bid from the Terre Haute team in the Three-Eye League.

That winter he did not go back to the woods, for reasons which he kept to himself, and when he stood in the yard late in April ready to leave for Terre Haute, the sixteen-year-old daughter of the house burst into sudden tempestuous tears and fled to the barn.

"For gosh sakes," her father said. "What's the matter with her?"

Bo did not enlighten him.

He liked playing ball in Terre Haute. It was a wandering life, full of action, and the adulation of fans put a cocky swagger in his walk. His name in the papers pleased him, the fellowship of the gang he played with was good masculine fellowship, with many afternoons in the icehouse cooling off on beer after a game, and many evenings of quiet, intent poker. He lost money, but he learned much. If it had not been for an accident he might have stayed on as a professional ball player, might even have moved up into the big time, because his hitting was consistent and powerful, and he was a good man behind the plate in the days when catchers worked with a thin fingerless glove. But late in the season of 1896 he tried to stretch a long hit, got tangled up in a plunging fight for the bag with the opposing third baseman, and came up limping with a badly wrenched knee.

That put him on the hospital list for the rest of the season, and he had to get another job. For a while he worked in a glass factory, gave it up because it kept him inside ten hours a day, went back to his old trade as carpenter, and quit that with pleasure at the beginning of the next season. But the third day of training he wrenched his knee again; in spite of bandages it felt as if it might cave under him, and it hindered his swing at the plate. Before the middle of the first month he had been released from the club and was selling beer on the road for a Milwaukee brewery.

His territory took in all of southern Minnesota, western Iowa, and South Dakota, and sometimes was stretched to include an illicit trip into North Dakota to pick off the blind pig trade. North Dakota was then a focal point for armies of immigrants and land seekers. The trains were full of Norwegian and Russian families burdened down with masses of belongings, the station platforms were piled with bundles and boxes and trunks and farm machinery, the station walls were plastered with posters, land was for sale everywhere, new lines were pushing across the fertile Red River country and into the western part of the state.

Something in the bustle of migration stirred a pulse in Bo Mason. He was not a lazy man; his activities had been various and strenuous since he was fourteen. But the boredom of carpentry, of towns, of regular hours and wages every Saturday and orders all the rest of the week, had always made him restless. Here in Dakota there was something else. Here everybody was his own boss, here was a wide open and unskimmed country where a man could hew his own line and not suffer for his independence. Obstacles raised by nature—cold, heat, drouth, the solid resistance of great trees, he could slog through with almost fierce joy, but obstacles raised by institutions and the habits of a civilized community left him prowling and baffled.

That was partly why he loved the feel of life in Dakota. Frequently he stopped over for a day or two to go bird shooting, coming home from the wide grasslands and sloughs with a buggy full of prairie chickens, sage hens, grouse, ducks. Those days he remembered, and he remembered the sniff of something remote and clean and active in the prairie wind, the flat country leaning westward toward the Missouri Plateau, the sight everywhere of new buildings, new plowing, new grain elevators rising along the new tracks on the edges of new towns. Saloon conversations were full of tales of fantastic crops. "Sixty bushel to the acre!" men said. "Sixty bushel. I seen it, I was at the spout of that threshing machine. My God, that wheat grows tall as Iowa corn." And from train windows Bo looked out over fields of flax in flower, acres and acres of blue, and then his brewery job, full of travelling as it was, seemed trivial, picayune, confining. He wanted breath in his lungs and the sight of a flock of prairie chickens rising over his gunsights.

"Things are going on out there," he told his boss on the next home stop. "Every time I go through there the towns along the line are bigger."

His boss sat pulling a bushy eyebrow with thumb and forefinger. "You want to quit?" he said.

"How did you know?"

"You've got the itch in you," his boss said. "I've seen it before. You can stay on if you want, glad to have you. I've got no complaints about your work or sales."

Bo said nothing.

"Planning to take up a homestead?"

"I don't know. Maybe."

"Don't," his boss said, and hauled himself straighter in his chair. "You take my advice and stay away from farms. I knew a lot of people went to Dakota and Nebraska in the old days. And the ones that made money weren't the ones that sweated themselves skinny farming. The ones that made money was the storekeepers and bankers and saloon-keepers. I don't suppose you know anything about banking."

"No."

"And you wouldn't like running a grocery store."

"No."

"Then it looks like a saloon," the old man said, and grinned. "And saloons are banned in Dakota."

"Not if you believe my sales reports," Bo said. They laughed.

The old man set the ends of his fingers together and brooded. "Looky here, son," he said. "I'll make you a proposition. You go out to some new town and set yourself up a place and I'll help you out. You can draw on me for fixtures and beer, and pay me off when you get going. I think you're the kind of guy might make a go of it."

"Thanks," Bo said, and rose. "I'll let you know. I want to go look around a little more first."

Two months later he wrote from Hardanger, saying that he had a good thing in a new town, no local police or anything to bother. He had bought half a building, was putting in bowling alleys himself, had three pool tables coming. He'd like a thirty-foot bar, mirrors to match it, and a shipment of beer, bottled beer. It was cleaner that way and it could be kept out of sight. "This town is only ten years old," he said, "and it's twice as busy now as it was two-three years ago. Five years from now I'll be buying out the brewery."

That was in the summer of 1899. Now it was 1905.

In September the roads were full of wagons, and on mornings when she worked around the house with doors and windows open Elsa could hear the shunt and crash of boxcars being backed under the spouts of the elevators. When the jolting and puffing stopped she could, by listening intently, hear the swishing rush as the dipped spout let go its river of wheat into the cars. Harvest excited her, as it had always excited her at home, and one afternoon, on an impulse, she left the house and went down.

There were dribbles of golden wheat below the spout, and at the bottom of the elevator wall a shining gold cone. She scooped her hand full and stood back watching, chewing and crunching the wheat kernels till they were sweet, rubbery gum in her mouth.

The last car was just being pulled away. Inside the elevator she heard the grunting of a separator engine and the occasional thud of a sack being thumped on the floor. She peeked in. A man she did not know, probably Bill Conzett's hired man, was separating seed flax, and Jud Chain, immaculate, dandified, wearing coat and vest even in the fall heat, leaned one shoulder negligently against the wall. He had his hat off, and a streak of sun through the elevator roof glinted on his blond hair.

"Hello," Elsa said. "I didn't expect to see you in an elevator."

"Come down a good deal," Jud said. "Bo and I are turning grain speculators. Buying flax this fall."

"Well," she said, and could think of nothing else to say to him.

"I'm daffy about flax anyway," Jud said. "Something about it makes me feel good. It's so slick and silky to feel." He ran his hand into the mouth of a sack and wriggled his fingers.

"We never grew it at home," Elsa said.

"Feel."

She pushed her hand into the brown flaky seeds. They slipped smoothly up her wrist, cool and dry, millions of polished, purple-brown, miniature guitar picks. She moved her hand and the flax swirled like heavy smooth water against her skin.

"That's nice," she said.

"It's something to see in flower, too," Jud said. "Acres of blue-bells."

Her quick look acknowledged something sensitive, almost feminine, in the expression of his face as he caressed the flax with his fingers. "It's like everything else that's lovely," Jud said. "Dangerous. Boy was drowned in a flax bin here a year ago. Fell in and it sucked him down before anybody could get to him. We had to empty the whole bin to get him." He rubbed his wrist with a flat white hand. "Nice boy, too," he said. "That's the kind things always happen to. A mean, tough kid, now, he'd never know enough to appreciate the feel of flax, and he'd never get caught in it."

"I guess so," Elsa said. She let her fingers move in the satiny, treacherous seeds.

"Seen Bo lately?" Jud said.

"Not for three or four days."

"I thought he spent all his time on your front porch."

"Oh, go along!" she said.

Jud lifted an amused eyebrow; his mouth puckered into an expression almost arch. "Don't make out that you don't know the conquest you've made," he said.

She blushed. "Oh, fiddlesticks!"

"Laugh," Jud said. "You've got poor old Bo roped and hogtied. You know what he's been like for the last three weeks? When the kid that sets them up in the alleys gets his pins up, he has to jump out of there and beat it over to rack the pool balls, and then fly up to serve somebody a drink, and then hike back to the alleys to set them up again. You know why? Because Bo is standing all that time out by the door watching to see if you won't be coming down the sidewalk."

Elsa's face was hot. "Oh yes," she said sarcastically. "He's just been a regular *preste-rompe*."

"What's a preste romper?"

"Preacher's tail. Somebody that's always tagging along. Like Bo."

"You don't mind, do you?"

"Oh no," she said. "I always feel sorry for strays. I pat him on the head once in a while."

His laugh was deep, moist, cavernous, like something alive down a cistern, a laugh that matched oddly with his polished and almost effeminate manners.

"Has Bo asked you anything lately?" he said.

She was startled. "No. What?"

"I guess he's been pretty busy," Jud said. "I know he's got it on his mind."

"Now you've got me curious."

"Oh well," Jud said. "I don't know why I shouldn't ask you. He'd get all tangled up in his tongue. How'd you like to go to Devil's Lake next Saturday?"

"Fine," she said. "What for?"

"State trap shoot. Bo's entered in the singles—would be in doubles too, but he can't stay away that long. We thought you and Eva might come along for the day. The fair's on, and there's a carnival in town. Big excitement."

"It sounds like fun," she said. "What if Bo forgets to ask me, now?"

"That," Jud said, "is the last thing he'd forget. He might forget his shotgun, maybe, but not you."

5

She saw him, from the parlor window, come up the walk with his derby already in his hand, and because they had a twenty-mile drive to make, and the shooting began at ten, she hurried to meet him at the door. He took the lunch box from her hand and held her elbow while she gathered her skirts for the step up to the axle of the buggy. "Here we go," he said, "if these old plugs can make it."

Settling herself, she said in surprise, "Why that's a beautiful team."

"Best old Handley had," Bo said. "If they ever caught up with the times in this burg they'd have horseless carriages for rent." He flicked the lines and the horses snapped into their collars; their trotting feet beat light and swift on the dust. Elsa knew they could make that twenty miles in two hours, easily. But it was like Bo to disparage anything he was proud of. Either he or Handley had worked over those horses. Their gray hides shone, their manes were roached, their forelocks tied, their tails curried smooth and glossy. She was glad they weren't docked; a docked horse was a pitiful thing when the flies were bad.

Jud was waiting in front of the hotel. Bo didn't slow down. Jud's great flat hand hooked the rail, his leg swung up, and he slid into the rear seat on the fly. The smell of bay rum came with him. "Must be in a hurry," he said. He breathed on the ruby ring on his left hand, rubbed it on his sleeve.

"Pony Express doesn't stop for anything," Bo said.

But they stopped for Eva. In front of her house Bo whistled and Jud whistled, but nothing happened. "Still snoring," Bo said. "Go on up and break the door down, Jud."

Jud climbed out. "Not Eva's door," he said. "I prize my health." He went up and rapped, bending to listen for movement inside.

"Make some noise, for God's sake," Bo said. He lifted his voice in a bellow that shocked down the quiet, weedgrown street. "Hey, EVA!" The echo bounced off Sprague's barn.

Jud knocked again. "Must be asleep," he said.

"That's just what I think," Bo said. "Eva! Hey, Eva! Wake up!"

An upstairs window opened and Eva stuck her head out. Her left hand held a flowered kimono close to her chest. "Shut up, you big loon," she said. "You'll wake Ma."

The window slammed. They waited five minutes, ten. Jud wandered across the porch, cut off a twig from a shrub with his knife, and began peeling it. In the buggy Bo looked at Elsa, then at his watch. "Fifteen minutes," he said, and muttered indistinguishable things under his breath.

"Maybe she misunderstood the time."

"Maybe my hip pocket is a gold mine. She just likes to keep people waiting."

At six-thirty Eva came out in a white pleated shirtwaist and a dark sport skirt that just cleared the ground. Her mouth was very red, and she walked briskly, as if unaware that she had delayed anyone. Jud helped her in, waited while she got over her despairing little laughs and helpless attempts to get her skirts arranged. Bo sucked a back tooth and looked bored, but Elsa reached back and gave Eva a hand. Men ought to consider that a girl with her waist squeezed at least four inches too small couldn't move very freely. Still, she supposed Eva could have left the corset a little looser.

"Get all prettied up?" Bo said.

"I didn't even stop to eat," Eva said. "Just on account of you and your noise."

"What were you doing, then? You had time for a ten course meal."

"You needn't act so nasty," Eva said. "I didn't keep you waiting long."

Bo clucked to the team, lifted his derby and ran a hand over his hair, tipped the derby on again at a cocky angle. "No trouble at all. Do the horses good to have that hour rest."

"Oh, an hour!"

"Cut it out," Jud said genially. "We're moving, aren't we?"

He moved Bo's shotgun case from under Eva's feet and folded the buffalo robe on the floor so that her feet wouldn't dangle. Eva was always complaining that all seats were made too high for short people.

As they drove along the road the mist was rising from a slough on the left, and a half dozen ducks turned and swam away into the tules as if pulled on wires. "Getting close to bird season," Bo said, and watched them with a nostalgic eye.

The grays lengthened out in a mile-eating trot across the flats. Flickertails jerked and ran and sat up with absurd little hands hanging on their chests. The light cloud of dust behind them hung a long time in the still air, so that turning at section corners they could see it for a quarter of a mile behind. They sang, the grays went crisply, perfectly matched, heads up and tails arching a little, the mist melted from above the sloughs and the sun burned warmer. They were pulling into the carnival grounds at Devil's Lake at nine-thirty.

Jud lifted Eva down, straightened his vest. "I don't suppose there'll be anything doing till later," he said, and looked at Bo.

"I wouldn't think so," Bo said. "Not till afternoon, anyway."

"I thought you started shooting at ten?" Eva said.

Bo wagged his jaw at her. "What? Little Eva remembering the time something starts?"

"How about a stroll through the carnival?" Jud said.

Eva looked around her at the long grass. "It looks wet," she said.

Jud kicked into it, inspected his toe. There were tiny drops of water across the waxed yellow shoe. Under the trees there was still a dewy early-morning smell. "I'll carry you," he said. "Over in the grounds it's dry."

Eva giggled. "I don't trust you. You're so lackadaisical you'd probably drop me in a puddle."

"You've got us mixed up," Bo said gravely. "That's what I'd do if I was carrying you."

Eva stiffened, but his face was bland. "Come on then," she said, and stuck her hand in Jud's high elbow.

Absurdly short and imposingly tall, they stepped through the grass toward the packed carnival street and the tents set in a long semicircle around the fringe of cottonwoods. Elsa, watching them, heard the early shouts of barkers, the sodden thump of a maul on a stake. She saw the gaudy flashes of color from kewpie dolls and pennants and prizes in a concession tent open to the sun. A merry-go-round squawked for a minute into a fast two-step and then stopped, and there were six shots, sharp and steady, from an unseen shooting gallery. Along the road from town people were beginning to come on foot and in buggies.

"You shouldn't tease her like that," Elsa said.

"Why not?"

"She might think you meant it."

"I do."

"That's all the more reason for not saying things like that."

Bo grunted. "She gives me a pain. Just because Jud gives her a little whirl, she thinks she's got a lifetime lease on him."

"Jud doesn't seem to mind."

"He never minds anything. If you went up and kicked him he'd turn around and beg your pardon for having his back turned on you."

"Oh well," Elsa said. "What do you have to do now?"

"Just have to register and get a number. There's a half hour yet."

"Let's go get it done," she said. "Jud says you're going to win a prize."

"I guess not. Too many good shooters here."

"You're a good shooter too."

He grinned. "Got confidence in me, hey?"

"Of course," she said.

With the shotgun case under one arm, he steered her toward the screened street of carnival tents. Though she was tall herself, she felt his size beside her, and it pleased her to be walking with him. It wasn't just his size, either. It was the width of his chest, the smooth nut-brown of his skin, the way he walked as if everything in him moved on ball bearings. She hummed, almost skipping, and laughed when he looked at her.

At the white tent marked "Shooting Headquarters," under a limp American flag, she waited while he registered. He came back with a big paper 13 pinned on his back. "Slipped me the unlucky number," he said. One eyebrow was raised in an expression of querulous protest.

"Why, are you superstitious?"

"No, but I'd just as soon have another number."

"Friday the thirteenth is my lucky day," she said. "I'll loan you my luck."

His shoulder bumped hers as he swung to look around at the white and brown and yellow tents, the sheds housing fair exhibits, the banners of linen-paper, the pennants, the flags. The barkers were opening up all down the street, the calliope had started again, the little painted horses of the merry-go-round were rising and falling through the yellowing leaves of the cottonwoods. At the far end of the grounds a great wheel began to turn, curving up against the cloudless sky, and a girl's squeal cut through the jumble of crowd-sound.

"What in heaven's name is that?" Elsa said.

"Ferris wheel. Haven't you ever been on one?"

"I never saw one before."

"Take you for a ride when the shooting's over," he said. The corners of his eyes crinkled with a smile of pure delight. "God," he said, "I like the smell of a place like this, even. When I was a kid I was always going to run away and join a circus. Minute I get near one I start snorting and pawing the ground."

They were in the midst of a pushing crowd. For a moment their eyes met, and they stood foolishly smiling, oblivious to the push of shoulders and the jabber of voices and the danger of having an eye put out by a parasol rib. Then he grabbed her arm and pulled her along behind him. "Come on. I don't think I can miss today."

"You'd better not," Elsa said. "I'll take a sandwich out of your lunch for every one you miss."

"Give me a kiss for every one I hit?"

"Ninny on your tintype," she said, and pulled her arm away. Ahead of them, dropping toward the low shore of the lake, was a dike of earth, and behind it a little distance a crowd was lining up, sitting on newspapers, robes, bare ground. They were men mostly, but there was a sprinkling of women bright against the yellowing trees and the gray earth. Below them, on the level ground behind the five dugout traps, three men sat at a table. Men with shotguns in their hands and numbers on their backs clustered around the shooting ground. A clay pigeon hissed in an experimental arc over the water and fell.

"I mean it," Bo said, and they were stopped again. A faint, teasing smile hung on his mouth. "I won't even shoot unless you promise."

"You might as well not unpack your gun, then," she said, but his look made her feel dizzy and absurd and hot and as if she were going to fly all to pieces. She had come to the point of meeting his eyes and trying to stare him down, both of them laughing, when the man with the megaphone began to announce the opening of the singles traps, for the championship of North Dakota.

"Promise!" Bo said. "Don't be a piker. I can't shoot for any such stakes as the championship of Dakota."

Elsa got hold of the disintegrating feeling and fingered the enamelled brooch at her throat. She was delighted and a little terrified. "We'll see," she said.

They found Jud and Eva sitting among the spectators behind the second trap. Eva had a kewpie doll in her lap. "Won it on a toy horse race," she said. "That's what comes of having a beau that knows the ponies. My horse never was behind." She reached out and pinched Jud's ankle, and he moved it calmly out of reach.

One of the men at the table read off the names of the first shooters, who lined up behind the traps. Bo leaned over and began explaining to Elsa. They shot in groups of twenty-five rounds. The first was the easiest, "known traps and known angles," the shooter knowing the source and direction of each bird. There would be a clump of possibles on this one. Then came twenty-five shots at known traps but unknown angles. The bird might come straight out or to either side. That was tougher. The third and fourth rounds the shooters went out singly. In the third round they shot "reversing," standing at number one trap and getting a crossing bird from number five, then standing at number two and getting a bird out of number four, and so on. The last twenty-five rounds was "expert." You didn't know which trap the bird would come from, or in what direction.

Her eyes were on him almost in horror, but she was laughing still. "You shoot a hundred times," she said, "and you're an extra good shot, and you have the nerve . . . !"

"A hundred isn't so many." She noticed for the first time what it was that made his face so changeful and interesting. His eyebrows turned up rather than down at their outside ends. Like a devil. He was a devil. A hundred times! "I might miss as many as six," he said slyly. "That'd only be ninety-four."

"Keep the gun in the case!" she said, and waved him away.

He laughed and leaned back. A white saucer whizzed out of the first trap, the first shooter caught it with his barrels, fired. The saucer shivered to fragments, its thin splashings as the pieces hit the water clearly audible even over the echo of the shot rolling back from the shore. "Good bird," said an official clearly. The scorer at the table echoed him, "Good bird." The second shooter stood ready. "Pull!" he said.

Bo kept score with a stick on the bare ground. If anyone missed more than two he erased the whole score. "Don't need to worry about them. Guy that wins this has to shoot a possible on the first two rounds."

A man with a sheet of paper in his hand went around reading

off the next names. "Simmons, number one; Carter, two; Shale, three; Gulbransen, four; Galbraith, five. Ready for the next squad. Simmons, Carter, Shale, Gulbransen, Galbraith."

"They run these off pretty smooth," Bo said. He opened the case and took out the stock and then the barrels, fitted the gun together, broke it and snapped it together again, his automatic hand going down to scratch in the tallies. He wiped off the stock, ran the ramrod through the shining barrels. His hands moved on the blue steel almost tenderly. Then he laid the gun across his feet and watched again.

"You'll be up pretty soon," Elsa said. He nodded, and she saw the tightening that had come over the muscles in his jaw and neck, the intent seriousness around his eyes. He seemed almost to have forgotten who she was, that she was even there.

Of the first two squads only two men had possibles, Carter and Olson. Bo watched Olson with a steady, almost basilisk look. "There's the guy to beat," he said. "He doesn't let down between shots at all. He's a shooter, that guy."

The squad hustler came around reading names, Bo's among them. When he stood up with the gun across his arm Elsa felt excited and nervous, weak with the desire to have him win. "Hit every one," she said, and had to hold her hands back to keep from reaching out to touch him.

He grinned at her absently. "Can't miss," he said. "See you after while."

"Five bucks you make a possible," Jud said.

Bo shook his head. "You'd jinx me."

He walked down to the table and joined the squad filling their pockets with shells. The last roar of number five's gun rolled along the shore, and number five walked back into the crowd. Then Bo was standing behind number three trap, hatless, his gun over his arm.

"Pull!" the first man said. The clay bird arced, the gun came up, the roar of the shot mushroomed in the still air. Then number two, then Bo. Each time Bo shot Elsa scratched a tally on the ground. Six, seven, eight, nine, ten, eleven, twelve. It took a long time, but every good bird was a little triumph. Glancing up from her tense concentration she saw Jud watching her. He lifted his eyebrows, and she made a face.

The thirteenth bird was coming. Thirteen! She stiffened herself, trying to loan him her luck. "Pull!" he said. The saucer shot out, but wobbly, weak, short. Bo raised the gun, hesitated, let the bird fall.

"No bird," the referee said. "No bird," said the scorer. Bo fished up a handkerchief swiftly and wiped his face. The handkerchief trailed whitely out of his side pocket as he half raised the gun again. "Pull!" he said. The bird whirred up, he caught it with the barrels quickly, too quickly, and missed it cleanly.

Elsa sat back with a noisily released breath. "Tough luck," Jud said. But Eva turned with an incredulous smile. "What do you know!" she said. "I never knew Bo was superstitious."

"He isn't."

"Don't tell me," Eva said. "He was nervous on that thirteenth one."

"He got a bad bird," Jud said. "Breaks of the game."

Bo was slow coming back. When he sat down beside them there was a clamp on his jaw and a shine of hard anger in his eyes.

"You did fine," Elsa said.

His laugh was hard and choppy, a disgusted sound. "I did fine all right. Let myself get jinxed on that thirteen ball."

"But only two hit them all," she said, "and only three others got all but one. You're tied for second."

"That isn't good enough," he said. "This Olson bird doesn't miss enough so you can afford to fool around." He sounded almost as if he were scolding her for saying he had done well. His voice was so snappish that she kept quiet.

It was after noon when he finished his second round. Going down still sore at the way things had broken in the first, he had missed the very first bird, and then in a cold fury that Elsa could see in his very shoulders and the set of his neck, had run out the remaining twenty-four as if each had been a personal enemy. Carter had dropped one, Olson none, and the rest of the field had dropped back so that Bo was third with forty-eight against Carter's forty-nine and Olson's possible.

His string of twenty-four restored his temper, and when Elsa took two sandwiches out of his lunch he groaned. "I'll be so weak I can't pull the trigger," he said.

"I guess the four you've had will keep you from starving. Besides, you lost them fair and square."

"I won forty-eight of something else, though."

"I never promised."

"What?" Eva said. "What did she promise?"

"I didn't promise anything."

"Now you're welching," Bo said.

"I'm not either welching. I never promised. Besides, you're not through yet."

"When I'm through you'll welch again."

"What I want to know," Eva said, "is what did she promise?"

"None of your business," Bo said bluntly, watching Elsa.

"You hit the next fifty and I really will promise," she said. "And when I promise anything I do it."

The full upper lids of Bo's eyes made his face look slitted like a mask, but he was smiling a fixed and concentrated smile. "Okay," he said. "I'll remember."

Jud hitched himself over until he had his back against a tree. He reached down and unlaced his yellow shoes. "What I hate about being up in the daytime," he said, "is that you have to wear shoes, and shoes hurt my feet something terrible." He pulled one off and sighed, reached for the other. Eva squealed affectedly. "Right at the table!" she said. "Put them on again, for Heaven's sake."

Bo's heavy-lidded eyes changed expression, were veiled with scorn. "I suppose you've never seen Jud's feet."

"Where would I have seen his feet?"

He shrugged. "Since he never wears anything but slippers, hardly, you might have seen them."

"Well, I don't go where Jud works," she said.

Jud sat looking down the immense length of his legs at his stockinged toes. He wriggled them experimentally. "You talk as if my feet were an everyday attraction," he said. "Not everybody has thirteen toes. I could make a good living in a sideshow with my feet."

"Thirteen toes!" Elsa said. "Has he?"

"I never bothered to count 'em," Bo said. "They look like a couple of cartridge belts."

Elegantly relaxed, his face bland and amused, looking more than ever like an actor, Jud continued to wriggle his feet. Elsa watched him, this remote and fastidious impostor who could quite easily, without showing it in the least, change the subject, get Bo and Eva away from their outspoken dislike, make everything smooth and casual again. "Want to see?" Jud said.

"You can't scare me," Elsa said.

He took off one sock and showed seven toes. The other foot, he said, had only six, though there was a little nubbin that with applications of hair restorer or something might be made to grow. Eva covered her eyes and squealed at him to cover up his awful old feet, he looked like a centipede.

From back on the grounds, over the faint musical wheezing of the calliope, came the dull boom of a shotgun. Bo looked at his watch. "I've got to be getting back," he said.

He helped Elsa stow the scattered remains of the lunch in the buggy. Jud put his shoes back on with unhurried deliberation, rose and stretched. Eva consulted her face in a little pocket mirror.

A man, small, dark, with a red birthmark smearing one side of his face, came through the trees. He passed clusters of picnicking people, looking at them sharply as if in search of someone. Then he saw Jud, and came directly over. Eva put the mirror away and straightened her dress, but the man threw only one brief glance at the others before he led Jud out of earshot. Jud nodded, lifted his head as if musing, nodded again. They laughed together, lighting cigarettes, and stood looking back through the grounds past the colored moving specks of the merry-go-round horses. The little man bent his arm, stuck the hand out at an angle, wriggled it, his bony white hand darting like a snake's head. Jud nodded, and the little man went away.

"Who was that?" Eva said.

"Fellow I used to know in Fargo," Jud said. "Joe Theodoratus."

"What is he, an Indian or something?"

"Greek, I guess." He bent over to brush his trousers, and as he bent Elsa saw a look pass between him and Bo.

"What did he want?"

"Got a deal on," Jud said. "Wants to talk to me a little while. You wouldn't mind going to watch Bo shoot, would you, birdie?"

Eva's brows gathered. "You mean you want to run out and leave me?"

"I have to attend to this," Jud said. "Bo and Elsa will take care of you."

"So I have to stick in the mud while you go off. How long will you be?"

"We're the mud," Bo said, and winked at Elsa.

"I'll be an hour or so," Jud said. His face did not lose its bland and mannerly smile, and his voice did not lift, but Elsa thought she caught something passing between them that she interpreted as a command. Eva turned away petulantly and gave in. "You'll have more fun watching Bo shoot, anyway," Jud said. "That's what we came up here for, to watch Bo shoot." He straightened his patterned vest and settled the derby on his neat head. "Well, if you'll excuse me for a little while."

"I never knew it to fail!" Eva said, and came along unwillingly with Bo and Elsa.

Walking on the other side from Eva, Bo took Elsa's elbow and squeezed it, and glancing up she saw the glow that had been in his narrowed eyes all during lunch. When he was excited or interested, she noticed, the cool blue-gray warmed in his pupils, and his square, almost expressionless face became lively and changeful. She remembered what Jud had said in the elevator the other day, and was trying to see evidences of it in his face when she caught herself. She was just an ignorant Norske girl from the sticks. He wasn't crazy about her. He couldn't be.

All the same, when his turn came up and she watched him go down alone, to stand in the lonely focal point between spectators and traps and break twenty-five straight, holding his fire sometimes until she almost yelled for him to shoot, but always shooting in time, picking off the birds close to the water when their swift flight had slowed in the drop—when she watched him like an infallible machine scatter the clay saucers one after another, she held her breath and felt something like a prayer on every shot. When his gun missed fire on the twenty-second bird she was in an agony for fear it counted against him, for fear it would make him nervous as the bad bird had in the first round. But they gave him another, and he broke it, and then the last three.

He came back with his face as expressionless as if he had just been for a drink of water, and when she clapped her hands he pulled down the corners of his mouth. "Lucky," he said. "I'll probably miss a dozen next round."

But his eyes did not think he would. They told her privately that he was going out there and score another possible. The last three men finished shooting, and the referee called out the running scores: Olson, seventy-three; Mason, seventy-three; Carter, seventy-three; Gulbransen and Smith, seventy-one.

"Tied for first!" Elsa said. He just rubbed his shoulder, pounded sore by the kick of the gun, and kept his eye on the shooter coming up.

"I wonder where that Jud is?" Eva said. She had hardly said a word in the hour and a half they had been sitting there. She twisted and fidgeted, looking through the crowd.

"I'm going to look for him," she said. "He gets gabbing and never thinks what time it is."

Bo paid no attention to her words or her departure. He sprawled back, watching Olson shoot. His actions were faster than in previous rounds. They had to be. The birds came at sharp angles, from unexpected traps, and almost every shot was a quartering one. He ran nine, snapped a hurried side shot at a saucer spinning wide from the fifth trap. A tiny fragment zinged from the clay, its click coming back after the roar of the gun. The bird fell solidly into the water. "Lost bird," the referee droned. Olson, red in the face, protested, but the official waved him back. "Dusted target is no bird," he said.

The hustler was coming through. "Condon up, Mason on deck, Williams in the hole."

"All right, honey," Bo said softly. "Hold your right ear and pray."

He went down early, sitting at the official table while Condon shot, and when Condon was through he went out and shot another possible, shoot, relax, shoot, relax, break the breech and kick the smoking shells out on the ground, reload, shoot, relax, snap up the barrels, find the spinning disc in the split second of its rise, hands and eyes working together surely, impeccably. When he reached twenty without a miss Elsa was on her knees. When he broke the last bird hissing out at a high angle she was on her feet.

"Harder they get the easier they are for that guy," a man next to her said. She nodded, waiting for Bo to come back.

"You did it!" she said. "Bo, it was wonderful!"

His eyes were warm and intimate, his voice a purr. "I had something to shoot for," he said. He took her hand and sat down beside her while the last two unimportant shooters finished out their rounds. Then they were calling Bo Mason back to the table, and a man was standing, bellowing through a megaphone. "The winna! Harry Mason of Hardanger, singles champion of North Dakota! Harry Mason wins the fifty-dolla cash prize and the silva cup with a score of ninety-eight. That's shootin', folks! Give him a hand!"

He dropped the megaphone to clap, stopped that to pump Bo's hand. The crowd clapped and cheered. The representative of a sporting goods house was introduced and presented Bo with a shiny new repeating shotgun. Bo made a play of trying it out, winced and staggered when the butt touched his shoulder. The crowd laughed. Elsa saw that they liked him. Men went up to talk to him, and he was still speaking over his shoulder as he walked up the slope. Behind him the referee was shouting, "Runner-up, Bill Olson of Mandan. Bill Olson . . ."

"Where'll we go?" Bo said. He held a gun under each arm, a packet of new bills in one hand. "This dough'll burn my pocket out."

"Anywhere," she said. "Bo, I think it's wonderful!"

"You do?"

"Well . . . some ways." They laughed.

"Where's Eva, do you suppose?"

Elsa stopped. "My goodness, we'll never find her, in this crowd."

"Serve her right," Bo said. "Jud told her where to stay."

"But where can Jud be?"

"Jud? Jud's in a poker game."

"Is that . . ."

"He'd be a sucker to pass up a carnival like this. We probably won't see him till late."

It wasn't very nice of Jud, Elsa thought as Bo dragged her off exuberantly toward the fair. If he was going to do that, what did he bring her for at all?

They deposited the guns in the headquarters tent for safe-keeping, and three quarters of an hour later they found Eva disconsolately eating Norwegian cakes and trying to make conversation with the booth attendant, a plump, rosy Norwegian woman who spoke only a dozen words of English.

"I got hungry," Eva said. "And I lost all my money on that horse race thing, and Jud isn't anywhere around. I looked all over. If they weren't giving these cakes away free I'd be starved by now, for all he cares."

The Norwegian woman pressed *kringler* and cups of coffee on them. They ate and licked their fingers. *"Mange tak,"* Elsa said to the woman, and smiled at her. The three of them went off down the street.

"Bo won," Elsa said. "Did you know that? He's champion of North Dakota."

"That's fine," Eva said. Her eyes were roving among the passing people. She stumbled on her skirts, and flew into a vixenish rage. "That's fine," she said. "Maybe you can shoot that big fool of a Jud for me when we find him."

"Hell with him," Bo said. He winked at Elsa. "Let's go have some fun."

They bought a bag of sunflower seeds from a Russian huckster and were experimentally trying out the peanut-like taste when the ferris wheel loomed in front of them. Bo hustled them into a swinging chair. Eva squealed as the wheel began to climb, carrying them up over the trees, over the fungus-growth of colored tents. The sun, which had been just down when they got aboard, showed like a thin red plate on the horizon. They reached the zenith, and the bottom dropped out of Elsa's stomach as they rolled down into the shadow.

"How do you like it?" Bo said.

"Wonderful!" she said. "It's like flying."

"Let's go around again."

They went around three times more until the thrill was worn off it. Eva declined. From the rising, swing-like seat climbing toward twelve o'clock position Elsa saw her below in the edge of the crowd with her head turning right and left in search of Jud.

She felt sorry for Eva. Such a frivolous, helpless, selfish thing. She must feel awful, being left that way.

But when they climbed out after their fourth ride Jud was there. "Oh-oh!" Bo said. "Now we'll have to referee a fight."

"I don't care!" Eva was saying violently. "You said you'd be back in a little while, and I waited hours. If there was any other way of getting home I'd go right now. I'd have gone hours ago."

"I'm sorry," Jud said. "I got detained. That was a pretty big deal Joe had up his sleeve. Turned out I made some money on it."

"What sort of a deal?"

"You wouldn't understand it, birdie," Jud said. "Business." He put his arm down around Eva's shoulders and she shook it off.

"Eva got tired watching us shoot," Bo said. "We found her a while back stuffing herself with Scandihoovian cake."

"I wouldn't have had even that if it hadn't been free!" Eva said.

"Well that's too bad, birdie," Jud said. "Let's go find something to eat right now."

"I'm not hungry now."

"Quit your wrangling," Bo said. "Let's go see the show."

Lamps and Japanese lanterns were on down the carnival street, and crowds milled before booths and tents and tables. The nasal rigmarole of a barker stopped them before a long, narrow tent lighted by a half dozen lamps that threw jigging shadows on the walls. At the end, thirty feet or so from the counter that closed the entrance, a grinning Negro face bobbed and grimaced through a hole in the back curtain painted to represent a jungle river. The Negro's head came right out of the spread terrific jaws of a crocodile.

"Hit the nigger in the head, get a good ten cent seegar," the barker said. "Three balls for a dime, folks. Try your skill and accuracy. Hit the nigger baby on the head get a handsome cane and pennant." His lips moved over the drone of words like the lips of an ape kissing, and he spoke on steadily through inhalation and exhalation, never varying the penetrating nasal whine.

"Want a cane?" Bo said. He stepped over to the counter.

"Me too," Jud said.

The barker shoved over six balls from a pile stacked like cannon balls. He stood back, indifferent to his present customers, his eyes on the passing crowd, his lips moving over the nasal pour of sound. Bo motioned to Jud. "Go ahead. Knock his head off."

The black grinning face in the crocodile's throat weaved and bobbled; the curtain billowed out and in. In the inadequate light it was a deceptive target. Jud removed his coat and folded it on the counter. Then he wound up and threw, awkwardly, Elsa noticed, like a girl. The ball dented a deep shadowy hole in the canvas and dropped. The grinning face opened its mouth, cackled. Then it became fixed, its mouth stretched wide, and Elsa stared, so perfect was the illusion of a succession of red gaping mouths swallowing one another.

"Take him," Bo said. "Your bird."

Jud threw again. The face weaved easily sideward. "There's a percentage in favor of the house," Jud said. His big hand went clear around the third ball as he squinted, aiming. Beside him Bo stood ready, and just as Jud let go he snapped a quick wrist throw. The balls travelled side by side. The swivel-necked colored boy rolled away from Jud's, saw Bo's coming, rolled back. Jud's ball hit him solidly on the skull and bounced clear to the tent roof.

"Got him!" Jud said. His incongruously masculine bellow of laughter filled the entrance. The Negro face pulled back in, leaving the crocodile a dark round hole for a throat. The barker stopped his bored droning and came over angrily. "What'sa idea?" he said. "You can't both peg at once."

"You never said we couldn't," Bo said. "Come across with a cane."

"I don't pay on that. You both threw at once."

Bo's neck and shoulders stiffened as he leaned over the counter. Elsa could not see his face, but she heard his voice, soft. "This guy hit the nigger on the head," he said. "You owe him a cane."

Peaked and white with anger, the barker glared at him. "Like hell!"

"You aren't very smart, fella," Bo said. He raised one hand as the barker started to speak. "And I wouldn't hey rube, either."

"Tough guy, uh?" the barker said.

"No. I just like to see people pay off when they lose."

After a minute the barker threw a cane onto the counter. Bo took it, laid down his two remaining balls, tossed two dimes on top of them so that they rolled off the board, and handed the cane to Eva.

Walking uncomfortably beside him, Elsa said, "Do you suppose the Negro is hurt? Jud threw that awful hard."

He laughed. "You can't hurt a coon hitting him on the head."

Almost immediately came the barker's voice. "Try your luck, folks. Try your skill and accuracy. Hit the nigger baby on the head, get a good ten cent seegar . . ."

"Bo," Elsa said.

"Uh?"

"Was it fair to throw both at once like that?"

He stared at her. "Sure. Every game in this carnival is a skin game. You got to out-smart 'em."

"The percentage is always in favor of the house," Jud said.

Bo took her arm and pointed. "There's a sample. Go on over and try your luck."

Curiously she crossed the street to where a small crowd had gathered around a table. A man at the table was manipulating three half walnut shells so fast that she couldn't follow his fingers. Bo stooped to whisper. "This is one of the oldest skin games in the world. Thimblerigger." He pressed a dollar into her hand and nodded to her, go ahead.

Elsa watched the man's hands. His mouth went constantly in an unintelligible flow of sound like a barker's at the throwing tent. Finally the hands came to rest, the shells in a neat row. A tall, gangling, hayseedy man in overalls threw down a silver dollar and put his finger on one shell. "Follered her all the way," he said. He turned the shell over, and the pea was there.

"Can't win all the time," the thimblerigger said. He threw a dollar to the man, and his hands went intricately among the shells, caressing, touching, turning, mixing. Now and again he opened his hand and showed the pea, or raised a shell to reveal it. "Can't win all the time. Sometimes a quick eye beats a quick hand. Down with your bets, folks. Nothing up the sleeve, an open game of skill. Try your luck again, mister?"

The gangling man grinned and shook his head and stuck his two dollars in his pocket.

"Shill," Bo whispered.

"What?"

"Tell you later. Go ahead and bet him."

Feeling horribly conspicuous, she stepped up and laid her dollar down. The man began shifting his shells, crooning. But she knew better than to listen to his talk. She kept her eyes on his hands, distinctly saw him put the pea under a shell and then shift the shells bewilderingly, but not so rapidly that she didn't keep her eye triumphantly on the right one. She reached out and put her finger on it. There was nothing underneath.

"But where was it?" she said when they were walking again. "I saw him put it there."

"Palms it in his hand," Bo said. "A clever rigger can make you think there's a pea under every one."

"But that other man won."

"He was a shill, a booster. When business is slack he comes around and wins once in a while to keep the suckers coming."

How he could tell that the man was a shill she had no idea, but he knew all about things like this and she knew nothing about anything. And he was the trap-shooting champion of North Dakota. He was also very big and good looking. She saw women turn to look at him in the street. But there was one thing she wanted to ask him, until she forgot about it in the excitement of the games they played all up and down the street. If games like these were always fixed in favor of the house, then what about the poker game that Jud had been in that afternoon? Was that crooked too? Or were poker games like that pure games of skill where a professional gambler like Jud would naturally win? There was a great deal she didn't know, sure enough. She listened to Bo's tutoring carefully whenever he bent to tell her something in that warm, intimate voice.

It was after ten, and black dark under the cottonwoods, when they groped back to the team. Elsa went quietly, guided by Bo's hand, full to the chin with new experiences. She had ridden on a ferris wheel and a merry-go-round. She had gone for a ride around a miniature race track in a horseless carriage, the first automobile she had ever seen, a stinking, explosive, dangerous-looking affair. She had been scared to death, putting on the ulster and goggles; when the man had gone behind and spun the crank and the explosions started right underneath her, she had jumped, she thought, a mile. After the dizzy whirl around the track she had climbed out shakily and pushed up the goggles, standing laughing under the hanging lanterns, and Bo had stopped laughing suddenly and stared at her. "God, your eyes are blue," he had said.

He was just dreadfully nice, she thought. It was his day, but it was hers too. Everything he had done had been shared with her, as if he didn't care about winning the championship and the money unless she had it too. She had collected kewpies, canes, pennants with "Devil's Lake, No. Dak." across them in yellow felt. She had won a box of chocolates, eaten candy popcorn and drunk lemonade and pop until she couldn't eat or drink any more. She had seen a show where a man in rube costume came out and sang a song about two rubes who went to a circus and got in a peck of trouble. Bo had liked that. He had stamped and clapped till the man came back and did the interminable song all over again, prancing around in his chin whiskers and straw hat and red topped boots and bandanna.

Bo was singing the song himself as he helped her over the rough ground:

He pulled Si's whiskers so all-fired hard
That his chin got as long as the neck of a gourd.
All at once I see Si grin and then
I knew his troubles was at an end,
And sure enough, with his knife so keen
He cut his whiskers close to his chin . . .

"Where's it go from there?"

She took a firmer hold on her plunder, each article of which she had vowed she would put away and never part with. "Something about throwing them out in a hurry? I don't know. I don't see how you remember so much of it."

"They don't get thrown out yet. Something about two girls fainting. I got it." He sang three or four lines more.

"That's wonderful," she said, genuinely impressed. "I never saw such a memory."

She stubbed her toe in a root and stumbled wildly in the dark. A doll slipped from her arms and Bo fumbled for it. When he rose his arms went around her suddenly, and he kissed her. Her arms were so full of bundles that she could only twist her face away. "Wait!" she said desperately.

He kept his arms around her. "Why? They're way up ahead."

"Please. Not now."

"Don't forget you've got to be a sport. No welching."

"I won't welch," she said. Whatever happened she wouldn't welch now. That was the thing he disliked Eva so for. She wasn't a sport.

His low laugh stirred in her hair. "Ninety-seven more," he said.

The rest of the way to the buggy she was silent, wondering how she could ever do it. Ninety-seven kisses, not in fun, not the kisses of a boy in a game, but the kisses of a man seven or eight or nine years older than she was, who had been all over and maybe had a past. And a saloon-keeper, a lawbreaker, really.

Briefly, as Jud's flaring match lighted a carriage lamp and the buggy emerged in the dim glow, she was reminded of the one admirer she had ever had, middle-aged mousy old Henry Mossman, who ran the hardware store in Indian Falls and who last spring had proposed to her at a picnic. He had sandy mustaches like a haycock, and he seemed always to smell of shoe-blacking, and he was meek, apologetic, at once gentle and ridiculous. He had proposed to her in the buggy as they drove home through the firefly-streaked darkness. The situation now was close enough to that other that she had a moment of dizziness, almost as if she were dreaming, as if she had been carried in a circle and washed up in a place and time where she had been before. But there weren't, she reminded herself, any fireflies here. And there was nothing meek or apologetic about Bo Mason. Imagine Henry Mossman working it so you had to kiss him a hundred times!

"What're you laughing at?" Bo said.

"I just thought of something."

"What?"

"Nothing you'd care about."

"I care about anything you care about."

"Well, you wouldn't care about this."

Jud came around and lighted the other lamp. Bo brought in the horses and hitched up. "Want me to drive?" Jud said.

"Sure. Go ahead."

The wheels crackled through leaves and twigs as they turned into the road, leaving the calliope still wheezing and the little colored horses of the merry-go-round still rising and falling in the torchlight glare of the shore. Then hard road, the beat of trotting hoofs, the yellow blur of the carriage lamps coasting alongside, the flow of cold air around the unequal silhouettes of Jud and Eva, and the snugness as Bo tucked the buffalo robe around her feet. His arm went around her shoulders and she did not move.

She saw the shadow of Jud put an arm around the shadow of Eva, and heard the murmur of low words. Eva must be over her peeve. That was good. It would be a shame to ride all that way home mad. It would be . . .

Bo leaned close and kissed her, holding it a long time. She heard Eva's clothes rustle as she turned in the front seat to look back, but she did not even have the impulse to free herself. Instead she leaned back further in the seat and smiled into the misty sky. "Two," she said, so softly that the front seat couldn't hear.

A long time later, when her hands were cold and her feet chilled and her lips bruised with Bo's kisses, the buggy stopped and she saw the gable of Karl's house. She had given up her attempt to keep count and hold him to the letter of her bargain. He might have kissed her a hundred or five hundred times.

No one made a move. Eva, muffled against Jud, squealed once in a stage whisper. Murmured words and a giggle came back, then a breathless, hushed squeak. Bo kissed her again, and when he let her go she saw his teeth in the misty dark.

"Don't!" Eva said from the front seat, and her shadow squirmed as if trying to get away.

"Why not?" Jud said, quite loud.

"Because you tickle."

"Isn't anybody getting off here?" Jud said.

"I hate to," said Elsa, and did not move. She looked at Bo, tried to make out his eyes. She pecked him with a swift kiss, pressed him back when he started to rise and help her out. "I'll just hop out and run," she said, whispering close into his ear. "It was a beautiful day." She pressed his hands, gathered her skirts, and jumped from the tire to the ground, half falling. When she popped up again she was right beside Jud, and caught his sudden movement. Eva huddled in her coat. She said goodnight to them and ran indoors.

There was much to think about in bed, many excitements, the memory of Bo's kisses, the eagerness and frankness of his admiration when he stopped laughing beside the automobile and said, "God, your eyes are blue!" He must like her, he must like her a lot. He wasn't the sort of person to pretend anything, and everything that had happened all day had said as plainly as it could be said that he was in love with her. That was a delicious thing to sleep with, a thought that could be hugged. But there was the other thought, the troublesome one, and the complete clarity with which she had seen what she had seen gave her a minute of sacred solemnity. Where was she going, and what kind of people was she going with? Because there wasn't any doubt: when she straightened up suddenly beside Jud after jumping from the buggy he had just been pulling his hand out from under Eva's dress.

6

"It isn't any of my business," Karl said. "I just got this letter from Nels. Or maybe it is my business. I don't know. I just thought I'd come and talk to you."

"What's the matter, is he scared I'll abduct his daughter?" Bo said.

"I don't know that he's scared of anything special. He just wants to know who you are and what you intend to do. He's pretty pious. I suppose he just wants to make sure of you."

"How'd he ever hear about me in the first place?"

"Probably she wrote home," Karl said. A man going out of the poolhall slapped Karl on the back, and he turned around and grinned and nodded. "In a way I'm responsible for her," he said to Bo. "Just how serious is this, anyway?"

He watched Bo take out his knife and begin carefully paring his nails. The heavy-lidded eyes were somber and the dark face expressionless. Then he looked straight up at Karl. "Why, if you come down to that," he said, "I guess it's pretty serious."

"You mean you're going to marry her?"

"I haven't asked her," Bo said.

"But you're going to."

"I guess maybe I am," Bo said, "if I ever get up the nerve."

"I can imagine how scared you are," Karl said. "She thinks you're a little tin god on wheels."

Bo lifted his eyes again, and Karl felt the glance like something heavy, like a pressure. "You sound as if she was making a mistake to think that," Bo said. "If she does."

Karl waved his hands helplessly. He didn't want to get into this. Nels ought to have written to Elsa, or to Bo himself, if he wanted to know so much. He put a man in a bad position. "She's an awful nice kid," he said.

"I never denied that."

"But she's just a kid," Karl said. "That's the only thing that bothers me. She's never been anywhere before, she don't know much. She's just a nice good-looking kid that some careless guy could take advantage of pretty easy."

"Thanks," Bo said, eyeing him. "Thanks very much."

"I never said you were taking advantage of her," Karl said. "I just said she didn't have any experience, she's got no way of judging people because all the people she ever saw were Norske farmers with their feet in a furrow."

"Just what is it you've got against me as her husband?" Bo said.

"I didn't say I had anything against you!" Karl said. His voice rose complainingly. "*Herregud,* I've been your friend for six years, haven't I? Only she isn't nineteen yet. She shouldn't be rushed."

"I haven't been rushing her," Bo said. "I've been making myself stay away from her for a week." His eyes were still cold, uncomfortably steady on Karl's face. "Spill it," he said.

"Oh hell," Karl said. He jingled the change in his pocket and looked toward the door. A wind blew scraps of paper and gray dust past the windows. "How am I going to tell Nels what you do, for one thing?" he said. "I can't just write and say, 'Bo's a good guy that runs a blind pig here in town.' Nels won't like it." He shook his head. "He might even try to stop it," he said.

"How would he stop it?"

"He might make her come home."

"I bet you any amount of money," Bo said, "that she wouldn't go. She ran away from him once, didn't she? He's got a hell of a lot of business trying to run her now."

"Do you want to take her in to live in a room in that hotel?" Karl said. "Can you see her as the wife of a guy that runs a pig? She's just the wrong kind for you, Bo. She's cut out to have a nice house and a bunch of kids and make somebody a good wife. Your kind of life would break her heart in a year."

"Suppose I told you I'm selling the joint."

"You are?"

"I might."

"Then what would you do?"

"I've been looking over a hotel in Grand Forks," Bo said. "If that's any of your business."

Karl wrinkled his forehead. "I don't want you to get sore at me," he said. "If I was doing the marrying I'd just as soon marry you. But I don't know that Elsa should, by God if I do. You're a rambler. You might both wish you hadn't."

Bo had finished paring his nails. He shut the knife with a snick and put it in his pocket. "You're an old busybody," he said. "Why don't you go back and tend to your store?"

Karl shrugged and pushed himself away from the bar. "Give me a beer first."

While Bo got out a bottle and glass Karl watched him. He was a nice guy. He was a hell of a nice guy. But what kind of a life would it be for that innocent of an Elsa, tagging him around from one thing to another? Bo wasn't a sticker. He chased rainbows too much. "You really gone on her?" he said. "You going to become a reformed character and settle down and be an alderman?"

Bo scraped the foam from Karl's glass with an ivory stick and dropped the bottle in a box under the bar. A man across the room was pulling the handle of the slot machine. "I told him," somebody back by the pool tables said loudly, "that I'd cut it for fodder before I'd pay any such cut to a thrashing crew . . ."

"Look," Bo said. "How many times do I have to tell you? I want to marry her. I'm not pretending to be something I'm not, but I'm not saying I'm going on here sitting on my tail in this little joint, either. If she wants to marry me on those terms, whose business is it but hers and mine? Write her old man and tell him anything you please. I'll write him myself if you want. I'm not trying to pull any fast ones. Sure she's a nice girl. She's so nice I can't believe it, considering the way she was brought up. She's a peach. She deserves a lot, I know it. I want to try to give it to her."

"Yeah," Karl said. "Well, nobody could ask for more than that.

I wasn't trying to break it up, you understand. It was just that I got this letter . . ."

He stopped. Bo was looking past him toward the man by the slot machine against the far wall. Moving swiftly, he raised the board and stepped out from behind the bar. He was almost at the man's shoulder before the other heard him, and turned. He was a tall, loosely-built man, a bum or an itinerant laborer with a ragged elbow in his coat. He turned and squawked almost in the same instant, and then Bo collared him.

Elsa looked up from the letter with puckered brows, looked unhappily out the window. It was a gray, unpleasant day, and the wind blew, rattling the window frame. The tight-lipped, strained face of her mother looked at her from the German silver frame of the daguerreotype. She felt miserable and discontented, and she hadn't seen Bo for days. Hardanger, her uncle's house, the people she knew here, were a foreign land and a foreign people. She had cut herself off from home, and now there was no real home here.

Her eyes went back to the letter. Sarah, Kristin wrote, was pretty hard to get along with sometimes. She was funny. One minute she'd be apologetic, and let Erling run all over her, and act as if she were a stray that had been let in, and the next she'd be snappish, trying to run the whole place. And she agreed with Pa that something should be done about Elsa, before she flew off the handle and married some good for nothing. Who was Bo Mason, anyway? Pa seemed to be worried about him. Was he nice? Where had she met him?

Elsa stood up. Let him think what he pleased. He would think the worst, because that was the way he was, but that didn't bother her. She knew Bo a lot better than he did, and if she chose to marry him—and were asked—she would. And what right had Sarah to talk! Marrying a man twice as old as she was, and then presuming to dictate the marriages of other people!

Angrily the girl threw on her coat and went outside. Until five in the afternoon she walked as fast as her legs would carry her, out through flattened weedy fields, across strips of summer fallow, over the corner of the dump-ground among wheels of old buggies, pieces of scrap iron, papers, tin cans rusted and plugged with bullet holes from the target-shooting of boys, the bones of a cow gnawed by dogs or coyotes. The slough confronted her, a saucer of stagnant water rimmed with tules, with mudhens floating close to shore and a wary flock of canvasbacks swimming out in the open water. She walked clear around it, feeling through her coat the coming of deep fall; the going away of warmth from the earth was like some loss of warmth and energy in herself.

And Kristin, wanting to get away from home too, asking if there wasn't someone in Hardanger who needed a girl—Kristin who couldn't bake, couldn't clean house without leaving the corners full of dust puppies and the wallpaper smeared where her broom had brushed down cobwebs. Indian Falls, the place she had called home and still unconsciously thought of as home, must be as bad as she had thought it when she left, if Kris wanted to leave too. But the sister she wanted to come to was lonesome in a strange and barren town.

Her feet kicked in flat brown reeds, sank in muck, squashed through wet hummocks of meadow, found dry ground again. How long would she go on living in someone else's house, eating someone else's bread, with never anything to call her own except the clothes she wore and the thoughts she thought? It would be nice, she thought irrationally, to take piano lessons. But there wasn't a piano in any house open to her. There wasn't anything she could do, no way she could use her time to improve herself, except by reading, and even finding books was difficult.

She kicked a pebble down the ruts worn by the dump wagons. What's the matter with you? she said, and impatience put length in her strides again. Mooning around like a calf, wishing you were somewhere else, or somebody else, and wanting things you can't have.

But I know what I want, she said. I want a place of my own where I can sit down and everything there is mine and everything I do means something.

And you want Bo in it, she said.

Well what if I do? she answered.

Her feet found plank sidewalk under them. She was on the prairie end of Main Street. At the confectionery she hesitated. An ice cream soda might be nice. But the wind whipping around the corner changed her mind. A cup of coffee at home would be better. She hurried faster. The fogged sun had gone completely, and the wind had a bite.

It was too bad, she thought as she neared the bowling alley, that Bo didn't run a place women could go to. She would have liked to drop in sometimes. She would like to right now, and see why he hadn't been over. But then he would think she was chasing him. With her head down against the wind she went past his door.

She was a half dozen steps past when she heard the uproar inside, and Bo's voice, saying, "All right. I'll just fix you so you won't be tempted again."

She shrank back into her uncle's doorway just as the swinging doors of the poolhall burst open and Bo, holding a man by the front of his coat, pushed him through and backed him to the edge of the sidewalk. Though the stranger was almost as big as Bo, he looked beaten. There was a ragged hole in the elbow of his coat. The crowd that had poured out after them stood in a cluster on the sidewalk. Elsa saw Karl, still in his store apron and his black sateen cuff protectors. "Now," Bo said, "how many times did you slug that machine?"

The man's quick eyes shifted from Bo to the crowd and back. He wet his lips. "I'll make it good, mister," he said. His hand fumbled in his pocket.

"How many times?"

"Just once." The tramp's hands quit fumbling, came up to lie lightly on Bo's wrist. "That guy was right close. He c'n tell you. I only did it once. I was hongry and needed a cup-a coffee."

"Why didn't you ask for a cup of coffee?"

"I didn't think you'd hand it out, mister. Honest to God, I'll make it good."

He almost babbled, his eyes on Bo's heavy dark face. It was so changed a face from his usual one that Elsa felt her stomach draw in. Bo kept his left hand rigid in the man's coat, teetering him on the eighteen-inch drop-off into the street. "Well, turn about's fair play. That's right, isn't it? Even-Stephen," Bo said softly. "That's all I'm going to slug you, see? Only once."

The crowd snickered, then someone grunted, a startled sound, as Bo's right fist smashed up. The tramp toppled backward into the street and lay where he fell, with a smear of blood on his mouth and his hat ten feet away from him in the dust.

Bo swung to go back inside, pushing through the men whose eyes still fed on the man lying in the street. Then he saw Elsa, flattened against her uncle's door. His expression changed, the hard, tough look left his face, and he took two steps toward her, but before he could come any further she turned and ran.

She did not look back, but she heard the windy *whoosh!* of the swinging doors as someone went through then, and the voice of someone in the crowd. "Jee-suss!" the voice said. "I'll just slug you once, he says, and then he socks him. Turn about's fair play, he says . . ."

Elsa, hurrying home with her stomach sick and her mind hot with outrage, saw nothing. Her mind was too full of the image of the fear-stricken face of the tramp and the abrupt stillness of his body in the street and the smear of blood on his mouth. He had been hit when he was begging for mercy, when he was making no attempt to resist, when he was offering to make good whatever it was he had done. Any man with a bit of pity in him would have let him go.

Too furious to think, she went and sat on her bed upstairs, stooped to run icy hands through the mass of her hair. Quite suddenly, not knowing she was going to do it, she began to cry.

He appeared so suddenly that there was no way to avoid him. It was eight o'clock. She had finished the supper dishes and was sweeping the kitchen, aware of the pipe smell from the parlor where Karl was reading, aware dimly that it had started to drizzle outside, and that she ought to shut the kitchen door. But she finished sweeping first, stooping with the dustpan, and when she rose he was in the doorway, rain dripping from the curled brim of his derby and the shoulders of his coat dark with wet.

For a moment she confronted him, dustpan in hand, as if he had been a burglar. He leaned against the jamb and said nothing, but his eyes were steady and his face serious. There was no trace around his mouth of the toughness she had seen that afternoon. She looked for it in the instant she faced him, but it was his nice face she saw, the smooth skin dark and healthy looking, the jaw square, the gray eyes lighted with somber warmth. She dropped her eyes to his hand, the hand that had been a brutal fist that afternoon, hooked in his lapel: a square brown hand with long square-ended fingers, a strong, heavy wrist.

With a twist of his body he straightened away from the jamb. "Hello," he said.

"Hello," she said. She stepped to the door, brushing him as she went by, and dumped the dustpan in the can, came back and shut the door, folded the tablecloth and put it away.

"I thought I'd better come over," he said.

"Oh?"

"I thought maybe I ought to do a little explaining."

"Is there anything to explain?"

"There's plenty to explain. You saw me hit that guy."

She faced him then, furiously. "Yes, I saw you hit him! I saw you hit him when he wasn't fighting back and was begging you not to."

Annoyance brushed his face, was smoothed away again. His voice was quiet, as if he were maintaining his patience and explaining something to a child. "There's only one way you can treat those guys," he said.

"He said he'd pay you back for whatever it was he did."

"Sure. Sure he'd pay me back, long as I had him. And you know what he'd do? Next place he went into he'd slug some other machine. Guys like that will go on slugging machines till someone shows them it isn't healthy."

"I suppose you did it just to teach him a lesson!"

Bo flushed. Leaning against the door, he breathed through his nose, pressing his lips together. She couldn't keep her temper now; she had to tell him what she thought of him. "What if he did slug a machine?" she said. "It's a gambling thing, isn't it?"

"Sort of."

She took her hands from her apron pockets, shoved them back in again hard because she couldn't keep them from shaking. "Remember what you told me at the carnival?" she said. "Remember what you said about it was all right to take advantage of a gambling game because any game like that was crooked? Any gambling game is crooked. Jud said so himself. What that tramp did was just what you and Jud did when you both threw at once."

"It isn't the same," Bo said. "It isn't anything like the same."

"I don't see any difference. You bullied the man at the carnival when he objected. What if the tramp had bullied you the same way?"

"He'd have got his head knocked off."

"He did anyway." Elsa opened her hands inside her pockets. They were sweating in the palms.

"I explained to you," Bo said. "You let these guys get away with things like that and they'll cheat everybody up and down the line."

She couldn't see him any more because her eyes were blurry. "That was the most brutal thing I ever saw," she said.

He did not speak for a moment, but when he did his voice was rougher. "You shouldn't have been around there," he said. "That's a man's place. It's no place for a woman."

She looked at him, almost stammering. "Excuse me," she said. "I didn't know the sidewalks were some place I shouldn't go. But I suppose you have to have them clear so you can beat somebody up every once in a while!"

"Listen, Elsa . . ."

"Listen nothing! I thought you were big and strong and fine, and now I find out that all you use your strength for is to hit people who beg you not to. If you'd shown any mercy at all, the least bit of pity . . ."

"Just because I sock a damn tinhorn that slugs my machine, I'm that bad."

"You're worse."

He laughed, the short, choppy, contemptuous sound that meant he was disgusted. "All right," he said briefly. "That's the way you feel about it." He pulled down his derby and ducked out into the drizzle.

Very slowly the fury drained out of her. Weakness wobbled her knees. She sat down at the table and bit her knuckles and stared at the wall. After a while she picked up the lamp and made her way through the parlor past Karl, who looked up with a discreet question in his eyes that she ignored.

7

Helm stood spraddle-legged, resting her weight evenly on both feet before the kitchen table she was using for an ironing board. The room was full of the smell of steam and starch. Helm's great bare arm, solid as a sawlog, moved with weight and authority back and forth, and her tongue moved just as heavily, just as authoritatively, with the same kind of bludgeoning dislike.

"Now this," she said, "is the shirt of Mr. Gerald Witwer, the druggist. Look at it. French flannel, fine enough to wrap a baby in. Summer times he wears silk and madras. His old lady never sends his underwear, and there are only two possible reasons why. Either she don't want to give away that he wears silk panties, or he can't hang onto himself and she's ashamed to send them with the wash. I don't know which choice I'd rather take. Maybe both."

She finished the shirt and folded it onto the pile in the basket. "Sometimes." she said, "I think I'd rather sit out in front of Bo's poolhall with a patch over my eye and a tincup strapped on my leg than wash the dirt out of clothes for people like them. Even when they're clean, those clothes are dirty. There's some kinds of hypocritical dirt you can't get out."

Elsa was only half listening. She sat by the window looking out, thinking that fall wasn't the pleasant season here that it was at home. There weren't any trees to change, for one thing. The land just got brown and then gray, and one night it froze, and then it rained, and froze again so that the roads were ridged with hardened tracks, and every change from summer to winter made the place look more desolate than it had before. And the wind blew interminably, holding you back, hustling you along, sweeping at you from around corners. You weren't free of it even inside, for it whined in the eavespouts and slammed doors and eddied down the chimney and made the stove smoke. It kept you tense all the time . . .

The realization that Helm had stopped speaking made her look up, Helm was watching her, smiling with her blackened teeth, her eyes soft and shining. "Honey," Helm said, "ain't you made it up with Bo yet?"

Elsa shook her head.

"Ain't you going to?"

Elsa shook her head again.

"It isn't like you to hold a grudge," Helm said.

"It isn't a grudge!" Elsa said. "I just can't like him after what he did."

"Well, what did he do?" Helm said. "He knocked down a tramp that had slugged a slot machine. That isn't anything to break your heart over, honey. If you try to find a man that never knocked another man down you're going to be left with nothing but guys like Gerald Witwer to pick from. I'd rather have one that *could* knock somebody else down, even if he had to do it once in a while to keep in practice."

"He did it in cold blood," Elsa said stubbornly. "That was what . . ."

"Bo hasn't got a drop of cold blood in him," Helm said. "Tell me he's got too wild a temper and gets disgusted too quick and despises people if they're clumsy or puny or hypocritical, but don't tell me he's cold blooded."

"He was that day. I saw him."

Helm released the catch and dropped a sadiron onto the stove, picked up another, upended it, spat on the smooth bottom. "Well, it sure hasn't helped your disposition, either one of you," she said. "You mope around like you didn't care whether you lit butter-side up or down, and Bo goes snarling around the place like a dog that's been kicked around too much and is going to bite the next guy tries it. Why don't you call it quits and give your friends a rest?"

"I'm sorry," Elsa said, and rose. "I don't want to be grumpy and bad company. It's the darned weather. I never saw weather stay so gray and disagreeable. I never could be cheerful in bad weather."

"Honey," the big woman said, "you're talking right through the top of your hat."

But Helm didn't know everything, Elsa thought on the way home. She hadn't seen Bo hit that man. Besides, Helm, for all her big heart, was used to rough men. She thought a man ought to be rough. But he oughtn't. A man could be strong and full of courage and still be generous and kind.

But what on earth shall I do? she said, and looked with distaste at the weedy vacant lot she was passing. While she had been dreaming her idiotic dreams about Bo Mason, Hardanger had been a vivid and exciting place, but now that those were put away it was a dreary little village on the desolate flats. And the only people she knew in it were in some way tied up with Bo. The Witwers and the Schantzes and the more "respectable" part of town kept to itself; there wasn't a friend to make the place bearable except those friends who were also friends of Bo's, and she never went to Helm's any more without dreading to find him there.

She heard the train whistle forlornly as she turned in at Karl's house. She felt as lonely as the train sounded, but inside the hall she took off her coat almost angrily. What she needed was work; if she didn't do something she'd be pitying herself until she blubbered.

When she went to the kitchen and started in she found the four mallards on the table. There was no note with them, but she knew instantly who had brought them. Karl never went hunting. Neither did Jud. There was only one other person who would have left them.

Well, she thought, if he thinks he can wheedle me out of it that way! But that was the second thing that came into her mind. The first was pleasure: the very sight of the ducks lying there, and the instant recognition of their giver, was a pure warm pleasure.

Three days later, when she opened the front door to sweep the first dry snow of the year off the porch, there were four more ducks hanging on the doorknob. They had not been there more than a few minutes, for their webbed feet were barely stiff, and the bodies of the ducks when she plucked them were still faintly warm. The tracks that led to and from the porch were large tracks, the imprints corrugated like the rubber sole of a wader boot.

Karl raised his eyebrows when he saw her plucking the second batch of birds. But she gave him no explanation. There wasn't any explanation she could give him. She told herself that she was not softening one bit, that he could go on leaving ducks as long as he chose and she would not change her mind about him. Still, she looked at both front and kitchen door every morning to see if anything else was there. On the Sunday following the first mallards there was a great Canada goose.

"Don't you think we ought to have company for supper?" Karl said. "If this buck Indian or whoever he is keeps leaving game in front of the wigwam we ought at least to let him come and eat some of it, hadn't we?"

Elsa was on the point of saying yes, and letting her anger and her dislike evaporate, but when she looked up into Karl's little knowing round blue eyes she shook her head. "I'd rather not, Uncle Karl."

He shrugged and let it go, and after he had left for the store she wondered if Bo had put him up to that question. It would be just like him, and then he could come swaggering in, on her invitation. If she made the first move then his pride would be saved. But the first move had already been made, she reminded herself, and he had made it.

Oh, I don't know! she said in vexation, and stormed through the house doing her housework as if every pillow were a face to be slapped. He did hit that man in cold blood, she said, but she couldn't fix the image of the sprawling body and the bloody mouth as definitely as she would have liked. Bo's eyes kept coming in over it, gray and steady and somberly warm, and once during the morning she found herself mentally moulding the blunt angle of his jaw, almost as if she were running her fingers along it.

The postoffice was at the far end of town, a frame shanty with a wall of boxes and a stamp window. Within the past two weeks the winter stove had been set up in the center of the room and a great pile of lignite dumped against the back wall outside. There were almost always two or three men sitting around on the bench, because on these cold days the postoffice was snug.

Elsa found herself anticipating that hot, tobacco-smelling cubbyhole as she walked through the light snow. Even the few blocks' walk from Karl's house could redden her nose and whiten her breath these days. She walked fast, noticing that all the houses were banked with dirt or had tarpaper tacked along the foundations; the smokes from all the chimneys had a warm, intimate look, and the town seemed friendlier now that its ugly weed-grown lots were covered with snow. There were stubby icicles hanging from the eaves of the postoffice.

She was not thinking about Bo at all when she opened the door and stepped in. If she had been, she might have been better prepared. As it was, she stopped dead still just inside the door, with her hand still on the knob.

"Morning," he said.

A swift look showed her no one else in the room except old Mr. Blake, puttering in the room behind the window.

"Hello," she said briefly, and went to Karl's box. He was right behind her; she felt his presence with a kind of stage fright.

"Look," he said. She took the one white envelope from the box, her mind automatically registering that it was from Indian Falls, in her father's spidery, old-world hand, and with the letter held helplessly in her fingers, she looked. His eyes were so sober, so warm, so compelling, that she was confused. She ought to walk right on out, bid him good morning and open the door . . .

"Call it quits?" Bo said.

"I . . ." Her confusion deepened. He was too direct and blunt. She fought the blood back from her face.

"I'll apologize," he said. "I'll admit I was wrong, if that's what you want."

"That wouldn't make it good to the poor man you hit," she said.

"I already made that good."

"You did?"

"As much as I could. I took him in and fed him and gave him money to get out of town."

"When?"

"Right after I saw you down there, right after it happened."

"But you didn't tell me," she said.

"You never gave me a chance."

"I . . ." Elsa said again.

"I still think there's only one way to treat a tinhorn," Bo said, "but after the way you looked I got worrying about him and went out and brought him in. I guess maybe I was already mad when I spotted him. Karl had been giving me the currycomb for a half hour."

"What about?" she said curiously. She couldn't imagine Karl doing anything of the kind.

"You."

"Me!"

"You," Bo said. "He'd got a letter from your father telling him to get you out of my clutches."

"Oh!" Elsa said furiously. She turned half away from his intent stare. The letter in her fingers was like a match held too long. She looked at it, wanting to drop it as she would have dropped the match before it burned her, but she did not drop it. When she looked up Bo was looking at it too.

"That another one from him?" he said.

She nodded.

"Kind of upset, isn't he?" he said, and laughed. In spite of her rage, she had to laugh with him.

"Sometimes," she said, "I could . . ."

"He made me a little mad myself," Bo said. "I guess I took it out on that bum. Shall we call it quits?"

Elsa looked into his face, dark and square, a little curl of smile at the corners of his mouth, his eyes smoky and glowing. "All right," she said. "I . . ." She shook her head. "Everything is such a mess," she said.

Bo held up his hand, and she saw that he too had a letter. He was grinning. "Between your family and mine," he said, "we've got a nice combination."

"Your family?" she said. "I didn't know you ever heard from your family." She craned to read the return address in the corner of the envelope: Hattie Mason, Black Hawk, Illinois.

"My sister's the only one ever writes. I don't even know where any of them are now, except her and Ma."

"Are they . . . well?" Elsa said. It was a silly thing to say, but she didn't want him to stop talking about them.

"They must be, the way their appetites hold out."

"You mean you support them?"

"No. They pull the hard luck story out of the bag about half a dozen times a year, and I send them something."

"I shouldn't think they'd have the nerve, after the way they treated you."

He was amused. "They treated me all right. Where'd you get that idea?"

"But you ran away from home."

"I ran away from the old man," Bo said. "He's been dead for ten years."

"Oh." She couldn't think of anything else to ask him, and they stood in the room's heat looking at each other. Mr. Blake stuck his gray head through the window, looked around, pulled it back in with a slow munching of toothless jaws. Bo put out a hand and touched her fur collar. "Thanks," he said. "You're a sport. I haven't felt as good as this for two weeks. That feud was getting my goat."

"Me too," she said, and blushed.

"Where you headed?"

"I was going over to Helm's and give her a loaf of fresh bread," she said, and lifted the newspaper-wrapped parcel under her arm.

"I got something to show you." He regarded her abstractedly, his tongue in the corner of his mouth. "You run on over, and I'll bust past the hotel and get it and see you at Helm's. How's that?"

"Good." She smiled at him, couldn't keep the smile from breaking into a laugh. "I'm so glad we've quit fighting!" she said, and started back along the sidewalk. She had gone only a dozen steps when her hat was knocked over her eye by a large soft snowball.

"One down, one cigar," Bo said as she turned. He was stooping for another handful. "Where you want this one?"

"Quit it." She shielded herself with the bundle of bread. The second snowball plastered itself against the newspapers, and she started for him. Instead of running, as she had expected him to, he grabbed a handful of snow and before she knew where she was had washed her face with it. "Keeps your complexion pretty," he said.

Sputtering, she grabbed snow and scuffled with him in the street. Mr. Blake came to the door of the postoffice and stood watching. "Hey," he said mildly. "What goes on, what goes on?"

Bo crunched a snowball within three inches of Mr. Blake's head and Mr. Blake retreated. Elsa, stooping, caught Bo off guard with a double handful of snow, wiped it around his face, grabbed her bread by the string, and ran. The snow melted on her face, and she wiped it off, looking back to make sure that Bo was not after her again. He stood beside the postoffice in a burly black dogskin coat, his teeth white in his dark face, and waved.

"Well," Helm said when she came in. "Roses in the cheeks."

"That big ape of a Bo," Elsa said. "He . . ."

She stopped, seeing Helm's smirk. "That explains everything," Helm said. "Don't bother to go on."

"He washed my face with snow!" Elsa said. "It isn't anything like you think."

"Don't bother explaining," Helm said. "He washed your face, and you're still mad. I could tell by the way you look you wouldn't speak to him on a bet."

"Oh, go to grass," Elsa said. "I brought you some bread. In a minute I'll wish I hadn't."

Still grinning, Helm waddled into the kitchen to put the bread away. When she came back Elsa said, "I didn't know he was sending money back to his family."

"Is he?"

"Every once in a while. They write and ask him for money and he sends it."

"What's wrong with that?"

"Nothing, only I wish I'd known it before. I think it's nice of him."

"Oh, he's cold blooded that way," Helm said. "Just sends money home as calmly as if he was cutting somebody's throat."

"Well, why didn't you tell me?" Elsa said. "You let me just go on . . ."

"Couldn't anybody tell you anything, last couple weeks," Helm said.

There was a stamping on the porch and Bo came in in his dogskin coat, looking as immense as a bear. He was whistling a bar of the rube ballad they had heard at the carnival. He made a pass at Helm and she lifted her great white arm.

"Feeling pretty horsy, ain't you?" she said.

"Isn't anything particularly wrong, is there?" he said.

"What's so right?" Helm said.

"Well, the *Svenske flika* has called off her dogs," Bo said. His mouth drew down as he looked at Elsa. "Then again," he said, "Jud and me just sold three thousand bushel of flax up twenty-seven cents from where we bought it."

"My goodness," Elsa said. "That's a lot of money."

"Chicken feed," Bo said. "Wait till we get going."

He was so pleased with himself and the world that he couldn't keep still. He sparred with two of Helm's boys in the kitchen, captured the pup and rolled him over to scratch his chest until the automatic hind leg was pumping, jumped up from that to go to his coat, thrown over the dining table, and bring out a package. "Forgot what I was going to show you," he said. "How do you like this?"

It was a silver shaving mug, ornately carved and moulded, with a grapevine curling around the rolled brim and three heavy clusters of metal grapes hanging down from the vine. In the unornamented metal on the side was engraved

Champion of North Dakota
Singles Traps
Harry Mason, 1905

"It's lovely," Elsa said, when she had looked it over. "I didn't know they gave you a cup too." She handed it back, but he put his hands behind him.

"Keep your property."

"What?"

"It's yours. Don't you spik the English?"

"Take it, for God sakes," Helm said, "before you make him cry."

Bo scowled at her. "Seems to me there's an awful lot of low class people around here," he said. "How about going for a walk?"

Helm stood with her hands on her hips and watched them get into their coats. She shook her head. "By God, it must be love," she said.

His hand under her elbow, Bo steered her down the beaten path in the snow. "Let's go out on the flats," he said. "I've been inside so much lately I need to get some wind through me."

She lifted her skirts and plunged with him, up to her shoetops in snow. The minute they were outside he had seemed to grow somber, and he said nothing all the way out past the last straggling shacks and into the open fields. The silence began to weigh on Elsa.

"Isn't Helm a funny old thing?" she said.

His head turned, his eyes met hers briefly. Then they looked away, ahead, anywhere, across the even white plain. Their feet found ripple-marked crust over a drift that almost held their weight, but not quite, and they staggered through it awkwardly.

"Funny?" he said.

"She says such funny things," Elsa said.

"She isn't as silly as she sounds," Bo said.

They were walking across the waves of a plowed field, ribbed brown and white. A yellow cat, tender-footed, delicate, obviously disgusted at the feel of snow under its pads, obviously out of place and irritated at whatever errand took it out into the fields on such a day, crossed in front of them, stopped with a lifted forefoot, opened its mouth in a soundless mew, went delicately forward again. Bo pegged a snowball at it and it flattened against the frozen furrow. Another, and it forgot its sensitiveness and leaped across the field in great muscular wild-animal bounds.

"What on earth would a cat be doing out here?" Elsa said.

His look was sober and intent, packed with some concentrated meaning she couldn't read. "I feel about as out of place as the cat," he said.

"Why?"

He stopped and faced her. "I want to ask you something."

Over his dogskin shoulder she saw the steely sky, misted, wintry, and back of him, spreading on all sides, the flat and wintry plain, spare yellow grass poking up in places swept clean by the wind, the surface irregular with miniature mounds tailed by flat cones of drift. She couldn't lift her eyes until he took her by the elbows. His hands were as rough as his voice.

"How about it?" he said.

"How about what?" she said, refusing to let herself know what he meant.

"How about marrying me?"

Her face cold in the wind, her mind stopped by the enormity of what was happening, she looked up at him. His face was paler than she had ever seen it, and there was no foolery in it. She nodded.

He moved so suddenly to kiss her that her feet tripped in the scored field and he fell against her awkwardly. They sprawled together. Instantly the constraint was gone; their laughter shouted into the wind, and they sat kissing exuberantly with cold lips in the middle of the waste of snow.

She held him away to look at him, noticing the subtle mingling of light and dark coloring in the pupils of his eyes, and the curving firmness of his mouth. Her shoulders drew up in an uncontrollable shiver. "You've got a nice mouth," she said, tracing it with her finger. "A nice mouth and dappled eyes."

It seemed that afternoon, when lunch was over and they had told Karl and had decided to be married right after New Year, and Karl had gone back to the store and left them alone to plan things, that all the trouble with Sarah, her father, Indian Falls, all the sense of uprooting and homelessness and the multiple problems that had invaded her life, were swept backward out of her mind like straw from a thresher spout, and her world was clean and new and spotless, to be made into what she would.

Bo told her that he was going to sell the poolhall. It didn't make enough money to satisfy him. Bill Conzett had offered him a price —not high enough, but it might be better to take it and get that money for speculating in grain. And there was the hotel in Grand Forks that he and Jud had been looking over. With that, plus the annual pickings they could make on grain, they ought to make a pile. He would build her a house in Grand Forks as soon as things got rolling good, and meantime, if the hotel deal went through, there was always a place to live.

She lay with his arm around her, thinking of that house they would build, of the lawn she would plant and the trees that would make it pleasant on warm afternoons in summer, and the roses over the trellis in front and the hollyhocks high against a white-washed back fence, and the grape arbor. . . .

"Oh goodness!" she said, and sat up suddenly. "I forgot all about that letter from Pa!"

She knew what would be in it, how much his world was set against the kind of world he thought she was getting into, and she was grateful when she opened it and saw that it was in Norwegian. Bo, looking over her shoulder, couldn't read it. All he could do was snort at the spidery hand and the unfamiliar tangle of letters. Outside the wind had risen, and pebbly snow lashed at the storm windows. Bo leaned further to see the cranky letters. "Hen tracks," he said. "What's he say?"

"He . . . doesn't think you're the right sort of man for me to be going around with," Elsa said. Her laugh was a little shrill, and she cut it off sharply. "He says anyone with a name like Bo is probably suspicious from the beginning, and Karl told him you ran a bowling alley. He doesn't want me to get mixed up with any rough crowd of people. Uncle Karl ought to take more care what people I know."

"Careful of you, isn't he?" Bo said.

"That isn't all," she said. "Listen. 'From what Karl says I do not judge this Mason the proper sort of man for you to marry. If you insist you will be going against my wishes. At the very least I hope you will bring him back here for a visit before you do anything rash.' "

Bo was fiddling with her hand, bending the thumb, releasing it. He looked up from under his upcurved eyebrows. "What's that mean? Do we take a trip to Minnesota to get looked over?"

Elsa compressed her lips. If she didn't do as she pleased now, she would never have the right of making her own decisions. "No," she said flatly. "He hasn't any right to have a say in my affairs. We'll go right ahead and let him lump it."

"That'll mean he'll disown you, or something else nice and high-minded."

"Maybe."

He snorted. He strode to the door and threw it open. The wind whipped snow in level, driving lines across his body and through the hall. "Go!" he said, pointing with a stiff finger. "Never darken my door again!"

Elsa laughed and bit her lip. "Shut the door," she said. "You'll have the hall full of snow."

" 'Tis kind of blowing, at that," he said. He shut the door and came back to nuzzle in her hair. "Does it matter much?" he said.

"It's just exactly what happened to him," she said. "He was not good enough for Mother, her folks thought, and they threw her out because she insisted on marrying him. Now he acts the same way they did."

"I'm perfectly willing to go see him."

"No," she said. "He never asked any of us when he was going to marry Sarah."

"So it's all set," Bo said. "New Year's day."

She nodded, and his eyes crinkled in the full-lidded smile that hardly moved his lips. "Any idea how good that makes me feel?"

"No," she said. "Tell me."

"Makes me feel as if I could settle down," Bo said. "Seems to me I've been on the move ever since I can remember. We'll find some good proposition and dowel ourselves in and keep our nose to the grindstone and make a pile."

Later he said he ought to run down to the poolhall and make

sure everything was jake. He'd be back for supper if she'd let him. She kissed him long and hard at the door, clenching her fingers in the hairy coat, begrudging even the hour or so he would be gone.

But he was not gone an hour. He had barely ducked into the wind, which now blew with heavy, gusty force, and she had barely settled down to look at her father's letter again, when he was back, stamping the snow off his feet, his nose red and leaking, his coat stiff with driven snow.

"This is going to be a buster," he said. "You can't see ten feet. The old poolhall can get along by itself. Getting cold as all billy hell, too."

"Can Uncle Karl get home, do you suppose?"

"He's a sucker if he tries it."

"Maybe we ought to get fixed," she said. "If it's going to be a bad storm."

"That's why I came back," he said. "We might be marooned three days if this keeps on."

He shouldered his way out the kitchen door with coal scuttle and bucket. It was five minutes before he came back. "By God," he said, and wiped the frozen clot from below his nose with a quick side glance of shame. "I got lost between here and the coal shed. This is an old ring-tailed roarer, let me tell you."

He dumped the buckets in the box and went out again, and a third time. When the box was full he brought in another load and filled the kitchen range and the heater, went out still once more for a last pair of buckets. Then he sat down in a kitchen chair and hung out his tongue with mock exhaustion, wiping the melting snow off his forehead with the back of his hand. His laugh filled the warm kitchen.

"How about some supper, wife?" he said.

They got into aprons and played housekeeping. It was six thirty by the time they had finished eating, and still Karl had not come. Elsa kept holding up her hand to listen for sounds. There was never anything but the pounding of the wind and the restless fluttering of the stove.

"Quit worrying," Bo said. "Karl's too wise a bird to start out in this. He'll stay snug in the store till it stops."

He was laughing, warm-eyed, the corners of his lips twitching with mirth. His big hands lay on the edge of the table before him.

"That isn't all I'm worrying about."

He leaned across the table to kiss her. "What else?"

She forced herself to meet his eyes. "If he doesn't come home, we'll be here together all night."

He laughed aloud. "Why not? We're going to be married pretty soon. And nobody can talk if people get marooned in a blizzard. It happens all the time."

He came around to her, put his hands under her chin, bent over her from behind. "It's been just like we've been married ever since this morning," he said. "Why should we worry if it keeps on?"

She shook herself loose and stood up, her chest tight and her face wrinkled as if with a pain. "Don't blame me," she said. "I . . . things come so fast, somehow. I seem to change my ideas about things from one day to the next." She put her hand on his arm. "It seems all right to me, now," she said. "Honestly it does. But can't you see what it would mean? After that letter from Pa, and the way he thinks you're not the right sort, for some reason? We'd just be giving him and people like him a chance to talk and say I told you so."

"I could slide out," Bo said. "When the storm started to let up I could vanish."

"Would you want me to be like Eva?" she said. "Do you want to be like Jud?"

For a moment he watched her face. Then he shrugged. "All right. But what if we can't help being cooped up here?"

"I don't know," she said helplessly.

His laugh chopped out, a short, mirthless recognition of the irony of what he had to do. "If I get my directions crossed and come back feet first you'll wish you'd been a little more tender-hearted," he said.

"What are you going to do?"

"Go get Karl, what'd you think?"

"Bo, you can't! You'd get lost, or frozen stiff."

"Probably will," he said amiably. "Got any rope around here?"

While she hung on his arm crying that he was insane, that he wouldn't get to the corner, that she never meant he should go out into the blizzard, she didn't know what she meant, he towed her around the kitchen poking into cupboards and drawers for rope. He was as stubborn as a mule. He was an idiot. He would die in the storm, and then how would she feel?

With a length of clothes line in his hand he looked at her quizzically. "When you convince me," he said, "you convince me for good."

"There must be some other way. Couldn't you go over to Con-zett's? That's closer." Then her temper let loose. "Anyway, I should think you'd be able to control yourself even if we were marooned."

He shook his head with a hanging, mocking grin. "Wouldn't promise a thing," he said. "Us undesirable characters can't be trusted."

"All right, then," she said, and let go of his arm. "Go on out and freeze to death."

She even went into the cellar hole and found him twenty feet of rope and a length of picket chain. But when he started out the front door (he had to put his shoulder against it and heave to move the storm door through the accumulated drift) she threw herself against the dogskin coat and clung. "Oh, be careful, Bo! If you can't find your way don't try too long."

By now, she saw, his stubbornness and recklessness wouldn't have let him stay even if she had begged him to. He grinned, kissed her, throttled her with an enormous bear hug, put his head down, and ran.

He must have run, she decided afterward, all the way to the store, taking a direction and plowing ahead blind. Probably he wanted to get there and back before she had time to worry; probably he also wanted to impress her with how fast he could do it. She was surprised; she was even startled, the stamping came on the porch so soon. She ran to open the door. Karl, his face muffled in a felt cap with earlaps and a broad chin band, with a yellow icicle in each nostril and his eyebrows stiffly iced, stumbled in. The rope around his waist was a smooth, velvety white cable.

The hall was full of wind and drift. *"Herregud!"* Karl said, and grabbed the storm door to keep it from blowing off its hinges. Bo loomed through the opaque, white-swirling darkness like a huge hairy animal.

When she had untied their lifeline she led them in, inspected them under the light for signs of frostbite, rushed Bo out into the hall while she scooped up snow and held it again the leprous spots on his cheekbones. He bit at her fingers, and she slapped him on the nose.

"That's a heck of a way to welcome a guy that's just risked his neck to go get a worthless old tumblebug like Karl."

"You hold still," she said. She scrubbed his face with snow till it glowed, looked to make sure all the spots were gone, and relaxed with a noisy sigh. "Oh, I'm glad you're back!" she said, and reached up to kiss his wet, beefy, ice-cold face, right in front of Karl. "How'd you ever make it?"

"Just spread my sails and coasted down. Wind lifted me right up and set me down square in front of the alleys. Ask Karl how we got back."

Huddling close to the stove with his neck still pulled into his shoulders, Karl grumbled. "Ask me!" he said. "Pulled me along like a steer. My belly'll be sore for a week."

Tall in the doorway, full of pride, Bo grinned at her. "Once," he said, "Karl got off the path and started off toward Fargo somewheres. I thought he was stuck in the snow, when it was only the rope caught around a telegraph pole, and I yanked him half in two before he backtracked and got straight again." He put an icy hand on the back of Elsa's neck. "Satisfied now?"

She squeezed the heavy muscles of his arm. Karl went into the kitchen, and she followed to get him his supper. Bo wandered after her. "What's the use of postponing this marriage till New Year?" he said. "Why don't we get a preacher and get it over with?"

"You sound as if it was like moving the furniture, or something," Elsa said. She couldn't get married in a rush like that. There wasn't anything ready, no towels, no sheets, no clothes, no anything to keep house with. But as she looked at his cold-reddened face and his smoky, laughing eyes, and thought how nice he'd been, really, to go out in a storm like that and bring Karl back just so she wouldn't get talked about, and because she wanted him to . . .

"I guess we can at least wait till the blizzard's over," she said.

It was almost the first time she had heard real mirth in his laughter, the first time it had sounded exuberant and full instead of short and half impatient. He pulled her onto his lap on the kitchen chair, while Karl grunted and grumbled over his supper, and scuffled with her, trying to take a toothy bite out of her between the neck and shoulder, where she was most ticklish. He was so boisterous and rough and strong that she struggled, but he held her arms and reduced her to helplessness.

"Hear that, Karl?" he said. "You can give the bride away about day after tomorrow."

"I'll be giving her away, all right," Karl said. "Might as well throw a girl to the lions."

"I'm tame," Bo said. "I'm completely house-broke. You tell him, Elsa."

"About like a dancing bear," she said. He set her suddenly on her feet and stood up.

"We have to consult the oracles," he said. "See if this marriage is going to be a success. I'll play you eleven games of casino to see who's going to wear the pants in the family. And if I win I'll play you eleven more for the championship of the Chicago stockyards."

Even after Karl had been long in bed and the kerosene in the parlor lamp had given out, and the lamp had dimmed, flared, sunk, flared up again, and gone out in a stink of coal oil; even after they had quit fooling around playing cards and had settled on the sofa with the rattle of granular snow on the windows and the house shuddering under the whining strength of the wind, there was a golden light over her mind, and her senses swayed with the swaying of a ghostly hammock in an idyllic grassy backyard with hollyhocks tall against a whitewashed fence, and a redbird was nesting in the grape arbor.

II

In one way
the accident
was a blessing,
for now, after she
had swept the broom
awkwardly, one-handed,
across the tenthouse floor,
had soused the dishes and
set them to dry, and had
stooped and pulled, making
the beds, while the blood rushed
painfully into her injured arm, there
was good time to rest. For an hour or
more in the mornings and for long quiet
periods in the afternoons she could sit on the
plank platform before the door and let the children
run in the clearing and simply relax, her mind still and
her senses full of the sounds and smells that the woods had
always had but that she had never had time to notice before.

Cradling her right arm, spiralled with thick bandage, in her lap, she could close her eyes and hear the tapping of woodpeckers off in the forest, and sometimes the drumming of a grouse. Her lungs loved the balsam air, and her body soaked up warmth, infinitely pleasant after the weeks of rain. It was as if a blessing had fallen suddenly on the half acre of stumpy ground. For five days there had been fine weather: every morning the sun tipped the firs and poured into the open, creeping from chip to chip until it filled the clearing, leaned its friendly weight on the tenthouse door. By the time Bo went to work at seven the shadows had all pulled themselves back toward the ring of woods, and while she did her housework she could feel the warmth growing on the canvas roof. When she handed out the carrots and greens for the two boys to feed to their rabbits, and came out to stand in the full sun, it was with a sense of peace and permanence so alien that she had to smile at her own perception of it.

More than anything else, it was the rabbits that gave her that feeling of home—they and the children digging in the dirt around a big stump. Home, as she imagined it and remembered it, had always meant those things, children, permanence, the recurrence of monotonous and warmly-felt days, and animals to care for. More than once, leaning her back against the wall, she fingered the bandage caressingly. It was odd you never realized how tired you were until something made you take a rest.

Even the pain beating in her arm from wrist to elbow with a steady nagging ache was good, because it reminded her that now there was a kind of fulfillment. The pain was like something left over from the rainy winter, lying in her like the things that she could not forget. But it would pass, and the things she had thought she could never forget she would forget. Unless she stirred too fast, or got impatient at her crippling, when it would leap instantly to an immense and throbbing pressure against the tight bandage, it was even a half-pleasant kind of pain. It would pass, but the peace would not pass. While you lay against the tent wall in the sun and the children dug endlessly and happily in the dirt Bo was working, and when the arm was better you would go back to work too, and the tenthouse would not always be a tenthouse. As you got ahead a little further it would become a house, with a barn behind at the edge of the firs, and the café would bring in a little money and you could have a garden and a few animals, a cow and some chickens, and that would be a good life.

In the sun, her face tipped back and her burned arm in her lap, she let down her hair and shook it over her shoulders, as thick and wavy and richly tinted as ever, lavish and rich and good to feel when it was well brushed. That was an odd thing too. In your childhood everybody teased you about your hair and yelled, "There comes a white horse, kid!" but now everybody seemed to think it was beautiful. You got more compliments on your hair than anything. As she brushed evenly down, pulling the hair over her breast to get at it with her good hand, she thought much about how their lives would be now, how Bo seemed to be over his disappointment and his restlessness. Seven years of hard times, and the crash of 1907, had humbled his ambitions. Perhaps that was good too. It didn't do to expect too much.

It was that hotel, she thought. Five years of butting our heads against that wall! Idly she watched a half dozen chickadees fussily busy at a crust of bread one of the boys had dropped. Her brush handle lay smooth and rounded and solid in her hand. She felt it there, something she could put down if she chose, but she did not put it down. She liked its solid familiar feel. That was the way with things you remembered. You could put them down if you chose, but you didn't quite choose. Every once in a while you took them up and found them familiar and well worn and intimate, and you kept them where you could touch them when you wanted to.

But that hotel. There was little you wanted to remember about that. The musty smell of the halls, the unpleasant work of cleaning rooms after the bank went and the help had to be let go, the unfriendly masculine atmosphere of the lobby, with its faint sour smell of whiskey from the bar that had gone in in spite of her protests (How can you run a commercial hotel without a bar?). It was funny, but the things you felt most vividly about that hotel, even more vividly than you felt the birth of Chester and Bruce in the first floor front suite where you lived, even more than you felt the loss of the first one, the girl baby born dead, were the evenings when Bo played solitaire and the time Pinky Jordan came around. Those things had weight in the memory; those were what was left when you boiled down six years in your mind.

The solitaire grew on him slowly in the days when receipts and expenses chased each other in an endless circle and the big companies took their drummers off the road and the bank had been cleaned out. It became a ritual, a kind of intent solitary fortune-telling game. Every evening he sat down at the table with cards and a tablet and pencil. The game never varied. He bought the deck for fifty-two dollars and got back five for every card he put up. For hours, some nights, she heard the stiff riffle of cards, the slipping noise as he thumbed the deck, the light smack as he laid them down. Looking up, she saw his dark, intent face, dark even in winter, bent over the game. When the last card was gone he leaned over and added figures to the long string on the tablet, adding or subtracting from his total gain or loss. Then the riffle again, the expert flip of the cut, the light smack of a new layout going down. Sometimes, cleaning up, she looked with baffled wonder at the columns of figures on a discarded tablet sheet, the thousands of dollars of mythical debt, and once in a while at top or bottom a string of aimless figures elaborately penmanlike, neat sevens and nines and twos with curly tails, or signatures with strong flowing downstrokes: Harry G. Mason, Harry G. Mason. 7 7 7 7 7 7, 2 2 2 2 2 2, 9 9 9—and the debt going up in fantastic figures from page to page. She learned to know that whenever the aimless signatures and the strings of numbers appeared on the pages, he was more baffled and restless and prowling and dissatisfied than usual, that somebody had ducked on his bill or that he and Jud had lost money in a poker game in the room behind the bar.

It did no good to laugh at him or get mad at him. He wanted, he said, to see how much he would stand to make from a solitaire game if he ever had a gambling house. When she asked him if he were planning on starting a gambling house he said no, of course not. But he wanted to know. She knew that he attached cabalistic importance to his figures. If he made money off his game one night, that meant that the next day the bar would do a good business, or there would be a couple more rooms rented. If he lost, the next day would be bad. So he did his best never to lose. He would play five games more just to see if he couldn't pick it up. When he lost on those he would play five more, and then ten more, and then fifteen more, just to make it an even fifty games for the evening, and if he had a string of games in which he did not win at all he became angry and intent and touchy, and went to bed angrily leaving cards and tablet sheets scattered over the table.

When he finally threw the deck down one night and said he had lost fifty-six thousand dollars on five thousand games, she thought he might be over that streak. But the next night he was playing solitaire cribbage, with the purpose, he said, of determining exactly what the average crib hand was. But cribbage too he used like a crystal ball. If he won as often as he lost, then the hotel would pull out of it and be a decent proposition. If he lost seventy-five out of a hundred games, it was a washout, they might as well sell it tomorrow, or give it away. If he won seventy-five out of a hundred, they'd make a mint.

She shook her head and smiled, remembering that. She couldn't remember how it had ended. So many evenings were blended into one composite recollection that she didn't know for sure whether he had been playing solitaire up to the time Pinky Jordan came to town, or whether he had stopped of his own accord. All she knew was that by the time Pinky Jordan came the hotel was a hopeless weight on their backs, that even Jud was getting the look of failure and defeat that it seemed to her now lay like mildew over all of them. And Eva still living with Jud in the hotel, not married but going by the name of Mrs. Chain, having attacks of her gall bladder trouble or whatever it was that ailed her, and needing attention like an invalid half the time. They were all tired out and low when Pinky Jordan came. Perhaps that was why he seemed like a comet across their horizon.

That day Elsa remembered as clearly as if it had been last week. (And why not? she said. If it hadn't been for him we wouldn't be here in Washington now, we wouldn't have gone back to Indian Falls that winter, we wouldn't have done anything, probably, except go on trying to make the hotel pay. Why wouldn't I remember an afternoon that changed our whole lives?) At the end of an opaque, telescoped gap in her life there was a little man with a nicked ear and a whiskey voice, a kind of Pied Piper who whistled one tune and up came all the roots of the people who heard him.

She was sitting in the chair behind the desk, resting after putting the children away for their naps and trying not to hear the random talk that came through the door of the blind pig, brazenly halfway open because of the heat. Chester had been down before going to bed, and Bo had swatted him with buggy pillows and tickled him into spasms and had ended by setting him on the bar and giving him a sip of beer. When she sailed in and rescued him, Bo had been disgusted, almost nasty. "Oh for God sakes!" he said. "What's the harm in that?" Jud, tending bar, winked at her and raised his shoulders eloquently. A couple of drummers had laughed.

Then as she sat behind the desk the screen door of the lobby opened and a little hatless baldheaded man came in. His face was a fiery rose-pink, and his bald red scalp was scrawled with bluish veins above the temples. His breath, when he leaned confidentially toward her, almost knocked her down. His voice was a whiskey voice. She had learned to recognize that. "I was told," said his hoarse whisper, "that a man could get a drink in here."

She jingled the bell for Bo, not even bothering to deny that they served liquor, as she ordinarily would have. This man was obviously no officer, but only a tramp or barfly wandering in on his way through town. Bo came hurriedly to the door, looked the man over, and motioned him inside. The door he left ajar.

She heard the clump of a bottle on the bar, and a low mutter of talk. Shortly the whiskey voice rose. "I'll have another'n of those."

Altogether he ordered five drinks in the course of an hour, in his hoarse, commanding whisper. The dead summer afternoon drifted on. A boy going past opened and slammed the screen door just to hear the noise. "Gimme another'n," said the whiskey voice from the bar.

Drowsily, without much interest but with nothing else to occupy her attention, she heard Bo come over and set one up for the stranger as he always did when anyone was buying freely. After a time the whiskey voice said, "How much, barkeep?"

Jud's voice said, "One seventy-five," and change clinked on the bar.

"Ain't got the change," the whiskey voice said. "You got a gold scale?"

"Hell no," Jud said, and laughed. "What for?"

"This's all I got with me." There was a sodden thump on the wood, and for once Elsa heard excitement and haste in Jud's voice. "I'll be damned," he said. "Hey, Bo, this guy wants to pay off in gold dust."

But the rapid steps, the noise of crowding, the exclamations, were at the bar almost as soon as he started to speak. "Where in hell did you get that?" Bo said.

"Klondike," said the superior, bored whiskey voice, "if that's any-a your business."

"No offense, no offense," Bo said. "We just don't see any of that around here. Pan it yourself?"

"Right out of the gravel, boys."

He must have poured some into his palm, for there were whistles and exclamations. Elsa strained her ears, but she needn't have. The men in the pig were almost shouting. "Jumping Jesus," a drummer said. "How much is that poke worth?"

"Oh—five, six hundred."

"Quite a slug to be lugging around," Bo said.

"More where that came from," the stranger said. "Plennnty more salted away, boys. Never carry more than I need."

"I'll go try the drugstore for a scale," Bo said. "How much an ounce?"

"Eighteen bucks."

Bo laughed, a short, incredulous chop of sound. "You have to spend your money with an eyedropper at that rate."

Pinky Jordan stayed all afternoon to soak up the admiration he had aroused. After she had brought the baby down in his buggy and set Chester to playing with his blocks, Elsa heard scraps of the tales he was holding his listeners with. Three more men had come back with Bo from the drugstore, and all afternoon others kept dropping in to have a beer and listen to stories of hundreds of miles of wild timberland, hundreds of thousands of caribou, hundreds of millions of salmon in suicidal dashes up the rivers; of woods full of bear and deer and otter and fox and wolverine and mink; of fruit salads on every tree in berry time. You didn't need to work for a living. You picked it off the bushes, netted it out of the river, shot it out of the woods, panned it out of the gravel in your front yard.

"You know how much a frenna mine got for one silver fox skin?" the whiskey voice was saying as she drew near the door once with the broom as an excuse. "For one, leetle, skin?" The voice was confidential and dramatic. "Four hunnerd dollahs."

There were whistles, clickings against the teeth. "Four hunnerd dollahs," Pinky Jordan said, "an' he traded it out of a halfbreed for a flannel shirt and a sheath knife. You wanna make your fortune, genlemen, you go on up to God's country. Flowin'th milk and honey."

It was nearly supper time when Pinky Jordan, drunk on his own eloquence and the uncounted drinks his listeners had poured for him, wobbled out of the lobby. Bo was at his elbow, telling him confidentially that sometimes they got up a little game in the evenings. Be glad to have him drop in. Just a friendly little game, no high stakes, but pleasant. They'd be glad to have him.

Pinky Jordan nodded owlishly, winked both eyes so that his naked red scalp pulled down over his brows like a loose slipping skullcap. From the desk Elsa watched him in the horizontal light of evening hesitating on the front sidewalk, a little man with a red bald head and a nick out of his right ear as if someone had taken a neat bite from it. Then he started up the walk, kicking at a crumpled piece of paper. Each time he came up behind it, measured his kick, booted it a few feet, and staggered after it to measure and kick again. On the fourth kick he stubbed his toe and fell into the street, and the men who had been looking after him from lobby and sidewalk ran to set him straight again. He jerked his kingly elbows out of their hands and staggered out of sight.

Pinky Jordan never returned for the poker game, though Bo tried all the next day to locate him around town. But he had done his work. He left behind him a few dollars' worth of gold dust in a shot glass behind Bo Mason's bar. He also left behind him a vision of clean wilderness, white rivers and noble mountains, forests full of game and fabulously valuable fur, sand full of glittering grains. And he left in Bo, fretted by hard times and the burden of an unpaid mortgage and the worry and wear of keeping his nose too long to an unprofitable grindstone, a heightened case of that same old wandering itch that had driven him from town to town and job to job since he was fourteen.

He was born with the itch in his bones, Elsa knew. He was always telling stories of men who had gone over the hills to some new place and found a land of Canaan, made their pile, got to be big men in the communities they fathered. But the Canaans toward which Bo's feet had turned had not lived up to their promise. People had been before him. The cream, he said, was gone. He should have lived a hundred years earlier.

Yet he would never quite grant that all the good places were filled up. There was somewhere, if you knew where to find it, some place where money could be made like drawing water from a well, some Big Rock Candy Mountain where life was effortless and rich and unrestricted and full of adventure and action, where something could be had for nothing. He hadn't found it in Chicago or Milwaukee or Terre Haute or the Wisconsin woods or Dakota; there was no place and no business where you took chances and the chances paid off, where you played, and the play was profitable. Ball playing might have been it, if he had hit the big time, but bad luck had spoiled that chance. But in the Klondike . . . the Klondike, Elsa knew as soon as he opened his mouth to say something when Pinky Jordan was gone, was the real thing, the thing he had been looking for for a lifetime.

"Let me show you," he said, and brought the shot glass containing Pinky Jordan's immortal dust. His mind was whitehot with visions, and he vibrated like a harp to his own versions of Pinky's yarns. There was a place without these scorching summers that fried the meat on your bones; there was a place where banks didn't close and panics didn't reach, where they had no rules and regulations a man had to live by. You stood on your own two feet and to hell with the rest of the world. In the Klondike the rivers ran gold and silver fox skins fetched four hundred dollars apiece and the woods were full of them.

She was not surprised when he proposed selling the hotel and lighting out. It took him only three or four days to arrive at that plan, but she was ready for it.

"Do you know what time of year it is?" she said.

His look was suspicious, as if he suspected her of plotting to throw hindrances in his path. "It doesn't take any astrologer to know it isn't Christmas," he said, and ran a finger inside the sweating band of his collar.

"No," she said, "but by the time you sell this place, and get to Seattle, and take a boat to Alaska or wherever it is you go, it will be Christmas."

His look this time was as heavy as a hand pushing against her. "What of it?"

"I believe you'd take those two little kids up there right in the dead of winter," she said.

"Winter's the fur season. Jud and I could go out trapping, and you and the kids could stay in town."

"Is Jud going?"

"Sure, if we do. He's all hot to go."

"Eva too."

"I suppose."

"So you've got it all planned," she said. "It's nice of you to come and tell me about it."

"Don't you want to go? Do you want to sit around here growing roots in your tail in this damned old hotel all your life?"

"That isn't it," she said. "I'm thinking about the kids."

"Yeah," he said gloomily. "Well, I don't know. Probably we couldn't move this joint with a derrick anyway."

But circumstances pushed them faster than they would have pushed themselves. Bo had just got her promise that she would go to Alaska in the spring if they could move the hotel during the winter when the police raided them, closed the blind pig, jailed

Jud, and missed Bo only because he was out of the hotel at the time and ducked out of town when he heard. Within two weeks of Pinky Jordan's meteoric passage Elsa and the two children were on their way to Indian Falls, going back ignominiously to the home she had run away from six years before, accepting whatever stiff charity her father's letter offered.

It was Bo who wrote in from where he was staying in a soddy with a homesteader and suggested that armistice with Indian Falls. Now it was a cinch they'd have to get out of the hotel, and they'd need all the money they could scrape together for passage in the spring. Couldn't they stay on her old man's farm, maybe, and earn their keep helping run the place?

Elsa made a bitter face and ruffled the bristles in her hairbrush, trying to decide how she ever humbled herself enough for that surrender, how Bo could have suggested it. It was the dream of what they would do in the spring, she supposed, the fire of that optimism melting everything else down until the only important thing was to get to the promised land. She supposed he would have stolen and cheated and lied to get there. When he slipped aboard the train a hundred miles out of Grand Forks and slid into the seat beside her he did not mention where they were going or remark on how mean it was to come sneaking back after defiance and repudiation to accept as charity what you had once refused as your right. All he said, breathing on the glass and rubbing a place clean to see out of, was that by God he'd never been gladder to get out of any place than he was to get out of that hotel.

The hairbrush slipped from her knees, and her quick jerk to catch it set the blood to throbbing in her arm. Carefully, with a morbid curiosity about what it looked like today, she unwrapped the bandage. The sight of the arm outraged her, and the smell made her wrinkle her nose in disgust. From above her elbow to her fingers the arm was one red piece of butcher's meat spotted with watery blisters. At the wrist the bandage stuck, and she yanked it loose; blood oozed in beady droplets from the skinned flesh.

It didn't feel better with the bandage off. It felt worse. But somewhere she had read that sunshine was good for hurts of any kind, and so every day she exposed it.

A burn was a nasty kind of injury, she thought, inflamed and disgusting. Once she had been proud of her arms, but when she stretched them out together now, the one hard, round, white, the other a peeled monstrosity, she grimaced. Maybe it never would look right again. She turned the other arm over, studying its fitness, and saw a slightly chapped spot on the elbow. She must get some cold cream to put on that. She didn't want elbows like Harriett Conzett's, or a goat's knees. Or Sarah's. The last time she saw Sarah she had been like a walking waxwork, submerged, buried, slipping into middle age before she had ever been young.

I'm only twenty-six, Elsa thought. That isn't old. And maybe now we'll be all settled down and get a house built sometime and the boys will grow up and go to school. I've got at least forty years ahead of me, she thought. It seemed a wonderful and dangerous idea. She contemplated it, shaking her head and smiling, before she got clean bandage and rewrapped her arm and got up to make the children their dinner.

2

The boys had been long in bed when she heard Bo's steps on the path, and rose to pull the curtain closer around their bed and turn up the lamp. She heard the scuff of his soles on the foot scraper. He was always careful about tracking in mud. Then the door swung inward and he came in with a lantern in his hand, a package under the other arm. As he lifted the chimney and blew out the lantern his big body blocked the door.

"You're late tonight," she said. "Any business?"

"Chicken feed. How's your arm?"

"Pretty good."

"Been picking at it any more?"

"Some more skin came off." At his frown she added defensively, "It just peels off in sheets. I can't leave it there."

"What'd you take the bandage off for?"

"It feels better."

He dumped the package on the table, keeping one hand on it. "You deserve to get blood poison," he said. "Let the doc take the skin off, if it needs taking off."

"I was just sitting out in the sun. It felt so tight I unrolled the bandage, and there was that loose skin, so I just snipped it off."

He looked at her and shook his head as if defeated.

"Have you eaten anything?" she said.

"I ate before I closed up."

"Well, what happened today?" she said, and settled back comfortably on the bed. This was the way it should be. It should be warm and pleasant and homelike like this, with your husband coming home from work and everything snug for the night and plenty of time to talk. Only it was a shame he had to work such long hours now that she was laid up. She saw his hand still protective on the package, and his eyes secret and sly. "What have you got there?" she said.

"Been bargain hunting."

"What is it?"

"Bombs," he said, and moved the package away from her reaching hand. "I joined the I.W.W.'s."

With a quick grab she hooked her fingers in the string. "Let me see!"

"Look out. It might go off."

"Oh, quit your fooling and let me see."

He surrendered the parcel and watched her, grinning, while she undid the string. "Save the store-cording," he said, and she rolled the string into a coil before unwrapping the package. Inside was a set of books in a red marbled binding, with dark red leather on spines and corners. "Complete Works of Shakespeare," the lettering on the spine said. Uncertainly she opened one and looked inside. It looked expensive.

"Well?" Bo said.

"Where on earth did you get them?"

"Fella came around. Selling bibles mainly, but I didn't think you'd want a bible."

Under her fingers the leather was smooth and cool. "How much?" she said.

"What does that matter? Do you like them or don't you?"

"Of course I like them." Her voice was low. "But I bet you paid more than we can afford for them."

Bo picked up one of the books and hefted it appreciatively, cracked back the spine in a way that would have infuriated her father, who always went through a book page by page pressing down the sheets so as not to break the binding. "Well, hell," he said. "I'm sick of not having anything decent around. We've got to have some books around the place, kids growing up and everything. I'd like to have a whole roomful."

She read him as plain as daylight. He was afraid he had been stung, he was scared she wouldn't like them, he knew he had been extravagant, but just suggest that the book peddler had skinned him and he'd blow up like a bullfrog.

"A roomful of books in a tent!" she said, before she thought. Then she saw that he was hurt, and got up and hugged him around the neck. "I love them," she said. "It was sweet of you to think of getting me something."

He pulled her down on his lap. "I don't like living in a tent any better than you do," he said.

"It's funny," she said, relaxing against him. "Since I got burned I'd loved it. Everything's been so settled and quiet it's like home all of a sudden." Through his shirt his body was like a stove. She felt warm and comfortable, cradled in affection so sure and easy that she rubbed against him. "You've been so nice lately," she said. "It's like it used to be before our luck got bad."

"It sure isn't any better now," he said, and she felt his body stir irritably. "I can't understand why that joint don't make money. It ought to, but it don't."

"It makes some."

"Some isn't enough."

"Isn't it?" she said, pulling herself back to look in his face. "Isn't it enough to make a living and get ahead gradually and make sure of things one after another and settle down in one place?"

"It'd be all right if you could make enough to live like a human being."

"It's slow," she said, "but we do make a little all the time, Bo. We'll have the fixtures paid for in a few more months, and then we'll make more. If we're careful we'll be all right in a year."

He grunted. "Being careful is what makes my tail ache. You get kind of sick of being careful after while."

"Oh, we'll make it," she said. "As soon as I'm well I'll take over and you can sleep for a week. You're all tired out."

"I'm not tired out. I'm just sick of that dinky little lumber town and seeing the same guys across the counter week in and week out."

"When we get the installments paid off we can hire somebody, maybe," she said. She kissed the side of his face. "Bo," she said, "you know you haven't got mad at either of the kids for a week?"

He grunted, but good-naturedly. "I must have forgot. I'll take care of it tomorrow."

"You watch them," she said. "They're three times better when they don't get punished a lot. They're as sweet as pie all day."

His wide chest swelled and sank under her. "Yeah, I suppose. It's been so long since I saw either of them I'll have to be introduced all over again."

"You *are* all worn out," she said. "I'll hurry up and get well so you can have a rest." Suddenly, weakly, she wanted to cry. She put her face against him and laughed instead.

"What's the matter?"

"I don't know. I'm just so happy things are as good as they are, even. After what happened in Seattle I guess I didn't ever think I could feel happy again." She smiled into his warming, half closed eyes and hugged him with her good arm. "Did you know you're a darling sometimes?"

"I've been told so," Bo said comfortably. "What am I darling about now?"

"Just being you," she said. "Just being the nice you." Her eyes went down to the book he still held in one hand. "Bo?"

"What?" As if he were methodically ringing doorbells, his fingers went down her back pushing each vertebra.

"How much did you pay for those books?"

"Eighteen dollars."

"Oh my Lord!" She lay digesting the enormity of the extravagance, but the more it grew in her mind the less she could reproach him. Because she was hurt and shut in, because he felt bothered in his conscience for letting her get burned, because he was galled by the tightness of money and needed to do something to express his contempt for penny-pinching, he spent more in one insane gesture than she had been able to spend on the boys' clothes all winter. There was nothing you could say to him when he did a thing like that. He never even said outright that they were a present for you, though you knew they were. And even if there had been a hundred presents more useful and acceptable, you had to like this one, and love him for it.

She got no news from him that night about what was happening in the settlement or the lumber camp, because she forgot to ask, but the next morning she saw him kneeling before the big black bureau he had built. He rummaged and felt in the back of a drawer. "What are you looking for?" she said.

"The gun."

"What do you need the gun for?"

"Want to load it up for you." Deliberately uncommunicative, he stooped and grunted, searching. Elsa sat up in bed. "Why should it be loaded for me?"

The boys, who had been having a pillow fight in their own bed, craned to look as Bo pulled the thirty-eight out of the bureau and slipped cartridges into the cylinder.

"I'm just going to leave it where you can get at it," Bo said. "Make you feel a little safer, maybe." Grinning at her, he laid the gun on a high shelf out of the boys' reach.

"Now tell me!" she said.

"Nothing to be scared of," Bo said. "There's been a cougar around prowling the camps, is all."

"A cougar!"

"Never bother a man. They're scared to death of a man. They just sneak around nights and steal fish and things. If you heard anything around at night you could shoo him away with this. One shot would have him high-tailing it for the next county."

Elsa looked sideways at the children, listening round-eyed. He could say all he wanted. She was scared, just the same. A cougar could get through a tent wall like nothing, and even if he was afraid of a man, he wouldn't be afraid of a child.

"Think I should keep the kids inside?"

"Akh!" Bo put the box of cartridges away. "They only prowl at night."

"Well, but . . ."

"Keep 'em around close if it makes you feel better. But there's nothing to be scared of. Bruce there could scare him clear into Oregon."

For the first hour after he left she kept glancing out into the clearing. It would be another fine day. She tried to imagine cougars lying in wait behind the sunny edge of the trees, but the thought in such fresh morning light was absurd. At mid-morning she had the children playing outside, and had settled herself with one of her new books on the step. Looking for something familiar, she found *Romeo and Juliet.*

Once or twice, lifting her head from the book to make sure that the boys hadn't strayed, she wondered about what she was reading. Shakespeare was something great and far-off, a vague magnificent name. She couldn't remember ever knowing anyone who had read any Shakespeare, though Bo had told her about one night in Indianapolis when he saw *Macbeth,* a long time ago, and about the flames flying around a dark stage and three old hags dropping the finger bones of children into their pot. Now she was reading one herself, and it was much like any other story, except that it was in poetry and there were some words she wasn't sure of. But it was a good story. She read again, and Romeo had just killed Tybalt in a street brawl when Bruce called.

He had to go to the toilet. Absorbed in her reading, Elsa told him to go by himself, he was a big boy now. Watching him with one eye, she saw him start unwillingly on the path that led back into the fringe of trees, looking back all the time, dragging his feet. He got half way, looked into the jungle of blackberry bushes, stopped, and began to cry.

Elsa put down her book. "Go on," she said. "A big boy like you shouldn't need help."

Chester, sitting on a stump swinging his legs and watching, said, "I go by *my*self, don't I, Ma?"

"Of course," she said. "All big boys do."

Bruce only wailed louder, and she stood up. He was a difficult child, cried for any little thing, grew afraid at nothing, got stubborn helpless streaks. No wonder Bo got mad at him. But it wouldn't do. You had to baby him or he got worse.

She walked out to him. "Come on, then," she said, and took his hand.

He hung back, staring fearfully into the woods.

"What are you afraid of?" she said, and pulled at him.

The child screamed and hung his whole weight on her hand. The effort of hauling at him sent a deep throbbing ache through her injured arm, and her impatience grew. "What *is* the matter with you?"

It was minutes before his screaming stopped. She had to give herself up to the job of quieting him, sit down by him, distract his attention, tell him a story. Then she took his hand again. "All right," she said. "Let's go do our business."

His round eyes swung to the woods again and his lip jutted. "Cougar'll eat me!"

"Ohhh!" Elsa opened eyes and mouth in understanding, pursed her lips and nodded. In a substratum of consciousness she felt irritation with Bo for making so much fuss about the cougar that morning. The first thing he knew, the child would be afraid to go ten feet by himself.

"The cougar's gone home," she said. "He lives way over by Lake Samamish."

"He does not," Bruce said. "He's in the woods and he's gonna eat me."

"No, he isn't in the woods." She rose, wincing at her throbbing arm. "Look, I'll go in first and show you."

She walked into the brush, slipped off the path and hid herself from him. Peeking from a thicket of blackberry she saw him sitting on the ground, his whole face set for a wail, watching where she had disappeared. After a moment she came back on the path. "See?"

"Isn't there a cougar?"

"Not a sign of one. Come on with me now."

Finally she got him to the privy and back, but her nerves were tried, and as she sat down again to read she thought in irritation that there wasn't much real peace in living in the woods a mile from town, with cougars running around robbing camps and your children afraid, almost justifiably, of being eaten by wild beasts. But that wasn't fair. Bo wasn't to blame for the way they were living now. If anyone was, she and the boys were. They had been a millstone around his neck, a jinx. If he had had only himself to think of, he would be in Alaska now with Jud, doing what he wanted to do, living the kind of life he loved, instead of working fifteen hours a day in a place he hated. Considering how much he had given up, it was no wonder he was sometimes irritable and brooding. The wonder was that he took his bad luck as well as he did. He had every excuse to be as miserable as he was that winter they went back to Indian Falls.

She couldn't remember much about the arrival home except a pattern of confusion, embarrassment, humiliation—and amazement at the change in Kristin and Erling. Kristin had grown up. Her selfishness and her lack of responsibility were gone. As for Erling, he was a great raw-boned man at eighteen, an inch over six feet and looking bigger because of his mop of red curls. He was obviously glad to see her and obviously not going to show it. She remembered the look of quick astonishment in Kristin's eyes, the sober, old-world courtesy in her father's manner, when she introduced Bo, and she remembered Henry Mossman, mild, getting a little bald, stepping up to shake Bo's hand and then stepping back as if he had just shaken hands with the President.

She felt the forced conversation as a guard against their saying what they really were thinking, and in the very quiet politeness of their manners she felt that they didn't like Bo. They had been prepared to dislike him, and now they did. He was only a big dark-faced man who had run a saloon or poolhall in North Dakota and tricked Elsa into marrying him. He was outside the pale of Christian society, son-in-law or no son-in-law. She knew also that Bo felt their careful courtesy for what it was, and that even before they reached the house he was despising them for a bunch of pious Scandihoovian hypocrites.

They were oil and water, though with the children Bo got on better. Kristin he won over to a kind of giggling liking by teasing her until she flew back at him, when he backed away waving helpless hands before him, and called her a hell-cat. She was never quite sure of him, but she thought he was lots of fun. Erling, after the first day on the farm, was his slave.

She remembered how that started. Bo, the first night, sat down after supper and lit a cigar and said well, he guessed they were set for the winter, and Erling, maliciously acute, said, "You mean stuck."

"All right," Bo said. "Stuck."

Erling was eating an apple, pounding the hard red Jonathan on the table to pulp it and then sucking the cidery juice through a hole in the skin. "You folks going to church regular?" he asked.

Bo blew out a cloud of smoke. "No."

"Swell. Then I won't have to."

"Don't go telling Pa we put you up to it," Elsa said.

"You've got the right idea," Bo said. He reached in his vest and handed Erling out a cigar. Erling took it, startled but game. Elsa started to protest, but decided to keep still. Let him play.

They sat in a haze of smoke for ten minutes. Erling took the cigar out of his mouth and looked at it, working his lips. "Good cigar."

"Just about got you whipped, hasn't it?" Bo said.

"Naw. I smoke a corncob generally."

"Not while Pa's around, I'll bet," Elsa said.

"He don't bother me. I'm running the farm myself now."

"You're the boss, uh?" Bo said.

"I'm the head man." Erling took the cigar out of his mouth again between thumb and forefinger and went to the door and spat, casually.

Bo laughed. "Got any work for a good farmhand?"

"You want-a work?"

"Sure."

"You'd get so lathered out in a field you'd drownd out all the gophers."

"Sweat's good fertilizer," Bo said.

Erling looked at him doubtfully, his little bright blue eyes squinting. Elsa could see him thinking. If this big guy wanted work, he'd sure give it to him. It would be fun to get him out and run his tongue out.

On the table lay a seed catalogue half an inch thick. Casually Bo leaned over, winked at Elsa, and seemed to be reading, paying no attention to Erling. Then he rose with the catalogue in his hand. "Through with this?"

"I guess so. Why?"

"Got to make a little trip," Bo said. He took hold of the upper corner with his other hand. The blunt fingers tightened, his neck swelled and his shoulders hunched. The catalogue tore slowly, reluctantly, until with a final twist he ripped it in two and went out without a word.

Erling's eyes bulged. He looked at Elsa, who smiled.

"Holy cats!" he said. He took up the remaining half of the catalogue and tried to tear it. It was like tearing a board. "My gosh he's strong," Erling said. "Where'd he get it?"

"Don't let him fool you," Elsa said. "Running a hotel he's got a little soft, but I've seen him bend pokers with his hands."

In her brother's transparent face she saw half-contemptuous toleration giving way to awed respect. She could see him beginning to like this big guy that Elsa had married. One gesture, and the boy was his. It was hard to explain, that knack he had of making men like him (and women, she said. Wasn't I just the same after one afternoon in Helm's parlor?). It was a kind of teasing and sultry and almost dangerous charm, a feeling of power you got from him as you got heat from a stove.

She remembered the way he worked during that fall, how he set himself to go Erling one better in everything they did, how he hid his blistered hands until they were toughened and callused, how every morning he and Erling wrestled out by the mill trough. Generally those bouts wound up with Erling going head-first into the tank. Big and agile as he was, he was lost if he let Bo's hands get on him. Then he yelped like a stepped-on pup, and after the ducking he came up streaming water and blowing promises of what he would do next time he got that big goof, and ran steaming through the cold to change his overalls.

Those were good clean sparkling mornings bright with color, with popcorn drying from the rafters of the porch, and Chester was growing into such a handful that half the time they were scared to death he would kill himself and half the time proud of his adventurousness. He was always wandering off into the cornfield by himself, or crawling up into the hayloft to burrow and growl at himself playing bear, or inducing visiting children, generally girls, to go swimming with him in the mill tank. In the evenings Bo sparred with him, "toughening him up," cuffing him on the ears as he sailed in, letting himself be flailed in return.

Bruce was a different problem. Sometimes Bo would induce him to come in and fight, but one or two light flicks on the ear would set him howling. Bo got impatient then. He never could abide a child's crying. Sometimes he roared at the boy to stop his noise, and once or twice he looked as if he might haul back and knock Bruce rolling if shame, or Elsa's presence, hadn't stopped him.

"You baby him too much," he said. "I never had any of this babying. I just got thrown out in the cold and had to get along. You've got Bruce so he bawls for any little thing."

"You let him alone," she said. "You can toughen Chet up all you want. He likes being knocked around. But Bruce is sensitive. You watch his face when you yell at him sometime. Just a little difference in your voice is enough to scare him."

"Yeah," Bo said heavily. "Yeah, I guess by God it is."

It was winter, the isolation and inactivity of just sitting and waiting for word from Jud, that frayed his temper. Even when the letter from Jud came, it helped little. He had an offer of three thousand, less than half what he and Bo had paid, and he was holding off to see if something better could be stirred up. When he read it, Bo got out paper and pencil and figured for an hour, and when he got through figuring he threw the pencil across the room and went outside. Next day, in a burst of activity, he sat down and wrote nine letters, more than he had written in a year, one to a steamship line in Seattle, two to fur houses in St. Louis, one to his sister, one to Jud, one to Sears Roebuck ordering some traps, two or three others she couldn't remember. Then he sat down and played solitaire till supper time.

Inactivity was like a disease in him. He needed the excitement of starting something, getting something going. Being cooped up in the house made him grit his teeth. Haunting the mailbox for letters that didn't arrive set him swearing. And when he lost thirty-five straight games of solitaire without winning once, he threw down the cards and glared, and she knew from the look in his heavy-lidded eyes that he made an omen out of it, it was bad luck for the Klondike project. Before she could think of a way of distracting his mind from it, he was back at the table again, swearing he would sit there and play till he beat it if it took him till spring.

But even after he had whipped it a good many times the omen was not conquered. He slept uneasily, woke up sweating and whimpering like a lost pup from frightful dreams. She remembered the dream he had had three or four nights in a row, that he worried over and tried to extract meaning from. He was a boy, fishing barefooted by the creek he had grown up on, with a watermelon on the bank beside him. He was there a long time, and caught a lot of fish that came up shining from the silvery water, almost as if they flew, weightless and beautiful, each one bigger than the last. Then people started coming, his sister and his mother and all his brothers and Elsa and the children and Elsa's father and Sarah, and they all sat down and ate his watermelon, pushing him away when he protested, and asking him for nickels. They caught in their hands the gleaming fish that flew upward when he pulled in the line. In disgust he got up and moved to another hole, and the fish poured again in a silvery stream, beautiful firm glittering slippery fish that he gloated over. Then they stopped biting suddenly, and he saw the cork riding motionless on the water. It grew and grew till it filled the whole stream, and he looked up to see the people coming again, and ran. He ran across a sand beach, and by that time it wasn't people that chased him any more, but some black Thing that swooped above the trees with edges that waved up and down in the wind like the swimming motion of a flounder, and his feet stuck, and the Thing was coming, and he woke up dripping wet when Elsa shook him and cried out to see what was making him moan so.

Inactive days, haunted nights, wore out his patience and drove him against the shut doors that he wanted to burst open. He cursed Jud for not finding anyone to buy the hotel. One day he cursed the piddling nincompoop who had offered a measly three thousand, and the next he cursed Jud for not having the sense to take it. He didn't care how much they lost, as long as they got a stake to go north on.

One day he sat in the kitchen and petted the gray housecat, rubbing behind its ears, stroking under its lifted chin, pulling its whiskers gently while it blinked and rubbed and purred. Elsa, turning at the stove to reach for the salt shaker, saw Bo's hand move down the crackling fur. The tom arched his back and tiptoed as the fingers stroked clear from ears to lifting haunches, up the raised and electric tail. Bo's face was passive, almost expressionless, and his eyes were half closed. Then the heavy thumbnail dug into the cat's tail with abrupt savagery. The cat yowled a startled, fighting yowl, turned and clawed and leaped free.

"God damn!" Bo was on his feet, his face dark with a wash of blood. "Claw me, you damn . . ."

The cat stood watchfully, yellow slit eyes on him, back humped, tail furred out and straight up. It leaped away from Bo's kick, slipped through the dining room door, dodged another kick, and vanished down the cellar stairs. Bo stood irresolute, fingering his scratched wrist. "Damn cat clawed the hide off me," he said, and sucked at the blood.

"You started it. You pinched his tail."

"Oh, the hell I did!"

"Bo, you did too. I saw you."

His heavy face, snarling, bullying, swung toward her. "And I say I didn't!"

Her blood jumping with anger, she turned away from him. She had seen his face when he pinched, the sudden, convulsive tightening of his mouth.

Through February and into a bitter March his irritability drove him from the house as if he couldn't bear to stay under a roof. He took to walking alone through the cornfield and down to the muddy little rill of water buried under the mounded snow in the creek bed, carrying a trap or two and looking for muskrat or fox or skunk sign. But all he caught was a half dozen muskrats and two skunks, and coming home from his fruitless prowling he would sit staring gloomily out the window, or try to lure Erling into a blackjack game, or get a deck and lose himself in solitaire. The sheets of tablet paper appeared again, and the strings of penmanlike signatures and figures, *Harry G. Mason, Harry G. Mason, Mr.*

Harry G. Mason, Mr. Harry G. Mason, Esq., with arabesques and flourishes, and pages of pictures of animals with bodies like frame houses and heads like gables and tails like chimneys with curls of smoke rising. The boys pounced on those whenever they found them, but the sight of them made Elsa feel cold and a little sick.

Brooding, the book forgotten in her lap, Elsa watched the children riding switches among the stumps, and even in the midst of the deep bird-twittering quiet she felt the frustration and restlessness of that winter. All that energy bottled up without a thing to occupy it. And then the spring, and the sale, and that wonderful week or two when they were really on their way and the world opened out westward into hope.

She pursed her lips and shook her head. You mustn't think about it, she said, and looked around startled to see if she had spoken aloud and the boys had heard. They were still playing horse among the stumps. But she mustn't think about it, anyway. It did no good to worry over things that were done and gone. But she wished with all her heart that it hadn't happened, that they had caught the boat as they intended, that Bo were doing what he would have loved to do, playing wild man in the wilderness. She didn't like to think of herself and the children as a hoodoo and a handicap.

3

That night after the boys were in bed she put the lamp on the table and sat down to read. But the light, reflected off the oilcloth, hurt her eyes, and before nine she was preparing for bed herself. After the light was out she opened the door and stood for a minute breathing the balsam air. It was very dark, the heavy trees a black impenetrable wall across the lighter cleared ground, their tops triangular blacknesses against the sky. She shivered. So lonely a place. The Klondike couldn't have been any lonelier. Ever since her marriage she had wanted for neighbors, in the hotel and on her father's farm and later in Seattle when they knew no one, but now for a moment the desire to have people nearby was like a muscular ache. If there were only a smoke in the daytime, a light at night.

Very carefully she bolted the door, looked at the unseen flimsy canvas roof overhead, listened for a moment to the easy breathing of the children, and slipped into bed.

No noises after dark, at least none like the sounds in a town, the hoarse calling of trains, the rattle of wheels and clack of hoofs and squeak of a dry axle in the street, the unfamiliar roar of an automobile coming around a corner and diminishing, softening, disappearing again down another street you could imagine, tree-lined, pooled with shadows, perhaps a single light in the gable of some house, and the dark pitch of roofs cutting off the stars. Nothing here but the soft continuous murmur like a sigh from the trees crowding the clearing, nothing but the padded blow of an erratic, tree-broken wind on the canvas roof, the faint rustle of needles falling from the fir at the back corner of the tent and skating down the canvas incline. No noises but inanimate creakings and rustlings that you strained to hear and were never satisfied with, stealthy noises that eluded identification and kept you straining for their repetition, noises too soft to be comforting, noises without the surety and satisfaction of trains calling or freight cars jarring as they coupled in the yards beyond the dark. You lay rigidly in bed and made your breath come shallowly, noiselessly, through your mouth, and your blood slowed and pounded until you felt its pressure like monotonous light blows on your injured arm. When you had listened for a sound until you were tightened to an unbearable tension, you heard it again, and it was only the needles falling, the sigh of the moving trees, and you relaxed in the bed and breathed once more. It seemed to you then that your present was a static interval like the pause between heartbeats, and when you lay thinking you thought of the past inevitably, because you couldn't help it, because the present was without the meaning of either past or future, because the past was the thing you knew well, in image and idea, because in the past your future lay.

You remembered how the future had looked on that trip west, close and touchable and warm as it had been only once before, in the early weeks of your marriage. You remembered the oceanic plains pouring behind, the mountains, the Elbow Pass above Banff and the Three Sisters immaculate in snow behind the smoky windows; the strange smothery feeling in the tunnels, and the way the children's noses bled in the altitude, and then Seattle, with Mount Rainier floating like a great smooth cloud high above where any mountain should be.

Everything about those days was full of a kind of drunkenness; it reeled in the memory. Even the cheap boarding house where you and Eva and the children stayed while Jud and Bo went to arrange passage, even Eva forgetting to have her pains, full of laughter. The things sweet to remember—the terrier puppy you bought for the boys, and the pictures you had taken to send back to Indian Falls: Chester with a clay pipe in his mouth, looking droll and eyebrowless, holding the puppy in his arms; the two boys posed behind a cardboard screen painted to represent the cutwater of a boat, with spray V-ing out on both sides and Bruce's hands on an artificial wheel, the whole thing so convincing to the boys later that Bruce's greatest boast even yet was that he had run a big motor boat all by himself.

The day when passage was arranged and the dog assured of a trip in the hold, and the actual tickets in Bo's hands to prove that it was really going to happen. He was exalted with excitement, jumpy, full of sudden exuberances. He stood by the window looking out to where workmen with great firehoses were washing away a whole hill to make way for a street, looking out and humming, breaking into song,

It was at the battle of Bunker Hill
There's where I lost my brother Bill.
'Twas a mighty hot fight, we'll all allow,
But it's a damn sight hotter where Bill is now.

Breaking into song, standing with his hands in his pockets staring out at the activity of the city and having crazy tunes come to his lips without warning, singing,

Oh the Joneses boys, they built a mill,
They built it up on the side of a hill
And they worked all night and they worked all day
To try and make that old mill pay. . . .

When a hurdy-gurdy man came by under the window, you remembered him breaking from the window to wheel you in a clumsy waltz around the room, catching heels in the old Brussels carpet, stumbling, roaring with laughter, singing,

Those six Canadian boys were drowned
But the oxen swam to shore . . .

Teasing the kids, wrestling the puppy, going out in the evening for pails of beer, and you all sat around in the scrawny room, full of fun and stories and songs, growing silent once in a while as you thought of the Promised Land. You remembered evenings when Jud and Eva had gone to their room, and those nights were full of warm, low talk in bed, and lovemaking like a second honeymoon.

Ah, that dream of escape, you thought now, lying in the dark tent hearing the whisper of needles and the light breathing of the boys. That dream of taking from life exactly what you wanted—you too, not merely Bo and Jud, but all of you, drunk on that dream. Then the fall, the cracking away of the well-brink just as you were climbing out. Ding, dong, bell, pussy's in the well, you thought, and made your face smile in the dark. Whose fault? Who put her in? Who pulled her out? You knew of no one responsible, unless whoever or whatever ran the world was really what it seemed sometimes, a mean, vindictive force against which you beat yourself to rags, so that sometimes you felt like a drowning sailor trying to climb into a lifeboat and having your fingers hammered off the gunwale time after time, until there was nothing to do except go down or make up your mind to stay afloat somehow, any way you could.

There was Bo's face the day he came back from buying supplies for the voyage that would start now in two days, and found you tending Chester, sick and whining with a sore throat—the swift, hot, suspicious look, the look of outrage, the look as you traced it over now almost of certainty, as if he had known all along that something would happen. "God damn it," he shouted, "he *can't* get sick now!"

But he did. The next morning there was red rash in his throat. By noon it had spread all over his chest. By afternoon the man was tacking up Scarlet Fever signs on the boarding-house door, and most of the boarders had fled, and the landlady was bitter and Bo, hearing the doctor's words, had flung out of the house like a madman, the doctor shouting after him.

You expected then that he would go without you, and were bitter at him, yet even then you couldn't have blamed him much. He had set his heart so on that voyage. You sat all afternoon and evening, and late at night he came back, his footsteps creaking on the stairs, the anger gone from him and only a look of such hopeless defeat in his face that it shook you with pity. You begged him then to go, to get Jud and Eva and go, and you would join him when Chester was well, but he wouldn't. He had fought it out with himself walking, and he would stick. Maybe they could go later, all of them. But the quarantine would be six weeks, and six weeks cut half the season away. Instead of agreeing to go, he went out to find another boarding place. In the morning he would look for a job. Should he get a nurse, he asked before he left. Could you get along with both kids to mind? But you didn't want a nurse. You didn't want to add that expense to what was already bound to be a disaster. You would stay afloat till another lifeboat came by.

But no more boats. Empty ocean with a fog on it. Chester sick only a week when Bruce came down, and the quarantine lengthening through two weeks, three, four, six, seven. Bruce was barely through peeling when his ear became infected and he howled with pain so that no one slept. You remembered Bo's coming one night, slipping in after his shift of running a streetcar was done, and you sat almost wordless, beaten and tired, though you hadn't seen him for almost a month.

Even then you still talked as if you might go. You would have exposed the children to any amount of cold winter if you could have gone that fall. But Bo had turned in the steamer tickets; doctors bills and living expenses had cut down their money. And then came Jud's first letter. It was a cautious letter. It didn't say definitely that there was nothing stirring. It said merely that from all Jud could find out, the way to get in on either the gold or the fur was to go way back in the wilderness, and Eva didn't like that idea much. Living was high as a kite. Just to fill in till he had located some likely proposition for them, Jud was dealing poker in a joint. If he kept his ears open, he expected that pretty soon he'd hear of something that was worth plunging on. Until then, Jud suggested that with a family to take care of Bo might do better to stay in Seattle. It was a hell of a lot cheaper to get along there than in Seward.

You saw, with the kind of slow, inevitable movement that a high wall makes in falling, that Bo's face lost its eagerness, sagged, set hard. He crushed the letter and threw it at the wall. After a while he picked it up again, smoothed it out and read it again, and broke into a fit of foul swearing, and looking at his eyes and mouth you knew he wanted to cry.

He wore that bitterness around his mouth for months, until he heard about the little café for sale in Richmond, out in the timber, and the prospect of getting away from the carline, from the rocking platform and the swollen feet and the irritation of working for someone else, checking in and checking out, keeping still when inspectors bawled him out, was too tempting to resist. He never looked into the café at all carefully. He simply quit his job and took what little money they had and bought it, spent ten days furiously painting and cobbling and cleaning up, bought new stools and coffee urn and equipment. You flicked the shutter open on that café, and your eye saw it as you had seen it for six months, clean and painted and neat outside, where the customers saw it, its poverty plain where the poverty wouldn't show. You saw the scuffed, softened, splintery fir floor behind the counter, the floor whose slivers found the holes in your shoes and drove in, stopping you sometimes as if you had stepped in a trap; the old cupboards that no amount of soda and scrubbing would sweeten.

But even so, you said, even so. It's better. It's steady, and it does make us a living, and since I've been hurt Bo seems to be willing to stick with it. That accident, unlucky as it seemed at the time, was a point of change, a climax of the bad luck, and since it was over things were better. You remembered old lady Moe at home in Indian Falls, and her belief that whenever she broke a dish she was bound to break three, and you remembered the day you saw her drop a saucer when she was serving afternoon coffee, and how she threw down a cup and another saucer on top of it, not angrily, not in a pet, but quite carefully, as if to finish a job. That was the way the burn was.

You were getting ready for the breakfast customers, you mixing pancake batter, Bo cleaning the coffee urn. He had emptied it, wiped it out, put in the fresh coffee, and heated the water in a pail. As you stirred the batter at the other end you saw him kick a low stool into place and climb up with the steaming water in his hand. He shifted the pail, reached down awkwardly for a dish-towel, wrapped it around his right hand, and took hold of the pail again to lift. The urn was high; he had to strain to hoist the pail. The lip caught under the flange of the urn top, and he hung there, teetering on the precarious stool. "Come here, quick!" he said.

You put down the bowl of batter, wiped your hands on a towel, started. "Hurry up!" he shouted. "This is scalding my hand!"

You were over to him in three steps, looking to see what he wanted you to do. "The stool!" Bo yelled. "The stool, the stool, the stool!" He could have lowered the pail and started over, but that was not his way. Convulsed with fury and strain, he shouted at you and kept the steaming pail jammed as high as he could reach. You grabbed the stool and held its teetering legs back on the floor, and Bo staggered, stuck his hand desperately at the wall, letting go of the bottom of the pail. Hot water slopped over him, and with a yell he dropped it and leaped back to save himself. The whole bucket of scalding water came down across your shoulder and arm.

And then Bo's face again—so many times the memory projected an image of his face, the exact expression. You stood there, your teeth in your lip and your body rigid with the shock. Your bare arm, in the time you could count ten, turned fiery, clear to the fingers. His face fallen in a kind of anguish, Bo stared at the arm and then at your face, and you held yourself rigid, not quite aware yet how badly you were hurt, and looked at him. He burst out as if he couldn't bear what he saw, "Yell! God damn it to hell, yell! Cry!"

Then he was grabbing the butter can and smearing your arm, roughly, angrily. Under his fingers the skin puffed in great blisters, growing while you watched. By the time Bo closed up the place and routed out a stage driver to take you down to the doctor's little office on the mill road, your arm was twice as big as normal and so hot and painful that you staggered getting out of the stage, and Bo picked you up and carried you into the office.

His face. It was almost as if you touched it, lovingly, seeing how strongly your lives had been welded together in spite of bad luck and bad temper, how behind all the violent irritability and the restlessness and the dissatisfaction you were his wife. You had never known what that meant, really, until you saw how it shook him to see you hurt . . .

In the bed Elsa stiffened. There was something, a sound not skating needles or sigh of trees or soft blows of wind on canvas. Rigid with listening, she waited. Again, like the stealthy pad of feet at the rear of the tent, a sound as if something were prowling around the little shed where they stored food, the trunk, clothing, everything that overflowed from the tent itself. Her eyes wide upon the sightless dark, her head half lifted from the pillow, she listened, and the heavy pound of blood began in her burned arm. There again . . . She strained her ears as she had strained them a hundred times at night noises, tight with fear that was not really fear but only apprehension that wanted to smile at itself, to take a long breath and relax again and know that what had brought it upright listening was only the wind or the settling of timbers in the house or the creak of a swaying door.

A long, furtive silence, the sigh of the wind, and then the noise of a stick of firewood falling on the woodpile.

It was as if a light had flashed on and made abruptly real all the fears that she hadn't really believed in. There was something out there, prowling in the dark, and if it was friendly it wouldn't prowl at this hour. Like a shutter that clicked three times, three swift thoughts went through her mind: the automatic question of what time it was and when Bo would be home, the realization that it couldn't be more than ten o'clock, and the thought of the cougar. Propped now on her elbow, she still listened. No more wood fell, but the soft sound of steps came through the flimsy canvas, and then unmistakably the rattle of the padlock against the hasp on the shed door.

Very slowly, so as not to make a noise, Elsa laid the covers back and inched her feet over the edge of the bed. The springs squeaked, and she waited with held breath. The noise outside was still there. It sounded as if the cougar, or whatever it was, had gotten into the shed. Even while she stood up she was wondering if she had padlocked that door, but she couldn't remember. She had been out to hang the ham on its hook just after supper. . . . For a moment, standing barefooted on the cold board floor, she cocked eyes and ears at the children's bed. Sleeping. She knew what she must do. It froze her with terror, but she knew. She must drive the thing away, frighten it so it would never come back, kill it if she could, for what peace would she ever have now when she had to leave the children alone, as she often had to do when she was helping at the café?

With her hurt arm held across her body she tiptoed to the bureau, felt for the revolver on the high shelf. Her teeth were locked, and her body shivered as if with cold, but she went on, over to the door. There she stooped, laid the gun on the floor, raised up and drew the bolt very slowly with her good hand, stooped again and picked up the gun. It was awkward left-handed, but it was better that way than trying to use the burned one.

On the narrow porch she listened again. Something bumped back in the darkness by the shed. The thing was bolder. All around her the dark ring of woods pressed on the less opaque darkness of the clearing, and she saw the cloudy sky above moving with the wind as silently and almost as invisibly as a thought moves in a mind. For a moment she wondered what she would do if the thing didn't scare, if it turned and attacked her, but she shut her determination down and clenched her teeth upon it. In her bare feet, feeling the needles and tiny twigs digging into her skin, she stepped off into the yard and a dozen steps to the side, to where she could see the blob of shadow that was the shed.

With all her will, knowing she must do it quickly or not at all, she lifted the gun and pointed it at the place where the shed door ought to be. Her hand wobbled, and she braced it with the hurt one. "Bo!" she cried out in a last forlorn hope. "Bo, is it you?"

There was a rush of movement, a half-seen moving shadow. The shed door banged back as the retreating animal bumped it, and with her teeth in her lip Elsa pulled the trigger.

The noise stunned her, the recoil threw her hands into the air and stabbed her arm with knives of pain. Slowly she let her hands come down with the gun, her mind still dazzled by the flash and the report and something else—the wild howl that still shivered against the ring of trees, an almost human howl. Before she realized that she had heard it, that the prowler had been real and that she had shot at it, perhaps hit it, she was back inside the tent leaning weakly against the slammed and bolted door.

Both boys were sitting up in bed, tousled and sleepy, shocked upright before they had had a chance to awaken. "What was it, Ma?" Chester said. His eyes, round with sleep and wonder, were on the gun hanging from her hand. Bruce whined, dug with his knuckles at the lingering sleep in his eyes. Then he too saw the gun, and his baby face slackened with the imminence of tears.

Elsa laughed, a squeaky, hysterical cackle. Forcing casualness over her panic like a tight lid over a saucepan, she went over and put the gun back on the shelf. "It was just an old skunk snooping around your rabbit pen," she said.

Chester knew about skunks. He sniffed.

"I scared him off before he had a chance to make a smell," his mother said, and laughed again, more naturally.

"D'you shoot him?"

"You bet I did. We don't want any old skunks bothering our rabbits, do we?"

Their solemn heads shook. "No."

"All right," she said, and went to tuck their covers back. "You go to sleep. If Pa comes home and finds you still awake he'll skin you alive."

They lay down again, punched one another for sleeping room, whispered together with secret giggles, and finally fell asleep. But Elsa, after playing at going back to bed, just to fool them, got up again and dressed, and she was sitting by the table with the light turned up bright when Bo's feet scraped on the steps.

She met him at the door with her finger on her lips, and when she told him what had happened he whistled low. "Scare you?"

She held up her left hand, trembling again now that everything was over and Bo was back. She could even laugh a little. "Half to death," she said.

"Did you hit him?"

"I don't know. He screeched bloody murder and ran away. I didn't even see him, just a kind of rush in the dark."

"Maybe you were seeing shadows."

"He was *not* a shadow! He yelled like old Nick. He was in the shed."

"How'd he get in there?"

"I don't know. Maybe I left the door open."

"Even if you did there's a thumb latch."

"I heard the latch rattle. Maybe the door wasn't caught."

He reached down the gun from the shelf, picked up the lamp, and took her arm. "Well, let's go see if we've got a cougar rug."

While Elsa held the lantern high, Bo, with the brighter light of the lamp, went into the shed and looked. Immediately his voice came, excited. "By God, there was something in here. Stuff's all scattered around."

"Did you think I was imagining things?"

"I did, sort of," he said. He came out and searched for tracks, but the ground was so littered it wouldn't have taken a clear print. Then Elsa stooped and picked up a chip at the corner. On one edge was a dark spatter, and when Bo rubbed it with his thumb it came off red. He looked at her. "You winged him, anyway."

He searched, stooping, the light silhouetting his head and shoulders and shining yellow on the side of his intent face. He seemed to sniff like a hound; there was excitement in him. Twenty feet from the corner he found another spatter of blood on a spruce twig. After that he found nothing. "I'll get up early and try it in the morning," he said. "No use in the dark."

His arm went across her shoulders, and she giggled without knowing she was going to, a sound as involuntary as a hiccough. "Old Mamma," he said. "Pops off a lion with one shot. How'd you ever get the nerve to go right out after him?"

"I wanted to scare him good, or kill him, so he'd never come back."

He paused, stooping for a last look. "This is the best place for tracks, where there's dust," he said. The wind flawed in the light, and he cupped a hand over the chimney. There were footprints all around in the dust, but no sign of animal tracks. Then Bo bent closer. "Ha!" he said.

"What?"

"Look."

He pointed to a large footprint, set his own foot down beside it and made a track. His print was an inch longer than the other. They stared at each other. The light spread around them dimly, shone on the side of the shed, was cut off at the corner as if a knife had sliced it. The woodpile was a jumbled and criss-cross pile of shadows.

"If that was a cougar you shot," Bo said, "he was wearing number nine shoes."

There was little sleep for her that night. In spite of Bo's reassurances that no court would hold her a minute, even if she had killed the prowler, the thought of having shot a man left her weak and sick. She imagined him out in the dark, hungry maybe, rummaging among the things in the shed while he listened for noises from the tent as fearfully as she listened from her bed. Then the shout out of the dark, the terror of discovery, the desperate running, the shot, the pain, the mouth wide on a scream. She imagined him dragging himself off into the woods, perhaps to die.

There was nothing she could do, because Bo said flatly he wasn't going to lose a night's sleep hunting for him in the dark. Besides, he might be dangerous, and as for his bleeding to death, there would have been more blood than they had found if she had hit him badly. The hell with going sleepless and maybe getting shot at out of pity for any burglar. She knew that he wasn't in the least afraid to go out, that he was merely tired and needed sleep, but she could not go to sleep as he did.

Five minutes after they were in bed he had started kicking the covers off his feet—and hers. His muscles twitched as he slept. In the other bed one of the children whimpered. Dreaming. It was comforting to know that nothing worse than dreams would touch him tonight. She should try to get to sleep. Bo rolled over, the bed sagging away under his weight, and she fought him for the covers. He was like an elephant in bed. You couldn't wake him up, and whenever he moved he stripped the whole bed bare. It took savage jabs in the ribs before he would even grunt and squirm and give you enough slack to pull over you.

The child whimpered again. Which one? Bruce? You couldn't tell. Never mind. Let yourself go, feel your weight relaxing into the bed . . .

The scream brought her out onto the floor in a single leap, confused, her heart shuddering after its first great bound. Where? What? The baby. He was screaming insanely, babbling, clopping his lips. Even when she felt across Chester and found Bruce backed against the wall, and took him up to hold his face against her shoulder and comfort him, he still choked and cried. As hard to waken as a mummy, Bo stirred and grumbled a question, but she didn't answer because she was busy crooning to Bruce, running her hand up and down his shivering wet back.

"There there there," she said. "It was just a dream. Nothing's going to hurt you. Mommy's got you safe."

He pressed against her and locked his arms around her neck. "Cougar!" he said. "Great big old cougar had me."

Finally, to quiet him, she lay down between the two boys and they jackknifed their little bottoms into her body and went to sleep again, but she lay as wakeful as ever, staring upward. That fool business of loading the gun and making such a fuss. It had already caused Bruce to be afraid of going fifteen feet from the tent, had made her shoot a man, had wakened the baby from his sleep drenched with nightmare sweat. Just once, it would be pleasant to live in a place where you felt safe and secure and permanent.

The canvas roof was dingy gray, and the birds were beginning off in the woods, before she fell asleep.

4

It was broad daylight when she awoke. The children were running naked in and out of the tent, and Bo was getting breakfast on the little iron stove. The good smell, mingled with the clean scent of the woods that blew in the open door, filled the tent. There was a golden patch of sun on the floor, and the roof was dappled with gold. For a moment, not remembering, she stretched luxuriously. It was good of Bo not to wake her early, because when you woke of your own accord there was pleasure in wakening. Every detail of the tent-house was intimate and precious, the four-foot board walls, the canvas patched near the ridge with two neat, seamanlike patches, the table and bench and stools and bureau, all of which Bo had made, the light pine wood worn smooth by the rubbing of hands and clothing. The whole day ahead was full of comfortable chores, home chores.

She watched Bo at the stove. He was a good cook—better than she was at some things, and he seemed to like to sneak out of bed before anyone was up. He turned the bacon, tipped the lid of the coffee pot to look in, flipped it down again with a light clank of metal. He was whistling under his breath. Still not aware that she was awake, he turned to watch the boys scuffling in the corner over a toy boat, and she saw the skin around his eyes wrinkle. As he turned back to the frying pan his whistle turned into a hum, the hum into a song,

> *My sweetheart's a mule in the mines,*
> *I drive her without any lines,*
> *Behind her I sit and tobacco I spit*
> *All over my sweetheart's behind.*

Just that little excitement last night could make him this way, she thought. Just one unusual thing, one break in the monotony, and he chirped like a bird. His movements were quick, almost jigging, like the movements of a Negro she had seen working on the docks at Seattle, as if at any minute he might break into a dance. The coffee pot began to steam, and Bo opened the lid so that a damp flaw wavered and clanged against the stovepipe like the "witch" in the throat of a fireplace. He sang,

> *Once upon a time, boys, an Irishman named Daugherty*
> *Was elected to the Senate by a very large majawrity . . .*

The bacon fizzed, and he turned it over, the song breaking and emerging again further on,

Oh they ate up everything that was upon the bill-of-fare,
And then they turned it over to see if any more was there.
There was blue fish, green fish, dried fish, and pa'tridges,
Fish balls, snow balls, cannon balls, and ca'tridges . . .

Then she remembered. "Bo!"

He turned around with a grin.

"Shouldn't we go out and look?"

He let his voice sink to sepulchral depths. "While you snored like a pig I already looked," he said. "I plow deep while sluggards sleep."

"Was there . . . ?"

"Not a sign," he said. "You couldn't have done more than scratch his hide. I've been all around clear out to the road."

"I guess I didn't get to sleep till pretty late," she said. She swung her legs over the side of the bed, saw Bruce watching her, and said, "You didn't help either, you little punkin. You had a nightmare and screamed as if you were being murdered."

Looking at Bruce, Bo said, "What'd give him nightmares?"

"You," she said, popping her head into her dress. "You and your fool guns and stories about cougars."

"He's got teeth," Bruce said. "He *woars!*"

Bo laughed. "He woars, does he?" Standing spraddle-legged, he winked at the child. "Tell you what. When you see that cougar poke his nose into the open, you sail right up to him and when he opens his mouth to eat you, stick your arm down his throat and grab his tail and yank him inside out."

Bruce's round face wavered in a grin. "He can't eat me," he said. "I'll kill him right down."

"That's the ticket," his father said. "Kill him right down. Pull off his leg and beat him over the head with the bloody end of it."

"You'll have them talking like toughs," Elsa said.

Bo was sitting down, cramming his mouth with bacon and fried bread. "Do 'em good. Make 'em so tough a cougar's teeth'd clinch right over if he tried to bite 'em." He made motions as if his jaws were glued together, frowned, pawed at his face, put his head down and bucked up and down in his chair, puzzled and wrathful. Both boys laughed. Bo winked at them, took a knife from the table, pried his jaws open, gulped half a cup of coffee and stood up. "Got to hustle," he said. "I'm late now."

This was her morning to go in and see the doctor. At ten o'clock she had the children washed and cleaned up, and started with them down the path toward the macadam road. They walked for a half mile under a roof of horizontal limbs, almost uniformly a dozen feet from the ground and so tightly laced over the old tote road that on rainy days it was possible to walk almost dry from the road to the tent. In that tight shaded aisle, and in the woods that thickened in brown tangles on both sides, there were no flowers brightening the mat of needles, but in the openings where the sun reached the color was spread in bright patches, flowers unfamiliar to her childhood, but looking as if they might be relatives of the windflowers and cornflowers of home. There was even one that looked like a furry-stemmed pasque flower. The boys had names for all of them, many of them the product of Bo's foolery. There was a little delicate blue blossom as low and hidden as a violet, that he had taught them to call a hocus-pocus crocus, and another, a rose blossom that grew on a sort of berry bush, which he called a blush-of-shame-for-a-life-ill-spent. If the boys ever did learn the names of things they would have to unlearn a lot of his teachings first.

Chester ran ahead, picking up cones and bending back the scales to look for seeds, but Bruce stuck close by her side, and she realized with a strange feeling of helplessness how the fear of the woods had taken hold of him. He had always been afraid of everything—horses, cows, streetcars, strange people, even the Santa Claus in the Bon Marche toy department in Seattle. Dark terrors seemed to drive him sometimes into propitiatory rituals, sending him round the tent before a meal touching with solemn babyish pats the bench, the bureau, the leg of the stove, the headboard of his bed. If he were hustled to his chair to eat, he lost his head completely, squalled, fought to get back and finish his compulsive ritual. Or he would turn against foods without warning so that one would have thought he was being offered offal, and not coaxing, not scolding, not spanking could make him eat one day what he had been ravenous for the day before.

He was a strange child. Now he clung to her skirts so closely that he hampered her walking, and she laid her hand on his head and kept it there because she knew that somewhere deep down in his prematurely old mind he lived with fear.

They came down onto the sun-dazzled white band of the macadam, and she pushed him on ahead to run with Chester, squared her own shoulders and stepped out briskly. It would be hard to know what to do with the children when she got well and went back to work, unless they could work out shifts that would let one of them be always at home. With Bruce this way, he couldn't be left alone. But she suspected that he shouldn't be left alone with Bo either. Bo wouldn't have any patience with his terrors. Maybe Bo could get permission to put an extension onto the café, and they could live there. The lumber company owned the whole town, and they hadn't been able to get any place before until Mr. Bane at the stage office let them camp on his timber tract. But if they could . . .

Oh fiddle, she said. It will all come out in the wash.

At the fork where the sawmill road turned off, she cut across the spongy meadow and entered the dirt road that ran straight as a yardstick through heavy timber. The doctor's office was visible an eighth of a mile down, a little frame shanty that he had put up midway between town and mill so as to be available to both. Just as she came into the road, a man went into the office door. That meant she would have to wait. She told the boys to play outside.

The little waiting room was empty, but the doctor poked his head around the inner door and said, "Good morning. I'll be just a minute."

She heard the noise of his moving around inside, and the mutter of voices. A high, nasal voice said, "Ow, for Christ sake!" and the doctor laughed. An instrument clinked in a pan, and after a few minutes the doctor's matter-of-fact voice again: "Leave that bandage on a couple of days, and then take it off and put on a clean one. Bake it in the oven if you can't get it sterile any other way. If it shows any signs of infecting, keep a warm wet pack on it."

The patient said nothing. The door opened and he came out, one ear and the side of his face along the temple swathed in bandage. He was a tall thin man with a peeled-looking skin and a bald head. The doctor, very young and growing a pale mustache to make himself appear older, leaned against the door and looked after him and laughed.

"How did he get hurt?" Elsa said.

"One ear hanging by a string," the doctor said. "These stiffs come in with some tall stories sometimes. An obvious bullet wound, a nice neat groove that creased his face and tore his ear half off, and he tries to tell me he snagged it on a nail in the dark, getting up to see what some disturbance was." He laughed again. "He'd have had to be going thirty miles an hour to do that on a nail."

Elsa was staring. "Do you know him?"

"No. He isn't one of the boys from the camp or the mill. Just a bum passing through. Some day he'll get shot and won't come out so lucky."

"Oh, I'm glad!" Elsa said.

"Glad?"

"You see," she said, and looked at him so radiantly that he batted his eyes. "You see, I shot him."

"Oh, come on!"

"Really. He broke into our shed last night and I thought he was a cougar."

The doctor leaned out to look up the road. "Do you want him pinched? We could still catch him, probably."

She shook her head, and he motioned her into the inner room. "Left handed?" he said as he began unwrapping her bandage. "I knew that bum was lucky. If you'd had the use of both hands he'd be worms' meat now."

Elsa shivered. "That's just what I was afraid of," she said.

Bo was alone in the café when she hurried in, and he leaned his elbows on the counter and winked at the boys. "Hi, kids," he said. "I was just hoping you'd show up."

"Why?" they said.

"Ice cream tastes funny this morning." He talked to them man-to-man, seriously. "Tastes funny as the dickens, for some reason. I need somebody to tell me what's the matter with it."

Chester's droll, eyebrowless face dropped open, and then he leered, scenting a hoax. "Which kind is it tastes funny?" he said.

"Both. Darnedest thing I ever saw. Chocolate tastes funny and vanilla tastes funny. Maybe you can tell me what's wrong with the stuff."

"I can tell quite a lot about chocolate," Chester said.

"Okay. How about you, Brucie?"

"I can tell more about vanilla," Bruce said.

Their father filled two cones and passed them over the counter. "Taste hard," he said, and waited frowning for their verdict. "Tastes to me as if they might have got a little skunk juice in them. Taste anything?"

Chester rolled his tongue in his mouth. "There's a little skunk juice in it, all right." Bruce was hesitating, not quite sure he wanted any of his.

"By golly," Bo said heartily, "that's just what I thought. Here, I'll throw them in the garbage pail for you."

He reached over the counter. Bruce, hesitating, was about to give his up, but Chester backed away, his eyes big over the suspended cone. "Don't you want me to throw the nasty thing away?" Bo said.

Chester took a lick, staying cautiously out of reach. "Aw, you're foolin'!" he said, and ran outside. Bruce followed him, the dubious cone still unlicked in his hand.

"Bo," Elsa said, "guess what I just saw?"

"What?"

"The man I shot at. He was down in the doctor's office with his ear half shot off."

"No fooling?"

"Yes. He wasn't hurt bad. He was a hobo, Miles said."

Bo's eyes across the counter were crinkling, the pupils warming. "Feel better, uh?"

"I should say so."

"Want an ice cream cone to celebrate?"

"All right."

She sat swinging her legs from the high stool, licking the cone, thinking how pleasant it was to drop into your husband's place of business and talk with him and have an ice cream cone, the way she had always wanted to in Hardanger when Bo ran the bowling alley.

"I heard something myself this morning," Bo said.

She looked at him. He had taken out his knife and was scraping absent-mindedly at the accumulated grease under the metal edge of the counter. The grease came off in a thin, curling strip. "Look at that," he said. "You'd think it would be clean, washed as much as it is." He flipped the curling strip in disgust to the floor. Elsa waited, knowing perfectly well that whatever was on his mind, it was not the grease under the counter edge. After a minute his eyes came up.

"Ever hear of the Peace River country?"

"Yes," she said slowly. "Isn't that that farming country up in Canada somewhere where people were going from Dakota?"

"Yeah. In Alberta."

Elsa had stopped licking her ice cream cone. As if someone had touched her and pointed, she saw the direction of his thoughts, and her muscles tightened with an instinctive antagonism, almost a fear. "What about it?" she said.

"Nothing about it," Bo said. "It's good country, that's all. About the best farm country anywhere, probably."

"Are you wanting to go up there?"

"Nope," Bo said deliberately. "It's all filled up." He shut his knife and slid it into his pocket. "But I know a place that's just as good or better that hasn't got a soul in it."

"But you're not a farmer!"

"I'm not a fry cook, either," he said.

"But where is it? Where is this place?"

"In Saskatchewan." They had been staring at each other over the counter almost as if they were about to quarrel. Now Elsa saw his face lose its dead expressionless stillness, the light come into his eyes, the animation appear. "There isn't a thing there but a few cattle ranches," he said. "Fella that comes in for breakfast lately was telling me. He was up through there three or four years ago drifting around working on ranches. Just wide open, big as all outdoors. But they're opening it for homesteaders, see? And the C.P.R. is going to run a branch line down through there from Swift Current. That opens it up, all that land that's as good wheat land as the Peace River country. See what that means?"

Elsa said nothing.

"It means," Bo said, watching her, "that the boys that get in there early and buy up land at the logical townsites are going to make plenty of money. In ten years there'll be dozens of towns along that line, and the ones that get in on the ground floor will be sitting pretty."

"I should think Dakota would have soured you on that kind of thing," Elsa said.

"Oh, Dakota!" he said. "You don't see the difference. The difference is that this is *new,* see? It isn't even scratched." He grew almost violent, trying to show it to her as he saw it. "Why, God knows what's up there," he said. "There might be coal, or iron, or oil, or any damn thing under that ground. Nobody but cowpunchers and the surveyors have ever been over it. And a railroad coming right through it."

When she still kept silent, he waved a pencil in the air. "Suppose you were up there and homesteaded a quarter section, somewhere along the right-of-way. And suppose you found coal on that quarter, say. Good God, all you'd have to do is snoop around a little and use your bean, and you could buy up all the likely-looking coal land and be on Easy Street in a year."

"What would you buy it with?" she said, not wanting to say it, not wanting really to throw cold water on his visions, but compelled to say it. They couldn't even afford a wooden house, and here he talked about Easy Street in a country hundreds of miles away, where they would have to start from scratch all over again and might never even get beyond their initial poverty. She saw the irritated jerk of his head when she said it, but she had to say it, and she had to keep insisting on it, because if she didn't he would drag them all off to some other get-rich-quick spot and they'd be back where they had started seven years ago, or worse.

"You've got about as much imagination as a pancake griddle," he said.

"It isn't a question of imagination," she said steadily. "It's a question of getting along. You can't just leave one place for another without knowing what's going to turn up in the new place. You wouldn't trade a sure thing for a gamble."

"I'd trade this sure thing," Bo said. "I'd trade this joint for almost any gamble you could name."

"And give up all the work we've put into it?"

"Look," he said. "I've been figuring this sure thing out for an hour, and there hasn't been a customer to interrupt me, either."

He leaned over with a sheet of paper, but she said defensively, before she would glance down at it, "It's always dead from ten to twelve. The mealtime crowds hold up."

"You'd never get rich off 'em. You know how much we still owe?" He stabbed the pencil on a column of figures. "Six hundred and twenty bucks."

"But that's pretty good," she said. "That's only half of what it was. We'll have it clear in a year or so."

"And what've we got when we've got it clear?" Bo said. "A business that brings you a hundred a month."

"It will be more than that when the payments are all finished."

"And then you'll have to spend that much more renovating."

"But we can live on it," she said. "We've been living on less."

"Out where the cougars sneak around and tramps raid the place and the kids get scared of their shadows," he said. "Do you call that living?"

He looked at the clock, turned to move a kettle onto the fire, took chalk and wrote neatly on the two-by-four blackboard, "Special Today, Irish Mulligan, bread, coffee, 20c. Ham and Eggs, 20c. Bacon and Eggs, 20c. Steaks and Chops on Short Order." He wrote a clean, neat hand, even on a blackboard.

"I worked on a railroad once," Bo said. "There's plenty of jobs for a smart guy if he keeps his eye open. Like bunkhouses. Sometimes the road puts those up, but lots of times they lease out the concession and the guy they lease it to gets it straight out of the men's pay. All clean, see. Then when the line moves on you knock down your bunkhouse and load it on a flatcar and set it up further down."

"I shouldn't think there'd be much money in that," she said stonily.

"That shows what you know about it. You know how many men a road has on a grading or steel-laying crew? Plenty. Two or three hundred. Furnishing bunks for two or three hundred stiffs isn't chicken feed, even if you flopped 'em for two bits a night. And when you're all through, in a new country like that, you can sell your beds and chairs and even your bunkhouse to somebody for almost as much as you paid in the first place." He was tapping with his finger on the counter, watching her. "There's another angle, too. What do you suppose those stiffs do for amusement at night, after work? There's no towns to go to. Suppose I wrote Jud to come on along. Don't you suppose a smart gambler like Jud could shake down a little loose change in a place like that? I just guess he could."

"You want to go awfully bad, don't you?" Elsa said. She felt sad, whipped, dependent. She was a millstone around his neck. That rough new country was where he belonged, really. But it would blow everything she wanted sky-high, uproot her again, take the children into a country where there weren't even schools.

Bo was watching her face. "And you don't," he said.

She shook her head. "No."

He shrugged and turned to getting things ready for the noon customers, and after a few minutes she went out to gather up the children and take them back for their own lunch. Bo didn't like them around eating in the café. They made it look as if they were eating up the leftovers, or something.

On Sunday Elsa was trying to wash clothes behind the tent. Laundry had piled up since she was hurt, Bo needed fresh shirts, the bed linen was soiled. She was sousing shirts in a tub of water and rubbing them one-handed on the board when she heard steps coming around the tent, and for an instant she froze with the fear of another tramp. Then Bo came in sight with his coat over his shoulder and his sleeves rolled up.

"Has something happened?" she said.

"Taking a vacation."

"Why?"

"*Why?*" he said. "It's about time, isn't it? I've been working sixteen hours a day seven days a week about long enough."

He seemed mad, sour, out of spirits. And he did need a rest, there wasn't any question. "Good," she said. "Did you just close up?"

"I made up about two dozen sandwiches and put 'em in a box and left a tin can with a slot in it on the doorstep," he said. "Maybe one out of three that takes a sandwich will pay for it. I don't give a damn if none of them do."

"Or if somebody steals the can," she said. "I don't either. It's nice to have you home for once. Soon as I get through maybe we can go for a walk."

He hooked his coat on the clothesline post, throwing it from six feet away, took off his shirt and threw it after the coat, and stretched in the sun in his undershirt, a languid, lazy, powerful stretch that moved the muscles under his milky skin. With his dark face and hands he looked like some odd cross-breed. He pushed her away from the tub. "You're an invalid," he said. "Let me swing that a while."

"I feel all right. It doesn't hurt."

"Go on," he said, and she had to back away.

"This is nice," she said. "I wish you could take a vacation more often."

He eyed her obliquely. "I'd just as soon take a good long vacation from that dump."

Instead of answering she went inside and got more laundry, and for a while they worked together, he washing and wringing shirts and children's clothes, twisting them so tight with his heavy wrists that she had trouble shaking them out to hang them up. She was standing on tiptoe at the high post-end of the line with her mouth full of clothespins when he said, "Thought any more about that Canada proposition?"

She hung the last shirt and took the clothespins out of her mouth. At this moment, when they were together, comfortable, with the sun on them and the children playing quietly in their own yard, wild enough and poor enough, God knew, but their own, he thought of nothing but getting away.

"Don't be mad, Bo," she said. "You asked me that before, and I told you what I thought. The café will keep us. We can clear it and live like other people instead of like gypsies."

"Uh," Bo said, and scrubbed a nightgown up and down the board. He said no more, but when she got the last batch of scrubbed clothes to hang up they were twisted as hard as sticks of wood, almost dry enough for ironing.

Bruce wandered into sight from the front yard and stood watching. He cocked one foot against his shin, shifted to stand on the other foot. "Ma," he said. "I got to go."

Elsa had a sheet half way on the line, and the wind pulled at it so that she had trouble keeping it in place with one hand. "You go on by yourself this time," she said over her shoulder. "You can do it."

Bruce shifted his feet, looked solemn, squinted his face, but did not move.

"Go on, bub," Bo said. "Do as your mother tells you. She's busy."

The boy moved a few feet, stopped, put his hands around the pole that supported the line, and swung on it. His eyes were on his mother. "You take me, Ma."

"Go on," his father said. "Ma's busy. You get on out there and back like a man. I bet you a penny you can't be back before I get this water dumped and the tub hung up."

Still watching his mother steadily, Bruce went a few feet, stopped to pick a flower and toss its petals into the air with a jerky little motion. He picked the leaves off the flower stem and did the same with them, very concentrated, very busy. He stood knock-kneed, holding his legs together.

"Now confound you," his father said sharply, "you move when you're spoken to! Get on out there before I have to make you."

Bruce went slowly out the path, tossing flowers and leaves and sticks into the air with his jerky, invariable motion. At the pile of slashings where the blackberry bushes grew thick he stopped. His father was hanging up the tub in the shed, out of sight. His mother was at the line. But back of him were the bushes, the shadows, and he had to walk another thirty feet into them alone to the privy. He didn't like the privy anyway. Wind blew up through the opening at the back, and flies crawled on your behind, and you didn't know what might be down there peeking at you, animals, cougars, snakes, faces with teeth . . .

Swiftly he pulled down his overalls and squatted in the weeds beside the path.

He had barely ducked when his father's yell startled him to his feet again, scuttling with hands clutching his overalls. But his father was after him. Heavy feet pounded the path. He heard his mother call out, but he couldn't get back to her now. Gasping, he scrambled into the privy and sat up on the children's hole. He cringed back when his father burst in. In one motion he was yanked upside down and spatted smartly on his bare backside.

"Now!" his father said, and slammed him back on the hole. "Now you sit there till you're through, and don't let me catch you squatting in the yard again."

Bruce bawled, and seeing his mother's face at the door bawled louder. But his father just went out and shut the door on him and he heard their steps going away.

"He's frightened," Elsa said. "That's why he doesn't like to come out here."

"Seems to me he's frightened of every damn thing in the world," Bo said. "You can't let him make a pigpen of the yard."

Elsa stopped. "I think I'll stay here and walk back with him," she said. "You've no idea how . . ."

Bo took her arm. "Let him walk back by himself."

"But he's scared, Bo."

"I was scared of water when I was a kid, too," Bo said. "That didn't keep my old man from throwing me in when I was about five, where it was ten feet deep."

"You never liked your father, either. You'll have that child hating you like poison."

"Then he'll just have to hate me," Bo said. "He's got to be trained if I have to bust his head for him on the way."

"You can't whip a child out of being afraid," she said in anger. "Bruce is sensitive, that's all. He's the most sensitive child I ever saw. But he's stubborn as a mule, too, just as stubborn as you are. You'll start something you can't finish."

"Let him keep on being stubborn," Bo said. "I'll guarantee to knock that out of him."

Still angry, she went back and finished hanging up the clothes, but after Bruce came back sniffling and Bo had started to putter in the shade of the shed, his jaw still set and a look on his face as if something smoldered in him, she didn't need to ask herself if his rage at Bruce had anything to do with the thing that had been on his mind when he closed up the café and came home for the afternoon, the proposition he had mentioned, glancing at her sideways, and then shut up about when she showed that her mind was still made up the other way.

Certainly, in the two weeks that followed, he showed less and less interest in the café. He always seemed to get there late in the morning, he closed up earlier at night, he shut up the whole place the following Sunday afternoon and made her come home when she said she would just as soon stay and take care of it. She was taking her regular turn now, relieving him at eleven o'clock and staying till the evening meal was ready. And while she was at the café, he was at home with the boys. That, she knew before two days had passed, wasn't good.

When she was at home she could take Bruce out to the privy, look after him, soothe his fears, get him interested in something else. But Bo was a martinet. The kid had been babied too much. All right, he would fix that. He made Bruce dress himself in the mornings, feed his rabbit by himself without even Chester's help, go out in back by himself, wash himself alone before meals. He insisted that Bruce eat exactly what was set before him and clean up his plate; if he didn't, it was taken away and he went hungry. When he went a whole day, stubbornly, without eating a mouthful, Elsa protested. Bo was being altogether too hard. It wasn't Bruce's fault he was finicky. The boys had been moved around from pillar to post ever since they were born. They weren't sure of anything, they had never had a home. You couldn't blame a child for feeling afraid and insecure.

But her argument got her nowhere. Look at Chester, Bo said. He hadn't had any different kind of life, and look at him. He wasn't afraid of anything. She had babied Bruce till he knew he could get anything he wanted, just by whining. Well, he would find out different.

"But he isn't even four years old yet," Elsa said, knowing with a kind of panic that she couldn't budge him. She could see him day by day getting further into that mood of restless irritability, of sullen, stubborn dissatisfaction, that had made the last months at Indian Falls a nightmare. Only this time, it seemed, it was to be Bruce and not the cat who suffered for it.

The first result of Bo's discipline was that Bruce began wetting and soiling himself rather than go out to the privy, though he had been broken of wetting for over a year. That only made things worse. If Bo were at the café, she could keep the accidents quiet, but once, when it happened during her shift, she came home to find the child sniffling against the back wall of the shed, and when she undressed him for bed she found the marks on his buttocks. Bo had used the razor strop on him.

That made her shout at him. "You can't spank a child into being dry! Haven't you any sense at all?"

He looked at her heavily. "Can't you see why he does it?"

"He does it because you've got him so scared he's half out of his mind."

"I can see pretty well," he said, "and that isn't what I see. He's doing it to dare me, by God."

"Oh, Bo," she said in despair. "You were so nice to them for a while, and they got along so well. Why don't you try being kind?"

"Sure I'll be kind, when he learns to do what he's told. Let him run over you and he'll run over you all his life. But by God he doesn't run over me." The words fell with solid, whacking emphasis, like chunks being chopped from a straight-grained block.

There was nothing she could do, unless she wanted to yield to what she knew bothered him, and take the children up into a place where Heaven knew what would turn up. So she kept quiet, but when, a few minutes later, she heard him say, "Well, I guess I'll go it one," and saw him take the deck of cards from the bureau and sit down, she wanted to scream. Solitaire was almost worse than bad temper.

On a Saturday, two weeks after Bo had first closed the café for the Sunday afternoon holiday, he came home at ten thirty in the morning. There was a barbecue over at the mill. Not a chance for a customer all day, he said. He seemed in a good enough humor, but restless. For a while he stood in the yard looking distastefully at the littered clearing. Then he called the boys and started them picking up chips and scraps of paper, piling tin cans over against the woods, straightening up the scattered woodpile. They did it lackadaisically, without thoroughness, but he didn't scold them. After a while he got hammer and nails and started repairing the porch.

"What's all the cleaning up about?" Elsa asked.

"Well, hell. Place looks like a boar's nest. If we got to live here the rest of our lives I might as well straighten it up a little."

Impulsively she put her fingers down and stirred his black hair. "Poor Bo," she said.

"Don't want to change your mind about Canada, do you?" he said. He hammered in a nail with four quick blows. "I had a letter about it the other day."

"Who from?"

"Friend of this Massey, that told me about it in the first place. I wrote him and asked for the dope."

"What did he say?"

"Said the road was coming through, all right. Already started grading."

For a moment she was almost tempted. It might be better, there might be a home there, certainly Bo would be happier if she didn't hold him back. After the way the Alaska business had fizzled, so that now Jud was still right where he had been at first, dealing in a gambling house, and after the way Bo had given up what had looked like a golden chance because of her and the boys, when Chester got sick, maybe she ought to say yes. But then her own desires would have to be sacrificed again, and the home she wanted for the children's salvation, for her own salvation, interposed itself like a fence.

She said, "If it weren't for the kids I'd say go anywhere."

He went on nailing down the loose boards of the porch, and when he had finished that he got up without a word and went to look at the well cover, which had rotted away at one side. He said nothing more about Canada, but she watched him unhappily, knowing that he was trying to do as she wished, and trying to accept the responsibility that his family laid on him, but that he still must feel chained and trapped.

Even after supper he did not mention the subject. He made an effort to be cheerful, creaking back in his chair with his pipe in his mouth and clipping Chester's ear with a back-handed cuff.

"Ow!" Chester said. He held his ear and scowled.

"Come on and fight," Bo said. "Anybody hits me, I hit him back. What's holding you?"

Chester lowered his head and sailed in, and Bo let him flail a few times before he clipped him on the other ear. As they scuffled, he got hold of Chester's wrist and bent it back, poking the tight little fist into its owner's eye. "What you hitting yourself for?" he said. "Hit me. It isn't good sense to sock yourself."

Chester squirmed and swung with the other hand. "You're doin' it," he said. "Let go and I'll . . ."

At the other end of the table Bruce sidled up to his mother, his eyes fixed steadily on the scuffling, and pulled her dress. She glanced down, saw his lips frame the words, "I got to go."

Her quick glance showed Bo still sparring with Chester, grinning, pushing the boy away with a big irremovable hand, holding him by the top of the head while Chester tried to bore in.

She nodded at Bruce, and led him quietly toward the door. Behind her Bo's voice came heavy and even. "Hey. Where you going?"

She turned around with a lie on her very lips before the absurdity of lying about such a thing made her meet his eyes. "Bruce has to go."

"Let him go by himself." Bo had quit sparring, and was holding the still-belligerent Chester at arm's length.

"It's getting dark," Elsa said.

"It isn't dark yet by a damn sight," Bo said. "He's been told often enough to go by himself. You just make him worse trying to sneak around and out-fox me."

Rebellious and angry, she hesitated. To stand around arguing about such a ridiculous thing! Why shouldn't she go out with him, if it made him feel safer? Why should he have to go out there alone when he was terrified of the woods and the dark? But Bo sat there, implacable and dominating. And that afternoon she had refused for the third time to do the thing he wanted. If this kept on, they would be at loggerheads over every little thing. . . .

"You can go out yourself like a big boy," she said. "Sure you can. Mommy's got to do up the dishes." She hated herself for that lame surrender, and saw Bruce hating her for it too. He twitched away from the door and tried putting his fingers around the lantern base.

"I don't need to," he said sullenly.

She looked helplessly at Bruce, then at Bo, and started clearing off the table without a word. But Bo half rose, and his voice was edged with a threat. "Oh yes you do. Skin on out there, right now."

Bruce's lip jutted, his eyes were dark with rebellion. "I don't need to."

The stool scraped as Bo stood up. "If you want a good hiding," he said, "just stand around there a minute more seeing how far you can go."

The child lingered at the door, his round baby face clouded with passion, but when Bo took two swift heavy steps toward him he bolted. Elsa said nothing. If Bo wanted to make that issue the most important in the world, just to assure himself that he was boss, she supposed he would do it. Bruce was trying enough. He made you want to scream sometimes. But it did no good to bully and spank. That only made the trouble loom bigger, and it was already ridiculously exaggerated. Let Bo go on and earn the hatred of his son. Secretly, she would almost have bet on the child rather than on Bo; Bruce would take scoldings, spankings, brutality, anything, and wail and howl and cry, but they wouldn't break him. All they would do would be to harden him under the surface fear and callous him to punishment.

The door opened and Bruce slipped in quickly. He shut the door as if locking something out. Bo took his pipe from his mouth and looked at him, the faint expression of petulance on his face overlaid by surface heartiness. "Get your business done?"

"Yes."

"Weren't any boogers out there, either, were there?"

"No."

"Sure not," Bo said. "Not a booger in sight. Even if there was, there's no call for a big guy like you to be scared. Chet here eats boogers for breakfast."

When he turned his chair squarely and fronted the child, his face, to his wife, was a curious mixture, as if the bluff good-natured heartiness with which he treated the children sometimes, and which he was trying to assume now, were an expression worn over at least two others, as if the underlying muscles of his face said at the same time that he was doomed and damned and leg-ironed by family responsibilities, and as if the eyes, quite independently, were appraising his youngest with an acid, prying look of contempt. But his voice was the playful voice of teasing fellowship. "Come on over and get pasted," he said. "I just toughened Chet up till you couldn't drive a nail in him."

Bruce hung close to his mother by the stove, his eyes sullen and unyielding. "I don't want to," he said.

The look of contempt for a moment obliterated the other expressions on Bo's face. He looked at Elsa, laughed a short, hard laugh, and stood up. "All right," he said. "All right, all right! You don't want to."

As he passed the stove on his way out of the tent Bruce crowded back against the box where his mother kept the dishes, and his eyes followed his father until the door shut behind him.

Elsa sighed. "You ought to play when Pa wants you to," she said, but Bruce turned his head aside and picked slivers off a stick of firewood with ritualistic care. "I don't want to," he said again.

"If you minded the first time he spoke to you you wouldn't get into trouble," she said. "Can't you try to mind better, Brucie?"

He went on picking slivers, and she turned from him to get at the dishes. After a few minutes she heard Bo's steps coming up the path, along the side of the tent. There was a surprised grunt. The footsteps paused while she might have counted five. Then Bo's voice, strident, high-pitched, insane with rage, was shouting curses. The baby jerked from behind the stove as if he were going to run, but in the middle of the tent he hesitated, his head swinging like a cornered animal's and his eyeballs distended with terror. Elsa had barely time to gather him in close to her before Bo burst in the door.

In the flash while their eyes met and held, while she crowded Bruce behind her back protectively, she knew that she had never seen Bo so furious. His face and neck were swollen and dark, his eyes glaring, his breath panting between bared and gritted teeth. His voice came in an incoherent, snarling roar.

"Of all the *God* damn, God damn! Right beside the path where I step in it! And lie about it! Right beside the path and then lie about it . . . !"

He was crouched on the threshold as if about to spring, and she backed up a step, holding Bruce behind her. "Bo! For God's sake, keep your temper, Bo!"

The swiftness with which his big body moved paralyzed her for a split second with utter terror that he would kill the child. Before she could put up her arm he had caught her shoulder and pushed her aside, and she fell screaming, trying with both hands to hang onto Bruce, feeling his fingers torn loose from her dress even while she fell, and hearing his thin squeak of terror. She screamed, "Bo, oh my God, Bo . . . Bo . . . !"

Moving with the same silent terrible speed, he was out the door again with Bruce under his arm, and she scrambled up, silent herself now, to hurl herself after him. Around the side of the tent the child's idiot babble of fear rose to a shriek, broke, rose again, cackled in a mad parody of laughter. In the near-dark she saw Bo bending over, the baby's frantic kicking legs beating out behind him as he shoved the child's face down to the ground, rubbing it around. "Will you mind?" he kept saying, "will you mind now, you damn stubborn little . . ."

She pulled at him, clawing, but one thick arm, powerful as a hurled log, brushed backward and knocked her down again, and she fell sideways on her half-healed arm. She never even felt the pain. Her mouth worked over soundless words. Like a dog, she screamed at him without making a sound, you treat your child like a dog! Her legs kicked her to her feet again so quickly that she might never have fallen. Bo was still rubbing Bruce's nose into the ground in a savage prolongation of fury.

Hatred flamed in her like a sheet of light. She wanted to kill him. Somehow her hand found a stick of stovewood in it, and with murder in her heart she rushed him. The first blow fell solid and soft across his shoulder. The second stung her hands as it found hard bone. Then she was wrestling with him, sobbing, trying to hit him again, screaming with helplessness and fury when she felt her wrist bent backward and her fingers loosening on the club.

Now finally the long moment when the madness burned out of both of them as suddenly as it had come and they faced each other in the heavy forest twilight with Bruce sobbing on the ground between them and Chester terrified and whimpering at the corner of the tent. Bo stared at her stupidly, his hands hanging. In the dusk she saw his mouth work, and bit her own lip, her body weak as water and her burned arm one long hammering ache. She didn't speak. Gathering the threads of her strength, she stooped and picked up Bruce and carried him into the tent, motioning Chester in after her and bolting the door.

Without pause or thought she went straight to the bed and lay down with Bruce tight against her, holding his moaning into her breast and trying by the very rigidity of her embrace to stop the shudders that went through his body. While she lay there Chester crept against her, so that she rolled a little and put her burned hand clumsily on his head.

There was no sound outside the tent. She caught herself listening tensely, and the anger touched her again like a rod of bare icy metal. The shivering of the child in her arms lessened gradually, but his breath still shook him into shudders, and at every catching intake of air she held him fiercely. Like a dog. Expecting a child to learn all at once, to be told and never afterward make a mistake, never to have any feelings of his own, but to jump like a trained animal. Even a dog he treated better, lessoned with endless patience, rewarded when it did something right. She blinked her dry eyes, scratchy as if they had been blow full of sand.

Poor child, she said. Poor baby! Her hand rubbed up and down his back, and she whispered in his ear. "Don't cry. Don't cry, baby. We won't let him do it any more."

(What instant outrage that she should have to say such a thing to him! We won't let him do it any more. His father!)

"Are you all right now?" she said finally. "Will you lie here and rest while Mommy lights the lamp?"

His hands clung, and she lay back. "Chet," she said, "can you light the lamp, do you think?"

He slipped off the bed, and she heard him bump against the table in the dark. Light leaped in a feeble spurt, went out, and he struck another match. Then the steadying glow of the lamp as he brought it back to the bed in both hands, carefully.

"Good boy," she said. "Set it on the chair."

Sitting up, she smoothed Bruce's hair back from his forehead and looked at him, and the cry that was wrenched from her came from a deeper well of horror and shame and anger than even the blows she had rained on Bo outside. Bruce's face was smeared with dirt and excrement and tears. Under that filth he was white as a corpse, his face shrunken and sharpened with terror. A nerve high in his cheek twitched in tiny sharp spasms, and his whole head shook as if he had St. Vitus' dance. But his eyes, his eyes . . .

"Look at me!" she said harshly, and shook him. "Brucie, look at me!"

The mouth closed on a thin, bubbling wail, the cheek twitched, but the eyes did not change. They remained fixed in mute impossible anguish, twisted inward until the pupils were half lost in the inner corners.

"Ma," Chester said, "is he cross-eyed, Ma?" He began to cry.

She shook Bruce again, her own eyes blind. "Bruce!"

His cheek twitched and his body shuddered. "Get me a pan of water and a wash cloth," Elsa said to Chester. She said it quietly, holding her voice down as if throwing all her weight on it. He mustn't be frightened any more, she mustn't shout at him, she must be soothing, soft, safe. Holding him cradled against her bad arm, she washed his face gently with the cloth, ran it over his eyes, pressed it against his forehead under the silky light hair matted with sweat and filth. Minute by interminable minute she washed him, and heard the sobbing smooth out under the stroking, saw the cheek twitch less often, less violently.

Chester was putting wood in the stove, being helpful, his solemn teary face watching his mother and brother on the bed. Elsa took a firm hold on Bruce's shoulders. "Look, Brucie," she said. "Look at Chet over there, getting supper for us like a big man."

While she watched, not breathing, Bruce's eyes wavered, rolled outward from that fixed and inhuman paralysis; some of the glaring white eyeballs, streaked with red, slid back out of sight and the whole pupils appeared briefly. Then, as if the strain were too much, as if normal focus were an effort too great for more than a moment, the pupils rolled back again. Elsa caught her breath with a jerky sigh. Maybe tomorrow, after he had slept . . .

But oh God, she said, to treat a child that way!

She had just laid him down on the pillow and started to get something to eat for Chester when Bruce was screaming again, eyes frantically crossed and cheek twitching, his hands clawing at his face and his voice screaming, "Mama, Mama, on my face . . . on my nose . . . !"

5

There hadn't really been any decision. As she dragged the round-topped trunk up the steps and propped its lid against the table, she was thinking that you never really made up your mind to anything. You simply bent where the pressure was greatest. You didn't surrender, because surrender was annihilation, but you gave before the pressure.

A light rain fingered the canvas over her head, and she knew the move would be unpleasant, sodden, miserable. But it didn't matter greatly. To leave on a sunny day would be inappropriate; a retreat should be made in weather as miserable as the act itself.

There wasn't much to pack. Bo's clothing she stowed in his brown suitcase and put aside. That could be left at the hotel for him, in case he ever came back. Apart from that there were only her own few clothes, the children's things, the bedding and table linen. Mr. Bane would have whatever else the tent contained—stove, beds, table, bureau, dishes. Mr. Bane had been very kind. He didn't really want the things at all. It was only to help her that he bought them.

Oh, and the rabbits. She straightened, brushing back the hair that fell damply on her forehead. What to do with the rabbits? They couldn't be left, and they could hardly be taken to a boarding-house room in Seattle. She shrugged and gave up thinking about them almost before she had begun. They could be taken along part way, perhaps given to someone along the road. Any child would be glad to get them.

Chester staggered in with a quilt huddled against his chest, dragging in front so that he tripped on it. Bruce came after him, also loaded. They were excited. The move to them was adventure. They didn't know it was retreat.

"What else, Ma?" Chester said.

"You'd better go feed your bunnies," she said. "There's some carrots in the shed."

Two minutes later they were back, breathless. "Ma, the bunnies are gone!"

"Are you sure?"

"The pen's empty."

She went to look. The screen had rusted away at one side of the board floor of the hutch, and something, either the rabbits or something digging from outside, had widened the hole. The boys looked up at her, and she hid her feeling of relief. She had to appear to be sorry.

"Why don't you look around the edge of the brush?" she said. "They're tame, they'd stay around. Take the carrots and call them."

She went back into the tent and packed the remaining things. In the bureau drawer, back under a collection of odd stockings, she found the tintype of her mother, stood looking at it a moment, curiously emotionless, emptied, unable to remember, somehow, the way she had used to feel when looking at that portrait. She snapped the case shut and laid it in the trunk.

She heard the buckboard come into the clearing, and went to the door. Emil Hurla, one of the bus drivers who lived in Richmond, waved from the seat.

"I'm practically ready," she said. "The trunk's packed now, if you want to get it."

Hurla, a great, lumbering man with a gray, pock-marked face, climbed down and got the trunk, muscling it through the door on his thighs. Elsa hurriedly crammed the last rags into her telescope and crushed it shut, strapping it tight. Hurla came in and took it off the table. She looked around at the stripped beds, the empty bureau with its drawers hanging open, the trash littered on the floor, discarded socks, frayed collars, hoarded mop-rags, all the souvenirs of flight. Deliberately, under a compulsion that was more than her ingrained neatness, that was something like a defiance in the midst of panic, she took the stubby broom and swept the whole place, dumping the refuse in the stove and setting fire to it. The boys and Hurla stood in the door and watched her.

"Our bunnies got lost," Chester said.

Hurla put his hands on his knees and bent down. "Is that right, now?" he said. "That's too bad."

"They got out of the pen," Chester said. "We hunted, but we can't find them."

"Well, now," Hurla said. "Maybe we ought to look once more."

He lifted his eyes to Elsa as if to ask if they had time, and when she nodded he went out, the boys after him.

She had pulled out the beds and swept up the dust puppies and had stood the broom back of the stove when she heard Bruce crying. She went to the door. Hurla stood with the well cover lifted on edge, and all three were looking down in.

"Ma!" Chester shouted. "Ma, the bunnies are down there."

Slowly she went out through the drizzle, her feet sinking soggily in the wet mould, the rain like fine mist in her face. At the well-edge she stopped and peered. Ten feet down, floating whitely, close together, their fur spread by the water like the fur of an angry cat, were the rabbits. The holes under the cover, she supposed, had tempted them in.

"Get a rope!" Chester shouted. "Get something. We got to get them out."

The sight of Bruce's immense, teary eyes as she turned away made Elsa grit her teeth with momentary fury, as if he were to blame. Then she pulled him against her and took Chester's hand. "It's no use," she said. "Your bunnies are drowned. It's a shame."

"But we can't leave them in there," Chester said. "Ma . . ."

She drew them away. Hurla let the cover fall, and Bruce burst out in a wild passionate wail. She lifted him into the buggy, letting him cry, ignoring Chester's worried "Ma, we can't . . . Ma." Hurla climbed up and took the lines. The mist had powdered the wool of his cap like a thin coating of flour.

He sawed the team around, and started out of the clearing. Elsa ducked her head to avoid the first low branches of the old tote road. She did not look back, but she could see in her mind every bush and stump in the clearing, every stain on the canvas roof, every detail of the place that had been home for a year and a half, that had still been home even after Bo ran off to Canada, that she had been fiercely determined to make home. But it was too much, she thought. She couldn't have tried any harder.

Behind her she heard Bruce's crying, furious now because she had not comforted him, and she felt in Chester's silence his grief for the death they left behind them in the well. She couldn't blame them any more than she could help them. There was too much that lay dead behind her. That well and clearing and abandoned tent-house neatly swept and locked against intrusion was a gravestone in her life. There had been other gravestones, but this was the worst, because it was more than a hope or a home that lay dead there. It was her marriage. Though she had not admitted it before, she knew that one reason she had tried so hard to keep the café going and to hold to the clearing was the hope that some day Bo would come back.

She did not look behind her, but she knew exactly how Bruce and Chester felt when they knelt at the lip of the well and saw the white, furred-out shapes of their pets floating, lifting motionless to the motionless lifting of earthbound water in a dark, earth-smelling hole under the rain.

Bo came out of the Half-Diamond Bar bunkhouse with Big Horn, the foreman, and stood picking his teeth in the watery October sun. Rusty, third son of a British earl, was stapling a broken bridle at the corner of the house. Another remittance man, the boy they called Slivers, was sprawled against the horse corral playing his mouth organ. Louis Treat, a half-breed Assiniboine, lounged against a low, rock-weighted stack of prairie hay and braided at a horsehair rope. A hundred yards up through the light, leafless growth of black birch and cottonwood, the stone mansion of Jim Purcell showed. Bo spat on the ground.

"How much money has old Purcell got, anyway?" he said.

Big Horn shrugged. "He's loaded with it. He give the C.P.R. ever' other house lot to survey a townsite here, and even if he'd of give 'em nine tenths of it it'd still have been a good proposition for him."

"How many head of cattle does he run?"

" 'Bout eight thousand."

"He'll have to cut that out, though, when the range gets homesteaded."

"Hell, he don't care about that," Big Horn said. "He must own forty thousand acres up the river. He was smart. He was buyin' land long before the road started down through."

"You've got to hand it to him," Bo said. "Still, he had the breaks, too."

Big Horn turned on him and laughed. "What's matter? You sore because you didn't think of it first?"

"I wasn't on the ground," Bo said. "That makes a hell of a lot of difference."

"Hell, if I had your bunkhouse business I wouldn't kick."

"I'm not kicking," Bo said. "I'm just wishing Purcell had left a little cream for the rest of us. That bunkhouse business won't last forever."

"Give you a job, thirty a month and grub," Big Horn said. "Christ A'mighty, what if you had to work? How'd you like ridin' line in a forty-below blizzard?"

"I told you I wasn't kicking," Bo said. "I'm just trying to figure some way a man could make a good thing out of this town Purcell's got started. There isn't much doubt it's going to be a town."

"Oh, it'll be a town, all right."

"Look at that Syrian peddler that's squatted here," Bo said. "Those guys are smart. They don't settle any place unless they see money in it."

"Tell me the Grain Growers' Association is going to build a elevator," Big Horn said. "Sure it'll be a town."

"There isn't anything it hasn't got," Bo said. "All that flat between the bends, that's plenty of room to grow in. Hills full of lignite, plenty of water. Hell, it'll draw trade for thirty miles around."

"Big as Chicago in ten years," Big Horn said comfortably. He yawned. "When it gets about as big as Shaunavon I'm movin' on. You and the rest of the promoters can run it then."

"Kiss my ass," Bo said. "You're scared it'll get big enough to support a cop."

"Cops don't bother me," Big Horn said. "Not Canadian cops. They're putting more Mounties at the post this winter, did you know that?"

"Sure?"

"Sure. Heard the old man talking about it the other day."

"Then that settles it," Bo said. "They aren't sticking in any new Mounties unless they're sure the place is going to grow." He looked through the trees at Purcell's stone house. There was the guy that had used his bean, gathered everything all in to himself. Stone house, forty-thousand-acre ranch, eight thousand head of cattle, real estate to hell and gone, Chink houseboy, big shots stopping in on the stage all the time to talk to him. "By God," he said, "I wish I owned about twenty lots in the middle of that flat."

Big Horn yawned. "It must be oncomfortable to be ambitious," he said. "Jaspers gnawin' at your pants all the time. Whyn't you leave all that ambition to the guys with a pack of kids to raise?"

Bo looked at him. "Maybe I have got a pack of kids to raise."

"Maybe you have," Big Horn said. "How would I know?"

Two cowpunchers, Slip and Little Horn, came across the open space between the saddle shed and the corral and stopped to listen to Slivers blow on his mouth organ. He was playing something sad and shivery, flapping his fingers to get a tremolo. Out of nowhere, apparently, a small boy appeared, a dark, black-eyed boy of about eight, with a dark birthmark on the very end of his nose. Little Horn said something to him, and he looked up with an impish, white-toothed smile.

"That's Orullian's kid, one of 'em," Big Horn said. "He's the guy with a pack of 'em. Must have six or seven."

"He'll raise 'em, too," Bo said. "I never saw a Syrian yet that couldn't make money if there was any to be made."

"There you go again," said Big Horn. "Why in hell don't you open a grocery store, if you think it's such a good thing?"

"I'm after something better than grocery stores."

The Orullian boy cackled loudly at something one of the hands said. Little Horn put his hand on the boy's head, and the boy ducked away with a scornful mouth. Little Horn laughed and started away toward the corral half hidden behind the saddle shed. In three minutes he was back dragging a lassoed calf, hauling it along with upturned muzzle and braced legs. The Orullian boy stood and watched. So did Bo and Big Horn.

Little Horn went and brought an old saddle girth, threw the calf and fastened it around him like a surcingle. The calf blatted and Little Horn let it up, holding it by the ears.

"Okay, cowboy. Lessee you ride him."

The boy approached carefully, sidling; hesitated as the calf backed away; tried to get around to the side. Slip braced himself against the calf's haunches and Little Horn held its head. "Climb aboard, cowboy," Little Horn said.

The boy leaned across the calf's back and scrambled and kicked himself up. His eyes were enormous and he hung tightly to the surcingle. The two punchers jumped back and yelled, and the calf went pitching across the lot. The boy hung on for about three jumps before he sprawled headlong. For a moment he lay where he fell, while the calf bucked off toward the river. Then he pushed himself up from the ground with his mouth drawn down in a tough leer. Little Horn, before he went after the calf, shook his hand and said he'd stayed sixty seconds. Then Slip shook his hand, then Slivers. The boy was very proud.

"Pretty tough kid," Bo said. Abruptly he threw away his toothpick and pulled down his hat. "Guess I'd better go see if my Chink has burned up the joint," he said, and walked away. It was some time before he could shake out of his head the memory of the way Chet used to swagger and leer when he had done something he thought he ought to be proud of. Chet was a good kid, full of beans. He'd be just about the Orullian kid's age now, maybe a little younger.

He walked across the mouth of the east bend, cut through a straggly patch of willows, and came out on the flat where the town would be. There were already three bare frame shacks, and two derailed dining cars set up along what would eventually be a street. The raw earth where the scrapers had been working showed against the foot of the south hill, and a hundred yards on from the end of the grade was his bunkhouse, sheathed with lathed-on tarpaper. Smoke rose from the stovepipes at both ends.

Inside, he found the Chink Mah Li sitting with his hands comfortably folded in his lap. The bunks were all neatly made, there was a full scuttle of lignite by each stove. Nobody else was in the place except old Hank Flynn, sick in the lungs. The crew would begin to come around after supper, which they took at McGrannahan's boarding house a quarter of a mile back up the line.

Mah Li smiled his beaming, wrinkle-eyed smile and pointed upward. "Light all bloke," he said.

Bo looked up. The mantles on the three hanging gasoline lamps were all in shreds. "How the hell did that happen?"

"Open door," Mah Li said. "Wind blowee, all bloke."

"Well, for Christ sake keep the door shut, then," Bo said. He found a package of mantles and climbed on a chair to take the first lamp down. Hank Flynn watched from his bunk.

"I seen what was goin' to happen when they started swingin'," Flynn said, "but there wasn't nothin' I could do, sick like this. I hollered at the Chink, but he didn't savvy."

Bo said nothing. He was carefully tying new mantles around the rings, evening the tucks so that no metal touched them. He scratched a match on his foot and touched it to first one mantle, then the other. The stink of burning cloth rose. When the mantles were shrunken and ash-white, he climbed the chair again and carefully hung the lamp on its wire.

"God this is a lonesome hole," Hank Flynn said, and rubbed his gray-bristled face. "I wisht there was some place a guy could go, poolroom or something. I ain't seen a soul since the boys left this morning, 'cept the Chink."

"You couldn't go out any place even if there was a place to go," Bo said.

Hank Flynn coughed. "Ain't it a hell of a note?" he said. His voice was a thin whine that grated on Bo's nerves. "Guy gets old and sick, when he'd ought to have a place of his own and a wife and kids to look after him, and what happens but he has to lie around a damn drafty bunkhouse all day without anybody but a Chink to talk to, and he can't talk."

"If you don't like the bunkhouse why don't you move to the hotel?" Bo said.

"Oh hell, it ain't the bunkhouse," Flynn said. "This is all right, all you could expect. It's not havin' anybody give a damn whether you're sick or not. I could lay here and die and rot and nobody'd even move my bones."

"Cheer up," Bo said. "We'd move you when you started to smell."

"That's right," Flynn said. "By God, that's about the only reason anybody'd give a damn whether I lived or died."

Bo had tied the mantles on the second lamp, and scratched another match. Through the windows along the east side he could see the crew streaming across the scraped and naked earth on the way to Mrs. McGrannahan's. The light outside was bleak and cheerless, a cold, early twilight. He wished Flynn would stop his whining. It was tough to be laid up, but that was no reason to crab and grouse all day. Nobody liked to hear a guy crab all the time.

"I prob'ly *will* die here," Flynn said. He sat up and rubbed at his face again, sitting with his head hanging and his elbows on his knees. "I sure never thought I'd wind up in the middle of nowhere without a friend or a soul that give a damn," he said. "I sure never did. I used to be strong as anybody. Ten years ago I could-a throwed anybody in that crew, straight wrastling, Marquis of Queensberry, or anything. You can sure see what sickness can do to a man. I used to have an arm on me . . ." He slipped up the sleeve of his winter underwear and pulled it high on his upper arm. "See that?" He flexed his muscle, and a hard white knob jumped under the skin. "It looks strong yet, by God," Hank said, staring at his muscle. Then he pulled the sleeve down and flinched his shoulder irritably, as if at a draft. "But it ain't," he said. "I ain't got enough stren'th left to pull my tongue out of the sugar barrel.

"If I had a sugar barrel," he added. He ran his hands over his whiskers and into his hair. "Sure is a hell of a life when you never laid nothing by," he said. "Just go hellin' around spendin' it as fast as you make it, and playin' the ladies and the horses and stickin' your feet up on bar rails. It sure makes you think when you get laid up and see what you made out-a all that stren'th you had once. You wisht you'd done a lot-a things different."

"Well, why didn't you?" Bo said.

Flynn looked surprised. "Hell, I don't know. Just hellin' around, takin' everything as it come. I don't know. When you're strong you don't ever think you can get old and sick. When you're in the jack you don't ever think you can go broke. When you don't give a damn for anybody you don't ever think you can get lonesome. But I'd sure do it different if I was doin' it over."

He stood up and scratched himself through the unbuttoned top of his underwear. "I s'pose I better get on over to the slop house," he said. "Nobody'd ever think to bring a guy anything when he's sick."

Bo looked at him, a stringy, gray-faced old man. He was pretty old to be working on a gypo gang, even if he wasn't sick. He stood there vaguely scratching his chest, mumbling under his breath and looking around for something, probably his shirt, in the mussed bunk.

"You really sick?" Bo said. "You really feel like hell, or are you just dogging it?"

Hank Flynn looked at him meanly. "I been tellin' you," he said. "I'm goin' to die right here, I know it. I'm sick as hell. I been coughin' blood for a month."

Bo looked at him steadily in pity and contempt. "Mah Li," he said.

The Chinaman was at his shoulder, smiling, bending a little forward.

"You ever have a belly ache?" Bo said. "You ever get sick, Mah Li? You're a long way from home. Ever get lonesome?"

"Lonesome long time away," Mah Li said. "Velly busy most time."

Bo grunted, eyeing the vague gray figure of Hank Flynn. "Yeah," he said. He had forgotten what he started to do. "Well, run on over to McGrannahan's and get some supper for this guy," he said. "Tell her to check it off his ticket." He turned away to prime and pump and light the lamps, turning his back on Flynn and shutting his ears to his whining and feeling a little sore, a little mad, scowling to himself with a dull pointless dissatisfaction. It was a hell of a hole, sure enough.

That night he sat at one of the two tables in the north end of the bunkhouse with a stack of papers before him and a neatly sharpened pencil in his fist. The other table was crowded with card players, seven or eight of them sitting in on one game, and he saw, when he looked up from his brooding abstraction and his figuring, that other men were hanging around as if they wished he'd clear out and leave the table empty for them. Ordinarily he would have got up and given it to them, or got up a game himself, but now he did not move. When somebody hollered for drinks he reached the key to the liquor box out of his pocket and handed it without a word to Mah Li. The Chink was good; he had savvy. He had never made as much as a ten cent mistake in the liquor sales.

He bent his head and looked at the figures before him, orderly as an accountant's books, plus and minus, expense and profit, stacked in neat columns. He was doing all right. Three months of bunking the crew, even on a sub-contract that cost him twenty percent of his profits, had paid for the lumber, the bedsprings and ticks, the stoves, lamps, tables. The liquor had brought him in two hundred dollars clear in the last month, and that was gravy. He wasn't supposed to sell it, but who was going to come around and close him up? Even the poker games that went on every night till after midnight totalled up into a surprising sum, because every game chipped in a kitty to buy cards and chips and pay for the lights. That was fair enough. He had thought a buck a game was enough; now it turned out it was three times more than enough. The accumulated kitties totalled forty-three dollars, and he had cards and chips enough to last a year. There was also the surplus that Mah Li turned up with every week. He got five dollars a week extra for dealing fan tan and monte as a house game, and he turned over his chips to the penny. In the month and a half he had been with Bo he had brought in a hundred and thirty dollars above his wages.

It was all right, he was out of the woods. He totalled up the checks he had just written and deducted them from his bank balance. He had six hundred dollars in the bank, he owned the bunkhouse and its furnishings, and he had built it so that it could be unbolted and loaded on a flat and taken on down the line on a day's notice when necessary. In three months of actual operations, with his liquor sales and gambling profits, he was that far ahead, and he had arrived in Swift Current with hardly a dime. It just went to show you that if you had any push and got into a new country you could coin money. Not the way Purcell was coining it, but Purcell hadn't started from scratch five months ago, either.

He sat hunched over his papers, hardly seeing the long smoky room with men sprawling in their bunks playing solitaire, reading magazines or newspapers, just sitting or lying, talking, arguing. He hardly smelled the thick smell of hot iron and bitter lignite smoke and tobacco smoke and socks and the heavy odor of fifty men jammed into one warm room. He hardly heard the jumble of talk, as thick and languid as the smells. Five months since he had pulled out of Washington. He hadn't written and he hadn't heard.

Well, how could she write? he said impatiently. How would she know where I was?

For a moment he had almost pulled the curtain that hung over that part of his mind, but he pulled it back. There'd be about one more month of working weather. After that there'd be only a skeleton crew on. But there'd be enough to break even, maybe enough so he could keep the Chink on to cook for him and take care of the place. He'd be close to a thousand dollars ahead of the game, and he could coast until spring, when the big gangs would be back and the steel would come on down from Ravenscrag.

Maybe another year of it, he said. Another year would leave him sitting pretty. His mind edged close to the thing he was trying to think of. If he went back to Elsa in a year or a year and a half with a good fat bankroll and a good proposition of some kind up here, would she . . . ?

Oh Jesus, he said, I don't know.

"Hey, Bo," somebody said. "You got any dice around?"

Bo looked up. Three men were standing under the lamp looking at him. "I don't know," he said. "Maybe I have."

He got up and went toward the cupboard at his back.

"We're gonna teach this heathen Chinee to shoot craps," the man said. "He's too God damn good at fan tan. That's his own game. He invented it."

Bo found a box of dice in the cupboard and picked out a pair. "You going to let yourself get trimmed, Mah Li?"

"No savvy claps," Mah Li said. "Fella can teach?"

He stood at the edge of the table in his black smock and baggy cotton pants, his yellow face bland and smiling.

Bo laughed. "Don't let 'em hook you, boy. You're playing for the house."

"Tly hard for Lady Luck," Mah Li said.

Bo sat down again. If he took part of that six hundred and bought a lot or two from Purcell he'd be paying Purcell a good profit. But the town was barely started, steel wasn't into it yet. Once the rails came in there would be a boom, and he ought to be able to sell off his lots easy. You had to keep money working or it got lazy on you.

But what about that other? he said. What about Elsa and the kids down there? Looking up at the jammed room, the bunks double-decked along both sides, the stoves squat and ugly at each end, the lamps hanging from their wires, he knew he couldn't bring them up to a place like this. He couldn't go down there and try to make things up and then bring them up to live in a bunkhouse with fifty men. He'd have to have a place to bring them to. Let it go a year and he could have a place, a good place.

And how do you know she'd come? he said. What does she feel like, left there to run that café alone with two little kids to take care of? How much does she hold that night against you? Maybe she'll never come back to you.

But good hell, she shouldn't hold a grudge like that, he said. I lost my temper, sure, but . . .

And you ran out on her, said whoever he was arguing with.

Because I was ashamed of myself, he said. Good God, how could I go back there that night? How could I go back the next morning, for that matter? How could I go back in a week, with my tail between my legs? And after I'd stayed away a week how could I go back at all?

You could have written a letter, the arguer said.

Yeah? he said. Saying what?

He looked morosely at the papers, swept them together and slipped a rubber band around them. He ought to be over seeing Purcell, or doing something useful. Or he might, as soon as the work stopped for the winter, go back to Swift Current or Regina and see what the railroad was holding its town lots at. They might sell cheaper than Purcell would.

Why didn't you write a letter? the arguer said. Why don't you write a letter right now? Are you going to let her sit there forever not knowing whether you're dead or alive? What are you afraid of?

He stared somberly at the little group between stove and bunk, down on their knees and shooting craps. Mah Li was shaking the dice against his ear. Lonesome was a long ways away, the Chink said. Velly busy most time. But how about the next six months when nothing was stirring and he had to sit in the very middle of nowhere without anything to be busy about? He'd be chewing the fat of this argument with himself every night for six months.

Well, hell, he said, and went and got a tablet from the cupboard. But when he sat down and looked at the plain white sheet it was an impossible job to put marks on it. What could he say? Go down on his knees and apologize?

Write her a letter, the arguer said. Tell her you're all right. Tell her you're thinking about her and the kids. Send her some money.

That's an idea, he said, and pulling his check book out he dated a check. How much? A hundred dollars? That would put him pretty short for any real estate deals. Make it fifty. Not expecting anything, she would be as pleased with fifty as a hundred, and it would leave him more to work with. They oughtn't to need more. They had the café, and living where they did they didn't have many expenses.

He made out the check and set the indelible pencil on the top of the tablet sheet. "Whitemud, Saskatchewan," he made the pencil write. "Oct. 17, 1913." Then he sat and looked helplessly at the white page. It was a long time, and his lip was stained with indelible violet, before he put down anything else.

2

When Elsa opened the door the statue on the stair post made her think of Helm, as it always did. The ragged boy had stood barelegged, lifting a bunch of cherries to his lips, in Helm's hall just as he stood here. Bo had always used it for a hatrack, slinging his derby from the hall and ringing the uplifted hand. And as always, she looked at it only a moment, because she knew that if she let herself remember she would make herself miserable.

Mrs. Bohn, the landlady, looked out from the kitchen door at the end of the hall. "Letter for you, Mrs. Mason. I put it on the hall table there."

"Letter?" Elsa said. She rummaged among the half-dozen envelopes and picked hers out. The face was scrawled with pencilled addresses, from Richmond through the three or four places she had moved to in Seattle, trying to find a place where the boys would be taken care of while she worked. But the original address was in Bo's hand, written in indelible pencil smeared and running violet from some time when a postman had walked in the rain.

For a moment she stood quietly, one hand on the stair rail under the varnished pedestal of the cherry boy. Then she went on up the stairs, tiredly, lifting herself as if she carried a burden on her back and pulling with her hand to help her heavy legs.

The window of her room looked out over a plateau of roofs, over the beetle-back shapes of the carbarns caught in a spider web of tracks. Beyond the barns the land rose to a wooded hill, a better residential district with white houses and spread green handkerchiefs of lawn. Under the ceiling of high fog the air was remarkably clear, with a cool grayness in it, no shadows, no contrasts, only the pellucid transparency that left every color and every detail clean and distinct.

She had pulled the rocking chair near to the window, looping back the curtains she had carried from boarding house to boarding house in an effort to make every room seem a little bit familiar, a little bit like home. Bo's letter lay in her lap, and a check for fifty dollars on a bank in Regina, Saskatchewan.

Everything in the letter, and everything behind the letter, was perfectly clear: his shame, his unwillingness to face the consequences of his own acts, his impatience at restraint and responsibility and the gnawing awareness that he was still responsible. He could neither accept those responsibilities nor run completely away from them. When he tried to shoulder them he was always chafing under the burden, and when he ran away his conscience bothered him, he worried, he finally sent a check to justify himself and persuade himself that what had happened was only an interruption, not a break. She knew too that the coming of the letter and the check would force a final decision upon her. She couldn't put it off or refuse to think what the ultimate end would be. She had to make up her mind.

The letter lay face up in her lap, and she bent her head to read it again.

Dear Elsa,

This is the first time I've had a chance to send on any money to help you out. I had to look around a while, and it took quite a while to get started up here, but I'm started now and doing pretty well. I'm running a bunkhouse for the grading crew on a sub-contract—I got in too late to pick up any contracts first hand, and probably I couldn't have got one anyway because you have to have a responsible business or post a bond, and I was pretty broke. But it's going to be a pretty good thing. Work will stop in about a month, and I'll hibernate till it opens again in the spring, and sort of keep my eye open for something permanent. This bunkhouse racket is good as long as it lasts, and will give us a stake, but I'll have to locate something to take its place when it folds up.

This is pretty fine country, flat like Dakota, with a nice river valley running through it, some timber in the valley and a nice stream. Every night when I go out and take a walk along the river I see beavers swimming around. The whole valley practically is owned by a fellow named Purcell, a big rancher. It used to be prime Indian country. A bunch of them are camped over in the bend now, with cow guts strung all over the tops of their shanties drying out. They smell like a stockyard and they'll swipe anything loose. My Chink that I've got working for me is scared to death of them, but they're harmless enough. I bought a pair of elk-hide moccasins from one the other day.

Well, Else, I hope the joint is going ok and that you've been able to clear off the payments I hope you and the kids are okay too. This winter, maybe, I can get away to come down and talk over everything with you. It's pretty lonesome up here, and I think about you and the kids a lot. I've got a lot to explain, I know, but I know we can straighten it out as soon as I get loose to come back to the States. I guess we both sort of lost our heads that night, and I'm sorry as hell for what I did. You can't ask any fairer than that.

Anyway, Else, this looks good up here, and the kids could have ponies of their own and have a fine time. I won a couple Indian ponies in a poker game over at the Half-Diamond Bar, that's Purcell's ranch, about a month ago. Won them from the son of a British earl, so they ought to be pretty hot-blooded nags. It looks as if this time we might get clear out of the woods. Let me know how you and the kids are getting along.

Love,

Bo

Through the window she watched a red streetcar crawl along a branch of the spider web and disappear under the barn. I hope the joint is going ok. If he had thought at all he might have known she couldn't take care of two children and run that place all by herself, when it was all the two of them could do when they were both there. He could make himself believe what he wanted to believe, that she was right where he had left her, secure enough, waiting to be taken back.

And what if she did go back, let him cart them off again to that wilderness he had found, a place full of cowpunchers and Indians and beavers and Chinamen and the sons of British earls? That would be giving in to what he had wanted in the first place, making herself and the children into something portable as property, like trunks left behind that could be sent for. Would it be any different up in Saskatchewan? Would there be any more permanence or satisfaction with what they had? Would he hang onto his temper any better, or forget to dream of some even better place over the hills somewhere?

"No," she said aloud, and the finality of the word in the empty room was at once proud and forlorn, so that she stood up with her breath hissing in a sigh. It was so final and awful a thing to think of doing. She knew he was sorry; there was not a doubt of that in her mind. She knew he was honestly sorry, and she knew how much it must have cost him to say so. It was hard for him to apologize. But she still couldn't risk it again. If there were only herself, maybe . . .

But if there were only myself, she said impatiently, there wouldn't have been any trouble in the first place. I could have gone with him anywhere. It's the boys that he's felt around his leg like a legiron, and he shouldn't feel them that way, he ought to be glad of them, and love them. . . .

3

Chet opened his eyes and looked straight up. His bed, the second story of a dormitory cot, was in the east gable, and the sun lay scrambled among the covers. Above him a great beam went from wall to wall, and above that was a criss-cross of two-by-fours bracing the roof. There were cobwebs in the angles of the two-by-fours, and directly above him was the dark spot on the under side of the shingles where the rain had come in once and Mrs. Hemingway had thought he had done it. He half closed his eyes, and the spot became a big boat with sails. Squinting, he twisted his head, trying to find the elephant that had been there yesterday, with his trunk in the air. There it was; if you turned the boat on its side it became the elephant.

"Elephant, elephant, elephant," he said, almost aloud, feeling the shape of the word with his lips. Then he pursed his lips and imitated Bruce. "Elphanut," he said. "Elphanut."

He snickered, peering down over the high edge of the cot, as high as the cutbank they slid down on the way to school. If you jumped off there you'd break your leg. That was what Mrs. Hemingway was always saying. You boys that sleep in the upper beds better not get frisky and jump around much. Fall off and break your leg and we'd have to shoot you. She was funny sometimes. But sometimes she walloped you, and then found out afterward that you hadn't wet the bed at all, it was the rain. But she was all right. It was Mrs. Mangin that gave him a pain. She had pretty fancy teeth, though. The gold in her teeth was worth a thousand dollars, probably. But that didn't make him want to kiss her any better. When Ma came on Sundays Mrs. Mangin always called you in and patted you on the head and stooped down so that her lavender beads clanked, and you heard her corsets creaking as she bent while she kissed you with her mouth that wouldn't quite close over her gold teeth. It was a funny feeling, being kissed by all that bare gold. The heck with Mrs. Mangin. She never kissed you when Ma wasn't around. Generally she went around with her pencil as big as a slingshot crotch, saying, "I'll *thump* you, Chester Mason! You mind now, or I'll *thump* you!"

Stretching his legs and kicking the covers off his feet, Chet made a face, pretending his lips wouldn't meet over his teeth. He bared his teeth so they would glitter goldenly.

Mrs. Mangin
Needs a spangin'.

Cautiously he stood up, reaching for the big beam overhead. The springs squeaked, and he looked around. Nobody was awake yet. The beam was six inches above his upstretched fingers, but by climbing on the iron headboard he could reach it easy. Treading gingerly on the cold round iron, he crouched and jumped, got his elbows over the beam, and wriggled himself up. It was dirty up there, but it was fine, like in an airplane. He wiped a black palm across his pajamas and with his finger pushed some of the deep layer of dust over the edge. It sifted down glittering through the sunlight. Way down below him, miles below where he sat comfortably in his airplane, all the kids slept in their beds. He took his hands away from the beam and flapped his arms, flying his airplane out over the ocean.

Look at the waves! Look at the sharks! Can't get me, sharks.

He stood perilously upright, a million miles above the waves and sharks, and balanced, walking over to the wall. Then he turned around and tightroped back. He saw his tiptoe tracks in the dust on the beam. Whee, he said, and wished somebody was awake to see him.

He started to yell to wake them up, but changed his mind. He'd keep right on going, around the world. From the end of the beam two two-by-fours, one above the other, stretched out to meet another beam coming across the center of the attic. Then two more two-by-fours cut back at the reverse angle into the adjoining gable, where the girls slept.

With his tongue between his teeth Chet inched out on the lower brace, hanging with both hands to the upper one. It was easy. But when he got out over the open floor, with no beds below, it looked a lot higher. If you fell from here, probably, you'd be an hour lighting. Experimentally he spit and watched the spit curve down, heard its light *splat* on the board floor. Hanging on hard, he looked across ten feet of space to the central beam. He was pretty near halfway around the world. The big beam was China, and then he could go on around the other side on the other two-by-fours. Before starting again he pulled his tongue into his mouth and carefully shut his teeth. Pa had told him that if he stuck out his tongue to do things, sooner or later he'd get jarred and bite it off, and then he'd talk like the idiot boy, *nyahh, nyahhh.* His feet crept and his hands slid until he reached the beam.

He wanted to yell and startle somebody, but first he had to get around the world. If he didn't get clear around the world and back to Seattle before everybody woke up and saw him, he'd . . . what? He'd be put in jail. Hastily he slid out on the braces leading into the adjoining gable.

His eyes were on the two-by-four under his feet, his tongue kept getting somehow into the corner of his mouth. But he was flying. He went faster than ever now, because if he didn't get clear around and back Mrs. Hemingway would come in and . . . No, if he didn't get clear around, there would be an earthquake and the whole world would get shaken down so there wouldn't be any place to land.

The next gable had a brace just like the one across his own. He reached it, seeing vaguely, unfocussed, the line of beds below him, a million miles down. Then he sat down on the solid back of the beam and wiped his black hands on his pajamas and breathed deeply, and looking down for the first time with intent to see something, he looked straight into a pair of wide-awake blue eyes.

The shock almost knocked him off the beam, and he grabbed the bracing rafters, ready to run. But the blue eyes—it was Helen Murphy, he saw, the new girl who had come only last week, and about his own age—winked rapidly at him, both eyes (he could wink with either eye, one at a time) and Helen's finger came up to her lips. On the brink of falling or flight, he hung on the beam and stared.

Helen slept in a top bed, like his. The top decks on both sides of her were empty, but the ones nearer the window were mounded with covers. Not a soul seemed to be awake but Helen. He must have waked up awful early.

He grinned at her, whispering, forming the words wide and round with his lips. "I'm a aviator. I'm flying around the world." He let go with one hand, then with both, and flapped his wings.

Helen lay quiet on her back, her eyes as steady as the eyes of a bird on the nest. Then she folded her arms over her chest and hugged herself, smothering a giggle. "You're dirty," she whispered. "You're dirty as a old pig."

Chet wiped his hands again, looking down at the broad smears he had made. "I don't care." He looked at his palms, evenly black, at the soles of his feet, the same way. Dust had sifted up between his toes.

"Mrs. Hemingway'll fix you. You ruined your pajamas. You'll have to sleep nekkid."

"I don't care," Chet said. He spoke too loud, and darted his eyes around. Nobody stirred. It must be awful early. With Helen giggling and watching him he had to do something. He stood on tiptoe and flapped his wings hard, making soundless crowing noises. The sharp eyes in the bed watched him, and when he sat down again she clapped her hand over her mouth and turned her face into the pillow. She was a nutty girl, he thought. Always acting silly.

One hand came out and a finger pointed at him. One eye, peeping up from the pillow, gleamed like a rabbit's, and there were muffled shakings of the bed. Now what? He stared at her, baffled.

The whole face came out again. The finger still pointed, and the face was twisted up with her silly laugh. "I see you," she said.

"Huh?"

"I see you. Your pajamas are unbuttoned."

He jerked around, saw that what she said was true, and buttoned himself up. When he looked back at the bed, doubtfully, she was still stifling giggles. A vague excitement stirred him. He swaggered from the waist up, straddling the beam, and wiped his hands again on his shirt.

Helen sat up. "You sure are dirty," she whispered. "You'll have to sleep in a nightgown, like a girl."

"Aw!" he said hoarsely.

"You'll have to sleep in a nightgown like me," she said. "Or nekkid." She shook with noiseless laughter.

Chet stared at her, his fingers prickling like growing pains. He ought to be getting back, before the earthquake shook everything down. He tried to imagine himself getting back too late and having no place to land on, but he couldn't quite imagine it any more. Helen was looking at him. She twisted around and looked at the other beds, turned back and winked both eyes at him. He winked back with one eye, to show her.

"Look," she whispered. Her eyes were like quarters, and her smile had got tangled up so that her teeth were over her lower lip. Squirming, she pulled her nightgown up around her neck and lay back on the bed.

Chet hung onto the beam with both hands. His heart went way up in the air without beating at all and then came down again, *kerchonk*. Then he grabbed for the rafter and fled, shuffling sideways out along the two-by-four, stretching and clawing to get across the angle where it joined the central beam, then on again, back to the beam above his own bed.

Win Gabriel, in a lower bed by the window, reared up in bed. "Look!" he screeched. "Look at Chet!"

In a minute all the kids were awake and staring, but Chet didn't stay on the beam to show them how he could fly. He let his feet down over the edge and dangled, feeling for the headboard, just as the six o'clock bell rang. His toes groped frantically, he twisted his head to try to see the thing. Mrs. Hemingway's steps sounded on the stairs, the bell in her hand ringing, ka-*dang,* ka-*dang,* ka-*dang*. Chet found the iron, let go with his hands, and threw himself sideward to alight on the bed. The springs bounced him right out again, and he was hanging by his elbows, scrambling to get back up, when Mrs. Hemingway came in and caught him.

There was no chance to think up a story or try to pretend he had just been getting out of bed. The evidence was all over him, and he didn't say a word when Mrs. Hemingway, after one indignant look, upended him and pulled down his pajamas and swatted his bare bottom a dozen times. She upended him again before he knew which end he was on and had him by the ear, leading him toward the washroom.

But at least, he thought, dragging along with automatic yelps when she yanked on his ear, she hadn't caught him on the beam up over Helen Murphy's bed. If she had caught him there, good night! Oh my!

The washroom was full of steam and the smell of soap and the noise of two dozen boys all washing at once. Chet crawled out of the bathtub where Mrs. Hemingway had dumped him and looked around for Bruce. He was supposed to make sure Bruce washed good every morning, because Bruce was afraid of soap in his eyes and didn't do it right. The kids were pushing him and yah-yah-ing him about getting paddled, but he didn't care. He was still groggy from what Helen had done. Mrs. Hemingway had swatted him pretty hard, though. He twisted to see if his bottom was red. It was, and he felt proud.

He found Brucie at the end washbowl dabbling his hands in the water. His face was dry, and he hadn't taken off his pajama top. "Come on," Chet said. "You're just a darn baby."

He grabbed the washrag and swabbed Bruce's face, splashing him, dripping on the floor. "You cut it out!" Bruce said. "I can wash."

"Hurry up then. It's pretty near breakfast time."

Boys flooded out through the door, racing upstairs again to get dressed and make their beds. Mrs. Hemingway stood at the door inspecting them as they went through. As Chet squeezed by with Bruce she caught him, looked behind his ears, cuffed him lightly. He looked up and saw her smiling. "Our big acrobat!" she said, and let him go.

His bed was tracked with dirt, and he brushed it off as well as he could. Then he went down to the end where Bruce slept in a lower bunk. Bruce had messed up the blankets worse trying to make the bed. He always did. Chet pushed him aside and yanked at the blankets. Little kids were a nuisance. They couldn't do anything.

The long tables in the dining room were already full when they got down. Chet caught a glimpse of Helen Murphy in the middle of the girls' table, but he ducked his head and ate. Mrs. Mangin moved ponderously behind the chairs, and he kept his head down, spooning his oatmeal. It was like a storm coming up to feel Mrs. Mangin creaking up behind you. He spooned desperately, sucking his lower lip to get the drip of milk. The storm moved close behind him and stopped. Chet ducked lower, his automatic elbow going. Any minute now that big pencil might come down on his head like a club, and he'd hear her say, "Ruining your pajamas, Chester Mason! There's only one thing to do with a disobedient dirty boy like you. *Thump* you!"

But it was Bruce she was after. "Eat your oatmeal, Bruce Mason," she said. Chet felt her there, one foot going, her lips as close over her golden teeth as she could get them. He smelled the faint flowery smell of her lavender beads, and heard her breath coming and going in her nose. Brucie would catch it if he didn't start eating his oatmeal.

"I don't like it," Bruce said.

Mrs. Mangin's hand came down across Chet's shoulder and took hold of Bruce's. "Eat it!" she said. "You know what I told you."

"I don't like it," Bruce said.

"Nonsense. It tastes good."

"It don't either."

"Bruce Mason!" Chet ducked until his chin was almost on the table, as Bruce was whisked out of the chair beside him.

"We learn to eat what's put before us," Mrs. Mangin said, "or we do without."

"I want some bread!" Bruce said. His voice started low and ended high and loud.

"Eat your oatmeal."

"No," Bruce said flatly. He started to bawl as Mrs. Mangin hustled him out of the room.

"Get out," she said. "Leave the room! Finicky, stubborn, insolent child . . ."

The storm cloud moved off and Chet straightened a little. He stole a grin at Win Gabriel, on the other side of Bruce's empty chair. Win was a year older than Chet, and could swear, and knew how to braid shoe laces into watchfobs.

"Damn old crab!" Win said, out of the corner of his mouth.

"Damn old stink!" Chet said.

They snickered, their eyes wary to spot Mrs. Mangin moving like a thunderhead along the back of the girls' table. Chet saw her stop behind Helen Murphy's chair.

"Comb your hair before you come to the table after this!" she said, and moved on.

Across the two tables Helen caught Chet's eye, and hunched over to clap her hand across her mouth the way she had done in bed. Chet looked away. When he looked back she was still watching him. She winked rapidly several times. Both eyes.

With his mouth full of bread and butter, Chet leaned over to Win and whispered, "I saw Helen Murphy without any clothes on."

"You're a liar," Win said.

"I ain't a liar. I did so."

"When?"

"This morning."

"I don't believe it."

"All right," Chet said. "Don't believe it then."

The bell rang to end breakfast, and they grabbed their plates to carry them to the kitchen. Just before the bread and butter plate was taken away Chet hooked a piece for Bruce. Ignoring Win, who trailed along behind him, he went to the door and out into the back yard, where he leaned against the wall and watched for Helen Murphy. Bruce was nowhere around, and before he thought Chet ate the bread and butter. He discovered his loss just before the last two bites, but there was no use saving two bites, so he finished them and licked his fingers.

"I don't believe you seen her at all," Win said at his elbow.

"Did so."

"Well, how?"

"Up on the rafters this morning. She just pulled up her nightgown and showed me."

At that minute Helen came out and went by as if she didn't see them, swinging her hands against the sides of her skirt.

"Shame shame double shame everybody knows your name," Win said. Helen jerked her head and went around the corner toward the teeter-totters.

"You're just a big liar," Win said. He stared at the corner where Helen had disappeared. "What's she *look* like?" he said.

A ten o'clock Mrs. Hemingway came to the door with the brass bell in her hand and waved it up and down, ka-*dang,* ka-*dang,* ka-*dang.* In the half minute during which she turned back inside to put down the bell and pick up the big granite dishpan, children materialized from everywhere. Up from the basement, pouring out of the sloping half-doors, stumbling and sprawling on the upper step; out of the orchard where they had been searching for left-over apples; up from the gully behind, where the bigger boys were digging a cave; around the corner from teeter-totters and sandpiles, they came like Indians from an ambush, forty of them in pell-mell haste, three- and four-year-olds galloping, six-year-olds with chests out and fists doubled, girls of all ages shrieking, their pig-tails whipping behind.

Chet had been digging in the cave. He was the first one up the bank, and as he ran he saw figures streaming from orchard and yard. Breakfast was pretty early at St. Anne's, and the oatmeal and bread-and-butter didn't hold you long. You were always hungry before Mrs. Hemingway came out on the step to ka-*dang* her bell.

Only the kids who had been playing in the basement beat Chet to the step. He rushed up, tiptoeing, crowding, to get his hands into the dishpan full of buttered crusts, pieces of dry bread left over, sometimes with single bites taken out of them, sometimes whole and untouched and precious. He jammed in close, tramped on a girl's heel, and edged ahead of her when she turned to yell at him. His right hand found the edge of the pan, and he felt Mrs. Hemingway brace herself backward to keep the whole thing from being torn out of her grasp. His first grab netted only a nibbled crust that someone had left under the edge of a plate. Dropping it, unable to see over the packed heads and reaching arms, he felt around frantically, feeling other hands, edges, the soft oily smear of butter. His fingers closed on a large piece of something and he caught a glimpse of it through the tangle. A whole half piece, unbitten. Before anyone could grab it from him he jerked his arm down and ducked out of the press, nibbling, smelling the breadbox smell of bread and faint mold and rancid butter.

There were still children hopping up and down, crowding to get close, when Mrs. Hemingway lifted the pan upside down to show that everything was gone, and disappeared inside. Chet stood against the wall with his slice, and as he nibbled around the edge delicately, like a rabbit, he saw Bruce. Bruce hadn't got anything. Chet watched him somberly. In a minute Bruce would start to blubber, prob'ly, and want a bite. Chet bit into the slice, deeply, just as Bruce saw him.

"Gimme a bite," Bruce said.

"Go on," Chet said. "You should of got here sooner."

"George Rising pushed me," Bruce said. "I was here early as anything, but he pushed me." He came close, his eyes steady on the bread in Chet's hand. "Just one bite, Chet," he said, and reached out. Chet pushed him away.

"You big pig," Bruce said. "Gimme a bite!"

"Go on, or I'll bust you one in the nose," Chet said. He turned to avoid Bruce's lunge, and made a threatening motion with his fist.

Helen Murphy, brushing crumbs from her hands, came swinging across the back of the house, humming to herself. She looked right through Chet, smiled as if at something she had thought of, and paused at the cellar doors. Chet watched her, pushing Bruce off with one hand. Win Gabriel was hanging around at the corner.

"Let's see now," Helen said, her finger against her cheek. "I'll play house, I guess." She smiled the vague smile that included Chet without recognizing him, and skipped down the stairs.

"I'll tell Ma," Bruce was saying. "I'll tell Ma you wouldn't give me any."

"Oh, for the love of Mike," Chet said. He shoved the remains of the slice at Bruce, wiped his hand across his mouth and went downstairs after Helen. He was on the bottom step when he heard Win Gabriel behind him.

They stood in the doorway a while watching Helen play house with two other girls. Helen was bossy, and she paid no attention to Chet and Win. "I'm the mama," she said. "You've got to be my two kids, and when I come home and find you messing up the kitchen, I spank you and then we get supper and then I'm the papa, and I come home . . ."

"You can't be mama and papa both," one of the girls said. "I want to be papa."

"You will not," Helen said. "First I'm mama, and then I'm papa."

Win looked at Chet. "My God," he said, like a grown man, and spit on the floor.

They climbed on boxes and jumped for the pipes running along under the floor. Win caught a pipe that was hot, and let go with a yelp. He hit a box and sprawled halfway across the floor.

"You're terrible," Chet said. "Watch a great acrobat." He jumped and caught a pipe and hung warbling, his eyes on Helen and the girls. But they still squabbled. Helen had a rag-plugged basin they were playing was a kettle, and another girl was tugging at it.

"I'll tell Mrs. Mangin," the girl said.

"Go ahead and be a tattle-tale."

"I *will!*"

"Go head. Go on and tattle."

The other girl started to cry and fight, and Helen pushed her so she fell down. Then both the other girls went out, the one crying and saying she was going to tell Mrs. Mangin and Mrs. Hemingway and everybody.

"Bawl-baby titty-mouse
Laid an egg in our house!" Helen said after her.

Win jumped and swung beside Chet, swinging with his knees bent, making faces. Helen put down her basin and put her hands behind her back. "You two are silly," she said.

Win dropped down, and Chet followed him. "I know what you did this morning," Win said.

"What?" Helen said, daring him. "You don't know anything."

"*I* know."

Win jerked her pigtail and they wrestled. In a minute he had her backed against the cement wall, penning her in with his arms. She giggled. "Chet ran away," she said.

"Aw, I did not," said Chet. "I heard Mrs. Hemingway coming."

"I bet you we wouldn't run away if you did it again," Win said. She stuck out her tongue at him, but she was smiling, watching Chet.

"I bet you would. I just bet you would!"

"Like fun," Win said. "I double-dare you."

Helen watched them both. She sucked her thumb briefly, looking up from under her eyelashes. She winked both eyes. "Not for nothing," she said. "You have to too."

Win looked at Chet, fished uncertainly in his pockets. "You're scared," he said.

"I'm not either scared," she said. "You do it and I will."

Win promptly slipped his overall straps down and let the overalls fall around his ankles. He was not wearing any underwear. Helen looked at him slyly, two little white teeth hooked over her lower lip. "Chet too," she said.

A glaze was over Chet's eyes. He moved jerkily, afraid and ashamed and shaken with excitement. "You first," he said.

"No. I won't till you do."

Through eyes strangely misted, Chet looked at her shining eyes, her red cheeks, her teeth hooked over her lip. Her breath whistled a little out of the corner of her mouth. "You're afraid," she said.

"Oh, I ain't either afraid!"

"Well, do it then."

"Come on," Win said, standing in the puddle of his overalls. "You're both a-scared. I'm the only one ain't a-scared."

Excitement grew in Chet until he could hardly breathe. Just as Helen was tossing her head and turning away in scorn he whipped down the overall straps and fumbled at the buttons of his underwear. He saw Helen reach up under her dress and pull her black drawers down, saw her hands gather the skirt and lift. Then he saw her face change, her eyes fix in a frightened stare. Her hands still helplessly held up the skirt, but her mouth dropped as if she were going to yell. Win jerked around with a squawk, grabbed for his overalls and started to run, and Chet did the same. But there was nowhere to run to. There was only one entrance to the basement room, and Mrs. Mangin was standing in that.

He was glad they had sent him out into the hall. He didn't want to stay in the company parlor and have Mrs. Mangin look at him as if she could just barely keep from vomiting, and he didn't like to see Ma sitting there. He hated Mrs. Mangin. That morning after she caught them she had taken them all up into the kitchen, just dragged them up with their clothes still hanging off them, and turned them up one by one and beaten them on the bare bottom with a yardstick. Chet wished he'd had as much nerve as Win, to fight her, even if he had got beaten over the head with the stick the way Win had. He wondered where Win was now, and Helen too. Prob'ly still locked up, the way he had been all day without anything to eat.

The hall still held the smell of supper, and he swallowed. He wished he had a belt to cinch tight, the way Indians did. Or he wished he had, right in his overalls pocket, a great big chocolate bar with peanuts in it. The vision and the taste came together, so delicious and overpowering that he felt in the pocket almost hopefully. There were only four slingshot rocks, a rubber band, a couple of carpet tacks he had been saving to put on seats in school, and an empty brass cartridge case.

Sitting on the hall seat in the dark he took the cartridge and blew in it experimentally. It made a thin, breathy whistle. He wished he had a gun. He'd put in this bullet and aim it right through the wall at where Mrs. Mangin was sitting inside talking to Ma, and he'd shoot it off and shoot a hole right through Mrs. Mangin. He aimed the cartridge, squinting. Bang, he said. Bang, bang, bang! There . . . I guess you won't ever lick me again, you old stink of a Mrs. Mangin.

His bottom was still sore from the whipping, and he shifted to get comfortable. He would be an Indian, and some morning he would come to the door with his gun under his blanket and say to Mrs. Mangin, "Last week you spanked Chet and Win and Helen right in the kitchen in front of everybody, and you're always going around thumping kids with your pencil. Well, I'll fix you." Then he would shoot her with his cartridge and whip out his scalping knife and snip off her scalp, zing, and pull out her gold teeth and sell them and give the money to the kids to buy marbles and candy with.

The voices in the parlor had grown louder, and he listened. It sounded as if Mrs. Mangin was mad. Carefully he slid off the hall seat and sneaked up to the door. By the time he got there and held his breath to listen, it was his mother's voice.

". . . that you're not being fair to him. You can't lay all the blame on him. He's not a bad boy."

Now Mrs. Mangin's, heavy and triumphant. "What do you call climbing on the rafters and peeking at the girls in bed? If that isn't bad . . ."

"You don't know he did that. Mrs. Hemingway doesn't think he did."

"What else would he be doing up there? I'm sorry to say it, Mrs. Mason, but I think we are dealing with a corrupt and filthy-minded child."

"Oh, nonsense!" Ma said, almost as loudly as Mrs. Mangin. "He's not quite seven years old yet."

Mrs. Mangin said, "My experience lets me know many more children than you can have known, Mrs. Mason . . ."

There was the scrape of a chair, as if someone had stood up, and Chet started to scuttle for the hall seat, but stopped when he heard his mother's voice again. "I know that when I brought Chester here he was as clean and nice a boy as anyone could ask for."

Mrs. Mangin's voice cut in, rising, "Mrs. Mason, if you mean to insinuate . . ."

"So if there's any evil in his mind now, he learned it at this home. I won't stand for your putting him in jail for two weeks, making him feel as if he's done something horrible. There's no evil in a child that age. The evil is read in by other people."

"There is only one way to treat a rotten-minded child," Mrs. Mangin said. "If our methods don't suit you . . ."

"There is only one kind of rotten-minded child," Ma said, almost shouting, "and that's the kind that exists in a rotten mind. You can just bet your methods don't suit me."

His ear against the wood, Chet shook his shoulders and crowed silently. Ma was just giving it to the old stink. "I looked at Bruce tonight, too," Ma was saying, and her words sounded jumbled and fast as if she were trying to say two or three things at once. "He's thin as a rail, all shoulder blades and eyes."

"If he won't eat his meals," Mrs. Mangin said, "he gets nothing else here. We don't coddle children, Mrs. Mason."

Ma didn't say anything for a minute, and Chet stretched his neck, trying to see through the crack in the door. But all he could see was the tiled fireplace, and the stone dog set above the opening. He jerked back when Ma's voice came, much closer to the door.

"There's not much point in discussing it, is there?" she said. "I'm taking the children out, right now."

Chet ducked back against the hall seat and the door opened, letting out a wide stripe of light across the hall. Ma stepped out and came over to him quickly. Her shirtwaist smelled like ironing as she stooped to hug him. "Wait here," she said. "I'm going up and get Bruce and we're going to get out of this place."

Ten minutes later she was down carrying Bruce; he was dressed, but sleep had not entirely left him, and his knuckles dug into his eyes. Mrs. Mangin stood in the parlor door, drawn up high, with her teeth not quite covered by her inadequate lips. Chet sidled past her, watchful for a thumping, till he got his hand in his mother's.

"I'll be back tomorrow for their clothes," Ma said.

Mrs. Mangin, with her wintry and goldenly-gleaming smile, watched them out the door. Chet stuck out his tongue from the porch, and then Ma set Brucie down and they walked together down the aisle of black spruces. It was the latest Chet had ever been out, and the yard looked funny in the dark. He wouldn't have known it was the same place.

"Where we going, Ma?" he said.

Her hand closed on his. "To my room."

"Are we gonna live there?"

"No."

"Is Pa coming back and get us?"

"No."

"What are we gonna do then?"

Ma sounded tired. "There's only one thing we can do," she said. "We'll have to go back and visit Grandpa."

4

That house—the dark, quiet little parlor, the library table stacked with Norwegian newspapers, the glass-fronted bookcases full of sets, Ibsen, Bjørnson, Lie, Kjelland, the folksongs of Asbjørnson and Moe, the brass-and-leather Snorre, the patriotic *landsmaal* songs of Ivar Aasen—she knew the feel and look of everything there, the wallpaper, the curtains, the stained dark woodwork. Nothing had changed a particle. She knew on what page of the great Snorre she would find the engraving of the death of Baldur that had made her cry as a child because Good was being destroyed by Evil, and she even felt some of her old hatred of the unstable and mischievous Loki. The most wonderful thing about the place was that sense of everything just where it had always been.

Kristin's arm was around her all the way upstairs, as if she were an invalid. The affection and sympathy in her sister's face was almost too much. She hadn't found it in her father or in Sarah; they were polite, dutiful, a little cold, and she knew they didn't want her, she knew their disapproval cut so deep that even now, in her desperation, when she had no other place to turn to, they suffered her merely, without real welcome. She smiled a little wearily, going upstairs, at what her pride had come to. Not once only, but twice, she had come back on them like a charity case.

Her room was just as it had always been. The roses still clustered in the wallpaper, the curtains hung crisply against the window whose bars were outlined by early snow, the carpet still took its streak of sun, and she saw the mark where it had faded through the years. On the wash stand was the big red and white bowl, the pitcher inside it, just as they had stood through her childhood, and through the misted window was the same quiet street and the same three white houses and the same gentle swell of open country dotted with bare trees.

Like smoke that rose and filled a room the feeling swelled in her that she had never breathed properly since she had run away from home. Dakota had been too open, a place of wind and empty sky. Seattle had been tenements in crowded streets and the interminable drifting rain. The tent-house where she had almost got the feeling of home had been huddled closely within a circle of woods. But here there was both shelter and space, here was home even if she was unwelcome in it. The changelessness of the house and the strip of quiet street and the swell of farmland was like an open and reassuring door.

She heard Kristin talking without being fully aware of what she said. There was a sad-sweet relaxation in all her bones, as if she had just taken off a rigid corset after hours of formality. Then Kristin's talk paused, and Elsa looked up to see her holding a dress she had just taken from the telescope. The dress was cheap, too-much-laundered, and the instant defensive words jumped to Elsa's lips. "I've had that dress ever since we lived in Hardanger. I ought to have thrown it away, years ago, but you know how you hang onto things."

"Yes," Kristin said quietly, and hung the dress in the wardrobe, but there was a vague hostility between them. Elsa had no idea what they all thought about her leaving Bo. Maybe they thought she had left because he wasn't a good provider, as if she were as disloyal and selfish as that! She shut the empty telescope and shoved it under the bed.

"Is there any hot water?" she said. "The boys ought to have baths."

"So should you," Kristin said. "They're out playing around the barn. You look after yourself first."

"Maybe I will," Elsa said. "A bath will feel good."

"I'll bring the tub up here."

"I can get it."

"Let me," Kristin said. "Please." She was out the door, and Elsa let her go. Slowly she unbuttoned her blouse and took it off, unhooked her corset, unlaced her shoes. Kristin labored in with two pails of steaming water, went out again after the tub. As she set the tub down she looked at Elsa, and Elsa saw her eyes widen and her mouth twist. She was looking at the burned arm. Elsa raised it and laughed a little.

"Oh, Else, how did you do it?" Kristin said.

"The coffee urn tipped over."

Kristin came up and touched the smooth whitish scar that prevented the arm's being completely straightened. "It must have been awful," she said. "Were you alone?"

"Do you want to blame that on him, too?" Elsa said.

Kristin stammered, flushing.

"He was there," Elsa said. "He carried me down to the doctor."

"Oh." Kristin stood twisting her engagement ring around on her finger.

"He isn't as bad as all of you always thought he was," Elsa said bitterly.

"I'm sorry, Elsa. Honestly, I didn't mean to . . ."

"Oh, let's not," Elsa said. "Please, Kristin. I didn't mean to snap at you, either. I just get tangled up. I can feel it all through the house, the way they blame him for everything. I'm as much to blame as he is."

"Do you know what Dad said to me after we got your wire?" Kristin sat down on the bed and took both of Elsa's hands. "He'd talked it all over with Sarah, and you know what he said? He said he wanted me to keep you occupied, and stay around and do things with you, because this whole thing was going to be pretty hard on Sarah. On *Sarah!* Oh, Else, she's still ashamed of marrying Dad, and she dislikes you for it, somehow, I know she does."

"Does she?" Elsa said. "I gave up disliking her a long time ago. She married Dad because she was alone and didn't have any place to turn. I couldn't dislike her for that very long. And besides, he's doing me a favor if he asks you to look after me. Isn't he?"

"I think Dad would be all right if it weren't for her," Kristin said. "She's just got so *good.* He missed you after you went away, but she keeps reminding him of all the sins she says Bo does. When you came back before she didn't want Dad to let you. That's the only time I ever heard him get mad at her and bawl her out."

"Oh well," Elsa said. "I'll try to find work somewhere, and then we won't have all this. I'm just so tired now I guess I don't care what they think."

"When George and I get married in April you come and live with us," Kristin said.

Elsa smiled. "I guess I don't want to wish that on you," she said. "I thought maybe I could keep house for Erling on the farm."

"You don't want to go out on that farm and get snowed in all winter. You stay right here. You've got more right here than Sarah has. I wouldn't let her drive me out."

"We'll see," Elsa said. She didn't, actually, want much to go out to the farm. The farm was the one part of home that was spoiled for her. The winter when Bo had nearly gone crazy out there would keep coming up and reminding her of things she didn't want to remember.

"You're thin," Kristin said, on the second morning. "You need to rest and eat a lot."

After that things were set beside her at the table casually, slyly. Her plate was heaped before she could refuse. She got second helpings she didn't want. She tried, she ate till she was stuffed, she let herself be supinely carried off for naps after lunch, but all the time she was aware that her father and Sarah were not a part of this plan. They were like strangers on a bench, making room for her to squeeze in, but asking no questions, inviting no confidences, interesting themselves in what had absorbed them before her arrival. They would not welcome her, but they would make room out of Christian charity.

Still she could forget, often, that they didn't want her. She could forget Bo and the café and Seattle and the orphanage, could look at the children and see them blooming, and be thankful at least for their sakes. Chester was in school, Bruce was teasing to go too, devoting himself for hours to crayons and slates, curled on the floor in the dining room. In the mild, brooding, early-winter days Elsa often sat in the dining room sewing and watched his absorbed play-learning and was grateful.

On Sunday afternoons her father took his nap in the dining room, on a couch crowded into the corner, his fingers trailing on the floor among the trailing fringes of the cover. The boys, unable to subdue themselves to Sunday, were in and out, pestering. They sneaked up to tickle Grandpa with feathers, and he played with them as Elsa had never seen him play with his own children. Even the unrelaxing sternness of his face, after the first few uncertain days, could not fool them. On the pretense of having protection against the flies, he took a fly-swatter with him to his nap, waving it up out of his doze occasionally. He seemed to sleep, his mustaches faintly blowing as he breathed, and the boys crept forward smothering giggles, stretching their feathers far out. They would be right at his nose, only an inch away, when one blue eye would open like a shutter, the stern eyebrows would scowl, and the fly-swatter would swish around their legs.

"Preacher's tails!" he would roar at them. "Mosquito-shadows!"

Watching that, or watching the boys playing with the neighborhood children, Elsa hadn't the heart to look for work yet. She couldn't take them away just when they were tasting normal childhood, making friends, feeling themselves secure. So she kept her own feelings quiet and made herself useful in the house. She helped preserve meat at butchering time, made head cheese and sausage and tried lard. And when there was nothing else to do she could help Kristin with her trousseau.

Most of her clothes had to be made, for her father would stand for no nonsense like shopping tours in Minneapolis. So Elsa made nightgowns and dresses and petticoats and blouses, hemmed sheets and pillow cases, crocheted lace, working as if it were her own hope chest that was being filled, and not her sister's.

"You're wonderful at sewing, Else," Kristin said once. "Why don't you make things for yourself, instead of helping me all the time? You could stand some new clothes."

Elsa bit off a thread, threaded the needle, and pulled the end down. "I don't need any new clothes."

"You do too."

"What for?"

There was no answer to that.

But even the unfailing recourse of sewing for Kristin could not occupy more than her hands, and to keep from thinking she often sang. Sometimes in the midst of a song she would break off abruptly, wondering why she sang at all. She wasn't happy enough to sing, certainly, only dormant, as if half of her slept. She remembered times when she had been happy enough to sing, the old days when she had sung alto in the church choir, evenings in Hardanger, even in Grand Forks, so miserably burdened with the weight of that hotel. She remembered evenings coming home from somewhere in the buggy, when she and Bo had sat together with their voices going up in old tunes. Bo had a nice voice, she thought wanly, full and rich. She remembered the nodding tip of the buggy whip against the sky, the windy freshness of the air of those lost evenings, and Bo's laughter, his rich, warm, possessive laughter, and the fool songs he knew, dozens of them, as if his mind were flypaper to catch all sorts of buzzing tunes. When she got that far in her remembering she always broke off, sang some other song, one that had no echoes except those that sounded down the green avenue of her childhood.

Sometimes Henry Mossman came to call, and everybody always

assumed that he came to see Nels Norgaard, and the two men sat in the parlor while the women worked or darned or chatted in the dining room. But Elsa knew why he came, and she sat sometimes studying his stooped, apologetic figure with a kind of regret, remembering that once he had wanted to marry her, that if she had she might have got what she now so desperately wanted. With a little shake of the head she would let amazement run through her mind at the way people changed. Nine years ago, silly and young and full of confidence that she knew just what she wanted to do with her life, she had run away from Indian Falls and Henry Mossman and the stodgy uneventful life of the town, and now she almost wished she had chosen the other way.

Henry was so mild and inoffensive and docile, so unwilling even to say straight out that he came to see her, not her father, and he sat in the parlor half a dozen evenings talking to Nels Norgaard and saying hardly more than ten words to Elsa. He was steady, incapable of a harsh word to anybody, kind, unattractive, dependable. She wished once, with a sigh, that Bo, with all his arrogant ease, his sharpness, his powerful and well-tuned body, might have had just a touch of Henry's dependable quietness. But before she had half thought it she was thinking almost proudly that Bo could never be like Henry. He wasn't a domestic animal, he wasn't tame, he couldn't like halters, no matter how hard he tried—and he did try, had tried, often. It just wasn't in him; she had probably helped along his unhappiness and her own by trying to turn him into something he was never cut out to be. Just by marrying him she had done that. Karl had known it, right from the beginning. Bo was a rambler, and the responsibilities of marriage would never sit easily on his back.

George Nelson, blond, laughing, very much in love with Kristin, came down from his Minneapolis law office and stayed for two days at Thanksgiving, and when he was gone Kristin folded up and put away the dress she had stolen out of her trousseau and threw herself into crocheting pillow-slip lace.

"You must be planning to spend all your life in bed," Elsa said. "You've already got six or eight pairs done."

Kristin blushed, let her hands stop, and looked up with her face strained as if she were about to cry. "I should think you'd hate me, Elsa."

"For goodness' sake, why?"

"Because I'm so happy."

Sympathy again, Elsa thought. Poor Elsa. But she wasn't angry.

Kristin was so full of her happiness and she had to be spendthrift, share it with everybody. "I'm as glad as I can be," Elsa said.

They were on the edge of the old forbidden ground. A silence like a drawn curtain came between them.

"You like George, don't you?" Kristin said from the other side of the curtain.

"Very much. I always did."

"You think he'll make a good husband, don't you?"

"I don't know anyone I'd rather see you marry," Elsa said.

Kristin picked at a knot in the lace, her eyes hiding. "I think he's wonderful," she said.

"So do I," Elsa said, crocheting steadily. "Not as wonderful as you do, but wonderful enough."

"I suppose every bridegroom seems wonderful to the bride," Kristin said. "Oh Elsa, I wish . . ."

"What?"

"I wish you were as happy as I am. You deserve such a lot, and you never got a thing."

"Maybe I don't deserve very much," Elsa said, "and how do you know I never got anything?" She straightened a square of lace and laid it aside. "That's fourteen," she said. "Eighty-two more and you'll have your bedspread."

Kristin stood up. "I've got to run down to the postoffice. George said he'd write the minute he got back."

She stood in the doorway, struggling into her coat. "Don't you think it's cute the way his hair curls up above his ears?" she said. She went out, letting the storm door bang.

In a few minutes the door slammed again, and Kristin blew in in a cloud of snow. She was some time taking off her coat and hanging it in the hall. Out in the kitchen Sarah was rattling pans. Then Kristin came in.

"Get your letter?" Elsa asked.

"Uh-huh."

"You don't seem very excited. Didn't he put any kisses at the bottom?"

"Oh, it's a nice letter," Kristin said. She went to the table and ruffled through the papers there.

"Is anything wrong?"

"No." Kristin turned around. "There's a letter for you, that's all." She took it out of her pocket.

"For me?" Elsa's hand came out halfway. Her eyes jumped to meet Kristin's.

"From him," Kristin said. She seemed unwilling to give it up.

"Oh, I wish he'd yet you alone!" she said. "When it's all over with, he ought to have decency enough . . ."

She threw the letter at Elsa and went out into the kitchen, leaving Elsa alone with the envelope a warm, speaking, dangerous thing under her fingers. The letter was postmarked Seattle. He had come back to Washington, then, and found her gone. She tore open the end and very slowly drew out the letter, a fat one. There was a money order folded into it. Two hundred dollars. Straightening the sheets, she read:

Dear Elsa,

If this letter doesn't reach you I don't know what I'll do. I've been about crazy since I came down here a week ago and found out you'd left the place in Richmond a long time back. I've been hunting all over Seattle, had a detective on the job and everything, and finally I found out you'd worked in that store, and got your address from a guy there, but the landlady said she didn't know where you'd gone. So I just have to shoot in the dark and hope you went home. You should have written me and told me about the cafe. I thought you'd make out there all right, and after you shut me out that night I was so mad and sick I didn't know what I was doing. I wrote a letter a month ago, with a check in it. Did you get it? Oh, damn it, Elsa, I don't know what to say. I'm getting along fine up in Canada, bought some real estate and ought to make some dough in the spring, but I'm lonesome for you and the kids all the time. If you've gone home to stay with your folks I wish you'd think it over, and in the spring come up here with me. I'm really in on the ground floor here, even if Purcell does own the whole valley. This road is opening up a country as big as Dakota, and there's plenty of homestead land open yet. I'm looking out for a half section in a good place, with water. Sometimes you can pre-empt another quarter along with the homesteaded quarter if the guy who homesteaded it first hasn't made his improvements. This land will grow wheat six feet high, and if we could get into some business in town and have a half section for farming in the summer we'd be set. This town, or this place where they will be a town, is going to have a lot of opportunities in it. As we get rolling we could buy up more land in the townsite and clean up a bbl. of money from the people who'll be flocking in here in six months. There is white clay along the river that a fellow from Medicine Hat says is just right for pottery. Coal too, lignite, the hills are full of it, and some fellows were around there when I left, snooping for oil. If we owned some land and oil was struck on it we'd be on Easy St. for life. We can't make any mistake on this place. It's what I've been looking for all my life. It isn't all skimmed off and gobbled up.

Elsa, I miss you and the kids, and this proposition looks so good I hate to think that now we stand a chance to make some money you aren't with me any more. Its no satisfaction to make money just for yourself. I can't seem to get steamed up about it alone. I guess if you're really set on leaving me I can't kick, because I had it coming the way I acted, but I wish you'd think it over. In a new country like that we could start all over.

This town will be a nice place to live. It's on the Whitemud River, and there'd be swimming and hunting and riding for the kids, and plenty of brush for them to run in. The country reminds me some of my old home town in Illinois, only there aren't any trees except in the river valley. I caught four beaver and a half dozen muskrats in traps in the week before I came down to the States. That shows you how wild it still is. Beavers swim right out in the river under the railroad bridge.

You think it over, Elsa. We don't want to go breaking up the family and not give the kids a chance. I have to go back to Whitemud right away, but if you get this, write me and let me know you're all right. I'm sending on some money, if you need more let me know and I can rake it up. I was going to invest this two hundred in another lot, but then I thought you'd probably need it, especially when I found out you hadn't been able to make the cafe go. And you'd better decide to come up here in the spring. I promise you nothing like that other will happen any more. I guess I learned something from that night.

All my love,
Bo

P.S. I want to send on something for a Christmas package. Can't tell much what you need, but I'll try to find something useful. I know you never did like jewjaws.

So he had finally struck something that promised to pay off. She had always believed that some day he would. If you tried enough things, sooner or later something was bound to turn out. But she mustn't, she thought almost desperately, she mustn't let herself be softened. It was a nice letter, and it made her want to do just what she knew she shouldn't do. But she would hang onto what she knew: she knew he couldn't promise to change what he was. The thing she feared in him, the thing that had made her shut him out that night, was still there, deep in his violent and irritable and restless blood.

Or was it? Was there a chance that only poverty, bad luck, dissatisfaction, brought that out in him? Was there a chance that in a new place, living the way he wanted to, making enough money to satisfy him, that side of him would never come out any more?

She looked up to see Kristin standing in the sliding doors between dining room and parlor. Her eyes were accusing. Pugnaciously she came in and sat down, her whole expression saying that she was not going to get up again until this thing was talked over and settled. Elsa sat still.

"What did he say?" Kristin said.

Elsa shrugged. "Sent some money. Wants me to come up to Canada in the spring."

"He would," Kristin said. "That's the kind he is. He'd abuse you for eight or nine years and then expect you to come crawling back for more. I wouldn't even have opened his letter."

"He's still my husband," Elsa said. "I wrote Dad once about helping me get a divorce, but he wouldn't do anything unless I had the one reason the church accepts. And Bo's never looked at another woman. You dislike him too much, Kris. He sent me two hundred dollars in this letter."

"It's a bribe!" Kristin said. "He'll send you money to get you back and then you'll have rags and beatings again."

"Beatings!"

Sitting forward on the edge of her chair, Kristin let her eyes bore into Elsa's. "He did beat you, didn't he?"

"My goodness, no."

Kristin sat back reluctantly, only half believing. "But you aren't going back to him, are you?"

"I was just wondering," Elsa said. She stared at the cherry-red mica squares in the door of the parlor heater and shook her head tiredly. "No, I don't think so."

"Because you don't know what he's done to you," Kristin said. "When you went away you were young, and pretty, and healthy, and everything, and you come back with your arm hurt so it'll always show, and without decent clothes, and . . ."

"And looking like an old woman," Elsa said.

"That isn't what I meant. You're pretty yet, only you look so tired, and thin. Sometimes when you don't know anybody's looking at you you look so worn out you scare me. Elsa, you look . . . just the way I remember Ma!"

She gave the spring handle of the poker a hard kick, and it rattled against the stove legs.

"I guess I can still manage to get around," Elsa said. "People needn't wear themselves out worrying about me."

"He's taken the heart out of you," Kristin said helplessly. "Even if he didn't beat you or burn your arm, he led you such a life that he's taken the heart right out of you. You used to be so spunky and independent, and make Erling and me toe the mark, and now you're so quiet and kind you make me want to cry!"

She was crying as she said it. Elsa put out a hand and touched her. "Then he's been good for me," she said. "At least I may have learned to keep my temper."

"It isn't a matter of keeping it. It's having it to keep. You don't seem to ever want anything for yourself any more, and that's not natural, Elsa."

"Let's not talk any more about it," Elsa said.

"Why don't you get a divorce in spite of Dad?"

Elsa laughed a little. "I don't know how. I don't even know how to begin, and I haven't any money for a lawyer."

"George would help you."

"And get him and you in dutch with Dad."

"George wouldn't care. Then you'd be free of him. You wouldn't always be getting letters . . ."

"One since I came," Elsa said drily.

". . . and worrying yourself about him. You're thinking about him all the time, and worrying."

"And then what would I do?" Elsa said, rising. "A divorce wouldn't change things any."

"You could get married again."

After a short, incredulous stare, Elsa laughed. "Don't be silly."

"Henry would still marry you."

"You make him sound very charitable," Elsa said. "I remember what you used to say about Henry."

She held the blue indignant eyes for a minute. "Don't you like Henry any more?" Kristin said.

"Certainly. I always did like him."

They stared at each other, and by a sudden emotional shift in the wind they were both close to anger. As they stared, Kristin's face changed, her eyebrows lifted, her lips came together.

"Elsa," she said, "you're still in love with Bo!"

Elsa turned away. "Well, what of it?" she said harshly.

5

Elsa stood above the kitchen range, the glow of its slow heat on arms and face, making Christmas pastry. It was the day before Christmas. Kristin, Sarah, and the boys were doing some last-minute shopping; her father had gone out to the farm after Erling.

On the table behind her a mound of sugar-dusted *fattigmands bakkelse* almost poured off on the floor, the back of the stove was sheeted with gray *lefse,* a wide crock in the cupboard was heaped with *goro brød*. She turned over a *lefse* sheet, browning in spots like broad freckles, and dropped a new batch of *fattigmand* into the kettle of fat. The kitchen was full of rich smells. She smiled a little, remembering how excited the boys were. This would be a Christmas they would remember, the kind of Christmas kids ought to have.

She thought too of what Bo's Christmas would be like in that raw little settlement in Saskatchewan: a few drinks with some other men, probably; perhaps a bowl of tom and jerry batter in his bunk-house the way they used to have it in Dakota. Just that, and her own futile, wept-over parcel with the knitted muffler and the gloves and the heavy home-made socks. One parcel to be ripped open in the postoffice or wherever he got his mail, and instead of the warmth and ritual and color, the tree and the decorations and the bountiful eating that brought the old country close that one day of the year, and the reunion of people tied by blood and traditions, there would be only his drinks with a few other men as lonely as himself in a little unformed unhistoried town of a half dozen frame shacks.

But that was what he wanted, that was the natural result of the itch in his bones and the restlessness in his mind. She thought it odd that he should be lonely, as his letter said he was, as she herself knew he was. For all his strength and violence he was oddly dependent in some ways, like a child. Like Bruce, she thought in surprise. He was really more like Bruce than like Chester, though they had both always thought Chet the image of him.

The doublings of her own mind wearied her. As she lifted the *fattigmand* brown and cake-smelling from the fat, she saw her bare right arm, the ridge of white scar in the bend of the elbow. She would always, apparently, wear Bo in her as she wore that scar, yet she had to make up her mind. She had to answer his letter, let him know what she would do. And she had to decide what to do about this house that echoed constantly of home but was home no longer.

The front door slammed, she heard the stamping of feet in the hall, Sarah's admonitions to the boys to clean the snow off their shoes. They all came in together, the boys rosy with the cold, Sarah pulling a wisp of hair up under her net, Kristin carrying packages. She dumped them on the floor by the cistern pump.

"Else," she said, "could you . . ." She stopped, looked at the piles of pastry, pulled off her gloves. "You're awful busy, though."

"I'm just about done. What is it?"

"George is going to be here at six o'clock, and that green dress doesn't fit right around the neck."

"Sure, just a minute."

Elsa moved the kettle of fat off the stove, gave a sugared *fattigmand* to each of the boys, standing with their tongues between their lips at the table, and shooed them out. Kristin picked up three or four big packages and followed her upstairs. While Elsa worked on the dress she said nothing, but when the collar was going back on, she jerked her head at one large parcel. "That came for you in the mail," she said.

They looked at each other, then at the square package. "Yes," Elsa said. "He said something about a Christmas parcel."

Though she wouldn't have shown it to Kristin, she was excited. Bo would have some part in this Christmas. He hadn't forgotten, and he wouldn't be forgotten.

She was so busy getting Kristin ready for George that she had no time to open it then, and later there was supper, and then the dishes, and then a quick change into a dress-up dress for the Christmas tree. But that was all right. Let it be a surprise, to her and to all of them. They thought he was so low and vicious, let them see right out in the open that he could be thoughtful too.

The house was full. Sarah's two sisters had come over, George was down from Minneapolis, Erling in from the farm. Groaning full with *ludefisk, kjodkager, risengrot, anschovy salat,* a half dozen kinds of pastry, pleasantly warmed by the grape wine traditional with Christmas feasts, they crowded into the parlor, sitting on chairs and floor wherever there was room. George and Kristin sat on the floor under the Christmas tree, Sarah on a straight chair, Nels Norgaard on the couch between Sarah's sisters. He quizzed them in Norwegian and smiled a little grimly at their halting and giggling answers. Erling had slipped out immediately after supper.

Chester stuck his head in between Grandpa and Hilda Veld. "There ain't any Santa Claus, is there?"

"Hoo!"

"There ain't any Santa Claus that comes down the chimney, is there?"

"I knew a boy once that didn't believe in Santa Claus," Grandpa said. "You know what he got for Christmas? An orange, and the orange was spoiled."

"Aw!" Chet said. He retreated to whisper with Bruce.

When Elsa came in Bruce ran up to her. "Mom."

"What is it?"

"Chet says he ain't going to come."

"Isn't. We don't say ain't. But he'll come. Chet's just trying to be smart."

"Aw, I know," Chet said. "*I* know!"

There was a knock on the door, and Elsa went to open it. It was Henry Mossman, stooping and smiling and apologetic. "Merry Christmas," he said. "Can I butt in on the celebration?"

"Sure thing. Come on in."

Henry bowed and spoke all around, the parcel he carried looking uncomfortably prominent in his hands. Elsa told him to put it under the tree.

"When do the festivities start?" he said.

"Any time now. Erling's out getting ready."

Henry looked at the boys, secretive in their corner. "They don't look half excited, do they?" he said, and laughed.

Elsa half turned away and smoothed the papers on the library table. For an instant a thought had sneaked into her mind. Just the sight of Henry's unaffected kindness, the way he looked at the boys as if he loved them both, made her see him for an instant as their father. They'd have walked all over him from the time they were born, but they would have loved him, they wouldn't ever have known what it was to hate or fear him . . .

Outside there was the faint jangle of sleigh bells. Nels Norgaard rose and shooed them all toward the kitchen, reached over and picked up the lamp. "All out," he said, "all out, all out. He won't come in if he sees us." The boys, frantic with excitement, hung back, escaped, had to be rounded up and herded. George and Kristin were hurriedly lighting the tree candles in their pink clamp-sockets. The tree glowed, the strings of popcorn gleamed white, there was a rich red glitter from the long festoons of cranberries, a shimmer from the glass bubbles and ornaments.

Motioning Henry to go in with the others, Elsa ran upstairs and collected her packages, piled her arms, stooped and caught her fingers in the cord of Bo's parcel, felt her way down the dark stairway again. Kristin was pushing packages under the tree. In the three minutes since the lamp had been removed the floor under the tree had been mounded with gifts. Elsa pushed her packages in with the others, turned and saw Erling's face grinning in through the window over a bushy white beard. "Hurry up," Erling said, his voice faint through the storm windows. "It's cold out here in this monkey suit."

The boys burst loose when she slipped into the kitchen. "Is he *here?*" Bruce said.

"I heard him up on the roof," she said. "He got stuck in the chimney for a minute or I'd never have got out in time."

She peered out the door. The partition between dining room and parlor cut off the tree, but she saw the flutter of its lights on the wall. There was the soft sound of the front door opening. She turned to her father. "Blow out the light," she said. "Then we can let the boys creep out and peek at him."

The kitchen went dark in a puffed breath. Sarah's sisters, somewhere in the dark, whispered and giggled. "Shhhhhhh!" Chester said fiercely, three times as loud as the whisper had been.

Taking the boys' hands, Elsa tiptoed them carefully into the dining room, where she stood with finger on lips and leaned to look through the double doors. Erling in a Santa Claus suit was standing in front of the fireplace cramming long scrolls of candy into the stockings. From a bag he poured streams of peanuts and butternuts and almonds, and crowned each stocking with a tangerine. The tree was barricaded with new packages, brightly wrapped. Candy canes hung from the tree, and there was a shimmer, a glitter, the whole fairy wonder of childhood, in the room. She pulled the boys close so they could peek.

They bent, stared; she felt their bodies rigid with awe. Even Chet, the unbeliever, did not breathe for minutes. Against their will they were tugged back into the kitchen. Sarah lighted the lamp again, and the roomful of people stood looking at the two boys, every pair of eyes watching the dazed entrancement in their faces. Bruce looked up at his mother, crowded against her legs, smiled wanly, and began unaccountably to cry.

Sleigh bells jangled again loudly, diminished as if moving away. "There he goes!" Chet said. They piled out of the kitchen, and the boys stopped short for a moment when they saw, well-lighted now and in plain view, the piles of gifts. Then they fell upon the loaded tree.

For a half hour there was pandemonium as they ripped open parcels, exposing Indian suits, revolvers, pencil boxes and crayons, tricycles (her father's gift, lavish, unheard of). The room was full of birdlike chirps of joy. Henry and George went around salvaging packages from the boys' rapacious hands and distributing them to their rightful owners. With surprise, Elsa found herself pressed with gifts. It had not occurred to her, in her desire to make this Christmas one that the children would always remember, that she would herself be remembered. Christmas before had always been a kind of hurried pushing-back of the world's leanness, a hasty and dutiful gift-giving always soured just a little by Bo's contempt for the whole business. (Spend a lot of money and get people things they'd never buy themselves and would never use.) She wished he could see this, the fine wholeheartedness of this feast. Her lap was full of things, gloves and a new dress from Kristin, a lavalière from Erling, a sternly practical sewing basket from Sarah and her father, even a brush and comb and mirror, backed with ivory, from Henry Mossman.

She stammered on her thanks, and her eyes betrayed her, so that she got up and began picking up scattered wrappings and feeding them into the heater. If Bo could only see it, just once, could only know just once that feeling of family loyalty and love and thanksgiving that was like a song sometimes, when Christmas went right, he would know what she missed, and why she missed it. Then she thought of Bo's package.

Chet collided with her, riding his tricycle around the room, and she caught his shoulder. "There's a package from Pa," she said, and steered him toward the tree. Bruce wheeled up, avid for more plunder, while she groped under the low branches and found the parcel.

The babble of voices went on behind her while she cut the string. The lips of the cardboard box spread apart. Wadded newspaper came first, then a package wrapped in brown paper. She wished she had had time to open the things first and re-wrap them prettily. Bo wouldn't have had any chance, where he was, to get nice wrappings, and now his presents looked shoddy by comparison with the others. She supposed Sarah and her father, even Kristin, would notice that and hold it against him.

The boys were clamoring at her shoulder. George Nelson, his eyes crinkled with a smile at the corners, bent to help her. For a moment, with the brown and dowdy package in her hand, she felt a twinge of fear, a tiny cold premonition. The voices behind her had dropped, and she knew they were all watching.

"It looks . . ." she said. "It looks as if it had been opened."

"Customs," George said. "They'd have to open anything coming in from Canada."

"Oh," she said, relieved. Her fingers unrolled the paper. A pair of overshoes came in sight, and her eyes went blurry, her whole body stiff with disappointment, as she looked at them. On her knees, the children over her shoulder, she hung as if clinging for her life. The overshoes were smeared with yellow mud from top to sole.

Frantically, telling herself it was a joke, a bad joke, but meant to be funny, she unrolled the second package. Another smaller pair of overshoes, smeared like the first ones. Bruce's voice, shrill, angry at being cheated, cut through the room. "Why they're *old!*" he said.

Elsa's face was hot as fire, her blood so wild with rage that she felt smothered. Violently she tore the paper off the third parcel and shook out the contents. It was a coat with a fur collar. There was mud spattered on it, and the collar, ripped half off, hung askew.

Not a person in the room said a word as she stood up. She fought to smile, fought to make her voice bright. "All right," she said. "That's all. They must have got dirtied by the customs inspectors. We'll wash them off tomorrow. Time for bed, now."

Henry Mossman picked up one of the overshoes and rubbed with his fingers at the dried mud. "That's about the worst I ever saw," he said. "Open packages and ruin everything in them." He looked at Elsa, and his eyes dropped. "I'll wash them off at the pump," he said. "They must have thrown them down in a puddle and stamped on them."

"Thank you, Henry," Elsa said. The stiff smile still on her face, she motion to Chet and Bruce. Chet looked at her solemnly, hanging to the handlebars of his tricycle. "Is that all Pa sent?" he said. "Is that all, Ma?"

Sick and humiliated, furious at the people in the room who sat silently and watched her shame, she herded them off to bed. She did not come down again, but went to bed to lie wakeful, bitter and raging, cringing at the thought of facing all of them tomorrow, beating against the brutal, unanswerable question of why he had sent things like that for Christmas gifts. Because she didn't believe, any more than the people downstairs did, that the customs inspectors were responsible.

Even the explanation, when it came, only made her bite her lips in vexation. That was the way Bo was, and there was no changing him. Everything he did was characteristic, blind, yet from one point of view reasonable, practical, full of insensitive logic.

The letter came two days after Christmas. The envelope had been stamped "Return to Sender," and stamps had been stuck on over the post office lettering. It was meant to reach her before the package, but he had forgotten the stamps, again characteristically.

She read it coming home from town, where she had fled to escape the house, get clear of Sarah's closed and vindicated face and the children's sullen reluctance to wear their scrubbed overshoes. The day before, she had sat a long time mending the ripped collar of the coat, and her whole mind had been one impossible question, Why? It was a nice coat, with a fox collar. It had cost a good deal. But the smears of mud, the rips. To buy new things and then spoil them before putting them in the mail.

Dear Elsa, the letter said.

There hasn't been any answer to my letter except that post card saying you were staying at home. What's the matter, honey? I've been up here working my head off to get a stake, and you won't even write more than a post card. I know you had a tough time in Richmond, but I honestly thought the joint would give you a living. Anyway I'm sorry, but I told you that before. You don't know how lonesome a place like this can be, just sitting around the stove and spitting in the door with a lot of section hands that don't know their behinds from thirty cents a week. The place is dead as a doornail, with winter here, and so cold you can't stick your nose out without freezing it off. The foreman of the Half Diamond Bar and I got the Chink cook to stick his tongue on a cold doorknob the other day and he like to tore all the hide off it trying to get away. You never heard such a jabber. But there isn't much doing. I've been drawing plans for a house I might build if you don't spoil everything by staying mad. Four gables, a bedroom in each one, and a big verandah. I've got three lots along the river on the high side where it won't ever flood out, and I'm sort of reserving one for us. You and the kids would like it up here. It's a swell climate in summer, sunshine sixteen hours a day.

I sent a box for Christmas today. When you open it you'll find the overshoes dirty and the coat torn a little, because I found out that new clothes sent across the line had a big duty slapped on them, but you can send second-hand ones without any duty. Money don't grow on trees so thick that I could afford to miss foxing the customs guys. The collar ought to sew right back on, and you can wash the mud off the boots easy. I got the coat when I came through Moose Jaw after I left Seattle. The collar is gray fox. I hope you think of me once in a while when you wear it, and that you'll write me a decent letter and say you'll come up here in the spring.

Love,
Bo

P.S. Merry Christmas. Tell the kids Merry Christmas too. If Chet is in school now maybe he has learned to write and can write his old man a letter.

Elsa leaned against a tree and sighed, and laughed aloud, and crushed the letter in her hand. Every word from him was full of the tangle of emotional pulls that had wearied her mind for months. He missed her, he missed the boys, he would love a letter from Chet—she could imagine his pride as he showed such a letter around—he honestly wanted her back, he would promise anything. And he sent her gifts that were not gifts, but slaps in the face that shamed her for him in front of everybody, yet the gifts had been well meant. It was only the saving of a few miserable dollars of duty that had made him spoil them. And his optimism, his incurable conviction that this time he was going to make his pile, the old, endless, repetitive story of his whole life . . .

A letter from him always weakened her resolution, made her wonder if she were doing right to stay away from him. Before she could soften herself too much with thinking she went home and wrote him a letter, a letter she could not help making kind. But she couldn't come back. The boys were coming out of their kinks, they had something like a home for the first time, they had friends and playmates and were healthy and happy. She was dreadfully sorry and unhappy, but she couldn't risk their futures any more. If he wanted a divorce she would agree, because she couldn't expect him not to want to be free under the circumstances. She had used the two checks he sent for the boys, and was keeping what was left to be spent on them when they needed things. He needn't feel any responsibility for her. The kids talked about him a lot, they hadn't forgotten him.

Across the bottom she wrote her thanks for the Christmas gifts, and she could not bring herself to mention how they had been received. It was a lovely coat, the overshoes were very useful in the deep snow they were having. The thought of how much he might be hurt if she told him the truth, how he had spent a lot of money on the coat and was staying up in a lonesome village hoping she might come back to him, kept her pen in the easy platitudes of thanks. She would lie before she would hurt him that way.

6

It was almost as if the necessity of protecting him, of keeping from him the knowledge of what a catastrophe his gifts had been, made the problem of living under the shadow of her family's unspoken condemnation harder to bear. She found herself on the brink of flaring out and defending him a half dozen times when their talk or their gestures or their very silence steered close to the disapproval they felt. They had known it all the time, their silence said, and now they were half pleased to have their judgment vindicated. Sometimes she felt like shouting at them, and as Kristin's marriage came closer she felt more and more how impossible it would be to stay on after her one friend was gone from the house. If it hadn't been for the children, she would not have stayed a week.

Then in mid-April Kristin was married, and after she and George had fled in a shower of rice and old shoes for a honeymoon in Florida that made Sarah lift her eyes in deprecation of such ungodly extravagance, the house was the dull burying ground she had known it would be. Her life went on from day to day by sufferance, not by any will or direction of its own. The weeks crept through their routine of housework and Sunday quiet, Sarah went beside her through the house like a mute, walked the four blocks to and from church like an automaton, spoke hardly ten words a day. Even the lavish flowering of the wild plum tree by the side of the house, and the misty green spread below her bedroom window, were tinged with the melancholy of something long-lost and past reclaiming. Her heart was no longer in this house, there was nothing for her here.

On the last day of April, when she was sweeping the porch, Henry Mossman came by and stood with his hat in his hand and asked her if she would like to bring the boys and come on a picnic the next Saturday afternoon. He asked her lamely, not knowing how she, a married woman, would feel about going out with him, humbly ready to assume that probably she wouldn't want to. "I just remembered that other picnic we went on once," he said.

"Pretty near ten years ago. When we had the buggy race and your dad walked on his hands."

"That was a lovely day," she said. "I've never forgotten it."

"Like to come this time? We might be lucky and get another perfect day."

"I shouldn't," she said. "I might get you talked about, Henry."

"That's what I was wondering," Henry said. "Not about me, about you."

"It wouldn't bother me."

"Then let's go," Henry said. "Nobody who ever knew you would talk about you a minute, and the rest of them don't matter." He lifted his face and smiled. She noticed how fine his eyes were, what a sweet and quizzical and gentle expression he always wore.

"The boys ought to have fun," Henry said. "I'll come around about one, then."

Standing with her back to the unfriendly house she felt the sudden trembling as if tears were fighting to emerge. She said, "I guess I've never known anyone as kind as you, Henry."

Henry quirked his lips in his half-humorous, self-derogatory smile. "I'd rather hear you say that than anyone I can think of," he said.

That was on Wednesday. On Friday the boy from the station came up with a telegram for Elsa Mason. It was from Bo, and he was in Minneapolis. He wanted her to meet him there Saturday afternoon.

"I'm dreadfully sorry, Henry," she said. "It's just that . . . he's come a long way . . ."

"Sure," he said. "Of course. You want to go."

He stood behind the counter of his hardware store in a black alpaca jacket, stroking the ends of his mustache, and her own uncertain state made her clairvoyantly sensitive to the stages by which he put away his disappointment.

"You were banking on it," she said. "I'm awfully sorry."

Henry reached out and swung the handles of three rakes hanging from the rafter. "Well, I won't say I'm glad he came just when he did."

She felt driven to explain, to justify Bo and herself. "I guess he won't come down here," she said. "He knows they don't like him. But when he comes all that way I can't just . . ."

"Why sure," Henry said. "You want to go right up. Don't worry about me."

Full of obscure and stubborn shame, Elsa started for the door. "Thank you, Henry," she said. She always seemed to hurt him, no matter how hard she tried not to. It always came down to a choice, and she always chose against him.

Henry came around the counter and followed her to the entrance. The street outside lay sleepily dead, a tired horse drooped on three feet a few doors down. "Elsa," Henry said.

She stopped.

"I want to tell you something," Henry said. "I had a half idea I might tell you at the picnic, sort of reproduce that one ten years ago." He was perfectly serious, perfectly self-assured. The awkwardness had fallen away, even his stoop wasn't noticeable. "I don't want to butt into anything that isn't my business," he said, "but I can't help knowing a few things. Maybe what I've heard is right and maybe it isn't. I don't care. I just want you to know what I think."

She watched him. "One thing I want to tell you," he said, "is that no matter what other folks think of your husband, I always liked him. I never saw Mr. Mason except that one winter a little, but I liked him."

Elsa wet her lips. "It's kind of you to say that."

"I don't know what's the trouble between you and Mr. Mason. That's none of my business either. Sarah said something once, but I didn't listen much." He looked out into the street. "I don't know what the trouble is and there's no reason I should know. Sarah said you wanted to get a divorce and couldn't. I don't know. But if you did do anything like that, and you didn't want to stay on with your folks . . ."

His face turned to meet hers. "I'm no better than I was ten years ago," he said, "and I'm not any younger. But I'd be proud to ask you the same thing I did then, if you should find yourself free."

Elsa bent her head. Every little thing lately seemed to make her cry.

"I like Mr. Mason," Henry was saying, "and you know I'm not prying at you to get you to divorce him. I just wanted you to know, just in case, so you would have it in mind as a possibility."

She was crying quietly with her head down.

"Don't," Henry said. "Please, Elsa. You don't have to say anything, or make up your mind, or anything. You go on up on Saturday and see him and I'll take the kids to the picnic."

It was that last kindness that put her to flight. She nodded and walked away before everything flew out of control.

It was different, telling Sarah. She simply announced that she was going up to see Bo in Minneapolis. Sarah stared at her, her placid, smooth face the color of dough, her slightly-bulging gray eyes hard and disapproving. She looked, Elsa thought, twenty years older than her real age, she looked unhealthy, like a fungus.

"Your father won't like it," Sarah said.

"I'm sorry," Elsa said. "Why should he object?"

"You know he doesn't want you to have any more to do with that man."

"Then why wouldn't he help me get a divorce?"

"You know why. You didn't, or said you didn't, have the Reason."

Elsa laughed, and she heard her laugh unpleasantly harsh in her own ears. "I had reason. I just didn't have the little narrow reason the church recognizes."

"Elsa!"

"Don't shout at me," Elsa said. "I don't know what you want me to be. I'm nothing the way I am. You won't help me divorce him, and you don't want me to go back to him, but still you act as if I were unclean when I come home to stay."

"I'm sorry," Sarah said stiffly. "We've been as kind as we know how to be."

"With a poker up your back," Elsa said. "You hush-hush around me as if he had given me some awful disease."

"He's not a good man," Sarah said.

Elsa sighed and shrugged. "Maybe not. I don't know what a good man is any more. But he wasn't all to blame. He . . ."

She stopped, looking at Sarah's faded hair, the plump colorless face, the quenched and somehow petulant look in the eyes. She said before she thought, "I loved him once, we were awfully happy at first."

Sarah turned away and went into the kitchen, and Elsa looked after her, thinking. As she went upstairs to dress for the train trip she knew that unhappy as she was she was not as unhappy as Sarah, and that seemed a strange thing.

She saw him before the train had fully stopped, and as people began crowding to the ends of the car she sat in the seat gripping the handle of her suitcase. Slowly, with a vise on her mind, she stood up. A porter took her bag and she let it go, though she would have liked it to hang to. The steps, the black hand helping her down, the momentary confusion of turning and searching among the crowd, and then Bo's eyes, gray and sober and intent. He stepped a half step forward, as if unsure of himself, started to speak and stopped, and then lifted her and held her close. His voice was whispering in her ear, "Oh, Elsa, Elsa!"

She shook her head, pulling away from him. Through the weak tears that came to her eyes she saw that he was well dressed, really handsome again in a good gray suit, and when she bent her head to blink the tears away she saw his hand, brown, scarred with signs of labor, still holding her elbow. The hand was more definitely Bo than the handsome man in the gray suit. She knew his hands, lovely big square long hands.

He drew her aside, she mindless and voiceless and almost without power to move her feet, rescued her bag from the porter, and stood her against a post to look at her. His eyes were warming, he was beginning to smile. "Ah, Elsa," he said, "you had me scared to death!"

She wet her lips, trying to grope back among the fragments of what she had been going to say to him. "Bo."

"Don't tell me you meant it," he said, and laughed. "Maybe you meant it when you wrote it, but you don't now. Where are the kids?"

"I left them at home. But Bo . . ."

"Come on," he said. "We've got a lot of talking to do. We're going to talk so much your tongue'll be tired for a month. You know what I've been doing the last three weeks?"

She wanted to tell him that he was taking too much for granted, that she was still determined, that she couldn't come back, but all she said, feebly, was "What?"

"Ever since the frost started working out of the ground," Bo said, "I've been building a house."

"A house!" She still had the feeling of idiocy, as if all she could say was senseless sounds, monosyllables, parrotings of his words.

"A two-story, eight-room house. When I left the foundation was in and the frame up. Full cement basement. Four bedrooms upstairs, living room, dining room, kitchen, big front hall. I sold the two lots and kept the best one for us."

"But Bo, I wrote you . . ."

They were outside the station. Bo raised his arm at a taxi and it pulled up to the curb. The street was of cement, and when they got in and started riding Elsa sat marvelling idiotically at how smoothly they went, not a bump or a sway. She brushed her hand across her mouth, trying to get hold of herself, forget how things had started falling in her mind the instant she saw him. But his voice was in her ears, warm, reassuring, and his arm lay across the seat above her shoulders.

"Look, honey," he said. "I started building the house in spite of your letter. We might have had a lot of hard luck, and what we did and said, me especially, might not be very pretty. But we're going to start all over, see? That's why I got the house going, just for a kind of guarantee."

"I don't know," she said. "I don't think . . ."

"I'll tell you something," Bo said, and pulled her around to face him. The taxi stopped in front of a hotel, but Bo paid no attention. "I'll tell you something. When I left Richmond I thought I was leaving you for good. I thought I really was, after that night. You know how long it lasted? About three weeks. I've been so lonesome and sick for you I can't sleep. Then when I thought I had a good start I came back for you and you weren't there."

He tightened his hold on her shoulders, and his eyes were so urgent that she wavered. "I just can't live without you," he said. "That sounds dippy, but it's true. And you can't live without me, either. Can you?"

She did not answer.

"Can you?"

"I . . ."

"How do the kids feel about it?"

"I don't know. Kids forget so quick."

"Meaning you can't forget," he said. His hands loosened, and he sat back. The little thing like a clock went on ticking in the taxi. The driver was looking straight ahead, whistling through his teeth.

"I'll tell you something else," Bo said. "I'll never let myself go like that again, as long as I live. I got on top of all that when I found out how much I missed you."

"But how can you promise a thing like that?" she said. "You'll forget, and lose your temper again, and there you'll be."

"All I can do is promise and mean it."

Because she needed time to think, and because she didn't like talking in front of the driver, she opened the door. Bo paid the driver and led her into the hotel lobby. It was one thirty by the clock over the desk.

"How about dinner?"

"I ought to be getting back," she said, and for an instant, looking at his face with her own absurd words slowly making their meaning plain, she laughed.

"What did you bring the suitcase for, then?"

She looked at the bag. In it she had packed nightclothes, a change of clothes, stockings, clean underwear. Her mouth was open and dry, and she swallowed. "I don't know," she said.

In the middle of the lobby he burst into loud, triumphant laughter, the kind of full, deep-chested laughter he so seldom voiced.

"See?" he said. "I told you you didn't mean it. You're coming back with me tomorrow."

"Oh no," she said. "No, I couldn't."

"Why not?"

There were a dozen reasons why not. She had been over them a hundred times. But when she opened her mouth her treacherous tongue betrayed her again. "Chester couldn't just leave school," she said.

Bo motioned her toward the dining room and she went as if sleepwalking. The waiter pulled out a chair for her and she sat down in it as if afraid it would collapse the way everything else had collapsed. Bo's eyes across the table were full of mirth, but warm, excited, loving, a look like those she remembered from years back, like the day they had become engaged, when they went walking in the snow and fell down in the middle of a field and sat laughing and kissing. "You've got a nice mouth," she had told him then, "a nice mouth and dappled eyes."

"Ah, Bo," she said, smiling at him, unable to think of a single one of the things she had been so resolutely going to say.

"If you come in June," he said, "I can have the house all finished for you." He reached for her hand across the table, and his face was twisted with a smile that looked as if it hurt him. "Lordy," he said, "you don't know how much you had me scared."

"Is it really good up there?" she said curiously. "Do you really think we can make some kind of a home there?"

"Listen," he said. "Canada's in a war, and they're howling for more wheat, more wheat, all the time. Homesteaders are already coming into that place by the hundreds. Know what I did? I homesteaded a quarter and pre-empted a quarter right next to it. That's a half section of wheat land, and wheat is going to be worth its weight in gold."

"But what about the railroad? I thought . . ."

"Oh, the railroad," Bo said. "That's died. Saving steel for war factories. The steel came into Whitemud and stopped. But it's all right. We've got a start, and a house and lot, and a farm. Wait till wheat gets to be three bucks a bushel and we have two hundred acres in and get sixty bushel to the acre."

In early June, 1914, Elsa loaded the children into the train under the brown eaves of the station, said goodbye to Sarah and George and Kristin and Erling and her father, all attending her dutifully as they would have attended her funeral, shook hands with Henry Mossman, holding his fingers in one last relinquishment of what he stood for and had offered her, and set her feet on the iron steps. The boys were already climbing on the seat inside and sticking their tongues out against the glass. For the third time (and each time forever, each time certain she would never return) she left home to hazard herself and her hopes in a new and unknown country.

And oh God, she said, looking through the windows at her family, Kristin with her handkerchief out, her father straight and grim with his hat formally off, Sarah placid with pursed mouth and hands folded across her stomach—oh God, let it be final this time! Let the house Bo is building be the place we'll stay in the rest of our lives, let it be the real home that the boys can look back to without a single regret.

Because she knew she was surrendering completely this time. She knew that she would stick to Bo now no matter what came. She had made her bed, and this time she would lie in it.

The train jerked. She waved, and as they moved up the platform she seized the window catches and shoved up the glass, and with her arm outside the window waved once more, the last time, at the place that had been home.

IV

In the summer it was the homestead, the little round-roofed shack that looked like a broad freight car with one side extended into a sleeping porch where the two beds were, the single room with the kerosene stove against one wall and the cupboards built up beside it, the table and the benches and the couch where the cat slept all day long, curled up dozing, but sleeping so lightly that a finger placed on one hair of him, anywhere, would bring him instantly awake with a *pr-r-r-rt!*

The homestead was the open, flat plain, unbroken clear to the horizon on every side except the south, where the Bearpaw Mountains, way down across the line in Montana, showed in a thin white line that later in summer turned to brown. In August, when the heat was intense, the mountains faded out of sight in the haze and heat waves, but almost any day in June and early July they could be seen, and they were an important part of the farm.

There were other important things about the farm, the intimate parts like the pasture, a half mile long and two hundred yards wide, fenced with three tight strands of barbed wire on peeled cedar posts, the whole thing a pride to Bruce because there was no fence anywhere near as tight and neat on the other farms nearby. His father was a thorough man on a job; when he put in a fence he put in a fence that he need not be ashamed of, he set the posts deep in the ground and tamped them in tight, he bought a wire-stretcher and strung the strands like guitar strings.

The pasture was cut diagonally by the coulee, and just below the house was the reservoir, and across the reservoir and through the fence was the long sixty-acre wheat field and the smaller field of flax, and the end of those fields was both the south line of their property and the international boundary. The farm was that feeling, too, the sense of straddling two nations, so that even though you were American, living in Canada, you lost nothing by it, but really gained, because the Fourth of July was celebrated in Canada and Canadian holidays like Victoria Day and the King's birthday were celebrated in Montana, and you got in on both. And you lived in Saskatchewan, in one nation, but got your mail in Montana, in another.

The farm was every summer between June and September. It was the long trip, in the first year by wagon but later by car, from Whitemud out; it was the landmarks on that trail, the Frenchman's house with a dozen barefooted children streaking for the barn, the gates that had to be opened, the great horse ranch where they travelled hours without seeing a living thing except herds of horses as wild as coyotes. It was Robsart, a little clot of dwellings with a boarding house that they generally tried to make for the noon meal, and then scattered farms again along the grass-grown wagon-track, and a couple of little streams to ford, and Gadke's where they always stopped while Pa talked things over with Mr. Gadke because Mr. Gadke was a smart dry-farmer, until finally the last gate and the last ford just past the twin tarpapered shacks that all the homesteaders called Pete and Emil, and then their own house, and the familiar-unfamiliar look of the fence and fireguard and pasture the first time in the spring.

Farm was the shut-up, mousy smell of the house, the musty smell of packed quilts, the mattresses out in the sun on the first morning. It was the oil that had to be wiped off his gopher traps, and the first walk out along the pasture fence to the edge of the field with the traps over his shoulder. It was trouble with water, sometimes, when the well-hole beside the reservoir had caved in and they had to haul drinking water in barrels for two miles, and stories like the one his father told about the Picketts, down in Montana. The Picketts had no well, only a little creekbed that often dried up on them, and then they hoarded water, according to Pa, like nothing you ever saw. A pan of water would be used to boil eggs in the morning. Then the dishes would be washed in it. Then all the family would wash, one after the other. Then the water would be strained to get the grease and dirt out, and saved to put in the radiator of the Picketts' old car. Pa swore you could tell whether the Picketts had had cabbage or beans or sweetcorn for dinner just by smelling the boiling radiator of that old McLaughlin.

Farm ordinarily was the things he and Chet did together, the guns they whittled out of sticks, the long campaigns in the coulee and the patch of sweetcorn when it got high enough to make good cover. It was the Russian thistle they hoed out of garden and fireguard, and the swearing his father did when the thistle got a good start in the wheat field. It was long days of blazing sun, and violent rains, and once it was a cyclone that passed a mile south of them. That was when they were still living in the tent, before Pa got the house built, and Pa roped them all down in the section hole until he was sure the twister wasn't going to hit them.

In this summer of 1918, because Chet was staying in town to be delivery boy for Mr. Babcock in the confectionery store, the homestead was isolation and loneliness, though he never felt it or knew it for what it was. Only when his mother looked at his father and said they should never have let Chet take that job, it left Brucie too much alone. Then he felt vaguely disturbed and faintly abused, but he never did really believe he was lonely, because he loved the homestead, and the Sunday school hymns he sang to himself down in the flowered coulee meant to him very definite and secret and precious things, meant primroses and space and the wet slap of a rare east wind, and those tunes would mean those things to him all his life.

Still he was almost always alone, and that summer he somehow lost his identity as a name. There was no other boy to confuse him with; he wasn't Bruce, but "the boy," and because he was the only thing of his kind in all that summer world he needed no name, but only his own sense of triumphant identity. He knew the homestead in intimate and secret detail because there was so little variety in it that the small things took the senses. He knew the way the grass grew curling over the lip of a burnout, and how the prairie owls nested under those grassy lips. He knew how the robins tucked their nests back under the fringes of the prairie wool, and their skyblue eggs were always a wonder. He could tell, by the way the horses clustered in a corner of the pasture, when something was wrong, as when Dick got wound up in the lower strand of the fence and almost cut his leg off trying to break loose. He could tell instantly when a weasel was after the hens by the kind of clamor they made. Nothing else, for some reason, ever caused that fighting squawk from the mother hens. He could tell a badger's permanent burrow from the one he made in digging out a gopher. The yapping of coyotes on a moonlit night was lonely and beautiful to him, and the yard and chicken house and fireguard and coulee were as much a part of him as his own skin.

He lived in his own world in summer, and only when hail or wind or gophers or Russian thistle threatened the wheat on which he knew his father yearly gambled everything, was there much communication with the adult world whose interests were tied down to the bonanza farming and the crop. Wheat, he knew, was very high. The war did that. And he knew too that they were not well off, that every spring his father scraped together everything he had for seed and supplies and hoped for a good year so that he could clean up. He knew that they had less than most of the homesteaders around: they didn't have a barn, a cow (they had two in town, but it was a hard trip to bring them out), a seeder, a binder, a disc, a harrow. They didn't have much of anything, actually, except a team, a plow, and a stoneboat. Anything he didn't have tools for his father either borrowed tools to do, or hired done. But that frantic period of plowing and seeding came early, before his senses had adjusted themselves completely to the homestead, and later, in the period when they did practically nothing but sit and wait and hope that the weather would give them a crop, he moved in a tranced air of summer and loneliness and delight.

At the end of the first week in this summer he caught a weasel in one of his gopher traps, and brought it, still twisting and fighting in the trap, to the house. His father and mother came to the door; his mother made a face and shivered.

"Ugh!" she said. "Ugly, snaky thing!"

But his father showed more interest. "Got something special, uh?" he said. He came down and took the ringed chain from the boy's hand, held the weasel up. The weasel hissed in his face, trying to jump at him, and he straightened his arm to hold the swinging trap away.

"You've got to hand it to them," he said. "There isn't anything alive with more fight in it."

"Take it and kill it," Elsa said. "Don't just keep it in the trap torturing it."

Bruce was looking at his father. He ignored his mother's words because this was men's business. She didn't understand about weasels. "Maybe I could keep him till he turns into an ermine," he said.

"Why not?" his father said. "You could get three bucks for his pelt, these days. We ought to be able to make a cage that'd hold him."

"Oh, Bo," Elsa said. "Keep a weasel?"

"Give Boopus here something to do," Bo said. "You've been telling me we ought to get him a pet."

Bruce looked from one to the other, wondering when they had talked over getting him a pet. "We've got old Tom now," he said.

"Old Tom," his father said, "is so full of mice his mind is all furry."

"We ought to get a dog," Elsa said. "Not a vicious thing like a weasel."

"Well, we've got the weasel, and we don't know any place to get a dog." Bo looked down at the boy and grinned. He swung the weasel gently back and forth, and it arched its long yellow body against the trap and lunged. "Let's go make a cage for this tough guy," Bo said.

"Can I have a dog too?"

"Maybe. If I can find one."

"Holy catartin," Bruce said. "A cat, a dog, and a weasel. Maybe I can catch some more and start a weasel farm."

"I'd move out," his mother said. She waved them away. "Hurry up, if you're going to keep that bloodthirsty thing. Don't leave it in the trap with its broken leg."

They made a cage out of a beer-case, screened under the hinged top and with a board removed at the bottom, leaving an opening over which they tacked a strip of screen. They had trouble getting the weasel out of the trap, and finally Bo had to smother him in a piece of horse blanket and spring the jaws loose and throw blanket and all in the cage. For three days the weasel sulked in the corner and would eat nothing, but when the boy said he didn't think it was going to live his father laughed at him. "You can't kill a weasel just by breaking his leg. Put a mouse in there and see what happens."

Next day the boy rescued a half-dead mouse that Tom was satedly toying with under the bed, and dropped it in the cage. Nothing happened, but when he came back later the mouse was dead, with a hole back of his ear and his body limp and apparently boneless. The boy fished the carcass out with a bent wire, and from then on there was no question of the weasel's dying. The problem was to find enough mice, but after a few days he tried a gopher, and then it was all right.

There had been a wind during the night, and all the loneliness of the world had swept up out of the southwest. The boy had heard it wailing through the screens of the sleeping porch where he lay, and he had heard the wash tub bang loose from the outside wall and roll on down the coulee, and the slam of the screen door, and his mother's padding feet as she rose to fasten things down. Through one half-open eye he had peered up from his pillow to see the moon skimming windily in a luminous sky. In his mind's eye he had seen the prairie outside with its woolly grass and cactus white under the moon, and the wind, whining across that endless oceanic land, sang in the screens, and sang him back to sleep.

Now, after breakfast, when he set out through the pasture on the round of his traps, there was no more wind, but the air smelled somehow recently swept and dusted, as the house in town smelled after his mother's cleaning. The sun was gently warm on the bony shoulder blades of the boy, and he whistled, and whistling turned to see if the Bearpaws were in sight to the south. There they were, a tenuous outline of white just breaking over the bulge of the world; the Mountains of the Moon, the place of running streams and timber and cool heights that he had never seen—only dreamed of on days when the baked gumbo of the yard cracked in the heat and the sun brought cedar smells from fenceposts long since split and dry and odorless, when he lay dreaming on the bed with a Sears Roebuck or a T. Eaton catalogue before him, picking out the presents he would buy for his mother and his father and Chet and his friends next Christmas, or the Christmas after that. On those days he looked often and long at the snowy mountains to the south, while dreams rose in him like heat waves, blurring the reality of the unfinished shack and the bald prairie of his home.

The Bearpaws were there now, and he watched them a moment, walking, his feet automatically dodging cactus clumps, before he turned his attention to the scattered stakes that marked his traps. He ran the line at a half-trot, whistling.

At the first stake the chain was stretched tightly down the hole. The pull on its lower end had dug a little channel in the soft earth of the mound. Gently, so as not to break the gopher's leg off, the boy eased the trap out of the burrow, held the chain in his left hand, and loosened the stake with his right. The gopher tugged against the trap, but it made no noise. There were only two places where they made a noise: at a distance, when they whistled a warning, and in the weasel's cage. Otherwise they kept still.

For a moment he debated whether to keep this one alive for the weasel or to wait so he wouldn't have to carry a live one all the way around. Deciding to wait, he held the chain out, measured the rodent, and swung. The knobbed end of the stake crushed the skull, and the eyes popped out of the head, round and blue. A trickle of blood started from nose and ears. The feet kicked.

Releasing the gopher, the boy lifted it by the tail and snapped its tail fur off with a smart flip. Then he stowed the trophy carefully in the breast pocket of his overalls. For the last two years he had won the grand prize offered by the province to the school child who destroyed the most gophers. On the mantel in town were two silver loving cups, and in the cigar box under his bed in the farmhouse were already seven hundred forty tails, the catch of three weeks. In one way, he resented his father's distributing poison along the wheat field, because poisoned gophers generally got down their holes to die, and he didn't get the tails. So he spent most of his time trapping and snaring in the pasture, where poison could not be spread because of the horses.

Picking up trap and stake, Bruce kicked the dead gopher down its burrow and scooped dirt over it with his toe. They stunk up the pasture if they weren't buried, and the bugs got into them. Frequently he had stood to windward of a dead and swollen gopher, watching the body shift and move with the movements of the beetles and crawling things in it. If such an infested corpse were turned over, the carrion beetles would roar out, great, hard-shelled, orange-colored, scavenging things that made his blood curdle at the thought of their touching him, and after they were gone and he looked again he would see the little black ones, undisturbed, seething through the rotten flesh. So he always buried his dead, now.

Through the gardens of red and yellow cactus blooms he went whistling, half-trotting, setting his traps afresh whenever a gopher shot upright, whistled, and ducked down its hole. All but two of the first seventeen traps held gophers, and he came to the eighteenth confidently, expecting to take this one alive. But this gopher had gone in head first, and the boy put back in his pocket the salt sack he had brought along for a game bag. He would have to trap or snare one down by the dam.

On the way back he stopped with bent head while he counted the morning's catch of tails, mentally adding this lot to the seven hundred forty he already had, trying to remember how many he and Chet had had this time last year. As he finished his mathematics his whistle broke out again, and he galloped down through the pasture, running for very abundance of life, until he came to the chicken house just within the fireguard.

Under the eaves of the chicken house, so close that the hens were constantly pecking up to its door and then almost losing their wits with fright, was the weasel's cage. The boy lifted the hinged top and looked down through the screen.

"Hello," he said. "Hungry?"

The weasel crouched, its snaky body humped, its head thrust forward and its malevolent eyes steady and glittering.

"Tough, ain't you?" the boy said. "Just you wait, you bloodsucking old stinker, you. Won't I skin you quick, hah?"

There was no dislike or emotion in his tone. He took the weasel's malignant ferocity with the same indifference he displayed in his gopher killing. Weasels, if you kept them long enough, were valuable. He would catch some more and have an ermine farm. He was the best gopher trapper in Saskatchewan. Why not weasels? Once he and Chet had even caught a badger, though they hadn't been able to take him alive because he was caught by only three hind toes, and lunged so savagely that they had to stand off and stone him to death in the trap. But weasels you could catch alive, and Pa said you couldn't hurt a weasel short of killing him outright. This one, though virtually three-legged, was as lively and vicious as ever.

Every morning now he had a live gopher for breakfast, in spite of Elsa's protests that it was cruel. She had argued and protested, but he had talked her down. When she said that the gopher didn't have a chance in the weasel's cage, he retorted that it didn't have a chance when the weasel came down the hole after it, either. When she said that the real job he should devote himself to was destroying all the weasels, he replied that then the gophers would get so thick they would eat the wheat down to stubble. Finally she had given up, and the weasel continued to have his warm meals.

For some time the boy stood watching his captive. Then he turned and went into the house, where he opened the oatbox in the kitchen and took out a chunk of dried beef. From this he cut a thick slice with the butcher knife, and went munching into the sleeping porch where his mother was making the beds.

"Where's that little double-naught?" he said.

"That what?"

"That little wee trap I use for catching live ones for Lucifer."

"Hanging out by the laundry bench, I think. Are you going trapping again now?"

"Lucifer hasn't been fed yet."

"How about your reading?"

"I'ne take the book along and read while I wait. I'm just going down by the dam."

"I *can,* not I'ne, son."

"I can," the boy said. "I am most delighted to comply with your request of the twenty-third inst." He grinned at his mother. He could always floor her with a quotation out of a letter or the Sears Roebuck catalogue.

With the trap swinging in his hand, and under his arm the book —*Narrative and Lyric Poems,* edited by Somebody-or-Other—which his mother kept him reading all summer so that "next year he could be at the head of his class again," the boy walked out into the growing heat.

From the northwest the coulee angled down through the pasture, a shallow swale dammed just above the house to catch the spring run-off of snow water. Below the dam, watered by the slow seepage from above, the coulee bottom was a parterre of flowers, buttercups in broad sheets, wild sweet pea, and stinkweed. On the slopes were evening primroses pale pink and white and delicately fragrant, and on the flats above the yellow and red burgeoning of the cactus.

Just under the slope of the coulee a female gopher and three half-grown pups basked on their warm mound. The boy chased them squeaking down the hole and set the trap carefully, embedding it partially in the earth. Then he retired back up on the level, where he lay full length on his stomach, opened the book, shifted so that the glare of the sun across the pages was blocked by the shadow of his head and shoulders, and began to read.

From time to time he looked up from the book to roll on his side and stare out across the coulee, across the barren plains pimpled with gopher mounds and bitten with fire and haired with dusty, woolly grass. Apparently as flat as a table, the land sloped imperceptibly to the south, so that nothing interfered with his view of the ghostly mountains, looking higher now as the heat increased. Between his eyes and that smoky outline sixty miles away the heat waves rose writhing like fine wavy hair. He knew that in an hour Pankhurst's farm would lift above the swelling knoll to the west. Many times he had seen that phenomenon, had seen Jason Pankhurst watering the horses or working in the yard when he knew that the whole farm was out of sight. It was heat waves that did it, his father said.

The gophers below had been thoroughly scared, and for a long time nothing happened. Idly the boy read through his poetry lesson, dreamfully conscious of the hard ground under him, feeling the gouge of a rock under his stomach without making any effort to remove it. The sun was a hot caress between his shoulder blades, and on the bare flesh where his overalls pulled above his sneakers it bit like a burning glass. Still he was comfortable, supremely relaxed and peaceful, lulled into a half trance by the heat and the steamy flower smells and the mist of yellow from the buttercup coulee below him.

And beyond the coulee was the dim profile of the Bearpaws, the Mountains of the Moon.

The boy's eyes, pulled out of focus by his tranced state, fixed on the page before him. Here was a poem he knew . . . but it wasn't a poem, it was a song. His mother sang it often, working at the sewing machine in winter.

It struck him as odd that a poem should also be a song, and because he found it hard to read without bringing in the tune, he lay quietly in the full glare of the sun, singing the page softly to himself. As he sang the trance grew on him again, he lost himself entirely. The bright hard dividing lines between senses blurred, and buttercups, smell of primrose, feel of hard gravel under body and elbows, sight of the ghosts of mountains haunting the southern horizon, were one intensely-felt experience focussed by the song the book had evoked.

And the song was the loveliest thing he had ever heard. He felt the words, tasted them, breathed upon them with all the ardor of his captivated senses.

The splendor falls on castle walls
And snowy summits old in story . . .

The current of his imagination flowed southward over the shoulder of the world to the ghostly outline of the Mountains of the Moon, haunting the heat-distorted horizon.

Oh hark, oh hear, how thin and clear,
And thinner, clearer, farther going,
Oh sweet and far, from cliff and scar . . .

In the enchanted forests of his mind the horns of elfland blew, and his breath was held in the cadence of their dying. The weight of the sun had been lifted from his back. The empty prairie of his home was castled and pillared with the magnificence of his imagining, and the sound of horns died thinly in the direction of the Mountains of the Moon.

From the coulee below came the sudden metallic clash of the trap, and an explosion of frantic squeals smothered almost instantly in the burrow. The boy leaped up, thrusting the book into the wide pocket of his overalls, and ran to the mound. The chain, stretched down the hole, jerked convulsively, and when he took hold of it he felt the life on the other end trying to escape. Tugging gently, he forced loose the digging claws and hauled the squirming gopher from the hole.

On the way up to the chicken house the dangling gopher with a tremendous muscular effort convulsed itself upward from the broken and imprisoned leg, and bit with a rasp of teeth on the iron. Its eyes, the boy noticed impersonally, were shiny black, like the head of a hatpin. He thought it odd that when they popped out of the head after a blow they were blue.

At the cage he lifted the cover and peered down through the screen. The weasel, scenting blood, backed against the far wall of the box, yellow body tense as a spring, teeth showing in a tiny soundless snarl.

Undoing the wire door with his left hand, the boy held the trap over the hole. Then he bore down with all his strength on the spring, releasing the gopher, which dropped on the straw and scurried into the corner opposite its enemy.

The weasel's three good feet gathered under it and it circled, very slowly, along the wall, its lips still lifted to expose the soundless snarl. The abject gopher crowded against the boards, turned once and tried to scramble up the side, fell back on its broken leg, and whirled like lightning to face its executioner again. The weasel moved carefully, circling, its cold eyes hypnotically steady.

Then the gopher screamed, a wild, agonized, despairing squeal that made the boy swallow and wet his lips. Another scream, wilder than the first, and before the sound had ended the weasel struck. There was a fierce flurry in the straw before the killer got its hold just back of the gopher's right ear, and then there was only the weasel looking at him over the dead and quivering body. In a few minutes, the boy knew, the gopher's carcass would be as limp as an empty skin, with all its blood sucked out and a hole as big as the ends of his two thumbs where the weasel had dined.

Still he remained staring through the screen top of the cage, face rapt and body completely lost. After a few minutes he went into the sleeping porch, stretched out on the bed, opened the Sears Roebuck catalogue, and dived so deeply into its fascinating pictures and legends that his mother had to shake him to make him hear her call to lunch.

2

Things greened beautifully that June. Rains came up out of the southeast, piling up solidly, moving toward them as slowly and surely as the sun moved, and it was fun to watch them come, the three of them standing in the doorway. When they saw the land east of them darken under the rain Bo would say, "Well, doesn't look as if it's going to miss us," and they would jump to shut windows and bring things in from yard or clothesline. Then they could stand quietly in the door and watch the good rain come, the front of it like a wall and the wind ahead of it stirring up dust, until it reached them and drenched the bare packed earth of the yard, and the ground smoked under its feet, and darkened, and ran with little streams, and they heard the swish of the rain on roof and ground and in the air.

They always watched it a good while, because rain was life in that country. When it didn't stop after twenty minutes or a half hour Bo would say with satisfaction, "She's a good soaker. That'll get down to the roots. Not so heavy it'll all run off, either." Then they would drift away from the door, because it was sure to be a good rain and there was another kind of satisfaction to be gained from little putter jobs while the rain outside made a crop for you. Elsa would carry her plants outside, the wandering Jew and the foliage plants and the geraniums stalky like miniature trees, and set them in the rain.

During that whole month there was much rain, and the boy's father whistled and hummed and sang. The boy lay in bed many mornings and heard him singing while he fried the bacon for breakfast. He always fried the bacon; he swore no woman knew how to do anything but burn it. And these days he always sang, fool songs he had learned somewhere back in the remote and unvisualizable past when he had worked on the railroad or played ball or cut timber in Wisconsin.

Oh I was a bouncing baby boy,
The neighbors did allow;
The girls they hugged and kissed me then,
Why don't they do it now?

He had a deep, big-chested voice, and he sang softly at first, rattling the pans, or whistled between his teeth with concentrated pauses between sounds, so that from the bed you knew he was slicing bacon off the slab. Then a match would scrape on the tin front of the stove, and he would be singing again,

Monkey married the baboon's sister,
Smacked his lips and then he kissed her.
Kissed so hard he raised a blister . . .

You lay in bed and waited, feeling fine because it had rained yesterday but today was fair, a good growing day, and you could almost feel how the wheat would be pushing up through the warm and steaming earth. And in the other room your father sang in great good humor,

She's thin as a broomstick, she carried no meat.
She never was known to put soap on her cheek.
Her hair is like rope and the color of brass—
But Oh, how I love her, this dear little lass!
Dear Evelina, Sweet Evelina . . .

After a minute or two he would poke his head into the porch and frown blackly, turn his head and frown even more blackly at the other bed where your mother lay stretching and smiling. "I plow deep while sluggards sleep!" he would say sepulchrally, and vanish. Then the final act, the great beating on the dishpan with a pewter spoon, and his singsong, hog-calling voice, "Come and get it, you potlickers, or I'll throw it away!"

It was fun to be alive and awake, and wait for your father to go through his whole elaborate ritual. It was fun to get up and souse in the washbasin outside the door, and throw the soapy water on the packed earth, and come in and eat, while Pa joked at you, saying he thought sure you were dead, he had been in there five times, pinching and slapping like a Pullman porter, but no sign of life. "You sure do sleep heavy," he would say. "It's a wonder you don't break down the bed. I better put some extra slats in there."

You joked back at him, and after breakfast you had a sparring match that left your ears all red and tingling, and then Pa went out to harrow to keep the earth broken up and the moisture in, and you went around your traps.

All through June there were good mornings, but the best of them all was the day Bo went down to Cree for the mail, and when he came back there was a dog sitting in the car seat beside him, a big-footed, lappy-tongued, frolicsome pup with one brown and one white eye and a heavy golden coat. The boy played with him for an hour, rolling him over and pulling his clumsy feet out from under him. Finally he lay down on the ground and the pup attacked his ears, sticking a red tongue into them, diving for openings, snuffling and snorting and romping. When the boy sat up, his mother and father were standing with their arms around one another, watching him. He went up very seriously and hugged them both in thanks for the pup.

"You'll have to teach him tricks," his father said. "A dog's no good unless you educate him. He gets the habit of minding you that way."

"How'll I do it?"

"Show you tonight." His father reached out and cuffed him on the ear and grinned. "Anything you can think of you'd like to do next week?"

The boy stared, wondering. "What?"

"What? What?" his father said, mimicking him. "Can't you think of anything you'd like to do?"

"I'd like to drive the stoneboat next time you use it."

"I don't think you know what fun is," his father said. "Don't you know what date it is?"

"Sure. It's June 27. No, June 28."

"Sure. And what comes after the week of June 28?"

The boy wondered, looking at first one, then another. They were both laughing at him. Then it hit him. "Fourth of July!" he said.

"Okay," his father said. He cuffed at him again, but missed. "Maybe we'll go into Chinook for the Fourth. Fireworks, ballgame, parade, pink lemonade sold in the shade by an old maid."

"Whee!" the boy said. He stooped and wrestled the pup, and afterward, when he lay panting on the ground, resting, and the pup gave up lapping his ears and lay down too, he thought that he had the swellest Ma and Pa there was.

That night his father showed him how to get the pup in a corner and make him sit up, bracing his back against the wall. For long, patient hours in the next few days he braced the pup there and repeated, "Sit up! Sit up! Sit up!" while he shoved back the slipping hind feet, straightened the limp spine, lifted the dropping front paws. You had to say the command a lot, his father said, and you had to reward him when he did it right. And you had to do only one trick at a time. After he learned to sit up you could teach him to jump over a stick, roll over, speak, shake hands, and play dead. The word for playing dead was "charge!" He would teach him, Bruce thought, to do that next, so they could play war. It would be better than having Chet there, because Chet never would play dead. He always argued and said he shot you first.

When he wasn't training the pup he was dreaming of Chinook and the ballgame and parade and fireworks, sky rockets, Roman candles, pinwheels. He was curious about pinwheels, because he remembered a passage in *Peck's Bad Boy and His Pa* where a pinwheel took after Pa and cornered him up on the sofa. But he was curious about all fireworks; he had never seen any except firecrackers. And the finest thing of all to imagine was the mountains, because Pa and Ma decided that since they were that close, they might as well drive up to the mountains too, and take the whole day.

His father teased him. Probably, he said, it would rain pitchforks on the Fourth. But his mother said Oh Pa, don't talk like that.

Then on the afternoon of the third they all stood in the yard and watched the southeast. Thunderheads were piling up there, livid white in front and black and ominous behind. Thunder rumbled like a wagon over a bridge.

"It'll pass over," Elsa said, and patted Bruce on the back. "It just wouldn't be fair if it rained now and spoiled our holiday."

The boy looked up and saw his father's dubious expression. "Do you think it'll blow over, Pa? Hardly any have blown over yet."

"Bound to blow over," his father said. "Law of averages. They can't all make a rain."

But the boy remembered three rains from that same quarter that same month that had gone on for twenty-four hours. He stayed in the yard watching, hoping against hope until the wall of dark was almost to the fireguard and the advance wind was stirring dust in the yard, stayed until the first large drops fell and puffed heavily in the dust, stayed until his mother pulled him inside with dark speckles all over his shirt. "Don't you worry," she said. "It'll be clear tomorrow. It has to be."

That night he stayed up until nine, waiting to see if the steady downpour would stop, hating the whisper of the rain outside and the gravelly patter on the roof. The tomcat awoke and stretched on the couch, jumped off with a sudden soft thud and went prowling into the sleeping porch, but the boy sat up. His parents were reading, not saying much. Once or twice he caught them looking at him, and always the house whispered with the steady, windy sound of the rain. This was no thunder shower. This was a drencher, and it could go on for two days, this time of year. His father had said so, with satisfaction, of other rains just like it.

When his mother finally sent him off to bed he went unwillingly, undressed slowly to see if the rain wouldn't stop before he got his shoes off, his stockings off, his overalls off. But when he was in his nightshirt it still rained steadily and insistently, and he turned into his pillow wanting to cry. A big tear came out and he felt it hanging on the side of his nose. He lay very still for fear it would fall off. He strangled the sob that jumped in his throat because that would make the drop fall, and while he was balancing the drop he fell asleep.

After the night's rain the yard was spongy and soft under the boy's bare feet. He stood at the edge of the packed dooryard in the flat thrust of sunrise looking at the ground washed clean and smooth and trackless, feeling the cool mud under his toes. Experimentally he lifted his right foot and put it down in a new place, pressed, picked it up again to look at the neat imprint of straight edge and curving instep and the five round dots of toes. The air was so fresh that he sniffed as he would have sniffed the smell of cinnamon.

Lifting his head, he saw how the prairie beyond the fireguard looked darker than in dry times, healthier with green-brown tints, smaller and more intimate somehow than it did when the heat waves crawled over scorched grass and carried the horizons backward into dim and unseeable distances. And standing in the yard above his one clean footprint, feeling his own verticality in all that spread of horizontal land, he sensed that as the prairie shrank he grew. He was immense. A little jump would crack his head on the sky; a stride would take him to any horizon.

His eyes turned into the low south sky, cloudless, almost colorless in the strong light. Just above the brown line of the horizon, faint as a watermark on pale blue paper, was the tracery of the mountains, tenuous and far-off, but today accessible for the first time. His mind had played among those ghostly summits for uncountable lost hours: today, in a few strides, they were his. And more. Under the shadow of those peaks, those Bearpaws that he and his mother always called the Mountains of the Moon, was Chinook, the band, the lemonade stands, the parade, the ballgame, the fireworks.

The pup lay watching, belly down on the damp ground. In a gleeful spasm the boy stooped to flap the dog's ears, then bent and spun in a wild wardance while the pup barked. And when his father came to the door in his undershirt, yawning, running a hand up the back of his head and through his hair, peering out from gummed eyes to see how the weather looked, the boy's voice was one deep breathing relief from yesterday's rainy fear.

"It's clear as a bell," he said.

His father yawned again, clopped his jaws, rubbed his eyes, mumbled something from a mouth furry with sleep. He stood on the step scratching himself comfortably, looking down at boy and dog.

"Going to be hot," he said slyly. "Might be too hot to drive."

"Aw, Pa!"

"Going to be a scorcher. Melt you right down to axle grease riding in that car."

The boy regarded him doubtfully, saw the lurking sly droop of his mouth. "Aw, we are too going!"

At his father's laugh he burst from his immobility like a sprinter starting, raced one complete circle around the house with the dog after him. When he flew around past his father again his voice trailed out behind him at the corner. "Gonna feed the hens," he said. His father looked after him, scratched his knee, laughed suddenly, and went back indoors.

Through chores and breakfast the boy moved with the dream of a day's rapture in his eyes, but that did not keep him from swift and agile helpfulness. He didn't even wait for commands. He scrubbed himself twice, slicked down his hair, hunted up clean clothes, wiped the mud from his shoes and put them on. While his mother packed the shoebox of lunch he stood at her elbow proffering aid. He flew to stow things in the topless old Ford. He got a rag and polished the brass radiator. Once or twice, jumping around to help, he looked up to see his parents looking at each other with the knowing, smiling expression in the eyes that said they were calling each other's attention to him.

"Just like a racehorse," his father said, and the boy felt foolish, swaggered, twisted his mouth down, said "Aw!" But in a moment he was hustling them again. They ought to get going, with fifty miles to drive. Long before they were ready he was standing beside the Ford, licked and immaculate and so excited that his feet jumped him up and down without his own volition or knowledge.

It was eight o'clock before his father came out, lifted off the front seat, poked the flat stick down into the gas tank, and pulled it out dripping. "Pretty near full," he said. "If we're going to the mountains too we better take a can along, though. Fill that two-gallon one with the spout."

The boy ran, dug the can out of the shed, filled it at the spigot of the drum that stood on a plank support to the north of the house. When he came back, his left arm stuck straight out and the can knocking against his leg, his mother was settling herself into the back seat among parcels and waterbags.

"Goodness," she said. "This is the first time I've been the first ready since I don't know when. I should think you'd have done all this last night."

"Plenty time." The father stood looking down at the boy. "All right, racehorse. You want to go to this shindig you better hop in."

The boy was up in the front seat like a squirrel. His father walked around to the front of the car. "Okay," he said. "Look sharp, now. When she kicks over, switch her to magneto and pull the spark down."

The boy said nothing. He looked upon the car with respect and a little awe. They didn't use it much, and starting it was a ritual like a firedrill. The father unscrewed the four-eared brass plug, looked down into the radiator, screwed the cap back on, and bent to take hold of the crank. "Watch it, now," he said.

The boy felt the gentle heave of the springs, up and down, as his father wound the crank. He heard the gentle hiss in the bowels of the engine as the choke wire was pulled out, and his nose filled with the strong, volatile odor of gasoline. Over the slope of the radiator his father's brown strained face looked up. "Is she turned on all right?"

"Yup. She's on battery."

"Must have flooded her. Have to let her rest a minute."

They waited, and then after a few minutes the wavelike heaving of the springs again, the rise and fall of the blue shirt and bent head over the radiator, the sighing swish of the choke, a stronger smell of gasoline. The motor had not even coughed.

The two voices came simultaneously from the car. "What's the matter with it?"

His brow puckered in an intent scowl, Bo stood back blowing mighty breaths. "Son of a gun," he said. Coming round, he pulled at the switch, adjusted the spark and gas levers. A fine mist of sweat made his face shine like dark oiled leather.

"There isn't anything really wrong, is there?" Elsa said, and her voice wavered uncertainly on the edge of fear.

"I don't see how there could be," Bo said. "She's always started right off, and she was running all right when I drove her in here."

The boy looked at his mother sitting erect and stiff among the things on the seat. She was all dressed up, a flowered dress, a hat with hard green varnished grapes on it pinned to her red hair. For a moment she sat, stiff and nervous. "What will you have to do?" she said.

"I don't know. Look at the motor."

"Well, I guess I'll get out of the sun while you do it," she said, and fumbled her way out of the clutter.

The boy felt her exodus like a surrender, a betrayal. If they didn't hurry up they'd miss the parade. In one motion he bounced out of the car. "Gee whiz!" he said. "Let's do something. We got to get started."

"Keep your shirt on," his father grunted. Lifting the hood, he bent his head inside. His hand went out to test wires, wiggle spark-plug connections, make tentative pulls at the choke. The weakly-hinged hood slipped and came down across his wrist, and he swore. "Get me the pliers," he said.

For ten minutes he probed and monkeyed. "Might be the plugs," he said at last. "She doesn't seem to be getting any fire through her."

Elsa, sitting on a box in the shade, smoothed her flowered dress nervously. "Will it take long?"

"Half hour."

"Any day but this!" she said. "I don't see why you didn't make sure last night."

Bo breathed through his nose and bent into the engine again. "It was raining last night," he said.

One by one the plugs came out, were squinted at, scraped, the gap tested with a thin dime. The boy stood on one foot, then the other, time pouring like a flood of uncatchable silver dollars through his hands. He kept looking at the sun, estimating how much time there was left. If they got started right away they might still make it for the parade, but it would be close. Maybe they'd drive right up the street while the parade was on, and be part of it . . .

"Is she ready?" he said.

"Pretty quick."

He wandered over by his mother, and she reached out to put an arm around him. "Well, anyway we can get there for the band and the ballgame and the fireworks," he said. "If she doesn't start till noon we can make it for those."

She said, "Pa'll get it going in a minute. We won't miss anything, hardly."

"You ever seen skyrockets, Ma?"

"Once."

"Are they fun?"

"Wonderful," she said. "Just like a million stars all colors all exploding at once."

His feet took him back to his father, who straightened up with a belligerent grunt. "Now!" he said. "If the sucker doesn't start now . . ."

And once more the heaving of the springs, the groaning of the turning engine, the hiss of the choke. He tried short, sharp half-turns, as if to catch the motor off guard. Then he went back to the stubborn, laboring spin. The back of his shirt was stained darkly, the curving dikes of muscles along the spine's hollow showing cleanly where the cloth stuck. Over and over, heaving, stubborn at first, then furious, till he staggered back panting.

"God damn!" he said. "What you suppose is the matter with the thing?"

"She didn't even cough once," the boy said, and staring up at his father's face full of angry bafflement he felt the cold fear touch him. What if it wouldn't start at all? What if, all ready to go, they had to unload the Ford and not even get out of the yard? His mother came over and they stood close together looking at the car and avoiding each other's eyes.

"Maybe something got wet last night," she said.

"Well, it's had plenty of time to dry out," Bo said.

"Isn't there something else you can try?"

"We can jack up the hind wheel, I guess. But there's no damn reason we should have to."

"Well, if you have to, you'll have to," she said briskly. "After planning it for a week we can't just get stuck like this. Can we, son?"

Bruce's answer was mechanical, his eyes steady on his father. "Sure not," he said.

His father opened his mouth to say something, looked hard at the boy, and shut his lips again. Without a word he pulled out the seat and got the jack.

The sun climbed steadily while they jacked up one hind wheel and blocked the car carefully so it wouldn't run over anybody if it started. The boy let off the brake and put it in high, and when they were ready he sat in the seat so full of hope and fear that his whole body was one tight concentration. His father stooped, his cheek pressed against the radiator as a milker's cheek touches the flank of a cow. His shoulder dropped, jerked up. Nothing. Another jerk. Nothing. Then he was rolling in a furious spasm of energy, the wet dark back of his shirt rising and falling. Inside the motor there was only the futile swish of the choke and the half-sound, half-feel of cavernous motion as the crankshaft turned over. The Ford bounced on its spring as if its front wheels were coming off the ground on every upstroke. Then it stopped, and the father was hanging on the radiator, breathless, dripping wet, swearing: "Son of a dirty, lousy, stinking, corrupted . . . !"

The boy stared from his father's angry wet face to his mother's, pinched with worry. The pup lay down in the shade and put its head on its paws. "Gee whiz!" the boy said. "Gee whiz!" He looked at the sun, and the morning was half gone.

Jerking with anger, his father threw the crank halfway across the yard and took a step or two toward the house. "The hell with the damn thing!" he said.

"Bo, you can't!"

He stopped, glared at her, took an oblique look at Bruce, bared his teeth in an irresolute, silent swearword. "But God, if it won't go!"

"Maybe if you hitched the horses to it," she said.

His laugh was short and choppy. "That'd be fine!" he said. "Why don't we just hitch the team to this damned old boat and pull it into Chinook?"

"But we've got to get it started. Why wouldn't it be all right to let the team pull it around? You push it on a hill sometimes and it starts."

He looked at the boy again, jerked his eyes away exasperatedly, as though he held his son somehow accountable. The boy stared, mournful, defeated, ready to cry, and his father's head swung back unwillingly. Then abruptly he winked, mopped his head and neck, and grinned. "Think you want to go, uh?"

The boy nodded. "All right," his father said crisply. "Fly up in the pasture and get the team. Hustle!"

On the high lope the boy was off up the coulee bank. Under the lip of the swale, a quarter of a mile west, the bay backs of the horses and the black dot of the cold showed. Usually he ran circumspectly across that pasture, because of the cactus, but now he flew. With shoes it was all right, and even without shoes he would have run. Across burnouts, over stretches so undermined with gopher holes that sometimes he broke through to the ankle, skimming over patches of cactus, soaring over a badger hole, plunging into the coulee and up the other side, he ran as if bears were after him. The black colt, spotting him, lifted his tail and took off in a spectacular stiff-legged sprint, but the bays merely lifted their heads and watched. He slowed, came up walking, laid a hand on the mare's neck and untied the looped halter rope. She stood for him while he scrambled and kicked himself up, and then they were off, the mare in an easy lope, the gelding trotting after, the colt stopping his wild showoff career and wobbling hastily and ignominiously after his departing mother.

They pulled up before the Ford, and the boy slid off to throw the halter rope to his father. "Shall I get the harness?" he said, and before anyone could answer he was off running, to come back dragging one heavy harness with the tugs trailing. He dropped it, turned to run again, his breath laboring in his lungs. "I'll get the other'n," he said.

With a short, almost incredulous laugh Bo looked once at Elsa and threw the harness over the mare. When the second one came he laid it on the gelding, pushed against the heavy shoulder to get the horse into place. The gelding resisted, pranced a little, got a curse and a crack across the nose, jerked back and trembled and lifted his feet nervously, and set one shod hoof on his owner's instep. Bo, unstrung by the heat and the hurry and the labor and the exasperation of a morning when nothing went right, kicked the gelding in the belly. "Get in there, you damned big blundering ox! Back, back up. Whoa now, whoa!"

With a heavy rope for a towline and the disengaged trees of the wagon for a rig he hitched the now-skittish team to the car. Without a word he stooped and lifted the boy to the mare's back. "All right," he said, and his face relaxed in a quick grin. "This is where we start her. Ride them around in a circle, not too fast."

Then he climbed into the Ford, turned the switch to magneto, fussed with the levers. "Let 'er go!" he said.

The boy kicked the mare ahead, twisting as he rode to watch the

Ford heave forward off the jack as a tired, heavy man heaves to his feet, and begin rolling after him over the uneven ground, jerking and kicking and growling when his father put it in gear. The horses settled as the added weight came on the line, flattened into their collars, swung in a circle, bumped each other, skittered. The mare reared, and the boy shut his eyes and clung. When he came down, her leg was entangled in the tug and his father was climbing cursing out of the car to straighten her out. His father was mad again and yelled at him. "Keep 'em apart! There isn't any tongue. You got to keep Dick over on his own side."

Now again the start, the flattening into the collars, the snapping tight of the tugs. This time it went smoothly, the Ford galloped after the team in lumbering, plunging jerks. The mare's eyes rolled white, and she broke into a trot, pulling the gelding after her. Desperately the boy clung to the knotted and shortened reins, his ears alert for the grumble of the Ford starting behind him. The pup ran beside the team yapping, crazy with excitement.

They made three complete circles of the back yard between house and chicken coop before the boy looked back again. "Won't she start?" he yelled. He saw his father rigid behind the wheel, heard his ripping burst of swearwords, saw him bend and glare down into the mysterious inwards of the engine through the pulled-up floorboards. Guiding the car with one hand, he fumbled down below, one glaring eye just visible over the cowl.

"Shall I stop?" the boy shouted. Excitement and near-despair made his voice a tearful scream. But his father's wild arm waved him on. "Go on, go on! Gallop 'em! Pull the guts out of this thing!"

And the galloping—the furious, mud-flinging, rolling-eyed galloping around the circle already rutted like a road, the Ford, now in savagely-held low, growling and surging and plowing behind; the mad yapping of the dog, the erratic scared bursts of runaway from the colt, the boy's mother in sight briefly for a quarter of each circle, her hands to her mouth and her eyes sick, and behind him in the Ford his father in a strangling rage, yelling him on, his lips back over his teeth and his face purple.

Until finally they stopped, the horses blowing, the boy white and tearful and still, the father dangerous with unexpended wrath. The boy slipped off, his lip bitten between his teeth, not crying now but ready to at any moment, the corners of his eyes prickling with it, and his teeth locked on his misery. His father climbed over the side of the Ford and stood looking as if he wanted to tear it apart with his bare hands.

Shoulders sagging, tears trembling to fall, jaw aching with the need to cry, the boy started toward his mother. As he came near his father he looked up, their eyes met, and he saw his father's blank with impotent rage. Dull hopelessness swallowed him. Not any of it, his mind said. Not even any of it. No parade, no ballgame, no band, no fireworks. No lemonade or ice cream or paper horns or firecrackers. No close sight of the mountains that throughout four summers had called like a legend from his horizons. No trip, no adventure, none of it, nothing.

Everything he felt was in that one still look. In spite of him his lip trembled, and he choked on a sob, his eyes on his father's face, on the brows pulling down and the eyes narrowing.

"Well, don't blubber!" his father shouted at him. "Don't stand there looking at me as if I was to blame for your missed picnic!"

"I can't—help it," the boy said, and with terror he felt the grief swelling up, overwhelming him, driving his voice out of him in a wail. Through the blur of his crying he saw the convulsive tightening of his father's face, and then all the fury of a maddening morning concentrated itself in a swift backhand blow that knocked the boy staggering.

He bawled aloud, from pain, from surprise, from outrage, from pure desolation, and ran to bury his face in his mother's lap. From that muffled sanctuary he heard her angry voice. "No," she said. "Go on away somewhere till he gets over it."

She rocked him against her, but the voice she had for his father was bitter. "As if he wasn't hurt enough already!" she said.

He heard the heavy quick footsteps going away, and for a long time he lay crying into the voile flowers. When he had cried himself out, and had listened apathetically to his mother's soothing promises that they would go in the first chance they got, go to the mountains, have a picnic under some waterfall, maybe be able to find a ballgame going on in town, some Saturday—when he had listened and become quiet, wanting to believe it but not believing it at all, he went inside to take his good clothes and his shoes off and put on his old overalls again.

It was almost noon when he came out to stand in the front yard looking southward toward the impossible land where the Mountains of the Moon lifted above the plains, and where, in the town below the peaks, crowds would now be eating picnic lunches, drinking pop, getting ready to go out to the ball ground and watch heroes in real uniforms play ball. The band would be braying now from a bunting-wrapped stand, kids would be playing in a cool grove, tossing firecrackers . . .

In the still heat his eyes searched the horizon for the telltale watermark. There was nothing but waves of heat crawling and lifting like invisible flames; the horizon was a blurred and writhing flatness where earth and sky met in an indistinct band of haze. This morning a stride would have taken him there; now it was gone.

Looking down, he saw at his feet the clean footprint he had made in the early morning. Aimlessly he put his right foot down and pressed. The mud was drying, but in a low place he found a spot that would still take an imprint. Very carefully, as if he performed some ritual for his life, he went around, stepping and leaning, stepping and leaning, until he had a circle six feet in diameter of delicately exact footprints, straight edge and curving instep and the five round dots of toes.

3

His father's voice awakened him next morning. Stretching his back, arching against the mattress, he looked over at his parents' end of the porch. His mother was up too, though he could tell from the flatness of the light outside that it was still early. He lay on his back, letting complete wakefulness come on, watching a spider that dangled on a golden, shining thread from the rolled canvas of the blinds. The spider came down in tiny jerks, his legs wriggling, and then went up again in the beam of sun. From the other room his father's voice rose loud and cheerful:

Oh I'd give every man in the army a quarter
If they'd all take a shot at my mother-in-law.

The boy slid his legs out of bed and yanked the nightshirt over his ears. He didn't want his father's face poking around the door, saying, "I plow deep while sluggards sleep!" He didn't want to be joked with. Yesterday was too sore a spot in his mind. He had been avoiding his father ever since the morning before, and he was not yet ready to accept any joking or attempts to make up. Nobody had a right hitting a person for nothing, and you bet they weren't going to be friends. Let him whistle and sing out there, pretending that nothing was the matter. The whole awful morning yesterday was the matter, the missed Fourth of July was the matter, that crack on the ear was the matter.

In the other room, as he pulled on his overalls, the bacon was snapping in the pan, and he smelled its good morning smell. His father whistled, sang:

In the town of O'Geary lived Paddy O'Flanagan
Battered away till he hadn't a pound,
His father he died and he made him a man again,
Left him a farm of tin acres o' ground.

Bruce pulled the overall straps up and went into the main room. His father stopped singing and looked at him. "Hello, Cheerful," he said. "You look like you'd bit into a wormy apple."

The boy mumbled something and went out to wash at the bench. It wasn't any fun waking up today. You kept thinking about yesterday, and how much fun it had been waking up then, when you were going to do something special and fancy. Now there wasn't anything to do except the same old things: run the traps, put out some poison, read the Sears Roebuck catalogue.

At breakfast he was glum, and his father joked him. Even his mother smiled, as if she had forgotten already how much wrong had been done the day before. "You look as if you'd been sent for and couldn't come," she said. "Cheer up."

"I don't want to cheer up."

They just smiled at each other, and he hated them both.

After breakfast his father said, "You help your Ma with the dishes, now. See how useful you can make yourself around here."

Unwillingly, wanting to get out of the house and away from them, he got the towel and swabbed away. He was rubbing a glass when he heard the Ford sputter and race and roar and then calm down into a steady mutter. His mouth opened, and he looked up at his mother. Her eyes were crinkled up with smiling.

"It goes!" he said.

"Sure it goes." She pulled both his ears, rocking his head. "Know what we're going to do?"

"What?"

"We're going to the mountains. Not to Chinook—there wouldn't be anything doing there today. But to the mountains, for a picnic. Pa got the car going yesterday afternoon, when you were down in the field, so we decided then. If you want to, of course."

"Yay!" he said. "Shall I dress up?"

"Put on your shoes, you'd better. We might climb a mountain."

The boy was out into the porch in three steps. With one shoe on and the other in his hand he hopped to the door. "When?" he said.

"Soon as you can get ready."

He was trying to run and tie his shoelaces at the same time as he went out of the house. There in the Ford, smoking his pipe, with one leg over the door and his weight on the back of his neck, his father sat. "What detained you?" he said. "I've been waiting a half hour. You must not want to go very bad."

"Aw!" the boy said. He looked inside the car. There was the lunch all packed, the fat wet canvas waterbag, even Spot with his tongue out and his ears up. Looking at his father, all his sullenness gone now, the boy said, "When did you get all this ready?"

His father grinned. "While you slept like a sluggard we worked like a buggard," he said. Then Bruce knew that everything was perfect, nothing could go wrong. When his father started rhyming things he was in his very best mood, and not even flat tires and breakdowns could make him do more than puff and playact.

He clambered into the front seat and felt the motor shaking under the floorboards. "Hey, Ma!" he yelled. "Hurry up! We're all ready to go!"

Their own road was a barely-marked trail that wiggled out across the burnouts along the east side of the wheat field. At the line it ran into another coming down from the homesteads to the east, and at Cree, a mile inside the Montana boundary, they hit the straight section-line road to Chinook. On that road they passed a trotting team pulling an empty wagon, and the boy waved and yelled, feeling superior, feeling as if he were charioted upon pure speed and all the rest of the world were earth-footed.

"Let's see how fast this old boat will go," his father said. He nursed it down through a coulee and onto the flat. His finger pulled the gas lever down, and the motor roared. Looking back with the wind-stung tears in his eyes, the boy saw his mother hanging to her hat, and the artificial grapes bouncing. The Ford leaped and bucked, the picnic box tipped over, the dog leaned out and the wind blew his eyes shut and his ears straight back. Turning around, the boy saw the blue sparks jumping from the magneto box and heard his father wahoo. He hung onto the side and leaned out to let the wind tear at him, tried to count the fenceposts going by, but they were ahead of him before he got to ten.

The road roughened, and they slowed down. "Good land," his mother said from the back seat. "We want to get to the Bearpaws, not wind up in a ditch."

"How fast were we going, Pa?"

"Forty or so. If we'd been going any faster you'd have hollered 'nough, I guess. You were looking pretty peaked."

"I was not."

"Looked pretty scared to me. I bet Ma was hopping around back there like corn in a popper. How'd you like it, Ma?"

"I liked it all right," she said comfortably. "But don't do it again."

They passed a farm, and the boy waved at three open-mouthed kids in the yard. It was pretty good to be going somewhere. The mountains were plainer now in the south. He could see dark canyons cutting into the slopes, and there was snow on the upper peaks.

"How soon'll we get there, Pa?"

His father tapped his pipe out and put it away and laughed. Without bothering to answer, he began to sing:

Oh, I dug Snoqualmie River
And Lake Samamish too,
And paddled down to Kirkland
In a little birch canoe.

I built the Rocky Mountains,
And placed them where they are,
Sold whiskey to the Indians
From behind a little bar.

It was then, with the empty flat country wheeling by like a great turntable, the wheat fields and fences and the weathered peak of a barn rotating slowly as if in a dignified dance, wheeling and slipping behind and gone, and his father singing, that the strangeness first came over the boy. Somewhere, sometime . . . and there were mountains in it, and a stream, and a swing that he had fallen out of and cried, and he had mashed ripe blackberries in his hands and his mother had wiped him off, straightening his stiff fingers and wiping hard. . . . His mind caught on that memory from a time before there was any memory, he rubbed his finger tips against his palms and slid a little down in the seat.

His father tramped on both pedals hard and leaned out of the car, looking. He swung to stare at the boy as a startled idiot might have stared, and in a voice heavy with German gutturals, he said, "Vot it iss in de crass?"

"What?"

"Iss in de crass somedings. Besser you bleiben right here."

He climbed out, and the boy climbed out after him. The dog jumped overboard and rushed, and in the grass by the side of the road the boy saw the biggest snake he had ever seen, long and fat and sleepy. When it pulled itself in and faced the stiff-legged dog he saw that the hind legs and tail of a gopher stuck out of the stretched mouth.

"Jiminy!" he said. "He eats gophers whole."

His father stooped with hands on knees to stare at the snake, looked at the boy, and wagged his head. "Himmel!" he said. "Dot iss a schlange vot iss a schlange."

"What is it?" the mother said from the car, and the boy yelled back, "A snake, a great big snake, and he's got a whole gopher in his mouth."

His father chased the pup away, found a rock, and with one

careful throw crushed the flat head. The body, as big around as the boy's ankle, tightened into a ridged convulsion of muscles, and the tail whipped back and forth. Stooping, Bo pulled on the gopher's tail. There was a wet, slupping noise, and the gopher slid out, coated with slime and twice as long as he ought to have been.

"Head first," Bo said. "That's a hell of a way to die."

He lifted the snake by the tail. "Look," he said, "he's longer than I am." But Elsa made a face and turned her head while he fastened it in the forked top of a fencepost. It trailed almost two feet on the ground. The tail still twitched.

"He'll twitch till the sun goes down," Bo said. "First guy that comes along here drunk is going to think he's got d.t.'s." He climbed into the car, and the boy followed.

"What was it, Pa?"

"Milk snake. They come into barns and milk cows dry, sometimes. You saw what he did to that gopher. Just like a suction pump."

"Gee," the boy said. He sat back and thought about how long and slick the gopher had been, and how the snake's mouth was all stretched, and it was a good feeling to have been along and to have shared something like that with his father. It was a trophy, a thing you would remember and tell about. And while he was thinking that already, before they got to the mountains at all, he had something to remember about the trip, he remembered that just before they saw the snake he had been remembering something else, and he puckered his eyes in the sun, thinking. He had been right on the edge of it, it was right on the tip of his tongue, and then his father had tramped on the pedals. But it was something a long time ago, and there was a strangeness about it, something bothersome and a little scary, and it hurt his head the way it hurt his head to do arithmetical sums without pencil and paper. When you did them in your head something went round like a wheel, and you had to keep looking inside to make sure that you didn't lose sight of the figures that were pasted up there somewhere, and if you did it very long at a time you got a sick headache out of it. That was the way it felt when he almost remembered, only he hadn't been able to see what he knew was there . . .

By ten o'clock they had left the graded road and were chugging up a winding trail with toothed rocks embedded in the ruts. Ahead of them the mountains looked low and disappointing, treeless, brown. The trail ducked into a narrow gulch and the sides rose up around them, reddish gravel covered with bunch grass and sage.

"Gee whiz," the boy said. "These don't look like mountains."
"What'd you expect?" his father said. "Expect to step out onto a glacier?"
"But there aren't any trees," the boy said. "Gee whiz, there isn't even any water."
He stood up to look ahead. His father's foot went down on the low pedal, and the Ford growled at the grade. "Come on, Lena," his father said. He hitched himself back and forth in the seat, helping the car over the hill, and then, as they barely pulled over the hump and the sides of the gully fell away, there were the real mountains, high as heaven, the high slopes spiked and tufted with trees, and directly ahead of them a magnificent V-shaped door with the sun touching gray cliffs far back in, and a straight-edged violet shadow streaming from the eastern peak clear to the canyon floor.
"Well?" his father's voice said. "I guess if you don't like it we can drop you here and pick you up on the way back."
The boy turned back to his mother. She was sitting far forward on the edge of the seat. "I guess we want to come along, all right," she said, and laughed as if she might cry. "Anything as beautiful as that. Don't we, sonny?"
"You bet," he said. He remained standing all the way up over the gentle slope of the alluvial fan that aproned out from the canyon's mouth, and when they passed under the violet shadow, not violet any more but cool gray, he tipped his head back and looked up miles and miles to the broken rock above.
The road got rougher. "Sit down," his father said. "First thing you know you'll fall out on your head and sprain both your ankles."
He was in his very best mood. He said funny things to the car, coaxing it over steep pitches. He talked to it like a horse, scratched it under the dashboard, promised it an apple when they got there. Above them the canyon walls opened out and back, went up steeply high and high and high, beyond the first walls that the boy had thought so terrific, away beyond those, piling peak on peak, and the sun touched and missed and touched again.
The trail steepened. A jet of steam burst from the brass radiator cap, the car throbbed and labored, they all sat forward and urged it on. But it slowed, shook, stopped and stood there steaming and shaking, and the motor died with a last lunging gasp.
"Is this as far as we can get?" the boy said. The thought that they might be broken down, right here on the threshold of wonder, put him in a panic. He looked around. They were in a bare rocky gorge. Not even any trees yet, though a stream tumbled

down a bouldered channel on the left. But to get to trees and the real mountains they had to go further, much further. "Are we stuck?" he said.

His father grunted. "Skin down to the creek and get a bucket of water." The boy ran, came stumbling and staggering back with the pail. His mother had climbed out and put a rock under the hind wheel, and they stood close together while Bo with a rag made quick, stabbing turns at the radiator cap. The cap blew off and steam went up for six feet and they all jumped back. There was a sullen subterranean boiling deep under the hood.

"Now!" Bo said. He poured a little water in, stepped back. In a minute the water came bubbling out. He poured again, and again the motor spit it out. "Can't seem to keep anything on her stomach," he said, and winked at the boy. He didn't seem worried.

The fourth dose stayed down. He filled the radiator till it ran over, screwed the plug in, and threw the pail in the back end. "You two stay out," he said. "I'll see if she'll go over unloaded."

She wouldn't. She moved two feet, strangled and died. The boy watched with his jaw hanging, remembering yesterday. But his father wasn't the same today. He just sat in the car and didn't swear at all, but winked at the boy and made a closing motion with his hand under his chin. "Better shut that mouth," he said. "Some bird'll fly in there and build a nest."

To Elsa he said, "Can you kick that rock out from under the wheel?"

"Sure," she said. "But do you think . . . Maybe we could walk from here."

"Hell with it," he said cheerfully. "I'll get her up if I have to lug her on my back."

She kicked the stone away and he rolled backward down the hill, craning, steering with one hand. At the bottom he cramped the wheels, got out and cranked, got in again, and turned around in the narrow road, making three or four angled tries before he made it. Then his hand waved, and there was the Ford coming up the hill backwards, kicking gravel down from under its straining hind wheels, angling across the road and back and up, and the motor roaring like a threshing engine, until it went by them and on up to the crest and turned around with one quick expert ducking motion, and they got in and were off again.

"Well!" said Elsa in relief. "Who would have thought of coming up backwards."

"Got more power in reverse," Bo said. "Can't make it one way, try another."

"Yay!" the boy said. He was standing up, watching the deep insides of the earth appear behind the angled rock, and his mind was soaring again, up into the heights where a hawk or eagle circled like a toy bird on a string.

"How do you like it?" his mother shouted at him. He turned around and nodded his head, and she smiled at him. She looked excited herself. Her face had color in it and the varnished grapes on her hat gave her a reckless, girlish look.

"Hi, Ma," he said.

"Hi yourself." He lifted his face and yelled with the pressure of happiness inside him.

They lay on a ledge high up on the sunny east slope and looked out to the north through a notch cut as sharply as a wedge out of a pie. Far below them the golden plain spread level, golden-tawny grass and golden-green wheat checkerboarded in a pattern as wide as the world. Back of them the spring they had followed up the slope welled out of the ledge, spread out in a narrow swampy spot, and ran off down the hill. There were trees, a thick cluster of spruce against the bulge of the wall above, a clump of twinkling, sunny aspen down the slope, and in the canyon bottom below, a dense forest of soft maple. His mother had a bouquet of leaves in her hand, a bunch of spruce cones on the ground beside her. The three lay quietly, looking down over the steeply-dropping wall to the V-shaped door, and beyond that to the plain.

The boy wriggled his back against the rock, put his hand down to shift himself, brought it up prickled with spruce needles. He picked them off, still staring down over the canyon gateway. They were far above the world he knew. The air was clearer, thinner. There was cold water running from the rock, and all around there were trees. And over the whole canyon, like a haze in the clear air, was that other thing, that memory or ghost of a memory, a swing he had fallen out of, the feel of his hands sticky with blackberries, his skin drinking cool shade, and his father's anger—the reflection of ecstasy and the shadow of tears.

"I never knew till this minute," his mother said, "how I've missed the trees."

Nobody answered. They were all stuffed with lunch, pleasantly tired after the climb. Bo lay looking off down the canyon, and the sour smell of his pipe, in that air, was pleasant and clean. The boy saw his mother put the stem of a maple leaf in her mouth and make a half-pleased face at the bitter taste.

Bo rose and dug a tin cup from the picnic box, walked to the spring and dipped himself a drink. He made a breathy sound of satisfaction. "So cold it hurts your teeth," he said. He brought Elsa a cup, and she drank.

"Brucie?" she said, motioning with the cup.

He started to get up, but his father filled the cup and brought it to him, making believe he was going to pour it on him. The boy ducked and reached for the cup. With his eyes on his father over the brim he drank, testing the water to see if it really did hurt his teeth. The water was cold and silvery in his mouth, and when he swallowed he felt it cold clear down to his stomach.

"It doesn't either hurt your teeth," he said. He poured a little on his arm, and something jumped in his skin. It was his skin that remembered. Something numbingly cold, and then warm. He felt it now, the way you waded in it.

"Mom," he said.

"What?"

"Was it in Washington we went on a picnic like this and picked blackberries and I fell out of a swing and there were big trees, and we found a river that was half cold and half warm?"

His father was relighting his pipe. "What do you know about Washington? You were only knee-high to a grasshopper when we lived there." He looked at Elsa, and she made a curious puzzled, almost-warning face. They were both watching him.

"Well, I remember," the boy said. "I've been remembering it all day, ever since you sang that song about building the Rocky Mountains. You sang it that day, too. Don't you remember, Mom?"

"I don't know," she said doubtfully. "We went on picnics in Washington."

"What's this about a river with hot and cold running water?" his father said. "You must be remembering some time you had a bath in a bathtub."

"I do not!" the boy said. "I got blackberries mashed all over my hands and Mom scrubbed me off, and then we found that river and waded in it and half was hot and half was cold."

"Ohhhh," his mother said. "I believe I do. . . . Bo, you remember once up in the Cascades, when we went out from Richmond with the Curtises? And little Bill Curtis fell in the lake." She turned to the boy. "Was there a summer cottage there, a brown shingled house?"

"I don't know," the boy said. "I don't remember any Curtises. But I remember blackberries and that river and a swing."

"Your head is full of blackberries," his father said. "If it was the time we went out with the Curtises there weren't any blackberries. That was in the spring."

"No," Elsa said. "It was in the fall, just after we moved to Richmond. And I think there was a place where one river from the mountains ran into another from the valley and they ran alongside each other in the same channel. The mountain one was a lot colder. Don't you remember that trip with the Curtises, Bo?"

"Sure I remember it," he said. "We hired a buckboard and saw a black bear and I won six bits from Joe Curtis pitching horseshoes."

"That's right," the mother said. "You remember the bear, Brucie."

The boy shook his head. There wasn't any bear in what he remembered. Just feelings, things that made his skin prickle.

His mother was looking at him, a little puzzled wrinkle between her eyes. "It's funny you should remember such different things than we remember," she said. "Everything means something different to everybody, I guess." She laughed, and the boy thought her eyes looked very odd and bright. "It makes me feel as if I didn't know you at all," she said.

She brushed her face with the handful of leaves and watched Bo gathering up odds and ends and putting them in the basket. "I wonder what each of us will remember about today?"

"I wouldn't worry about it," he said. "You can depend on Bub here to remember a lot of things that didn't happen."

"I don't think he does," she said. "He's got a good memory."

He picked up the box. "It takes a good memory to remember things that never happened. I remember once a garter snake crawled into my crib and I used it for a belt to keep my breechclout on. They took it away from me and I bawled the crib so full of tears I had to swim for shore. I drifted in three days later on a checkerboard raft with a didie for a sail."

The boy stood up and brushed off his pants. "You do too remember that river," he said.

His father grinned at him. "Sure. Only it wasn't quite as hot and cold as you make it out."

It was evening in the canyon, but when they reached the mouth again they emerged into full afternoon, with two hours of sun left them. Bo stopped the car before they dipped into the gravelly wash between the foothills, and they all looked back at the steep thrust of the mountains, purpling in the shadows, the rock glowing golden-red far back on the faces of the inner peaks. Elsa still held the bouquet of maple leaves in her hand.

"Well, there go the Mountains of the Moon," she said. The moment was almost solemn. In the front seat the boy stood up to look back. He felt the sun strong against the side of his face; the mountains sheering up before him were very real and solid. In a little while, as they went north, they would begin to melt together, and the patches of snow would appear far up on the northern slopes. His eyes went out of focus so that he saw the mountains as they would appear from the homestead on a clear day, a ghostly line on the horizon.

He felt his father twist toward him, but the trance was so strong that he did not look down. When he finally did, he caught his mother and father looking at each other, the look they had for moments when he had pleased them or made them proud of him.

"Okay," his father said, and stabbed him in the ribs with a hard thumb. "Wipe the black bears out of your eyes."

He started the car, and as they bounced down the rocky trail toward the road he sang at the top of his voice, bellowing into the still, hot afternoon:

I had a kid and his name was Brucie
Squeezed black bears and found them juicy.
Washed them off in a hot-cold river,
Now you boil and now you shiver.
Caught his pants so full of trout
He couldn't sit down till he got them out.
Trout were boiled from the hot-side river,
Trout from the cold side raw as liver.
Ate the boiled ones, ate the raw,
And then went howling home to Maw.

The boy looked up at his father, his laughter bubbling up, everything wonderful, the day a swell day, his mother clapping hands in time to his father's fool singing.

"Aw, for gosh sakes," he said, and ducked when his father pretended he was going to swat him one.

4

There were days in July when they went out together along the wheat field, the long narrow strip stretching almost a mile from the pasture fence to the Montana line. They all carried pails of wheat wet and swollen and sweet-smelling from strychnine, and dropped a tablespoonful at every gopher hole they found. This was the crucial time, as far as the gophers were concerned. The wheat was a foot high, and the gophers liked it best at that stage, when they could break down the spears and get at the tender joints. Already, in spite of the boy's trapping and snaring and poisoning, there were patches as big as a table along the edges of the field where the wheat was broken and eaten down close to the ground.

"You ought to get out here with your traps more," Bo said. "You spend too much time in the pasture, where it doesn't matter."

"They come down for water, though," the boy said. "There's one hole by the dam where I've caught nineteen already."

"Well, you aren't catching them all," said his father. "If this poison doesn't thin them down you'll have to trap all up and down this field."

"I'll get 'em. I sort of hate to poison them because then I don't get the tails."

"Forget about the tails. You've got to keep this field from looking as if it had the mange."

They went clear to the line, to the heavy iron post that marked the international boundary, along the foot of the field, and back up the other side between the wheat and the flax. Bo was sweating heavily under his wide straw hat. "I was a sucker to make that field so long and narrow," he said. "It'd be a lot handier if it was wider and not so long."

Elsa looked at him and smiled. "You wanted to plow a furrow a mile long and straight as a string," she said.

"Well, I plowed her. Maybe I'm no farmer, but I plowed her a mile long and six inches deep and straight as the team could walk."

"I know," she said, and lifted her straw hat from her red hair to let the wind cool her. "You've done fine with it."

Reaching down for a clod, he crumbled it between his fingers. "Dry pretty far down," he said. "We could stand a rain."

"It'll rain," she said. "It has to. Even so, I think the wheat looks awfully good." She wiped her forehead on her sleeve and smiled.

"It better," he said. He looked down the green shimmer of the field and set the edges of his teeth precisely together. "By God," he said, "if it doesn't make for us this year I'll . . ." He could think of nothing bad enough to do. "It sure better rain," he said. "With wheat two and a half a bushel it better rain."

"If we get a crop will you fix up the house a little?" she said.

"Fix it up how?"

"Paint it, maybe. And rig some kind of water system so I could plant flowers and things."

"Old Mama," he said. "Wants a cottage with roses round the door."

"Well, I do. It's so barren the way it is. It's like camping in the place. Ever since we went to the mountains I've had the itch to fix it up."

"I tell you one thing," he said, "if we don't make it this year we won't even be camping in it. We'll be going some place where we can make a living."

"We've made a living. Even with the drouth last year and the rust the year before we made a living."

He stooped to lay a spoonful of poison at a gopher hole. "When we came up here," he said, "we didn't come up just to make a living. We came up to make a pile."

They watched the sky those days, watched the southeast where the June rains had come from. Nothing but the fitful glare of heat lightning rewarded their watching, but even without rain the wheat grew strongly. From day to day the boy thought he could see the difference, for the days were warm and endless, and when he dug into the ground it was warm for five or six inches down.

The gophers were under control, though there were still hundreds of them. He had almost fifteen hundred tails in the cigar box, tied into bundles of a hundred so that he didn't have to spend all afternoon counting them. And he had taken to drowning out gophers along the coulee by the dam. There were always some there, now that the dry spell was on, and it was fun to sic Spot on the hole while he ran with buckets. Spot learned fast. He would stand quivering with excitement, with his nose down the hole, while the boy was gone, and when the water came he backed up one step and waited, whining and watching the hole. When the gopher popped out, wet and slick and dark with the water, Spot would snap once, and that was the end of Mister Gopher.

There were days, during that hot July, when they got into the Ford and went down to the little stream by Pete and Emil and had a swim in the lukewarm, barely-running water. Those were good days. But as July passed and the rain held off a tension came into the house. His father sang less at breakfast-making, and he was likely to stand in the door facing another cloudless morning and swear under his breath. His mother went around often with her lips pressed together and her eyes worried, and he saw how she avoided talk whenever she could.

When thunderheads did build up, the tension pulled harder, and there was a difference in the way they stood and watched. In June they had waited confidently, because if this one blew over the ground was still good and moist, and there would be another one soon anyway. But now there was a half expectation that the clouds would come to nothing, because there had been false alarms a half dozen times. Once or twice they watched storms get near enough to drop a few heavy pellets of rain in the baked dooryard, and whistle their winds through the screens of the porch so that they ran to roll down the canvas blinds. But by the time they got the porch snug the pelting would have stopped, and they would stand in the doorway again and see blue sky coming like a falsely-smiling enemy behind the hopeful dark of the cloud.

That tension invaded the private life of the boy, too. The farm was no longer a world invented simply for his exploration and delight. Seeing his father glum, his mother silent, he felt a compulsion to do something. The only thing he could do was to destroy gophers, and though they were not the real danger now, their decimation at least gave him the sense of helping. He was in the pasture and along the field three or four times a day, and from his lookout in the sleeping porch he kept the coulee bank always under his eye when he was in the house. The minute a gopher showed on the tawny slope he was out with a bucket as if he belonged to a volunteer fire company.

"By God," his father would say irritably, looking up at the brassy summer sky, "there isn't a drop of rain in a thousand miles."

The boy's mother told him privately that there wasn't enough for Pa to do. If he had had stock to care for, or odd jobs to do, or anything, he wouldn't be so nervous. On an ordinary farm, if one crop failed, others would come through all right, and you would have your hogs or your cattle or your cowpeas or whatever even if your big crop didn't make. But here it was just sit and watch, and it was pretty hard on Pa, and if the wheat didn't make there was nothing.

He took to going out into the field alone, and they would see him walking along the edge of the wheat, green-bronze now, stooping and straightening and taking little excursions into the grain that reached around his waist like green water. The first year they had come out, his mother said—1915, that was—the wheat had been higher than Pa's head. He had just walked into Gadke's field and disappeared. Ever since then Pa had had a great respect for Gadke as a farmer. But he hadn't had much of a field in that year himself, just twenty acres, because he was building the house and getting the fence in and getting the sod broken and everything. Even so, they had made over a thousand bushel of wheat that year, more than they had made since with two or three times the acreage in.

The boy dreamed about the wheat at night now. Once he dreamed that he went out across the coulee and there was the grain grown enormously, a wilderness, a woods of wheat, taller than tall, with great fat heads nodding far above him, and he ran back to the house with his mouth shouting words, calling his father to come and see, but when they got back the wheat had shrivelled and blackened and died, and the field looked like a dark and smoky place that fire had passed over. His father flew into a rage and cuffed him for lying, and he awoke.

As August moved on day by cloudless day, they began to watch the southwest rather than the southeast. The days were hot, with light hot fingering winds that bent the wheat and died again, and in the evenings there was always a flicker of heat lightning. The southwest was dangerous in August. From that direction came the hot winds, blowing for two or three days at a time, that had withered and scorched the wheat last year. They were like Chinooks, his father said, except that in summer they were hot as hell. You couldn't predict them and you couldn't depend on their coming, but if they came you were sunk.

What a God damned country, his father said.

The boy heard them talking in bed at night, when they thought he was asleep, but even without that he couldn't have missed how his father grew darker and more sullen and silent. The good humor was less frequent and never lasted. Even when he proposed a swim down by Pete and Emil he did it as if it were a last resort to keep from flying all apart with worry and impotence. "Let's get out of here and do something," he would say. "Sit around here much longer and the roof'll fall in on us."

"It's just this not being able to do anything," the boy's mother said. "It's this sitting, without being able to do anything but sit . . ."

That was why, the boy knew, she proposed the visit to the Garfields, who had come two years before to take up a homestead four miles east of them. "We ought to know our neighbors better," she said. "They've lived there two years and we've never even met them."

"I've met him," Bo said.

"Where?"

"Down at Cree. He's a prissy-faced long-nosed Englishman."

"Well, but he's our nearest neighbor. And she might be nice."

"Have they got any kids, Ma?" the boy asked.

"I don't think so. I wish they had." She looked at Bo and wheedled him. "You'll drive us over on Sunday, won't you?" she said. "Just to be neighborly. It'll do you good."

He shrugged and picked up a magazine, four months old and dog-eared from long use.

The boy was excited by the visit to Garfields'. The hot afternoon was still and breathless, the air harder to breathe than usual. He knew there was a change in weather coming, because the ginger-snaps in their tall cardboard box were soft and bendable when he snitched a couple to stick in his pocket. He could tell too by his father's grumpiness that something was coming. If it was rain everything would be dandy, there would be humming and singing again before breakfast. Maybe his father would let him ride the mare down to Cree for the mail. But if it was hail or hot wind they'd have to walk soft and speak softer, and the crop might be ruined, and that would be calamity.

He found more than he looked for at Garfields'. Mr. Garfield was tall and bald with a big nose, and talked very softly and politely. The boy's father was determined not to like him right from the start.

When Mr. Garfield said, "Dear, I think we might have a glass of lemonade, don't you?" the boy saw his parents look at each other, saw the beginning of a smile on his father's face, saw his mother purse her lips and shake her head ever so little. And when Mrs. Garfield, prim and spectacled, with a habit of tucking her head back and to one side while she listened to anyone talk, brought in the lemonade, the boy saw his father taste his and make a little face behind the glass. He hated any summer drink without ice in it, and kept his own beer at home deep in the cellar hole where it would keep cool.

But Mr. and Mrs. Garfield were nice people. They sat down in their new parlor and showed the boy's mother the rug and the gramophone. When the boy came up curiously to inspect the little box with a petunia-shaped horn with a picture of a terrier and "His Master's Voice" painted on it, and when the Garfields found that he had never seen or heard a gramophone, they put on a cylinder like a big spool of tightly-wrapped black thread, and pushed a lever and lowered a needle, and out came a man's voice singing in Scotch brogue, and his mother smiled and nodded and said, "My land, Harry Lauder! I heard him once a long time ago. Isn't it wonderful, sonny?"

It was wonderful all right. He inspected it, reached out his fingers to touch things, wiggled the big horn to see if it was loose or screwed in. His father warned him sharply to keep his hands off, but Mr. Garfield smiled and said, "Oh, he can't hurt it. Let's play something else," and found a record about the saucy little bird on Nellie's hat that had them all laughing. They let him wind the machine and play the record over again, all by himself, and he was very careful. It was a fine machine. He wished he had one.

About the time he had finished playing his sixth or seventh record, and George M. Cohan was singing, "She's a grand old rag, she's a high-flying flag, and forever in peace may she wave," he glanced at his father and saw that he was grouchy about something. He wasn't taking part in the conversation, but was sitting with his chin in his hand staring out the window. Mr. Garfield was looking at him a little helplessly. His eyes met the boy's and he motioned him over.

"What do you find to do all summer, young man? Only child, are you?"

"No sir. My brother's in Whitemud. He's twelve. He's got a job."

"So you came out on the farm to help," Mr. Garfield said. He had his hand on the boy's shoulder and his voice was so kind that the boy lost his shyness and felt no embarrassment at all in being out there in the middle of the parlor with all of them looking at him.

"I don't help much," he said. "I'm too little to do anything but drive the stoneboat, Pa says. When I'm twelve he's going to get me a gun and then I can go hunting."

"Hunting?" said Mr. Garfield. "What would you hunt?"

"Oh, gophers and weasels. I got a pet weasel now. His name's Lucifer."

"Well," Mr. Garfield said. "You seem a manly little chap. What do you feed your weasel?"

"Gophers." He thought it best not to say that the gophers were alive when he threw them in. He thought that probably Mr. Garfield would be a little shocked at that.

Mr. Garfield straightened up and looked around at the grown-ups. "Isn't it a shame," he said, "that there are so many predatory animals and pests in this country that we have to spend our time destroying them? I hate killing things."

"I hate weasels," the boy said. "I'm saving this one till he turns white and then I'm going to skin him. Once I speared a weasel with a pitchfork in the chicken house and he dropped right off the tine and ran up my leg and bit me after he was speared clean through."

He finished breathlessly, and his mother smiled at him, motioning him not to talk so much. But Mr. Garfield was still looking at him kindly. "So you want to make war on the cruel things, the weasels and hawks," he said.

"Yes sir." The boy looked at his mother and it was all right. He hadn't spoiled anything by talking about the weasels.

"Now that reminds me," Mr. Garfield said, rising. "Maybe I've got something you would find useful."

He went into another room and came back with a .22 in his hand. "Could you use this?"

"I . . . yes *sir!*" the boy said. He had almost, in his excitement, said, "I hope to whisk in your piskers."

"If your parents will let you have it," Mr. Garfield said, and raised his eyebrows at the boy's mother. He didn't look at the father, but the boy did.

"Can I, Pa?"

"I guess so," his father said. "Sure."

"Thank Mr. Garfield nicely," his mother said.

"Gee," the boy said. "Thanks, Mr. Garfield, ever so much."

"There's a promise goes with it," Mr. Garfield said. "I'd like you to promise never to shoot anything with it but the bloodthirsty animals, the cruel ones like weasels and hawks. Never anything like birds or prairie dogs."

"How about butcher birds?"

"Butcher birds?"

"Shrikes," said the boy's mother. "We've got some over by our place. They kill all sorts of other things, snakes and gophers and other birds. They're worse than the hawks, because they kill just for the fun of it."

"By all means," said Mr. Garfield. "Shoot the shrikes. A thing that kills for the fun of it . . ." He shook his head and his voice got solemn, like the voice of Mr. McGregor, the Sunday school superintendent in town, when he was asking the benediction. "There's something about the way the war drags on, or maybe it's just being in this new, clean country," Mr. Garfield said, "that makes me hate killing. I simply can't bear to shoot anything any more, even a weasel."

The boy's father turned cold eyes away from Mr. Garfield and looked out the window. One big brown hand, a little dirty from the wheel of the car, rubbed against the day-old bristles of his jaws. Then he stood up and stretched. "We got to be going," he said.

"Oh, stay a while," Mr. Garfield said. "You just came. I wanted to show you my trees."

The boy's mother stared. "Trees?"

He smiled. "Sounds a bit odd out here, doesn't it? But I think trees will grow. I've made some plantings down below."

"I'd love to see them," she said. "Sometimes I'd give almost anything to get into a deep shady woods. Just to smell it, and feel how cool . ."

"There's a little story connected with these," Mr. Garfield said. He spoke warmly, to the mother alone. "When we first decided to come out here I said to Martha that if trees wouldn't grow we shouldn't stick it. That's just what I said, 'If trees won't grow there we shan't stick it.' Trees are like the breath of life to me."

The boy's father was shaken by a sudden spell of coughing, and his wife shot a look at him and then looked back at Mr. Garfield with a light flush on her cheekbones. "I'd love to see them," she said again. "I was raised in Minnesota, and I never will get used to a place as barren as this."

"When I think of the beeches back home in England," Mr. Garfield said, and shook his head.

Bo lifted himself heavily out of his chair and followed the rest of them out to the coulee edge. Below them willows grew in a thin belt along the almost-dry creek, and farther back from the water there were perhaps twenty cottonwoods a half-dozen feet high.

"I'm trying cottonwoods first because they can stand drouth," Mr. Garfield said.

Elsa was looking down with all her longing plain and naked in her face. "It's wonderful," she said. "I'd give almost anything to have some on our place."

"I found the willows near here," Mr. Garfield said. "Just at the south end of the hills they call the Old-Man-on-His-Back, where a stream comes down."

"Stream?" the boy's father said. "You mean that spring-month trickle?"

"It's not much of a stream," Mr. Garfield said apologetically. "But . . ."

"Are there any more there?" Elsa said.

"Oh yes. You could get some. Cut them slanting and push them into any damp ground. They'll grow."

"They'll grow about six feet high," Bo Mason said.

"Yes," said Mr. Garfield. "They're not, properly speaking, trees. Still . . ."

Bo Mason looked at the southwest. "It's getting pretty smothery," he said, rather loudly. "We better be getting on."

This time Mr. Garfield didn't object, and they went back to the car with Mrs. Garfield and the boy's mother exchanging promises of visits. Bo turned the crank and climbed into the Ford, where the boy was sighting along his gun. "Put that down!" his father said. "Don't you know any better than to point a gun around people?"

"It isn't loaded."

"They never are. Put it down now."

The Garfields were standing with their arms around each other's waists, waiting to wave goodbye. Mr. Garfield reached over and picked something from his wife's dress.

"What was it, Alfred?" she said, peering.

"Nothing. Only a bit of fluff."

The boy's father coughed violently and the car started with a jerk. With his head down almost on the wheel, still coughing, he waved, and the mother and the boy waved as they went down along the badly-set cedar posts of the pasture fence. They were almost a quarter of a mile away before the boy, with a last flourish of the gun, turned around to see that his father was not coughing, but laughing. He rocked the car with his joy, and when Elsa said, "Oh, Bo, you big fool," he pointed helplessly to his shoulder. "Would you mind," he said. "Would you mind brushing that bit o' fluff off me showldah?" He rocked again, pounding the wheel. "I cawn't stick it," he said. "I bloody well cawn't stick it, you knaow."

"It isn't fair to laugh at him," she said. "He can't help being English."

"He can't help being a sanctimonious old mudhen, either," he said. "Braying about his luv-ly, luv-ly trees. They'll freeze out the first cold winter."

"How do you know? Maybe it's like he says—if they get a start they'll grow here as well as anywhere."

"Maybe there's a gold mine in our back yard, too, but I'm not going to dig to see. I couldn't stick it."

"You're just being stubborn," she said. "Just because you didn't like him . . ."

He turned on her in a heavy amazement. "Well my God, did you?"

"I thought he was very nice," she said, and sat straighter in the back seat, speaking loudly above the jolting of the springs and the cough of the motor. "They're trying to make a home, not just a wheat crop. I liked them."

"Uh huh." He was not laughing any more now. Sitting beside him, the boy could see that his face had hardened and that the cold look had come into his eyes again. "So I should start talking like I had a mouthful of bran, and planting trees around the house that'll look like clothesline poles in two months."

"I didn't say that."

"You thought it, though." He looked irritably at the sky, misted with the same delusive film of haze or cloud that had fooled him for three days. "You thought it all the time we were there. 'Why aren't you more like Mr. Garfield, he's such a nice man.'" With mincing savagery he swung around and mocked her. "Shall I make it a walnut grove? Or a sugar orchard? Or maybe you'd prefer orange trees."

The boy was squinting down his gun, trying not to hear them

quarrel, but he knew what his mother's face would be like—hurt and a little flushed, and her chin trembling into stubbornness. "I don't suppose you could bear to have a rug on the floor, or a gramophone?" she said.

He smacked the wheel hard. "Of course I could bear it if we could afford it. I'd love it. But I don't know what you think is going to give us the dough for things like that if a wind comes up out of that heat-hole over there. And I'd a damn sight rather do without than be like that old sandhill crane."

"I don't suppose you'd like to take me over to the Old-Man-on-His-Back some day to get some willow slips, either."

"What for?"

"To plant down in the coulee, by the dam."

"That dam dries up every August. Your willows wouldn't live till snow flies."

"Well, would it do any harm to try?"

"Oh, shut up!" he said. "Just thinking about that guy and his fluff and his trees gives me the pleefer."

The topless Ford lurched, one wheel at a time, through the deep burnout by their pasture corner, and the boy clambered out with his gun in his hand to slip the loop of the three-strand gate. It was then that he saw the snake, a striped limp ribbon, dangling on the fence, and a moment later the sparrow, neatly butchered and hung by the throat on a barb. He pointed the gun at them. "Lookit!" he said. "Lookit what the butcher bird's been doing."

His father's violent hand waved at him from the car. "Come on! Get the wire out of the way."

The boy dragged the gate through the dust, and the Ford went through and up behind the house framed by the fireguard overgrown with Russian thistle. Walking across that yard a few minutes later, the boy felt its hard heat through his sneakers. There was hardly a spear of grass within the fireguard. It was one of his father's prides that the dooryard should be like cement. "Pour your wash-water out long enough," he said, "and you'll have a surface so hard it won't even make mud." Religiously he threw his water out three times a day, carrying it sometimes a dozen steps to dump it on a dusty or grassy spot.

Elsa had objected at first, asking why they had to live in the middle of an alkali flat, and why they couldn't let grass grow up to the door. But he snorted her down. Everything around the house ought to be bare as a bone. Get a good grass fire going and it would jump that guard like nothing, and if they had grass to the door where would they be? She said why not plow a wider guard then, one a fire couldn't jump, but he said he had other things to do than plowing fifty-foot fireguards.

They were arguing inside when the boy came up the step to sit down and aim his empty .22 at a fencepost. Apparently his mother had been persistent, and persistence when he was not in a mood for it angered his father worse than anything. Their talk came vaguely through the boy's concentration, but he shut his ears on it. If that spot on the post was a coyote, now, and he held the sight steady, right on it, and pulled the trigger, that old coyote would jump about eighty feet in the air and come down dead as a mackerel, and he could tack his hide on the barn the way Mr. Larson had one, only the dogs had jumped and torn the tail and hind legs off Mr. Larson's, and he wouldn't get more than the three-dollar bounty for its ears. But Mr. Larson had shot his with a shotgun, anyway, and the hide wasn't worth much even before the dogs tore it.

"I can't for the life of me see why not," his mother said inside. "We could do it now. We're not doing anything else."

"I tell you they wouldn't grow!" his father said, with emphasis on every word. "Why should we run our tongues out doing everything that mealy-mouthed fool does?"

"I don't want anything but the willows. They're easy."

He made his special sound of contempt, half-snort and half-grunt. After a silence she tried again. "They might even have pussies on them in the spring. Mr. Garfield thinks they'd grow, and his wife told me he used to work in a greenhouse."

"This isn't a greenhouse, for Chrissake. Go outside and feel that breeze if you think so."

"Oh, let it go," she said. "I've stood it this long without any green things around. I guess I can stand it some more."

The boy, aiming now toward the gate where the butcher bird, coming back to his prey, would in just a second fly right into Dead-eye's unerring bullet, heard his father stand up suddenly.

"Abused, aren't you?" he said.

His mother's voice rose. "No, I'm not abused! Only I don't see why it would be so awful to get some willows. Just because Mr. Garfield gave me the idea, and you don't like him . . ."

"You're right I don't like him. He gives me a pain right under the crupper."

"Because," his mother's voice said bitterly, "he calls his wife 'dear' and puts his arm around her and likes trees. It wouldn't occur to you to put your arm around your wife, would it?"

The boy aimed and held his breath. His mother ought to keep

still, because if she didn't she'd get him real mad and then they'd both have to tiptoe around the rest of the day. He heard his father's breath whistle through his teeth, and his mincing, nasty voice: "Would you like me to put my arm around you now, *dear?*"

"I wouldn't let you touch me with a ten-foot pole," his mother said. She sounded just as mad as he did, and it wasn't often she let herself get that way. The boy squirmed over when he heard the quick hard steps come up behind him and pause. Then his father's hand, brown and meaty and felted with fine black hair, reached down over his shoulder and took the .22.

"Let's see this cannon old Scissor-Bill gave you," he said.

It was a single-shot, bolt-action Savage, a little rusty on the barrel, the bolt sticky with hardened grease when he removed it. Sighting up through the barrel, he grunted. "Takes care of a gun like he sets a fence. Probably used it to cultivate his luv-ly trees."

He went out into the porch, and after a minute came back with a rag and a can of machine oil. Hunching the boy over on the step, he sat down and began rubbing the bolt with the oil-soaked rag.

"I just cawn't bear to shoot anything any more," he said, and laughed suddenly. "I just cawn't stick it, little man." He leered at the boy, who grinned back uncertainly. Squinting through the barrel again, his father breathed through his nose and clamped his lips together, shaking his head.

The sun lay heavy on the baked yard. Out over the corner of the pasture a soaring hawk caught wind and sun at the same time, so that his light breast feathers flashed as he banked and rose. Just wait, the boy said. Wait till I get my gun working and I'll fix you, you hen-robber. He thought of the three chicks a hawk had struck earlier in the summer, the three balls of yellow with the barred mature plumage just showing through. Two of them dead before he got there and chased the hawk away, the other with its crop slashed open and wheat spilling from it to the ground. His mother had sewed up the crop, and the chicken had lived, but it always looked droopy, like a plant in drouth time, and sometimes it stood working its bill as if choking.

By golly, he thought, I'll shoot every hawk and butcher bird in twenty miles. I'll . . .

"Rustle around and find me a piece of baling wire," his father said. "This barrel looks like a henroost."

Behind the house he found a piece of rusty wire, brought it back and watched his father straighten it, wind a piece of rag around the end, ram it up and down through the barrel, and peer through again. "He's leaded her so you can hardly see the grooves," he said. "But maybe she'll shoot. We'll fill her with vinegar and cork her up tonight."

Elsa was behind them, leaning against the jamb and watching. She reached down and rumpled Bo's black hair. "The minute you get a gun in your hands you start feeling better," she said. "It's just a shame you weren't born a hundred years sooner."

"A gun's a good tool," he said. "It hadn't ought to be misused. Gun like this is enough to make a guy cry."

"Well, you've at least got to admit it was nice of him to give it to Bruce," she said. It was the wrong thing to say. The boy had a feeling that she knew it was the wrong thing to say, that she said it anyway just to have one tiny triumph over him. Even before he heard his father's answer he knew Pa would be mad again.

"Oh sure," he said. "Mr. Garfield's a fine man. He can preach a better sermon than anybody in Saskatchewan. God Almighty, I get sick of hearing his praises sung. If you liked it so well why don't you move over there?"

"If you weren't so blind stubborn . . ."

He rose with the .22 in his hand and brushed past her into the house. "I'm not so blind," he said heavily in passing. "You've been throwing that bastard up to me for two hours. It doesn't take very good eyes to see what that means. It means I'm no good, I can't do anything right."

She started to say, "All because I want a few little . . ." but the boy cut in on her, anxious to help the situation somehow. "Will it shoot now?" he said.

His father said nothing. His mother looked down at him, sighed, shrugged, smiled bleakly with a tight mouth. She moved aside when his father came back with a box of cartridges in his hand. He ignored her, speaking to the boy alone in the particular half-jocular tone he always used with him or with the dog when he wasn't mad.

"Thought I had these around," he said. "Let's see what this smoke-pole will do."

He slipped in a cartridge and locked the bolt, looking around for something to shoot at. Behind him Elsa's feet moved on the floor, and her voice came purposefully. "I can't see why you want to act this way," she said. "I'm going over and get some of those slips myself."

There was a long silence. The angled shade lay sharp as a knife across the baked front yard, and a breeze stirred in the Russian thistle of the fireguard. Bo's cheek was pressed against the stock of the gun, his arms and hands as steady as stone.

"How'll you get there?" he said, whispering down the barrel.

"I'll walk."

"Five miles and back."

"Yes, or fifty miles and back. If there was any earthly reason why you should mind . . ."

"I don't mind," he said, his voice soft as silk. "Go ahead."

Close to his mother's long skirts in the doorway, the boy felt her stiffen as if she had been slapped. He squirmed anxiously, but his desperation could find only the question he had asked before. His voice squeaked on it: "Will it shoot now?"

"See that sparrow out there?" his father said. "Right out by that cactus?"

"Bo!" Elsa said. "If you shoot that harmless little bird!"

Fascinated, the boy watched his father's dark face against the rifle stock, the locked, immovable left arm, the thick finger crooked inside the trigger-guard almost too small to hold it. He saw the sparrow, gray, white-breasted, hopping obliviously in search of bugs, fifty feet out on the gray earth.

"I just . . . cawn't . . . bear . . . to . . . shoot . . . anything," his father said, his face like dark stone, his lips hardly moving. "I just . . . cawn't . . . stick it!"

"Bo!" his wife screamed.

The boy's mouth opened, a dark wash of terror shadowed his vision of the bare yard and the sharp angle of shade. "Don't, Pa!"

The rocklike figure of his father never moved. The thick finger squeezed down slowly, there was a thin, sharp report, and the sparrow jerked and collapsed into a shapeless wad on the ground. In the instant of the shot all its clean outlines vanished. Head, feet, the white breast, the perceptible outlines of the folded wings, disappeared all at once, crumpled together and were lost, and the boy sat beside his father on the step with the echo of the shot thin in his ears.

He did not look at either of his parents. He looked only at the crumpled sparrow. Step by step, unable to keep away, he went to it, stooped, and picked it up. Blood stained his fingers, and he held the bird by the tail while he wiped the smeared hand on his overalls. He heard the click as the bolt was shot and the empty cartridge ejected, and he saw his mother come swiftly out of the house past his father, who sat still on the step. Her hands were clenched, and she walked with her head down.

"Ma!" the boy said dully. "Ma, what'll I do with it?"

She stopped and turned, and for a moment they faced each other. He saw the dead pallor of her face, the burning eyes, the not-quite-controlled quiver of her lips. But her words, when they came, were flat and level, almost casual.

"Leave it right there," she said. "After while your father will want to hang it on the barbed wire."

The boy dropped it and went straight away, as if by inspiration, to run his trap line. He hated his father and he would not even stay in the same yard with him, and he hated him all up through the pasture and back along the north end of the wheat field where the grain drooped in the withering sun. The wind, by the time he got back to the house toward evening, was blowing quite strongly from the southwest.

5

So the year that began in hope ended in bitterness. The rains that came after the blistering winds were ironic and unwanted, the crop was ruined, the prospect of a hard winter was there again, like an old unwelcome acquaintance come upon around a corner.

For the boy, the farm was spoiled. The reservoir had dried up almost completely, and now was a smelly, hoof-pocked, muddy hole. The creek by Pete and Emil was almost as bad. The trapping had palled, and the smell of his almost-two thousand tails when he opened the cigar box filled the sleeping porch and sickened him. There was no water for drowning gophers out, he had no more cartridges for shooting at hawks. And one night, in a blustering wind, the weasel's cage got tipped over and the weasel got away.

Everything was stale. Because his father went down to Cree three or four times a week now and spent all afternoon talking with other lost and prowling homesteaders, there were practically no trips to the store any more. The only thing that saved him from empty moping was the advent of the Fall Sears Roebuck catalogue and the coming of the thresher crew to rescue the remnants of the wheat.

But then nothing again, the lackluster hours of hanging on the pasture gate and looking south toward the Bearpaws, without pleasure particularly, without longing, without anything but a dull wish that they'd go into town pretty soon.

"What's the matter, son?" his mother said to him. "You go around looking like a lost soul."

"I don't know," he said. He ran a finger up the rough face of a stud behind the sofa where he lay, got a sliver under the nail, and listlessly pulled it out again. "When we going into town, Ma?"

"Right away, soon as Pa can get the rest of the wheat hauled. You anxious to get back?"

"Uh huh. I guess so."

"Oh Lord," she said. "Me too. The change would do us all good."

Then his father came back from his trip with the wagon crews, so bitter that he wouldn't even say how much he had got for the little wheat the winds had left him, and the morning after that he said they were going to get out of this God-forsaken buffalo-chip flat as quick as they could pack.

They worked all that day stowing in the bed of the wagon quilts, clothes, odds and ends of furniture needed in town, spare cans of gasoline and kerosene, some sacks of wheat saved for chicken and cow feed. The wagon box was more than level full when they went in to supper, and when the boy went to bed that night and lay thinking about the loaded wagon outside, the trip coming up tomorrow, the excitement of town again, school again, Chet again, the house in town and the river and the brush and Hallowe'en again, it seemed to him that the lonesome whining of the wind through the sleeping-porch screen, the lonesome slatting of a half-unrolled canvas curtain, had in them all that frightened and depressed him about the homestead. It was so big outside, the stars so high and cold, the land so flat and mysterious lying still as a shadow-earth under the remote sky. You could go out in the yard and stare in every direction and never see a light unless one of the few neighbors within five miles was out in the yard with a lantern, or an infrequent car was moving on the Cree road, and then it was almost worse than seeing no light at all, because it was such a faint lost glimmer that it spread the horizons further than ever and deepened instead of lightening the loneliness of wind and dark and stars and empty prairie.

And tomorrow would be the fifty-mile trip in, Gadke's and the horse pasture and the Frenchman's, La Pointe's, and all the kids peeking around the stone foundations of the barn, and then there would be the south bench, the dipping of the road that angled down into the flat river valley, and below them the green belt of willows crooked as a snake-trail in sand, the dull glitter of the river and the folded brown draws down the north bench opposite, and then the town, almost a hundred houses, dozens of kids, greetings and late shivery swims and playing run sheepy run again, and hare and hounds through the river brush.

Before daylight he was awakened by his father's swearing and stamping around in the other room. He lay listening. The stove had run out of kerosene, and all the spare coal oil was packed far down under the mass of household goods in the wagon. The boy got out of bed and dressed swiftly, not wanting to be yelled at for oversleeping on a busy morning. But the morning was pretty well spoiled. Pa had got up on the wrong side of bed.

The sun was not yet up, and the prairie outside lay gray and desolate. He turned from the screen and went into the other room, hardly responding to his mother's good morning. There was a dull and dispirited weight on his mind. He couldn't wake up properly, and his mouth kept opening in jaw-cracking yawns.

His father came inside with the kerosene can, saw him standing there stupidly, and told him sharply to do something, for God sake. Did he think the world moved on wheels to get his breakfast and carry him into town? Go up and get the horses.

He went sullenly in the gray light, searching the corners of the pasture for the outlines of the team. In the east light grew, and turning his head he saw the pearly band along the horizon touched with rose. He stumbled in a badger hole and cursed like his father, kicking the mounded earth.

When he returned with the team, breakfast was on the table and his mother was already eating. His father was frying slices of bread in bacon fat. The boy slid into his chair, and his father turned to glower at him. "Have you washed?"

"No," the boy said sullenly. At the bench outside, in the full rosy light, he dabbed his face and hands and threw out the water. The sun's glaring saucer slipped over the flat horizon and touched him. That, and the dash of cold water on his face, made him feel better. The headachy feeling he had waked up to, the sort of feeling he had when a bilious spell was coming on, was almost gone. In a little while, his mind said, they would be heading for Whitemud, and that would be fine.

"Are we going to leave right after breakfast, Mom?"

"I am. I'm going to start with the wagon, and you and Pa are going to finish up here and then you're coming in the car."

The boy looked toward the stove. His father's dark face, even in profile, looked grouchy, dissatisfied, mad. "Ma, I want to go with you."

"I'm afraid you can't," she said. "Pa needs you to help him." She smiled at him, squinting her eyes and warning him, reminding him —not to make a fuss, not to whine, not to get Pa's temper started. He understood her look but he fussed anyway. The prospect of riding all the way with his father was suddenly dreadful to him.

"Well, I want to!" he said. "I want to go in the wagon with you."

"You do as you're told," his father said, and slapped another slice of bread into the pan. The boy sat pouting, accusing his mother silently. She had betrayed him. Her face was weary as she reached out to pat his hand.

"Don't worry," she said. "I won't get very far before you catch me. You can change off then."

He was carrying old boards up to the house for shuttering when his mother climbed into the wagon seat atop the monstrous load and gathered up the lines. He dropped the boards and ran to open the gate, and as the wagon went through with his father walking at the wheel his mother smiled down at the boy and blew him a kiss off the ends of her heavy gloves. She looked so funny up there with a straw hat on that he laughed.

"Don't try to hurry it," his father said. "You've got a heavy load and a colt along. Let the team make its own speed. We'll probably catch you the other side of the horse pasture somewhere."

"All right." Sitting on her high seat, she smiled down on them. " 'Bye, son." Her eyes went back to the little round-topped shack on the other side of the coulee, and she stood up to raise an arm. "So long, homestead," she said. "We'll be back!" She met Bo's eyes briefly, held them, and flapped the lines over the horses. The laden wagon creaked heavily, rocking through the burnouts. A hundred feet away she turned and waved, and the boy waved back, mechanically, watching the wagon crawl into the blazing east.

"All right," his father said. "Let's get a move on."

Back at the house he started nailing boards over the two windows, rolling down the porch blinds and cleating them fast. He sent the boy for the three chicken crates saved from the spring, and they ran down all the hens and put them squawking into the boxes. The boy loaded them in the Ford while his father lugged the rain barrel and all the loose tools inside. The plow went into the chicken house, the stoneboat was leaned up against the wall.

Then there was the last-minute gleaning of the house, the loose bundles of odds and ends, the left-over food in a cardboard box, the cat, the dog, the almost-forgotten cigar box of gopher tails, and finally the moment when they stood in the door looking back into the darkened, unfamiliar cave of the house, and the last shutting of the door.

"Want anything to eat before we start?" his father said. He had the box of left-over food, ready to load it into the Ford.

"No," the boy said. "I don't feel very good."

His father looked at him sharply, and his brows drew down. "What do you mean, you don't feel very good?"

"I feel kind of sick to my stomach," the boy said, and stood lugubrious and resentful under his father's harsh glare.

"Oh Jesus," his father said finally. "You would. Well, get in."

The boy walked out to the gate, closed it when the Ford passed through, and climbed in. His father needn't act as if a person got sick just for fun. He belched, testing himself, and thought with forlorn satisfaction that he would probably have to throw up pretty soon. He could feel his insides rolling as the Ford lurched, and he tasted deep inside himself for that old familiar awful bitter taste of a sour stomach. He thought that the belch had had it, just a little.

"How're you feeling?" his father said as they passed Pete and Emil.

"Kind of sick," the boy said. He tasted again, thinking how bad it was that his mother had gone off and left him, and now here he was going to have a bilious spell, and nobody with him but Pa, who didn't ever have any patience with sickness even though he had plenty of sick headaches himself. He belched again, and the gall burned his throat. Misery went through him. He was sick, and all Pa would do about it was to get mad and think he did it on purpose to make things unpleasant. Brine flooded his mouth, he swallowed, belched again, felt the blood drain from his face, and hung onto the side of the car.

"Pa," he said. "Pa, I got to throw up!"

Through his fear and misery he saw his father's sideward face, the exasperation, the irritation just short of swearing, but no sympathy, no pity. He began to bawl, and as the Ford rolled to a stop in the narrow wagon-track he leaned out and vomited over the side.

When Elsa turned to look back for the last time she saw the broad body of her husband, the slight one of her son, standing together at the gate, and behind them the shanty and the vanishing line of fence dipping down the coulee. Bruce's figure looked thin, spidery, somehow pathetic, and she waved, watching his arm come up. His face remained steadily fixed in her direction. Poor lamb, he'd had a lonesome summer. It would be a treat for him to get back to town.

The sun's glare was bright in her eyes, and she bent her head away from it. Almost fifty miles to go, and no roads to speak of for the first fifteen, just wagon tracks that split and branched and wandered through the buffalo grass. It would have been much nicer if Brucie could have come with her. Someone to talk to. And he didn't want to ride with Bo. He'd been a little sullen with Bo ever since the shooting of the sparrow. She sighed, wondering if all boys held things against their fathers as a kind of natural reaction against authority, or if Bruce were going to be a grudge-holder, or if maybe—she thought of the hot-cold river and the picnic in the Bearpaws—if he might remember something about that time back in Washington.

She put her foot on the trailing lines and wriggled out of her coat. Letting the team plod on, she pushed up her sleeves and opened the throat of her blouse. It was already hot. The scar on her right arm caught her eye. In six years the shiny red had faded, but it always reacted to sunburn violently, and was redder than the tan of the unharmed skin. There was a ridge of tight scar in the elbow that wouldn't quite let her straighten the arm out. That was one relic of the days she wanted to forget. Could there be, she wondered, another relic in the mind of that child? Would he, at four years, have hatred and fear so burned into him that the scar would never leave?

She laughed at herself and picked up the lines. Put me by myself, she said, just let me sit alone for a few hours, and I'll sure worry something up.

She sat looking at the base of the wagon tongue, watching the singletrees jerk, staring half-seeing at the black hairs snagged in the bolt of the doubletree. Her mind doubled on itself, avoiding things as a horse shies. She didn't want to think of those things. But there was the look on Bruce's face as he watched his father, the old familiar feel in the air of hard times and restlessness, as definite and recognizable as a weather change to a rheumatic old man.

The prairie lay around her, withered and pitted and brown like a very old face, but she didn't see it. Her eyes were fixed on the space between the horses, and her mind went back, beyond Washington, beyond Dakota, back to Minnesota where it started, back to Indian Falls when she was eighteen and had run away from what she couldn't bear, or thought she couldn't bear. Her mother might have stayed and borne it and made some kind of triumph out of it, but when you were eighteen you didn't know what you knew when you were thirty-two, and because you were eighteen and proud and blind and full of high notions you ran away like a coward and called it the only decent thing to do.

She couldn't run away from this, and wasn't going to. Only she wished that the still, breezeless air didn't carry that threat of storm, and that the rheumatic joints of her old worrying mind didn't ache with the fear of something.

She looked up. She was approaching Gadke's, and Mrs. Gadke was in the yard, her apron full of chicken feed. She came to the road to meet the wagon, her greeting so warm and hearty that Elsa heard the loneliness and isolation in it. Farm women were always lonely. There were never enough visitors to satisfy their itch to talk, and up here there were probably not a half dozen a year. She leaned down to shake Mrs. Gadke's hand.

"Well, well!" Mrs. Gadke said. "Moving in again."

Elsa took off her hat and fanned herself and laughed. "Seems like we're always loaded up going somewhere."

"I wish I was," Mrs. Gadke said. She looked at the loaded wagon with envy. "Come in and have a cup of coffee and a bite."

"I shouldn't," Elsa said. "Bo and Bruce are coming in the car, and I ought to be covering ground."

"Oh, come on in," Mrs. Gadke said. "You can spare twenty minutes. We don't see you folks more'n twice a year."

Elsa let herself be temped down. She sat in the kitchen and had a cup of coffee and looked at Mrs. Gadke's brilliant row of geraniums, more than a dozen, in a wooden box under the window. "Your plants are pretty," she said. "Moving as much as we do, I can't seem to keep flowers going. I just get some nice plants started in town and we have to leave them with somebody or bring them out here, and if we leave them they get forgotten and die, and if we bring them they get broken."

"They're a comfort," Mrs. Gadke said. "But if I could talk Gadke into going in for the winter I'd sure be glad to do without."

"I notice you've got a rose bush outside."

"Gadke put that in for me last spring. It seems to be doing all right. I dump my dishwater on it every day. It's a climbing kind, white blossoms."

"It'll be lovely when it blooms," Elsa said. "There are some people over by us, some English people named Garfield, that have planted trees in their coulee. He used to work in a greenhouse and he thinks they'll grow."

She knew while she said it that she was envying Mrs. Gadke her geraniums and that rose bush, and that she envied the Garfields their trees. But what she really envied in both of them was the permanence they had. They had both made up their minds to settle down and stick, they weren't bonanza farmers gambling against the rains. Or if they gambled, they risked their whole lives, and it was only on that assumption that you could be comfortable in a place.

She rose. "I really have to get on," she said. "It's a long drive in the wagon."

"I s'pose you'll be out again come spring," Mrs. Gadke said. "Plan to stop off and stay the night. Then you could get a good start and have the morning to shake down in your own place."

"Thank you," Elsa said. "That's nice of you." She put her foot on the hub and took hold of the dusty iron tire, hoisting herself up. "I don't know," she said, looking down. "Bo's so discouraged about the crop this year that I don't know whether we'll ever be out again. I had a kind of feeling this morning when I drove off that I was saying goodbye for good."

"Of course you'll be back," Mrs. Gadke said. She stood back as the wagon started, and Elsa turned three times to wave to the stout aproned figure before she dipped down into the first rolling country and climbed off to open the horse-pasture gate. Ahead of her was fifteen miles without house or field, just one immense pasture with herds of horses thundering away from the wagon, standing on high ground to stare with ears up, whickering loudly, curiously, and putting the team into a state of nervousness and scaring the colt so that he hugged his mother's side.

The wagon rocked, the road over the rolling ground was rougher and rockier, and the seat was hard. She folded her coat and sat on it, and the team went steadily. The trees seesawed, the tugs slacked and tightened, the doubletree bolt squeaked, and she felt the weight of the wagon like a falling thing whenever the wheels rolled solidly over a hump and jounced down.

You never like what you've got, she was thinking. Mrs. Gadke, with something permanent and good started there, wanted to leave it and come to town for the winter. You had to stay in a place to make it a home. A home had to be lived in every day, every month, every year for a long time, till it was worn like an old shoe and fitted the comfortable curvatures of your life.

It was almost eleven before she heard the tooting of the Ford's horn, and looked back to see it behind her. She turned off the road and stopped, and Bruce got out of the car and into the seat beside her. Elsa took one look at his greenish-white face and wrapped her arms around him.

"Oh, what's the matter?" she said.

"Sick to his stomach," Bo said from the car. His lips went down in a wry, deprecatory grimace.

Stroking the boy's thin back, Elsa said, "Maybe he should go on with you. I'll be hours behind."

"He doesn't want to go with me," Bo said, and pressed his lips together.

She saw that he was irritable, sore, exasperated, ready to bite. "All right," she said. "You go on then."

She watched him pull ahead in the trail. Bruce lay down with his feet in her lap and his straw hat over his face. Within a mile they came to the other edge of the pasture. Bo had left the gate open, and she knew from that how cranky he was. He was usually as fussy as an old woman about gates.

When she got up again after closing it, Bruce was sitting up, looking forlorn and pinched around the mouth.

"Feel better?"

"No," he said sullenly.

"You'd better lie down again."

"I don't want to lie down."

She let him have his contrary way while they rocked over the last mile of ruts to the junction with the Robsart road. He wanted, she knew, to be sympathized with, and if he wanted that, he wasn't as sick as he pretended to be. When he got a real sick headache he was in bed for two days.

Bruce squirmed sullenly. He said, "Pa got mad at me for being sick."

"You couldn't help being sick," she said. "He wouldn't get mad at you for that."

"Well, he did."

"Pa's just disappointed about the crop," she said. "He's got a lot of worries on his mind. He wasn't mad at you."

The boy pulled his straw hat down over his eyes and glowered under the brim. "I hate Pa!" he said.

Elsa reached out and shook him hard. "I don't want you talking like that. Understand?"

His shoulders contracted under her hands, and bending to look at his face she saw his old expression of stony, stubborn implacability. It was useless to try to talk to him when he wore that look, but she shook him again anyway, and said, "Pa's doing the best he can. That's all any of us can do. We've all got to do the best we can and help all we can."

She said no more to him for a long time, and there was nothing on the road to interest him. He sat for a while slumped, lurching with the wagon, thinking how he hated his father and how when he got big enough he would run away and after a while he would come back rich and well dressed and grown up, and take Chet and Ma away to live with him, and if Pa wanted to come too he'd just turn his big McLaughlin around and drive off and leave him standing there.

After a time he lay down, and his mother said, "Feeling sick again?"

"No."

"You might as well keep lying down anyway," she said. "It'll be three hours at least before we're there. You can go right to bed when we get back."

"I feel all right."

He lay quietly, his straw hat over his face and his legs sprawled over the boxes piled in front of the seat. His mind slipped away from how he hated his father, caught for a spiteful minute, wandered off again to consider what he would do when they got to town. The thought of town made him squirm his back and keep his eyes shut the way he did when he was having a nice dream and didn't want to wake up. He nursed the pictures that came to him, went painstakingly around and through everything that town meant, and everything that made summer and winter different.

In summer it was the farm, and freedom and loneliness and the clean sharpening of the senses, the feeling of strong personal identity in the midst of a wide, cleanly-bounded world; but the rest of the year it was the town, sunk in its ancient river valley hemmed in by the bench hills, and that was another life.

That life centered around the three houses on the cutbank side of the west bend, and the bath houses behind, on the bank, that the boy got to use only for a short time in the spring. In winter they were used as storehouses by the three families in that end of the town. His feet knew the path, rutted hard with frost or deep in snow, that went out past the barn to the bath houses; his fingers knew the cut of the bail and the icy slop of water as he lugged buckets from the chopped hole in the river ice, staggering lopsidedly up the dugway from the footbridge head. His fingers knew too the sticky bite of a frosty doorknob, they knew the clumsy fumbling with the bath house key when he was sent out to bring a chunk of frozen beef or pork in from the still, cold, faintly urine-and-wet-bathing-suit-smelling shanty. His nose knew bath house smell and barn smell and kitchen smell and the smell of baking paint behind the redhot parlor heater, and those were town.

Town was Preacher Morrison and the Sunday school parties where they played beanbag and crocinole. It was birthday parties the girls gave, and the bolt of hair-ribbon that Mr. Orullian cut from when you went in to spend your two bits for a present. It was McGregor's hardware store with the smell of stove blacking and turpentine and the tallowy smell of the baled muskrat skins on the back counter. It was the Pastime Movie Theater where every Friday night there was a new installment of *The Black Box* or *Tarzan of the Apes* or *The Red Ace*. It was the boys, Weddie Orullian or Preacher-Kid Morrison that the cave caved in on last spring, or Bill Brewer or the Heathcliff kids from across the river, the bunch he went skating with around the river's bitter bends, spreading his mackinaw to the wind on the way back and skimming like a bird up to the fires and slush and noise by the cutbank.

Town was many things, was the irrigation dam of old man Purcell where they trapped muskrats and weasels and once a mink, the willow breaks where in late fall the gang of little kids built huts of branches, playing they were holing up for the winter—huts which the Big-Kid gang, Chet among them, always discovered and tore down. It was the smell of dry willow leaves crushed and rolled in tissue paper and smoked, the taste of wild rose hips nibbled on an October afternoon, the numb blue-white of snow moons when the crowd of them rode on a bob behind Pete Purcell's pony up the long Swift Current hill, their handsleds stretched out in a black line behind. It was the game they played after a heavy blizzard, when they tunneled down through the overhanging drifts piled against the cutbanks, making a smooth packed burrow through which they could dive in a breathless belly-ride and skid snowy and yelling onto the river ice.

The town was Whitemud, Saskatchewan, what Bo Mason, when he was disgusted, was likely to call a dirty little dung-heeled sagebrush town. But to the boy it was society, civilization, a warm place of home where his mother sat sewing long hours under the weak light of the north windows, singing sometimes to herself, making dresses for girls who were going to be married or for women who lived up on Millionaire Row. The town was school, the excitement of books, the Ridpath *History of the World* that he had read entirely through by his eighth birthday. His mother, telling that to neighbors, always spoke with awe in her voice, and her pride in his brains sent him scrabbling for anything else in the old bookcase upstairs that he had not already read. Mostly it was novels like *The Rock in the Baltic* and *Graustark* and *The Three Musketeers.*

Town, home, was that and more. It was the steel engravings in Ridpath, the "Rape of the Sabine Women" that he puzzled over and finally asked his mother about, to be told that he shouldn't be so everlastingly curious. It was the sixth grade room where they sang "God Save the King" and "In Days of Yore from Britain's Shore" and "The March of the Men of Harlech," and the boy sang with tears in his eyes because the songs were heroic and Miss Crow's brother was in the army and Canada was at war with the Huns.

Bruce was a better scholar than Chet, but Chet was a better singer, and in all the cantatas the school gave. Chet was strong, too, and had licked Weddie Orullian and Pete Purcell and had almost licked Tad McGovern.

Town was things that had happened, like the time he had shot himself through the toe with Chet's .22, the numb moment before he knew he was hurt, when he thought somebody had hit him in the foot with a rock, and stood there with the .22 in his hand wondering what had made the noise, until he saw the sole ripped clear off his shoe, and the leather bloody.

Town was winter, the river ice full of air bubbles like silver coins, and the wonder of a Chinook in the midst of bitter cold, when he woke to the wail of a blizzard and looked out to see no blizzard at all, but a thaw, the eaves of Chance's house dripping, the roof melted black, the ground a lake of slush and water, and the wind coming through the three little portholes of the storm windows warm as milk. Town was the four-gabled white house his father had built when the town was first settled in 1914, the room where he and Chet lay in bed making pictures of dragons and trains and animals and angels among the blotches left by the firemen's chemicals when the attic had caught fire. It was the parlor downstairs, the piano his mother was so fond of, the big-bellied Round Oak stove with the asbestos pad underneath and the scuttle of lignite behind it.

It was his mother darning, and sometimes his father reading or reciting Robert W. Service:

This is the law of the Yukon, and ever she makes it plain.
Send not your foolish and feeble, send but your strong and your sane . . .

Sometimes too it was stories, when his father was feeling good, exciting stories about the Wisconsin woods and the Terrible Swede and little Pete the Wanigan boy and Paul Bunyan and Hot Biscuit Slim. When the boys were finally shooed off to bed, going reluctantly up the cold stairs and looking back wanting more, Bruce always had a strong feeling of home and warmth and security on nights like that, when his father was jovial and full of yarns. He knew his mother liked those too. She never had the tired look in her shoulders, the puckery squint around her eyes, the habit of looking as if she saw something through the wall.

His mother's hand touched him, and she said, "Well, son, there's the big city."

He sat up and looked. They were starting down the dugway. Below them lay the river valley and the looping bends, and at the top of the big U-bend the houses of Whitemud. He pushed his hat back and watched as they went down carefully, the wooden brake shoes sizzling on the tires like sandpaper, the horses' rumps hunched back, braced into the breeching against the push of the load. The colt limped along beside Daisy, fell behind, trotted tiredly to catch up.

"Poor little thing," Elsa said. "That's an awful trip for a poor little colt."

Bruce snapped his fingers and whistled at the lagging colt. "Come on, Peggie," he said. "We're pretty near there."

"Glad?" his mother said.

"Uh huh."

"So am I," she said, and laughed. "Or I would be if I knew what we were going to live on this winter."

V

What, said Bo to himself, sitting and thinking, trying to figure away the winter that stretched ahead, would an Indian do to make sure of eating for those seven months? How would some pioneer off in the wilderness provide for his family?

There were the cows and the chickens. He had already figured them, one cow fresh and one due to freshen in two months. There might be a little milk to sell, and there might be a few extra eggs from their dozen hens. But that was almost all. The jobs he could do he had done. He had spent three frantic weeks cutting fall hay on the north bench, had borrowed a baler so that he'd be able to get more into the small loft he had. There might be some of that to sell, if he turned the horses loose on the range and kept only the cows and the colt inside. And he had hauled five wagon-loads of lignite from the hillside west of the railroad bridge, enough to keep them warm for the winter. It was lousy fuel, half ash and half rock, but it was better than nothing, and it was free.

So, he said, figuring, they could keep warm and they could depend on milk and eggs. They might make a dime a day from their extra milk, maybe thirty cents a day when the muley freshened. There might be thirty or forty dollars' worth of extra hay. The town owed him ten dollars for his annual job of taking out the footbridge before the river froze over.

And that was all. That was absolutely, by God, he thought angrily, that was absolutely all. The little money he had got from the wheat would pay their bills and buy a few necessities, but there wouldn't be anything left in the spring for seed, for summer supplies, for anything.

Grind your own wheat? he said. Slaughter your own hogs? If you had a hog. Might be a good idea to try picking one up, even this late. It was cheaper on the hoof than it was in Heimie's shop. A beef was out, but he might find some farmer who was slaughtering and had a quarter to spare. But what else? There had to be something else. What would an Indian do?

Game? He considered it, weighing the cost of shells against the possible addition to the food supply. In Dakota they had sometimes frozen ducks and geese down. And fur. There were all those traps of the kids', and the north bench was full of muskrat sloughs. And fur was high. It would be small pickings, maybe, but better than sitting on your pratt.

He rose from the table, went to the window and looked into the square of front yard that two years ago had been hopefully seeded to lawn. The two spruces that he had gone clear up to the Cypress Hills for stood withered and dead at the corners of the house. That was the way with everything in the whole damn town. It started out big and just dwindled away.

He compressed his lips, breathed in a great lungful of air, went to the cellarway and took out his shotgun. The hell with just sitting around wondering and figuring. He would fill that bath house so full of meat, by God, that they'd eat duck three times a day and have some left over for the Fourth of July.

So through the waning days of mid-October, in the chill, leaden, snow-spitting weather, he spent days on the north bench after ducks. He built a blind and sat patiently for whole mornings at a time with his feet slowly going dead through the heavy socks and waders, watching the sky and the bobbing decoys riding the shallow, riffled water. He sat in the wind with the mangy dogskin coat around his ears, and when a flock circled and came back he crouched lower, shaking the coat off onto the packed damp tules, and as they came in he let them have it, taking no chances, trying no fancy shots, letting them come clear down even, shooting sitting birds, because there was no limit in this kind of hunting. He was after a winter's meat.

The first day, red-nosed and windburned, he brought in fourteen ducks. The next day he got only eight. The day after that he had a carful of teal and mallard and spoonbill, and one goose. In a week he brought in over a hundred birds. They had eaten duck until the very sight of one turned their stomachs, Elsa and the boys had plucked ducks until their fingers were sore (because duck down, Bo said, made good pillows, and pillows were things people always wanted. Elsa could get some ticking and make a lot of pillows and you ought to get a buck apiece for them).

He was driven by such a furious compulsion to fill the house with game that Elsa laughed at him, asking him when he was going to start saving tea-lead and string, and he was irritated and hurt that she couldn't see how necessary it was to save every penny. For himself, he was a miser. The thought of all the money he had squandered in the past ten years tortured him. The necessity of saving everything, making use of everything, living off the land, was an obsession that hardly let him sleep. Elsa tried to make him stop. People were talking about the flu that was spreading around the country. John Chapman said that if it came anywhere close he was hitting for California. It would be a hard and cold and long winter even if the flu didn't get to them, and Bo's going out and catching pneumonia in a slough wouldn't make it any easier.

She might as well have saved her breath. He kept up his hunting, she picked a dozen or two dozen ducks every day, there were gunny sacks full of duck feathers waiting to be made into pillows when she got time. The ducks themselves they hung out to freeze, and then strung up in long lines in the bath house, but it was early in the season for freezing down meat, and Elsa eyed them dubiously, afraid they might all spoil.

They did. The weather turned warm, the frozen ground softened and turned to mud. Bo was in a frenzy. A hundred ducks out there, enough for fifty meals, two months' meat, and the damned thermometer jumped up to forty-five degrees. He rushed down to Heimie Gross to see if they could be packed in Heimie's ice-house, but Heimie's ice-house was nothing but damp sawdust. There wouldn't be any ice until the river froze.

"God damn!" Bo said. He stood for a minute, thinking, and then started toward home, took the key from the kitchen door, and went out to the bath house. It felt cold inside when he stepped in, but not cold enough. He felt one of the ducks hanging from the wire. Beginning to soften. He swore again, his eyes darting around the bare room with the benches, the dirty inscriptions, the nails where clothes and bathing suits were hung in the summer.

There was a step outside, and Elsa looked in. "How are they?" she said. She held her hand up, feeling the air. "It feels pretty cold yet. Maybe they'll last till night, and it'll get colder then."

He shook his head, looking at the strings of ducks, fat, meaty, their necks stretched from hanging and their webbed feet dangling. "Have you got any empty fruit sealers?"

"A dozen or so, maybe." She looked doubtfully at the ducks. "Would that work?"

"Well, something's got to work!" he shouted at her. "Have you got any better ideas?"

"It seems a shame," she said. "The jars I've got wouldn't save more than a few."

"I know that." He clicked his teeth, wanting to cut loose and kick the bench away from the wall. Violent impulses jumped in his hands and feet, and he went abruptly outside. Elsa came after him.

"I'll go get the jars boiling," she said hurriedly, and with a side glance at him went back to the house.

Bo stood where he was, looking out over the cutbank, across the river to the low thick scrub of willow and alder and black birch. It never failed. You worked your head off and then something went sour. His mind groped for an object to curse, something to vent his anger on. A tin can lay at his feet, and with one swing he booted it thirty feet into the river.

Well, there were only four ways of preserving meat that he knew of. Freezing was out because of the thaw, canning would take care of only a few ducks, and jars were too expensive to buy. Drying was out of the question in this weather. So there was only smoking left. He had never heard of smoked duck, but by God there was going to be plenty of smoked duck this winter. He locked the bath house door, and lurching in his haste, started for the barn to get tools and boards to knock together a smokehouse.

At the end of five days he gave up. The ducks which had hung in the smoke, wizened, dried, blackened things, were rubbery and evil-tasting. The combination of gamy flavor and smoke was enough, he said, to turn the stomach of a vulture. He tasted them raw, and they sickened him. He boiled one, and the smell drove him from the house. Finally he threw the whole lot of them in the river, and all they had from his furious hunting was a dozen jars of canned duck and a few of duck soup.

By October 28 the river was filmed with brittle ice under the wagons coming down from the bench and fording below Purcell's. There were many wagons. Bo, driven to prowl the town and sit in Anderson's poolhall, saw two dozen men he did not recognize, and the street was full of strange women and children. The town wore a look of unaccustomed activity, as if for Thanksgiving or Christmas, but there was little holiday feeling. Faces were long and talk somber, and they talked of three things: the war, the price of food, and the flu.

Bo had been too busy to pay any attention to the flu, but listening to the farmers who hung around the poolhall he heard the fear in their talk. Out on the prairie, miles from town or a doctor, a man got thinking. There was never a winter that some homesteader didn't get snowed in, or break his leg or cut himself with an ax and then sit there in his shanty unable to help himself, sitting with his sheepskin on and all his blankets over that, hoarding his fuel, while his wound festered and swelled and the shack got colder, and almost every spring some such homesteader was found frozen stiff. Suppose, then, a whole family got sick with this flu, and no help around, and winter setting in solid and cold three weeks early?

It was supposing things like this that drove in the homesteaders in wagons piled with goods, to settle down on some relative or friend or in vacant rooms. Three families had gone together and cobbled up a shack, half house and half tent, in the curve of the willows east of the elevators. Even a tent in town was better, in these times, than a house out on the bitter flats.

The papers they read didn't reassure them. On both coasts the hospitals were jammed, the army camps were crowded with sick soldiers, whole inland parts of the country were virtually isolated. Because there was no safe place to run to, people stayed, but they took it easy about going outdoors, they doctored colds as if they were pneumonia, they kept their children home from school if a sniffle was heard in the primary room, they soused their handkerchiefs with the eucalyptus oil that Henderson the druggist said was a preventative. And they sat in Anderson's poolhall and talked.

Once Bo sat for a solid hour hearing how the disease turned you black as ink just before it killed you, and how people in the last stages rose from their beds and ran screaming and gibbering through the streets, foaming at the mouth and biting anyone who got in their way. Bo hawked in disgust and got up to take a drink from the waterpail in back. As he lifted the dipper he saw the yellow-green moss coating the tin bottom, and dumped the water angrily on the floor. With his fingernail he traced a skull and crossbones in the bottom of the dipper, digging the scum off clear to the stained metal, and hung the thing up again. No wonder these guys were scared of the flu. They had a right to be, with things like that left around to drink out of.

Back at the bar, sticky and smelling sweetly of strawberry pop, he drummed his fingers on the counter and looked at Ed Anderson. Ed had had an eye knocked out by an exploding pop bottle the year before, and wore a black patch. "I don't suppose you've got a bottle of beer in the joint," Bo said.

Mopping off the counter, Ed turned to spit at a hidden spittoon. "I would if I could, boy," he said. "You just can't get it, even if the cops would let you sell it."

Bo drummed again, looking out the dirty windows into the street. He turned his head and inspected the half dozen men hanging around the front end, and cleaned his teeth with his tongue. Bunch of dung-footed dirt farmers. He contemplated them with contempt, wondering if it would do any good to try getting up a little stud game. But he gave it up immediately. If they were too leaded to play pool, they wouldn't play poker. They didn't even have spirit enough to crab about the prohibition law that kept them from having a schooner of beer.

"What's the matter with this town?" he said irritably. "Isn't there anybody in it with gumption enough to start a blind pig, even? What's the matter with you, Ed? You don't look like a Christer."

"I ain't any Christer," Ed said. "But I'm telling you, you can't get it. Where'd I buy it?"

"There must be somebody got it for sale. When I was selling beer on the road in Dakota I did my whole business with blind pigs."

The half dozen loungers were all looking at him. "What I wish," one said, "is that you could get a bottle of good strong liquor-sauce in this place. If that old flu lights around here I want to crawl in bed with a bottle."

"Ain't it the truth," Ed said. "If I had ten cases behind this bar I could sell out in three days."

"You could get five bucks a bottle for it, too," Bo said.

Ed's one eye, pale, with strained red streaks in it, opened in agreement, and he jerked his head sideways to shoot at the spittoon again. "You tell 'em," he said. "If a guy wants something bad enough, he'll pay anything."

Bo stood up. "Well," he said, "if bullshitting around would get a man a drink, I'd be stiff as a plank now. Anybody want to shoot a game of pool?"

Nobody did. Dissatisfied and aimless, he got into the dogskin and wandered outside. Weddie Orullian's great wife, thick and pillowy and wide as a sidewalk, the mother of nine children and enormous now with her tenth, went up the street on the other side and waved a bulky arm, grinning and yelling at him. Bo waved back. That old squaw, common as manure, but she had fun. About the only cheerful thing in the whole damn town.

He was disgusted, vaguely grouchy, irrationally sore at the farmers who sat around Anderson's all day and couldn't think of anything to do but tell bear stories about the flu. Every one of them wanted a drink or a bottle, but would they do anything to get it? They'd sit on their behinds and cry, that was all they'd do. It was only a hundred miles to Chinook, less than that to some of the smaller Montana towns. If they wanted a drink as bad as they said, they could drive over any time, get a carload, bring it back into Canada over any of a hundred little unwatched wagon-track trails . . .

In the middle of the plank sidewalk he stopped short. An incredulous laugh burst out of him. "Holy jumping Jesus!" he said softly. "I've been sitting right on top of a gold mine!"

Briefly, automatically, he wished for Jud. Jud was the only partner he had ever had, a guy you could depend on to come in on anything worth a gamble. But Jud was dead in Alaska, and there was nobody in town he could go to for money, nobody he wanted to cut into this proposition. The only possibility was Chapman, at the bank, and Chapman would have to be talked to like a Dutch uncle.

As he passed McKenna's store on the way to the bank another thought struck him, and he turned up the stairs to Dr. O'Malley's office. The doctor was in, sitting on his desk. He had a young, fresh face and an easy grin, and his sleeves, even in the chilly office, were rolled up above the elbows. Bo noticed that his arms were brown and corded with muscle. The kid was more man than he looked.

"Want to ask you a question," Bo said.

"Shoot."

"About this flu."

O'Malley's eyebrows lifted. "I've been answering that one for three weeks. Stay out of drafts, avoid catching cold, don't go outside when you're overheated, don't hang around in crowds or go to the picture palace." He grinned. "And pray," he said.

Bo grunted. "That isn't the question. I want to know if whiskey is good for the flu."

"Whiskey's good for almost anything," O'Malley said. "Except d.t.'s. Why?"

"It's a medicine, isn't it? You'd say it was good medicine for this influenza."

O'Malley laughed. "I guess it must be medicine. The druggist's the only person in town allowed to sell it. I've worn out a prescription pad helping him."

"That's all I want to know. Thanks."

The doctor's puzzled frown followed him to the door. With one hand on the knob Bo turned. "How's your own stock?"

"I haven't got any," O'Malley said. "I'm not in the liquor business. Sell you some nice ipecac."

"I don't want to buy any. I'm asking you if you want to buy any." He shoved his hands deep into the pockets of the dogskin.

"They've been saying that if the flu hits here the town'll be quarantined. Is that right?"

"Yes."

"And if it's quarantined there won't be any trains in or out."

"No."

"And if there aren't any trains there won't be any more supplies for Henderson."

"I asked him already to lay in a lot of salts and quinine and eucalyptus oil. We'll be cut off for a while, sure."

"But you didn't have him lay in any whiskey. Want me to bring you some?"

O'Malley sat down on the desk and slowly rolled down his sleeves, buttoning them neatly around his wrists. "It's against the law, you know."

"This is an emergency," Bo said.

"If it weren't," O'Malley said, "I wouldn't be talking to you. How much do you want for Irish?"

Bo guessed, guessing plenty high. "Six dollars a bottle."

"I'm used to paying around three and a half," the doctor said.

"But you haven't been able to get any."

The doctor stood up and reached for his coat on the hanger. "How much for a case?"

"Make it to you for sixty-five."

O'Malley rummaged in a drawer, came out again empty-handed, and faced Bo. "All right," he said. "Only there's this. Are you going to Montana after it?"

"I didn't say."

The doctor's voice sharpened. "I have to know, just the same. A lot of towns in Montana are quarantined already. I can connive to break the liquor law in an emergency, but if you're breaking quarantines to bring this whiskey in, I'm out."

"You needn't worry," Bo said. "The place I'm getting this isn't quarantined."

O'Malley held his eyes a minute. "All right," he said shortly. "A case of Irish, Bushmill's or Jameson's."

Bo nodded and went downstairs again, his mind jumping with figures. It was a dead immortal cinch. If he couldn't buy a case of Irish for thirty-five at the most, he'd kiss a pig. Maybe less, if he bought a lot, ten cases or so. His mind jumped again. Ten! The old Lizzie ought to carry twelve or fifteen. Maybe get a pony cask and decant it, sell plain old corn for three bucks a bottle . . .

John Chapman was sitting alone in the bank, peeling an apple carefully, the unbroken spiral peel hanging like a shaving as he turned the fruit. Bo watched him till the peel fell into the waste-basket, watched him halve and then quarter the white meat, and then asked for his loan: two hundred dollars for two weeks.

Chapman deliberated. There was already a mortgage on Bo's house, and no payment on the principal for a year and a half. "What security?" he said.

"How about my team?"

Very tall and bulky, Chapman sat and spread his hands. "If you didn't meet your obligation I couldn't get two hundred for a team. I couldn't get a hundred, this time of year."

"Listen," Bo said. "This is no bread-and-butter loan, see? I'll have that money back to you in a week, maybe less. You can have the team, the colt, two cows, and anything else you think you want if you'll let me have two hundred right now, American money."

"You sound pretty sure of yourself," Chapman said.

"It's foolproof," said Bo. "I don't even give a damn what interest you charge me, because I'll be paying this back before you know it's out of your safe."

A half hour later he went home carrying a bag of American silver dollars and some bills, all the American money Chapman had.

He kept the bag hidden under the hall seat until after supper, when the boys were sent up to bed. Even then he did not bring it out, but sat figuring. He ought to be able to get fifty dollars a case for good liquor, and if he couldn't buy it for around twenty-five there was something wrong. He could double his money. And suppose he got a twenty-gallon keg of corn. It shouldn't cost more than five dollars a gallon that way, and he could get three dollars a quart just like spitting in a stove door. Gold mine! he said. I hope to whisk in your piskers it's a gold mine.

He lifted his eyes and looked at Elsa, her head bent over her darning. "How much money have we got?"

She smiled. "Figuring again?"

"There's nothing wrong with knowing where you stand. Have we got any left?"

"I paid McKenna and the hardware store," she said, "and I laid out what we owe Hoffman for seed. There's not much left."

"Well, let's count it up and see. The less there is the easier it is to count."

While she was upstairs getting her purse he slipped into the hall, got the bag, and concealed it under his chair. Elsa came down and laid the purse on the table. "There's our worldly wealth," she said, and laughed.

Bo opened the purse and counted out a hundred and twenty-two dollars. The hundred he smoothed out, folded, smoothed again, and laid aside. The twenty-two he put back in the purse. Elsa watched him. He could see the curiosity and the anxiety in her face.

"What would you say," he said, "if I told you I could turn that hundred into two hundred and forty in three days?" He lifted the bills between his fingers, passed the other hand over them, waved his fingers. "Nothing up the sleeve," he said. He opened his right hand. "Nothing in the hand. Presto, chango, pffft!" He palmed the bills and showed her his empty hands and grinned. "Three days from now I'll make it return with a hundred and forty more."

The anxiety had not left her face. "You've got some deal on. What is it?"

"Starting with three hundred dollars," he said, "I can be worth over six hundred by the end of the week."

"But you haven't got three hundred to start."

He reached under the chair and got the bag, set it with a metallic clump on the table, untied the neck and poured a flood of silver dollars on the cloth.

"Well, where on earth . . . !" she said.

Expertly he stacked two piles of dollars, shuffled them, melted them into one pile with a smooth drawing motion. "We're out of the woods," he said.

She was facing him with her hands on the table, as if ready to rise. "Where did you get this?"

"Borrowed it."

"Who from?"

"Chapman."

"But . . ."

He got up and went around to her. "This is how it is," he said with his hands on her shoulders. "The flu'll hit us sure. It's already in Regina. And when it comes there won't be any way of getting in and out, or of bringing medicine in. So I'm going after some, to Chinook. I talked with the sawbones this afternoon."

"But why should you have to borrow all this money?"

"Because I'm making the profit. You know what the best medicine for flu is?"

"Eucalyptus oil?" she said. "I don't know."

"Good old-fashioned corn whiskey. So I'm going out like an old St. Bernard with a keg around my neck."

He felt her stiffen under his hands, and she leaned forward. "Whiskey business!" she said.

"It isn't whiskey business," he said in irritation. "Their damn fool prohibition law might kill off the whole town. Ask Doc O'Malley. He wants a case of Irish himself."

She stared across the table at the stacks of dollars. "What if you get caught?"

"Oh, caught! Who's going to be running around that prairie trying to catch anybody? Anyway it's a medical emergency."

When she said nothing for a long time he pulled her chair sideways and looked at her face. "You still don't like it," he said.

"I hate to see you get into that illegal business again," she said. "And it's dangerous. What if a blizzard came up, or you got sick on the road?"

"I might dislocate my jaw yawning, too," he said. "Hell, I can drive over there and back in less than two days."

"I wonder," she said. "I bet you it's snowing right now."

He went to the window and looked. The yellow panes of Chance's house, next door, were streaked with wavering white. "It isn't even the end of October yet," he said. "This'll be gone by morning. Even if it isn't I can wait a day."

Elsa came up and took his arm, and he looked down at her worried face. "Bo," she said, "I wish you wouldn't."

For a moment he stood, almost hating her, hating the way she and the kids hung on him and held him back, loaded him with responsibilities and then hamstrung him when he tried to do anything. His teeth clicked, but he waited till the anger passed. "Look," he said wearily. "This town's played out. It played out two or three years ago. Do you think I'd be sticking around here if it wasn't for you and the kids? I'd be off somewhere where there was money to be made, wouldn't I? Well, I'm sticking here, but you can't expect me not to make a living any way I can."

"You brought us up here," she said. "You said you didn't want to live anywhere without us. I believed you then, Bo."

In spite of himself he heard his voice rising, and he faced her, shaking-handed. "I'm sticking," he shouted. "I haven't run away, have I? I built you a house and made you a home, didn't I? But how in hell are we going to live in it without any money?"

Elsa looked at him, silent for a moment. "All right," she said. "I said when I came back that I'd never try to interfere with you again. I made up my mind that I was your wife and I'd stay your wife, no matter what. But I just want you to remember, Bo, that I never asked for more than we had. I'd have been satisfied with just a bare living, if we could only keep what we've had up here. So don't ever say you did this for me or them. Don't ever forget that I was against it."

Their eyes held for a moment, and he turned half away to look out the window. After a minute Elsa's hand touched his arm lightly. "Poor Bo," she said. When he turned back her eyes were shining with tears.

"Poor Elsa, you mean," he said. "Oh damn it, honey, you think I like to see us down to a hundred bucks with a whole winter ahead?"

"I know you don't," she said. She moved against him and he put his arms around her. "What you don't see," she said, "what you'll never see, is that there are things ten times worse than being poor."

"I guess I never will," he said. "Maybe you think it would be fun to go hungry, but I don't."

"So you still think you'll go."

He held her tightly against him, looking over her head at the open sack of money on the table, and his mind shut hard and tight. "I've got to," he said. "Whether you see it or not."

It still snowed in the morning, not heavily, but persistently, with a driving wind. For a few minutes Bo contemplated going away, but it was too thick, and with all the homesteaders crowded into the towns there would be no place to stop along the road if anything went wrong. So he spent the day canvassing the town discreetly, getting orders for five cases more without even propositioning the crowd at Anderson's. They were bulk-rye prospects anyway.

That afternoon he worked on the Ford in the shed. Under the seat he put a half dozen cans of canned heat, two spare sparkplugs, a couple pair of chains, and a little bottle of ether, trying to prepare for any sort of emergency. When a car wouldn't start, he had heard, a little ether in the sparkplug wells was like turpentine on a balky mule. With all that whiskey aboard he wasn't going to run any chance of getting stuck. He even cut up an old horse blanket, doubled it, and sewed it into a crude cover for the radiator. If the weather turned cold the radiator could freeze even with the motor running, and you wouldn't know it till you cracked the head or did some real damage.

There was gasoline left from the drum to fill the tank and a five gallon can. At the last minute, looking around for final preparations, Bo took out the back seat and set it against the wall. The car would hold more with the seat out.

After supper he sat in the kitchen while Elsa fried a chicken for his box lunch. It was Hallowe'en, and the boys were both out. Bo kept going to the door and looking out. The snow had stopped, but the ground was humped with drifts, and it was still blowing. From the direction of town he heard the distant yelling of kids.

"If those shysters come horsing around the shed and bung up that car I'll fill their behinds with birdshot," he said.

"It's locked, isn't it?"

"Locks don't stop kids when they get going on a tear."

"I'll stay up and watch," she said. "You should get to sleep early."

He looked at her curiously, wondering how much she still objected, how much she was swallowing. She had a habit of swallowing things, and then years later you discovered that she hadn't forgotten them.

The kitchen door swung open, and Chet and Bruce rushed in. Their noses were red and leaking with the cold, their eyes starting out.

"The flu's hit town!" they said in a breathless burst. "Old Mrs. Rieger's got it."

Bo shut the door. "How do you know?"

"Mr. McGregor said. We were out behind the Chinks', and he called us and said not to play any tricks because the flu was in town, and now all the kids are distributing flu masks and eucalyptus oil and we're going back right now."

"No you're not," Bo said. He looked at Elsa. "You chase these snickelfritzes up to bed. I'm going uptown to see what's going on."

"You won't be able to go now," she said, and the relief in her voice made him mad. "The town will be quarantined."

"That quarantine's nothing but a word," he said. "The town really needs the stuff now."

"Go where?" Chet said.

His father pushed him into the dining room. "None of your beeswax. Go on up to bed, both of you."

An hour uptown told him nothing he didn't know. Nobody would be allowed in or out of town, but that just made him grin. He could imagine people sitting out along the roads in the cold to warn people. Like hell. They'd be sealed up tight in their houses. At ten o'clock he went home from the darkened and deserted main street, stoked the parlor heater for the night, and went up to bed. All the actual coming of the flu did was to make it surer that he could sell all the whiskey the Ford would carry.

2

In the clear, gray-and-white morning he carried blankets and lunch box out to the shed. The snow had blown during the night, and a foot-deep drift with a deep bluish hollow at its inner edge curved around the corner of the barn. The thermometer read twenty-two above zero. The Ford smelled cold; it was hard to imagine that anything so cold would ever start.

Dumping the blankets and lunch, he went back to the house, dipped two steaming pails of water from the waterjacket of the range, and lugged them back out. They took careful pouring in the tiny hole, and he squinted in the gray indoor light, concentrating. When he had the radiator full he bent to feel the crank, engaged it, tried a half turn. It was like trying to lift the car with one hand. The cold oil gave heavily, reluctantly, to the crankshaft's turning. Whistling through his teeth, he went around to adjust spark and gas levers and switch the key to battery. Then with one finger hooked in the choke wire he bent and heaved, fighting the stiff inwards of the motor around. On his cheek he could feel the dim warmth of the water he had poured in.

Three minutes of laborious heaving loosened the crankshaft a little. He pulled the choke full out and threw his whole weight into the spin. After two ponderous twirls the motor coughed.

"Ha!" he said. He spun again, and again it coughed. It was a good feeling to have that stubborn frozen block of complicated metal giving before his pressure. He felt strong, heavy, able to twist the Ford any way he wanted to. The muscles hardened in his shoulder, and he heaved.

The motor coughed, caught, roared, died again in spite of his frantic coaxing of the choke wire. Another spin and it roared again, banging his knuckles against the mudguard. He choked it in quick bursts, laid his shoulder against the radiator to hold back the Ford's trembling, nuzzling eagerness, and watching his chance, ran around to pull down the spark and push up the gas lever. Only a frantic grab at the choke kept it from dying, and he nursed it carefully, leaning far inside the side-curtained darkness of the front seat. The switch to magneto was crucial: she survived it. He slipped the gas lever up and down, and she roared.

Okay, you old bugger, he said, and leaving it running, went back to the house sucking his skinned knuckles.

The boys were up, crowding their bottoms into the oven door and regarding the preparations with blurred and wondering eyes. Bo warmed his hands briefly before pulling on the big double mitts. When he picked up the bag of money he met Elsa's sober look.

"Now don't you worry, Sis."

"How can I help worrying? A thousand things could happen."

"You never saw me get into anything I couldn't get out of, did you?"

"There's always a first time," she said.

"Where's Pa going?" Chet said.

"Just on a little trip," Elsa said. She reached up to touch Bo's cheek. "Be awfully careful," she said.

He bent and kissed her, sparred a moment with the boys in farewell, and eyed them all seriously from the doorway. It wouldn't do to get into any trouble on this trip, with the flu in town. "You stay close," he said to Elsa. "I ought to be back tomorrow night, but if I'm not, don't worry. Something might hold me up till the day after."

He ducked out, swinging the heavy bag of dollars, and ran down the path, feeling light, agile, like a boy again. As he drove out of the shed and bucked through a drift into the road up past Van Dam's toward the oil derrick he booped once on the rubber horn to Elsa, standing in the doorway with her arms folded across her breast and watching him.

The wind had blown from the north all night, and the dugway up to the south bench was almost bare. But on the bench the snow lay in long, ripple-marked drifts, not deep, but deep enough to hide the road in spots. There had been no guard or hindrance, not even a sign, along the road as he left town. Bo folded a blanket on the floorboards to set his feet on. It was cold, but not too cold, and he was glad for the absence of wind. The sun, flat along the bench, burned on the crests of the drifts and the air in front of the car glittered with sunstruck motes of frost.

Close in, the fences and the Russian thistle jammed against them had kept the road fairly clear, and even where the fences gave out the drifts were nowhere more than a foot deep. The snow was so granular, almost like coarse sand, that he rode over it as he might have over a hard-packed beach.

There was no sign of life, no smoke, in the homesteads he passed; the pastures were empty of stock. As the farms thinned out and the fences broke off at right angles to leave the road unmarked, the drifts were more frequent, and he had to look far ahead to the spots blown bare to make sure of staying on the trail. Once, bucking across a long drift, he dipped down in a swale and bogged down. Three minutes after he had shovelled out he ran smack into a fence, and there was no gate.

He got out to look around, but there was nothing to tell him where he was, only the dazzle of sun on snow and the patches of beaten and frozen grass. Climbing in again, he cramped the wheels sharp left and bumped along the fence. Within a half mile he came to a gate, and recognized it. He was at the edge of the horse pasture. That wasn't so bad. He'd be at his own homestead by noon, could stop off and have lunch inside, warm up a little before going on. Experimentally he moved his toes inside the heavy socks and elkhide moccasins. Not cold yet, just a little stiff from sitting still.

He was lost twice in the horse pasture, finding his way back into the road each time by following the water ditch. Once he had to shovel out. When he pulled up toward Gadke's at eleven-thirty he decided to stop there rather than go on to the homestead. Any story would do to tell them. He was being sent for flu medicine, that was all.

But there was no one at Gadke's. The barn doors were nailed shut with cleats, the blinds in the house were drawn. Bo swore, kicking his numb feet together, and pulled out again. It was the homestead for lunch after all.

For a while he pounded his feet on the blanket and sang to keep warm, but it was too hard to follow the trail and sing at the same time. The biggest branch of the trail turned off just past Gadke's, and left only a pair of shallow ruts. In undrifted snow he could have followed them, but the drifts changed everything. In ten more minutes he was off the road again.

He swung left in a wide circle, but there were only drifts and bare grass. Under one wheel the bottom fell out of a drifted burnout, and the shock rattled his teeth. The motor died and he had to get out and crank. It infuriated him to be lost in a country he had driven through two dozen times. It was the damned snow; everything looked different.

All right, he said, and climbed in again. Lose the road, drive by ear. The sun was straight ahead of him. He couldn't go far wrong if he headed straight south, unless he hit a coulee he couldn't cross. The burnouts were enough to kink his neck, but if the Ford could stand them he could.

Within a mile he came to the edge of a coulee ten or fifteen feet deep and a hundred wide. "Damn!" he said, and sat peering through the windshield. The snow was deep in the coulee bottom, too deep. So it was go around. He cramped the wheels to the right and bucked drifts along the top till he got to the rounded, windswept edge where the grass was bare. All the coulees in this country ran east and south. If he went far enough west he ought to head this one.

He came to the head and saw the shack at the same time. It was a one-room, slant-roofed leanto, covered with tarpaper outside and striped vertically with lath. He had pulled into the yard, his eye on the thin smoke from the stovepipe, before he recognized the place as Ole Pederson's. He swore unbelievingly. He was within six miles of his own farm, and hadn't recognized a thing till he bumped into Ole's yard. But at least he was somewhere. Ole Pederson was a dumb Swede, but his fire was as warm as anybody's.

Feeling good again now that he had passed the bad part, now that Montana lay ahead of him, with marked roads, he hammered on the door. Inside he heard movement: he hammered again. "Hey, Ole!" he said.

The door opened and Ole Pederson, taller than the door by a good two inches, stood there stooping. He wore a black sweater with a wide orange stripe around the middle like the stripe of a Poland hog. His pale hair was wispily on end, as if he had been lying down, and his eyes were suspicious.

"Hi," Bo said. He started in, but Ole half closed the door, keeping his long melancholy face in the crack.

"Ay don't tank you batter coom in har," he said.

"Why, what's the matter?"

"Anyt'ing," Ole said wearily. "Ain't anyt'ing matter. But Ay don't tank you better coom in."

"What the hell?" Bo said. He peered at Ole's pale, long-cheeked face. "You sick?"

"No," Ole said. "Ay ban't sick. Ay yust don't vant to gat sick. Ay don't vant to run you out, but you batter go on."

"Hell," Bo said. "I couldn't give you the flu. I haven't got it."

"Var you coom from? V'itemud?"

"Yeah. And there's no flu there. Come on, let me in, I'm cold."

"Val, Ay don't know . . ."

With one quick step Bo crowded into the shack. "Hell's afire," he said. "You don't need to be scared of me. I'm healthy."

Ole backed up till he sat down on the bunk in the corner. He ran a great splay hand through his hair. "Ay vish you didn't coom in har," he said.

Bo had his mitts off, warming his hands over the stove. "Take it easy. How long have you been holed up?"

"Two veeks."

"Haven't you seen anybody all that time?"

"Two farmers," Ole said. "Ay rather be alone than catch flu."

Bo eyed him half in contempt. His fingers tingled with the heat, and he felt his toes, stiff and deeply aching when he set his weight on one foot or the other. Opening the box of lunch, he spread bread and butter and chicken on the table. A half sandwich went down in two bites, and he sank his teeth in a drumstick, cold and meaty and succulent. "Help yourself," he said with his mouth full.

Ole looked, but made no move, so Bo picked up the other drumstick and tossed it to him. He caught it clumsily in his lap and sat holding it, lugubrious and stubborn. Bo dropped the leg bone in the pail behind the stove and started on a second joint.

"Why don't you go into town where the doctors are, if you're scared of the flu?" he said.

Ole shook his head. "Ay don't vant to go to town." His face, which had been pale as cheese when Bo came in, was flushed now, clear to the roots of the yellow hair. Maybe the big dumb guy was sick and didn't know it.

"I'm going into Chinook, if you want to come along," Bo said.

When Ole shook his head again, Bo shrugged and pulled on his mitts, rolling the remains of the chicken in its napkin. "Well, that's your lookout," he said. "Thanks for the hospitality."

Ole sat on his bunk and with obvious relief watched him get ready to go.

"How do I get to the Chinook road?" Bo said. "Up along your fence?"

"It's a half mile," Ole said. "Turn right at the corner."

"Sure you don't want to come in?"

"Ay tank Ay stay har."

Bo shrugged and left him. He bumped down across the flats, turned right at the fence corner, and found the road. Fifteen minutes later he was on the narrow graded road coming up past Cree, in Montana, and with a contented sigh he settled back to let the Ford plow ahead. It was easy from here. Three hours and he'd be in Chinook. Eight hours for the whole hundred miles. That was good time, considering. And coming back he'd have his own tracks to follow.

At four o'clock, the sun already a dry yellow ball in the haze, he pulled into the empty street and stopped before the Palace Hotel. With the bag of money under his coat he climbed out, stiff and clumsy with cold, and stepped up on the plank sidewalk. It was funny there wasn't anyone around. Not a man, not a horse, not a sleigh or a car, was in the street. The hotel front was blank; he saw his own fur reflection coming to meet him in the front window. And the door, when he thumbed the latch and put his shoulder against the panel, was locked.

"Well I'll be . . ." he said. He cupped a hand over his eyes and put his nose against the glass. The desk was there, deserted. The chairs were there, the big-bellied stove, but there was no sign of life. Bo stepped back, his chest beginning to churn with slow rage. Now what if the flu had closed up the whole place? What if the saloons were closed? With narrowed eyes and lips compressed he started walking.

He saw the white flutter of paper on the saloon door before he reached the corner. "Closed while the flu is on," it said. "City Ordernance."

Savagely, his feet beginning to ache as walking brought the blood back, he cut across the deserted street to the other saloon where he had bought beer last summer. There was no sign up, but the doors were locked.

Involuntary swearing broke out of him. No place to sleep. Not a joint in the whole stinking, cowardly town open. No place to buy the whiskey he had driven a hundred cold miles for. But by God, somebody would have to open up, or he'd beat their door down.

He had knocked without success on three doors, up the street past the business section, when he saw a man hurrying along the opposite sidewalk. The man wore a white mask over his face, and his head was covered by a heavy fur cap with deep earlaps. Bo crossed over.

"What's the matter around here?" he said.

The man's eyes, sharp black holes between brown fur and white mask, darted at him, looked him up and down. "Where'd you come from?"

Bo let his face go dead and stupid. "I just come in off the farm. What's the matter, there ain't a place in town open."

"We got the flu," the man said. "The place is quarantined."

"Good gosh," Bo said. "Is that right?" He kept the man standing impatiently while he fingered his chin. "Hell, I wanted to buy me some whiskey," he said. "I heard there was this flu around, but I didn't know it was in town here."

"Everything's closed," the man said. "You can't even leave town, now you're in." He seemed rather pleased to see Bo stuck. "You got to get a mask, too. That's orders."

"How'd I get a mask if nothing's open?"

"Hospital," the man said. "Block up the first cross street on the right."

He started off, but Bo laid a hand on his arm. "Look," he said. "If I can't get out of here I still want a bottle or two. Where's a barkeep or somebody live?"

The man laughed. "The whole bunch from the Last Chance is in the hospital."

"Isn't there another one?"

"There's the Silver Dollar. Frank Selby lives right back of the joint. But you won't get him to open up."

"Well, I guess I'll try anyway," Bo said. He watched the man's slight hurrying figure go up the street, and wrinkled his lip and spat in the snow.

The Silver Dollar saloon ran back from a two-story false front for seventy or eighty feet, a bare blank wall for half its length. At the back end, where it became living quarters, there were two windows and a door approached by three wooden steps. The green shades were drawn on the windows.

Bo went up the steps, the bag of money under his coat, and knocked. For two minutes he waited without an answer. He banged on the storm door with the whole weight of his fist. One of the blinds, he thought, twitched slightly, but no one came to the door. He lifted his fist and thundered on the wood.

"Who's there?" a woman's voice whined suddenly. She must have tiptoed to the door, for the voice came directly through the boards in front of him.

"I have to see Frank Selby," Bo said. "It's important."

"He isn't seeing anybody," the woman said.

"He's got to see me," Bo said. "The doctor sent me."

There was a moment's silence, then the inner door was opened and the woman's face looked at him through the little window in the storm door. She had a red, wet-looking harelip. "What's the doctor want?" she said.

"I'm from Harlem. The doctor there sent me over for whiskey for medicine."

The woman shook her head. "You'll have to get it somewheres else. We're closed."

Quietly, out of her sight, Bo put his thumb on the storm-door latch, depressed it gently. As she started to shut the inner door he opened the outer one swiftly and stuck his foot in the crack. The woman confronted him furiously, shoving at the blocked door. "Go away!" she said. "You can't come butting in here!"

Bo took the bag from under his coat. "Look," he said. "I was sent over here in an emergency. I want three hundred bucks' worth of liquor for that whole town. And I'm not going back without it. You think I drove over here for fun?"

The woman stared at the bag, then at him. She licked the red split in her lip. Still exerting pressure on the door, she called, "Frank!"

In a minute her husband's face appeared over hers in the crack, a fat face, bartender-pale, with drooping sandy mustaches. "What is this?" he said. "What you trying to do?"

Lifting the bag before the man's hard eyes, Bo said, "I was sent over from Harlem for a carload of whiskey. They need it for flu medicine."

Both faces remained stuck behind the door's edge. "Jesus, man," Frank said, "I can't sell you nothing. The law's closed me up on account of this-here epidermic."

Bo rattled the bag. "I guess three hundred bucks ought to be worth opening up for."

"What's the matter with Joe's place in Harlem?"

"He's burned down. That's why I had to come over here."

Frank eyed the bag again. "All right," he said finally. "You wait right there." Bo took his foot out of the door and it closed smartly. He laughed. In five minutes Frank came out, a sheepskin around his ears, the strings of a flu mask dangling inside it and a muffler wrapped around mouth and nose.

"Afraid of freezing your handlebars?" Bo said.

"Go ahead and laugh," said Selby, through the muffler and mask. "You stay six feet away from me if you want me to sell you anything. Where's your car?"

"In front of the Palace."

"Drive it around behind the joint, clear around the house part and halfway up the inside. I don't want anybody snooping around."

When Bo brought the Ford around Frank opened a side door and backed away to a safe distance. "All right," he said. "What you want, now?"

"Got any kegs of rye?"

"Couple."

"How much?"

"I'd have to figure," Frank said. He figured. "Ninety-six."

"Okay. One of those. How about Irish?"

"How much you want?"

"Case."

"I'll see." He rummaged among a stack of case goods against the wall. The air in the storeroom was still and cold, full of the smell of whiskey and straw and burlap. "Here she is," Frank said. He swung the case out by its burlap ear. "What else?"

"Seven cases middle-price bourbon," Bo said. "What you got?"

He took a bottle of beer out of an opened barrel and yanked the cap off on a nailhead. The beer was icy cold and faintly skunky. "You ought to keep the light off beer in white bottles," he said. Frank, lifting cases around, only grunted through his muffler.

"I'll have to split up on you," he said finally. "I ain't got seven cases all one kind."

"Okay, long as it isn't rotgut." Sitting on a box, Bo tipped the beer and watched Frank pull cases together, watched him roll a keg from behind some barrels of beer.

"How much does that come to?" he said.

Frank figured on a barrel head. "Two hundred and ninety-four even."

"Sharpen your pencil a little," Bo said. "This is a wholesale deal."

"I already figured it wholesale. I don't make more'n a buck or two a case at that price."

"Tell you what," Bo said. "If it was for me, I'd never buy a bottle of it till I got a jobber's price. When a town buys whiskey for medicine it ought to get the lowdown. But you throw in another case of bourbon and I'll give you three hundred even."

Frank shook his head. "I couldn't do it. That's a whole case for six bucks. I wouldn't make a dime."

"That's the only kind of a deal I'm interested in," Bo said. "I went over to the hospital and talked to the guy from the Last Chance, because I couldn't raise anybody out in front here. He wanted to sell me the stuff, but I'd have to hunt up a relative of his to get it. I thought it'd be easier here. But if you don't want to talk business . . ."

Frank backed away further. "You been over to the hospital?" he said. His voice was a squawk. "What the hell do you come around me for?"

"You don't want to do business, uh?"

"All right, take it," Frank said. "Take your nine cases and get out of here."

"Now you're talking sense," Bo said. He held out the bag, but Frank put his hands behind him. "Put it on the table," he said. He stood back while Bo carried the sacks outside. "I'm not sticking my nose in the car you're driving, even," he said.

Bo worked swiftly in the late gray light. The seat took three flat cases neatly, and three more on top of those brought the load level with the sides. The keg, heavy and clumsy, he wrestled into the footspace in front of the back seat, and one of the three remaining cases he wedged beside the keg, padding it with a blanket. The last two he put in front, one in the seat and one on the floor. Then he covered the whole load with blankets and threw the gasoline can on top.

Frank was still standing back. "You count out the money," he said. "I'm not touching it till the wife bakes it in the oven."

"Okay," Bo said. "Strike a light."

Selby lighted a candle, and very carefully and contemptuously Bo counted out the stacks of dollars and the roll of bills. "Okay?"

"Okay," Selby said. "Dump 'em back in the bag."

The last thing Bo saw, as he backed out of the alley, Frank was carrying the sack before him as if it might explode. He would probably bake the glove he had touched the bag with, too. Bo laughed. As he bumped across the intersection of alley and street he whistled. The springs hit bottom on the slightest jar. No batting over burnouts on the way back. That was another reason for not starting back now. He'd need daylight to find the road and keep on it.

He slept that night at the livery stable, where he found two men taking care of a whole barnful of stock belonging to people in the hospital. They didn't want him at first. He loosened them up by going back to the car and breaking out a bottle of bourbon. After that they let him drive into the grain shed and make himself a bed of hay beside the car. When he lay down in his clothes, the fur coat wrapped around him under the blankets, he heard their voices loud through the partition, heard the stamp and blow of horses and the knocking of a cow's horns against the stanchions. The hay he had piled on the floor rustled under his weight, and sometime during the night he heard a dog sniffing under the shed door. The thought of food for tomorrow crossed his mind, but he let it drift. There was some bread left, and a wing of chicken, and if he got an early start he'd be back in Whitemud by early afternoon. Everything was jake. The bottle to the stablemen was a good investment. Keep them from getting too curious.

It was barely daylight when he woke. There was a yellow-spoked wheel directly in front of his eyes, and he lay wondering for a minute. His shoulders and hips were stiff and his feet cold. The wheel revolved a little, stopped, went around a little the other way, and he blinked his eyes clear and saw the car, the crack of light under the shed door.

He stood up, stamped his feet, swung his arms. A look into the Ford showed him the load untouched. In the other room he heard the stablemen snoring. Driven by ravenous hunger, he went through the partition door and into the stable. There were a half dozen milk pails on a bench. Four cows, in improvised stanchions, swung their heads to look at him. He hunted up a stool, tipped straw out of a pail, and sat down to the nearest one. The quart of milk he drew down was foamy and warm and slightly sickening, and it spilled on his coat as he tipped the pail to drink, but it laid the devil in his stomach. He drank it all, resting between gulps.

The stablemen were still asleep when he went through to the shed. There was the question of warm water for the Ford. He turned the radiator petcock and went out in back with a pail. The pump was there, a wide smooth icicle hanging like a white tongue from its mouth. The pump complained stiffly, but finally brought up water, and with the bucket in his hand he went in and started a fire in the sheetiron stove. When he came in with a second pail one of the stablemen was sitting up. His face was contracted and his eyes bloodshot. He looked incuriously at Bo for a few minutes and lay down again with his face to the wall. The other one snored on. They were still in their bunks when Bo poured the hot water into the rust-smelling gullet of the Ford and bent to crank.

At eight o'clock he was headed out of town, following his own solitary tracks of yesterday. There was not a soul anywhere about except for a woman who pulled back her front curtains to look as he went by.

It was not as clear as it had been the day before. The sun, straight ahead of him for the first two miles, before the north road switched off, was pale behind a thin screen of mist. Occasional snake-trails of snow moved in the road, wriggled a few yards, and died. Inside the side-curtains it did not seem cold.

As he drove, Bo was juggling figures. Sometimes, having difficulty keeping them straight in his head, he took his hands off the wheel and drew them in the palm of his mitt. The case to Doc O'Malley would bring him sixty-five; the keg, at three dollars a quart, would be another two hundred and forty. That was his original investment, right there. The whole eight cases of bourbon were gravy. At four dollars a bottle—and there were ninety-six bottles, or ninety-five since he'd given one to the stablemen—and four times ninety-five was. . . . He figured on his mitt, one eye on the road. Three hundred and eighty, all clear profit. Not so bad, he said to the Ford, not so bad. He remembered the time only a couple of weeks ago when he had nearly lost his mind because his ducks had spoiled. That all seemed very childish and primitive, something out of the backwoods. One good break, and he was past all that scrabbling for a living.

He ate the fragments left in the lunch box and threw the box out the window. There were no tracks on the straight road except his own. The sun, on his right now, was barely visible through the mist. He took a firmer grip on the wheel and pulled the gas lever down a notch. It might snow, and he needed those tracks. Ahead of him the erratic wind lifted a trail of dry snow across the road.

His feet, unprotected now by a folded blanket, felt the cold first. When he stamped them he realized that they had been getting colder all the time. In one way cold was good. There wouldn't be much snow if the temperature dropped. But the road ahead was now crawling with lifting ropes of drift. He swore. Wind was just as bad, worse. It would cover his tracks in an hour if it blew. The sky was grayer now, too, the whole world darkening over the white waste. He dropped the gas lever another notch.

Where the road turned off to Cree he stopped, hesitating between choices. He ought to stop somewhere and get warm, have a cup of coffee, before tackling the last fifty miles. But there might be no one left at Cree. His own place would be like an icehouse, and the kerosene stove wouldn't do more than warm his hands. The only place he was sure of was Ole's, and Ole wouldn't be tickled to death to see him. He jammed his foot hard on the low pedal. Ole would see him anyway.

Rather than risk losing his way he followed his own tracks, going carefully across the roadless flat and stopping in Ole's yard. The wind blew smoke down to the ground, making him turn his head. The barometer must be clear to the bottom, if smoke wouldn't rise.

Ole didn't answer his first knock, and he put his shoulder against the door. Locked. He pounded again, listened. "Coom in," the Swede's voice said.

"The door's locked!" Bo yelled.

He waited, leaning his weight impatiently against the homemade door. In a minute the latch clicked and Ole, still in his orange-banded sweater, backed away to let him come in. The minute he looked at the Swede's face a slow, climbing rage tightened in Bo's stomach and chest. Ole's face was drawn and sick, his eyes glittering like blue ice, his mouth chapped and stained in the corners.

"What's the matter?" Bo said sharply. "You sick?"

"Ay don't feel gude," Ole said. "Ay ant felt gude for couple days."

"Well for Christ sake why didn't you come into Chinook with me yesterday?"

Ole didn't answer, and Bo stood with his hands spread over the stove, watching the drawn face. He was sick all right. He was sick as a horse. His hands shook, and when he stooped to sit down in the bunk he had to reach back and ease himself down. So now, Bo said, I suppose I've got this big ox on my hands with the Ford already so loaded she hits bottom on every bump!

"You were a damn fool to stay out here alone in the first place," he said.

Ole shook with a heavy chill, grabbed his hands together and held them to still their trembling, but said nothing.

"Got any coffee?"

Ole's eyes lifted to the stove. Bo took the top off the pot, saw that there was a good pint of black liquid inside, and shoved it onto the hot part of the stove. While he waited for it to boil he went out and got a bottle of bourbon. "Where's your corkscrew?" he said.

"Ay an't got vun."

"Oh for . . . !" Angrily Bo pawed through the half dozen knives and forks and spoons on the cupboard shelf. Nothing, not even a paring knife. He tipped the bottle neck down and gave the bottom a stiff, flat-palmed smack, hitting it so hard that pain jolted up his wrist. You had to hit it just right to jar the cork loose, and it was a damn fool stunt anyway. He had seen a man cut his hand half off trying it. But if this big dumb Ole didn't have a corkscrew there was nothing else to do. He jolted the bottle again, savagely. On the fifth try he caught it right. The cork started a quarter of an inch, and he got the blade of his knife under it and lifted carefully till it came out.

He poured a tin cup a third full and handed it to Ole. "This is supposed to be medicine," he said. "See what it does for you."

He had a swig himself out of the bottle, corked it and stuck it in the pocket of his coat. The coffee pot was steaming, rocking a little on the stove.

"Got a cup or anything you haven't used lately?" Bo said. Ole's mouth opened helplessly, he wrinkled his forehead, looking at the cupboard.

"Well, what the hell," Bo said. He found a saucepan and poured coffee into it for himself, filled the Swede's cup. "Drink that damn quick," he said. "We got to get out of here."

His own coffee was black and bitter, with grounds floating in it, but he drank it in gulps, scalding hot. In ten minutes he had the bundled Swede outside with a quilt around him. The two cases of whiskey in the front seat had to be shifted to the back. That was bad, because they were loose and might bounce and break, but there was nothing else he could do. He boosted Ole inside and tucked the quilt in, went inside to snatch two blankets off the bunk, dumped the coffee pot into the fire and kicked the draft shut, and closed the door.

There was a definite wind now, a creeping, close-to-the-ground wind that he could feel as a steady pressure from the northwest. The drifting didn't seem to be much worse. The snow was packed, and only the top dust blew. But it was cold. It was cold as all billy hell. And if it hadn't been for this jinx Swede he'd be almost to

Gadke's by now. As he climbed in he looked with distaste at Ole's muffled face. A guy that big ought to be all man.

Ole was definitely a jinx. At the first coulee head, still within sight of his shack, they had to run through a shallow swale drifted a foot deep on one side. Bo took it charging, but something under the snow, burnout or badger hole, rocked them with a solid, bouncing shock, and the Ford hit bottom and died in the drift. The inside filled with the smell of whiskey.

"*God* damn!" Bo said. He yanked the sidecurtain loose, ripping one of the eyelets, and swarmed over the side. God knew how many bottles were busted. There wasn't even time to look now. That wind was too dangerous. Hard pebbles stung his face, and he looked up to see that they were not drift, but snow.

Shovelling like a dynamo, he cleared the wheels and threw the shovel inside. "Can you drive?" he said to Ole.

Ole shook his head. "You're going to anyway," Bo said. "Shove over here." He showed Ole how to let the brake off and push down on the low pedal, feeding gas at the same time. "When I say go, let her have it," he said.

He braced himself against the body, said "Go!" and heaved forward. The Swede jammed on the pedal, forgot to feed gas, and killed the engine.

"Gas!" Bo yelled. "Give it the gas!"

Ole dropped his hands from the wheel and leaned away. His face was pitiful, as if he were going to cry. Bo took a deep breath and swallowed his rage, cranked, braced himself again. "Now take it easy," he said. "When I say go, let her in slow and give her plenty of gas."

This time the Swede gave her too much, and went roaring and spinning up the coulee side, out of control, scared to death and with his foot frozen to the gear pedal, so that Bo, encumbered with his heavy coat, had to sprint alongside and jump on the running board to yank on the hand brake. He was breathing hard when he climbed in, and his mind was red hot. The air inside the curtains was so thick with spilled whiskey it was almost intoxicating.

By the time they reached Gadke's the tracks were drifted half full, only the top edges clear, and the gray sky was spitting snow as hard as hail against the windshield. The wind increased steadily, pushing against the bellied sidecurtains, pouring in the V-shaped hole where Bo had torn the eyelet. And it was getting colder. He could feel it getting colder by the quarter-hour, feel it in his bones and in his mind. This was going to be a regular old he-blizzard, and he was still forty miles from home. At the horse pasture gate he stopped long enough to fit the radiator blanket on, thanking his stars he had had sense enough to make it.

There was no worrying about the trail now. The best he could do was to follow his yesterday's tracks, hoping to God they held out. His jaw clenched on him automatically as he drove, and at intervals he sat back and loosened it. Then the tense concentration of trying to see ahead through the drift and the murky white darkness crept into his muscles again, until he came to and forcibly relaxed once more. Ole sat beside him, humped in the quilt.

They passed through the horse pasture faster than Bo had been able to go coming out. The not-quite-covered tracks did that for them, at least. But at the far gate of the pasture Bo stood outside the Ford, his eyes slitted against the drift, and wondered whether to stay with the tracks, off the road, or try to pick up the trail. He hadn't been far off that time. If he started straight out from the gate he ought to hit his tracks again within a half mile. It was taking chances, but there wasn't much time. The wind by now was a positive force, a thing you fought against. Drift and falling snow were indistinguishable, the air was thick with stinging pebbles, the visibility hardly fifty feet. It was so cold that his eyes stung and watered, his nose leaked. When he wiped it with the back of his mitt he felt the slick ice on the leather.

He piled in beside the Swede. "How do you feel?" he said. "Okay?"

Ole nodded, and they started again. Bo was driving partly by sight, partly by feel now. The wind was from the northwest. He wanted to go almost exactly northeast. If he kept the wind square against the left sidecurtains, kept them stiff and strained as a sail, he couldn't go far wrong. The minute they flapped or slackened he was circling. Either that or the wind was shifting. But you didn't think about that.

Ahead of him was a whirling blur of light, the whole world driving, moving, blowing under his wheels. It was like driving on fast water, except when bumps or holes or burnouts bounced them clear down to the axle. Bo squinted, peering, his stiff hands clenched on the wheel. There were almost-effaced tracks ahead. He'd hit it, right on the nose. But the tracks turned off left, and the slack in the sidecurtains when he started to follow them stopped him. He had almost followed his own tracks the wrong way. That would have been a nice one. He backed and started in the other direction.

He knew he was off the road. The feel of the tires told him that. But as long as he kept the wind there, he'd eventually run into the graded road paralleling the south bench. He'd get her in, by the gods, if he had to drive the last twenty miles by ear.

The tires hit the road again. He could feel it, smooth and hard and sunken, though his eyes showed him no difference. Within five minutes the ruts were gone. He swung into the wind, feeling for them like a blind man, his body tense, one with the body of the car. And in the moment when he turned, feeling, the wind burst furiously against the sidecurtain and tore it loose, and he was blinded and muffled in cloth and icy isinglass.

Cursing, he stepped on the pedals and fought the frantic flapping thing out of his face. The eyelets were all ripped now, and there was no fastening it down. Wind and snow drove into the hole, hammering his eyes shut, peppering his face. His fury ripped out of him in shouted swearing as he twisted, trying to fasten the curtain somehow. The Swede was a hindrance to his movements, and he shoved him over in the seat with one fierce hunch of the shoulder. Eventually he had to grope in the back seat and find one of Ole's blankets, poke it up over the metal bar along the top, pull it down through, and sit on both ends. It wasn't as good as the curtain, and it made the car almost as dark as night, but it kept that paralyzing wind out of his face while he drove.

The thing became a nightmare. He sat within the dark cabin of the car, his numb feet ready to jump on the pedals, his mitt slipping up and down the smooth wheel to feed or retard gas, his eyes glued on the flowing, dirty-gray-white world ahead. In an hour he was on and off the road a dozen times.

The strain and cold stiffened his legs and arms, but the excitement got into him, too. He turned to look at Ole, only his long nose and white eyebrows showing above the quilt, and in the steady motor-sounding and wind-sounding and snow-pebble-sounding silence of the car he opened his mouth and yelled.

"Yippee!" he yelled. "Powder River, let 'er buck!"

The Swede jumped six inches, and his lugubrious, startled face turned. "You tank ve make it?" he said.

Bo laughed, jamming the Ford recklessly through a drift. "You're God damned right Ay tank ve make it," he said. He leaned back, stretching, relaxing his tightened muscles for the twentieth time. The whirl of snow visible through the windshield lifted briefly, showing him a drift deeper than most, long and crested and fringed with blowing tatters of snow. He stepped on the low pedal and dragged down the gas, and then when they were halfway through the drift, slugging through it like a boat through a wave, he saw the fence dead ahead.

His hands yanked the wheel around and his feet stabbed at

brake and reverse at the same time. The Ford shuddered, swung, skidded, caught, hit something big and solid under the drift, and very slowly, as if careful not to hurt or break anything, turned over on its side.

The Swede's two hundred pounds came down on Bo, smashing him against the blanket curtain. He felt the snow under the blanket crush and give, heard bottles smash, and then he was fighting back against Ole's dead weight, reaching out through the clumsy coat and mitts and blanket to turn the switch and cut the motor, still running on its side.

"Get off!" he roared. "Get your damned dead carcass out of here!"

3

Elsa saw the storm coming by mid-morning. At noon, when she was certain it was going to be bad, she sent the boys out after buckets of lignite, and herself went out to the barn, broke open two bales of hay with the pliers, and tumbled the packed dusty slabs down into the mangers. If the wind blew hard for very long she might not be able to get out for a while.

The wind was up strong when she closed the barn doors; she had to wrestle them with all her weight. Worry about Bo drove her to sit by the kitchen window afterward, staring across the vacant lot toward the south road. The air was striated and thick with driving snow. Sometimes such a gust drove in from the river bend that Van Dam's house and shed and the low windmill tower were blotted out, and only the madly-whirling blades remained in sight. Jim Van Dam ought to do something about that mill. It would blow to pieces if he didn't.

She was about to call Chet and send him over to tell them their mill was up, but another look at the wind and snow outside made her hesitate. And the boys should be kept in because of the flu. She reached for her coat, stooping to see if the blades were still there.

"I'm going over to Van Dam's," she called into the other room. "You stay in the house, both of you."

Her eyes screwed shut, body doubled against the gusts, she made her way across the lot and up to the Van Dam's kitchen door. Her knock went rattling down the wind. No one could possibly have heard it. She pushed on the knob, and the wind blew her into the kitchen.

Jim Van Dam, a lumpy quilt around him, was sitting on the oven door with a dishpan between his feet. He did not look up, but his wife, holding his forehead, turned a white face and made a sick grimace with her mouth. Then he gagged and retched, and she clung to him, holding him upright.

"He just took sick this morning," Mrs. Van Dam said. "He was all right till after breakfast, and then he said he felt queer and I gave him some calomel, and he's been throwing up for a half hour."

She didn't say, "Now he's got it!" but she might just as well have. Elsa took off her coat. "Where's little Jimmy?" she said.

"Upstairs. I wouldn't let him come down too close."

"Haven't you got a couch in the parlor?"

"Yes."

"We ought to get him to bed," Elsa said. She looked at Jim Van Dam, contracted in a heavy chill. But when she stooped to help Mrs. Van Dam get him to his feet and lead him in to the couch, the other woman's eyes met hers. "Oh Lord," Mrs. Van Dam said. "Now you've got close to him."

"I'd have got close, one way or another," Elsa said. "None of us can hide away, I guess."

She stayed until the sick man was in bed. Then she brought in a good supply of coal and kindling and two buckets of water from the well. The windmill, she saw, was already ruined, its whole broad tail gone. But it was no time to be worrying about windmills. When she sat inside again having a cup of coffee with Mrs. Van Dam she tried not to see the tears that dropped on the oilcloth, or the scrawny thinness of Mrs. Van Dam's arms. But even more than that she tried not to see the picture that her mind kept trying to uncover, a picture of Bo fighting his way back through this blizzard, maybe sick himself. If Jim Van Dam was all right at breakfast and was this sick by noon, Bo could have had the same thing happen . . .

"I'll go call up Doctor O'Malley," she said. "He'll probably want to send a rig to take Jim to the schoolhouse. They've got the schoolteachers nursing, and he'd get better care there."

"Thank you," Mrs. Van Dam said. "I guess that'd be better. I'm no good. When I knew he had it I just went all to pieces. I . . ."

"Don't worry," Elsa said. "Give him a hot lemonade and some salts when he can hold them down, and I'll see if I can't get somebody. They may not be able to get around till tomorrow, if this keeps up, but I'll run over and see if you need anything."

It was not until the odd jobs, the telephoning, the grim preparatory look through the medicine cupboard, were all done that worry crept up on her and stayed. It came obliquely, discreetly, while the wind leaned its weight against the house, howled around the eaves, strained the frame until the walls creaked. No car could get a mile in such weather. She had confidence in Bo, he could get through if anyone could, but that was just the trouble. He might very well have started from Chinook while there was only that pre-storm haze, that ominous coppery blurring over the sun, thinking that he could run through before it broke. And once it broke he wouldn't stop. He'd butt right ahead, stubborn as a mule, no matter how cold it got or how the wind blew.

She went to the front window and looked at the thermometer hung on the outside frame. Two below. An hour ago it had been five above, at noon ten above. The longer he drove—if he was driving—the worse it got.

Her nervousness wouldn't let her sit still. She went to the sewing machine and got out the dress she was making for Freda Appleton, who was getting married next month. One way to keep from worrying was to stitch buttonholes. But every few minutes during the two hours she sat sewing she kept getting up to stoke the stove, shake down ashes, walk to the window and see the temperature down to four below, to five, to eight. The boys squabbled over the Erector set on the dining room table, and she separated them and punished Chet with only half her mind on what she was doing. If Bo had started after breakfast he ought to be in now. The clock said a quarter to five. Still, he hadn't promised to be home tonight. He would certainly have stopped along the road, at Cree or Gadke's, or maybe at Robsart if he had chosen that road. He was probably sitting by some fire not two hours away from home, waiting for the storm to blow out.

But suppose the snow blocked the roads and stayed. There would be no moving the car till spring.

Oh fiddle, she said. He can take care of himself. He could get a bobsleigh or something.

With all that liquor aboard? her mind said. What would he do with that? Suppose he stopped somewhere and they called in the police . . .

She spun it back and forth, stitching steadily at the monotonous buttonholes that went from neck to waist down the back of the dress. The stove glowed dull red in the corner, but over where she sat under the lamp, needing light now to see, it was cold. Occasionally attention stiffened her body as she thought she heard noises that were not the wind. Once she was sure she heard a car, but the window showed nothing, and when she tried to look out the back door it was nailed fast by the wind. For a minute she stood listening: the sound did not come again. Before she quite gave it up she went out on the front porch, half blocked by an angled drift laid in on the side-swipe of wind, and stood for a minute with the snow buzzing in the air around her, settling on hair and dress.

He wouldn't try to come through today. There was no use worrying. Besides, it was time to get the boys' supper. Shut in, they did nothing but eat. They had been piecing all day, and still they said periodically, every ten minutes, "Ma, when do we eat?"

Still she went back to the buttonholes for a few more minutes, unwilling just yet to break her listening. But what if, her mind said slyly, Bo stopped somewhere along the road and they had the flu there? Or what if he got so sick on the road he couldn't make it to shelter?

For one catastrophic instant she saw the image of cattle frozen by the roadsides in the spring, still frozen but bloated, horrible, obscene as the spring thaws softened them for the final decay, and she gritted her teeth and stood up. It was then that she heard the unmistakable thumping on the porch.

When she opened the door a short, involuntary cry was wrenched out of her. A man was stretched out on the steps, feet trailing in the broken snow, and another man was pulling at his shoulders, trying to drag him. He turned his head at her cry, and his grim face, only nose and eyes showing from the fur cap, brought her flying out to help him. Together they dragged the heavy figure of the other man into the hallway. The boys were in the door. "Get out of the way!" Bo said harshly, and shouldered through them.

They laid the man down, and in the light from the front room Elsa recognized Ole Pederson. His cheeks and nose were leprous white, and he had evidently been crying, because his eyelids were stuck fast with ice. Her eyes darted to Bo. "Oh, I was afraid . . . !" she said. "Where . . . ?" She was noticing twenty things at once —the rattling icicles beaten into the hair of the dogskin coat, the monstrous hulk of Bo's shoulders, the harsh jut of brows and nose from the fur cap, the way he stood with feet wide apart, swaying, the telltale white patches on cheeks and nose. In one quick glance, while she moved to shut the door on the curving lee-side wind, she saw all those things, and her hands and feet and voice leaped into action all at once.

"Lie down on the couch," she said to Bo. "Chet, get a dishpan full of snow. Bruce, run upstairs and get some blankets and quilts, anything." Reaching outside, she scooped a handful of snow and slammed the door. The boys were still stupidly staring at Ole's corpse-like body; Bo stood in the hall door, swaying a little and grinning at her. She hustled the boys off, slapped the handful of snow into his face and held it there. He stood for it quietly, and when the last white patch had disappeared, wiped his face clumsily on a towel, his hands still cased in the icy mitts. He was stooping to look at Ole when Elsa got the pan of snow from Chet and came up. He motioned her away.

"Stay away from him, all of you," he said.

Deliberately, as if contemptuous of his own samaritanism, he smeared snow in Ole's face with a mittened hand, found it clumsy, and held out his hands to Elsa. "Pull these off," he said.

The leather was frozen stiff, curved from the wheel, and the mitts came off hard. When they came, Elsa cried out again. Bo's fingers were white clear to the second joint. She tried to push them down in the pan of snow, but he snarled at her and brushed her away. She watched helplessly while his frozen fingers rubbed snow on the frozen cheeks and nose and chin of the Swede. In a minute she had started forward to pull at him. "Let me," she said, "if he has to be fixed first."

"Get back!" he said. He waved at the boys, crowding on the stairway to look down. "You too. Get away on back."

"What's the matter with him?" she said. "Is he hurt?"

Bo didn't answer. He tried to take off Ole's mittens, could not grip them with his own wooden hands, and ended by pulling them off with his teeth. Ole's hands were all right.

On his heels beside the Swede, Bo squatted and washed his hands in the pan. "I don't know what to do about this big sucker," he said finally. "I don't want you tending him. He's got the flu, I guess."

"Chester," Elsa said without turning her head. "Call up Doctor O'Malley and tell him if he's going to pick up Jim Van Dam as soon as the storm stops, he'd better pick up Ole here, too."

"Van Dam got it?" Bo said.

"I was over there helping this afternoon."

Their eyes met, and Bo shrugged. "Then I guess there's no use taking care. I didn't want to bring him home, but there wasn't anything else I could do with the guy."

"Brucie," Elsa said, "you start taking off Pa's moccasins. Chet, soon as you telephone, get a new pan of snow and a bucket of water."

Leaving Ole on the floor under a quilt, she led Bo in to the couch. He walked awkwardly, his face fiery red now, and his hair on end. Coming out of the bearish bulkiness of the coat, his head and neck had a curiously frail human look that made Elsa shake her head. You got used to thinking of Bo as capable of anything, but this drive must have been close. She steered her mind away from how close it must have been. His hands and face frozen, maybe his feet . . .

"Hurry!" she said to Bruce. "Hustle!"

Her own hands were busy kneading his fingers in the pan of snow, working them, stripping them like the teats of a cow, rubbing down the wrists. "Feel anything?" He shook his head.

"Let's get a little closer to the fire," he said. He started to rise, but she pushed him back.

"You stay away from the fire!" She rubbed at the cold, curved, inhuman fingers, and relief brought tears to her eyes. "Oh Bo!" she said. "You shouldn't have tried to come through!"

Bruce was pulling with both hands at the heavy socks, their tops stiff frozen. One came off, and Elsa, looking down, winced. The feet too, waxen and ribbed by the ribs of the socks like something hardened in a mold. She looked at Bo's red, unshaven face, and he winked at her, drawing down the corners of his mouth. "Too many patients for you, Mama," he said.

Elsa dumped snow in Chet's pail of water, rolled up Bo's trouser legs, and set both feet in the pail. The water slopped over, but she went on working, shifting from fingers to toes. "Feel anything yet?"

"Hands a little. I haven't felt my feet since we tipped over."

That brought her head up. "Tipped over? How did you get in then?"

"I drove in," Bo said. His mood seemed to have changed suddenly; he looked and sounded savage, as if the very memory made him mad.

"But," she said, still rubbing. "If you tipped over . . ."

"I tipped it back up," he said harshly. "Don't ask me how. I don't know how. I don't know how I got in, either, so you needn't ask me that. I didn't know I was here till I ran into the fence."

"Oh my Lord," Elsa said softly. "You're lucky!"

He grunted irritably. "Yeah. I'm lucky I ran into that big dumb Ole and had to bring him in. I'm lucky I froze my face and hands and feet. I'm lucky I broke God knows how many bottles of hooch. I'm lucky as hell, all right."

She kept still, and later, when the pain came like fire into his hands and feet and he roared at her to let him alone, she did as he asked. There was nothing she knew about the care of frost-bite except to keep it from thawing out too fast, to prevent gangrene. Maybe he'd get gangrene anyway. It had taken a long time to get the blood back into his feet. And all, she said in one spiteful instant, for a load of whiskey and a few dollars!

Because Bo was in too much pain now to put his weight on his feet, she got the boys to help knock one of the upstairs beds apart and set it up again in the dining room. Ole Pederson came out of his stupor and moaned, and she tugged and dragged and rolled him onto the couch in the parlor. Then she fed the boys and sent them off to bed.

Curiously, that night was one of almost blissful peace. Her worry was gone, Bo was home and safe. The blizzard whined and howled and pounded around the house, and the thermometer on the porch dropped steadily until at ten o'clock it hovered around twenty below. But the parlor stove was brick red, there was a comfortable, lazy smell of baking paint from the asbestos mat in the corner. She sat on the edge of the bed in the dining room and talked to Bo quietly, remembering the other time she had had to rub his frosted face with snow, the day she and Bo had decided to be married. Ole Pederson, in the other room, drank the duck soup she fixed for him and sank into a light, mumbling sleep, and with the lamp blown out she and Bo talked.

He told her about Chinook, and the fear that was chasing everybody inside to hibernate.

"A lot of people wouldn't have brought Ole in," she said, and smoothed the hair back from his forehead.

Bo grunted. "All this running away. If it's going to get you it's going to get you."

"Funny," Elsa said. "Once it comes right into your own house you're not scared any more. It's just like any sickness, and it doesn't paralyze you the way it did at first."

"If you're not scared you're the only person in Saskatchewan that isn't." He reached out to pull her down for a kiss, and flinched back. She felt the jerk of his body, and a slow, warm, tender amusement filled her. He could overcome almost anything, do almost anything, but give him a little pain and put him in bed and he was the biggest baby on earth. A woman could stand twice as much. It was like the way the flu seemed to take the biggest and strongest men, as if their very strength was their weakness.

She moved, and Bo hissed at her through gritted teeth to go easy. When she dragged the covers over his feet that way she liked to killed him.

"What will you do about the things in the car?" she said. "You can't walk, and you can't hold anything in your hands."

"I don't know. Unless maybe you and the kids can get it in. None of it's very heavy but the keg, and that'll roll."

"We'll get it," she said. "Are you sure it's all right out there tonight? Won't it freeze, or something?"

He roared with laughter that clicked off against his teeth when the pain hit him. "Old Mama!" he said. "It'll freeze about as quick as the thermometer will."

"How about the car radiator?"

"Have to get a new one," he said. "That'll be froze solid before now. I wasn't in very good shape to drain her when I pulled in."

"No," she said, and stooped carefully to kiss his raw, hot face. "You couldn't have gone on much longer, could you?"

"It was pretty touchy for a while."

"Mmmm," she said, quiet now, at rest, warm and peaceful and in possession of her husband and her home, and not afraid of anything because somehow they'd pull through it. They always did. She lay down beside him, and he turned to nuzzle in her throat. His lips nipped softly at the skin under her jaw.

"Take off your clothes," he whispered.

"How about Ole?"

"He's dead to the world."

"Don't talk that way. He might really be."

"He's all right. Take them off."

"But your hands," she said. "Your feet . . ."

"I don't need any hands or feet."

"Well," she said, softly laughing. "If you want to hurt yourself . . ."

"I want to hurt you too," he said, and bit her suddenly in the side of the neck. "I want us both to lie here and love and hurt together and then I want to sleep for twenty-four hours."

But in the morning the peace was gone, along with the violence of the wind. When she slid out of bed, Bo still slept, one swollen hand up to his cheek. His breath was quick and noisy. She started to feel his forehead, but didn't for fear of waking him. In the other room Ole Pederson was blazing with fever, his voice so weak that she could hardly make out what he said. Blood had oozed in tiny droplets through the pores of his cheeks and nose, and the inert helplessness of his body alarmed her. In slippers and robe she padded into the kitchen to make up the fire and get some breakfast going.

The rattling of the stove when she shook down the ashes woke Bo. He felt hot, he said, and his eternally God damned hands and feet were killing him. His back felt as if a log had dropped across it, and his bones ached. For a while she went on trying to believe that his fever was from the frost-bite and the terrible trip, but after breakfast he gurgled frantically, waved his arm, grew purple. She ran with a pan and he leaned out of bed to vomit, every joint tortured with retching, his eyes shut and the sweat standing out on his forehead in great drops. She remembered Jim Van Dam yesterday, the big man helpless as a stunned calf, and she couldn't pretend any more.

The sleigh from the livery stable came just after she and Chet had finished getting the liquor in from the Ford. The house stank with the smell from the seven broken bottles when Lars Poulsen knocked on the door and said to get the patients ready, he'd go get Van Dam and be back. He stood on the porch and chewed tobacco rhythmically, watching her from under his felt cap.

"See your car got left out."

"Yes."

"Bo out driving when the wind come on?"

She hesitated a moment. "Yes."

"Where's he now?" Poulsen said. "Like to see him a minute."

"Come in," she said. "He's sick. I was just going to ask you to take him in to the schoolhouse."

Poulsen came in, stood at Bo's bedside. "Fella told me you had some hooch for sale," he said.

"Who told you that?"

"I dunno. One of the guys." He lifted his head and sniffed. "Smells like he had it about right."

"What do you want?" Bo said. "I'm sort of laid out. Sis'll get it for you."

"How much is it?" Elsa said. "I don't know anything about it."

"I can tell you, can't I?" he said. "Get a pencil and I'll make you a price list. You'll have to run this thing if I'm getting lugged off to the hospital."

She got paper and pencil and made a list at his dictation, and sold Lars Poulsen a half gallon of rye and watched him tuck it carefully under the seat of the bobsleigh and turn his horses toward Van Dam's. It was almost funny, the way her dislike for the whiskey business boomeranged. She was the operator of a blind pig now, all by herself. She could be arrested if anyone wanted to turn her in. But there was no time now to worry about that.

Poulsen was a long time at Van Dam's. When everything was ready for him she sat on the bed. "I hate to see you go up there," she said. "I'd rather take care of you here, but I think for the kids' sake . . ."

"You'd be up all night," Bo said. "You stay home and take it easy and I'll be back in a few days. This isn't anything but grippe."

"It's worse than grippe. You be careful, and do what they tell you to up there. I can imagine you ranting around and refusing to take your medicine."

He grunted. "Some of that hooch ought to be delivered," he

said. "The sawbones gets the case of Irish, and there's a list of guys who get bourbon. In my pocket, somewhere."

She found the list. "I'll see that they get it."

"Chet could take it on his sled," he said. "But tell him not to leave it without the money. Not for anybody."

"I won't be sending Chet," she said. "I won't have the kids mixed up in this."

For a minute he looked at her, red-faced and puffy-lipped. Then he grunted.

But he was tender with her when Poulsen's knock sounded. "Take it easy," he whispered. "I got a hunch that as soon as we get past this flu we're out of the woods."

Her lip was trembling, and she bit it down. "Bo, get well right away. Do what they tell you, and don't get mad at anything."

"What would I get mad at?"

"You always get mad when you're sick. You get mad at people for trying to help."

"Oh bull!" he said, grinning. To Poulsen he said, "How you going to get me out there? Got another man?"

"Nope. Can't you walk a few steps? I'll hold you up."

"My feet are froze," Bo said, instantly irritable. "Walking out there would be like walking on broken glass. Why the hell can't they send two men on a job like this?"

"Ain't got 'em to send," Poulsen said. "How about riding on my back? How much you weigh?"

"Two ten," Bo said. He snorted, a short, violent sound. "Feel like lugging two ten out there?"

"Now come on," Elsa said. "I can take your feet if Lars will take your shoulders."

They got him out finally, and he lay in the hay of the wagonbox with his forehead white and dewed, his jaw tight and his eyes furious. Then Ole, almost as heavy, but easier to carry because they didn't have to be careful of hands and feet. Poulsen climbed to the seat and Elsa leaned against the tailgate, looking at the bundled sick men, all of them big, strapping men, and she thought again of the thing people said, that the flu took the strongest first, the ones with the deep chests and wide backs. The tears in her eyes were like pebbles of ice.

"Goodbye," she said. "Get well quick, all of you." She said it to all, but she looked only at Bo. She saw his jaw relax a little. "Take it easy, Mama," he said. "I got enough meanness in me to poison any germ."

"John Chapman died this mornin'," Poulsen said from the seat.

Bo sat up, and the stab he made to catch his balance with his hand made him grit his teeth. "What did you say?"

"John Chapman's dead. Funny thing, Doc O'Malley says his heart was all out of place, clear over on the right side. Been that way all his life. Never think it, a big tall guy like that."

Bo's eyes sought Elsa's. "By Godfrey," he said, "I almost forgot about something."

"Shall I do anything about it?" She too had forgotten that they owed Chapman two hundred dollars. Now Chapman was dead. But they could pay it back as soon as she delivered those cases . . .

"No," Bo said. "Let it go. Everything's closed up anyway. Let it go." He lay back on the hay and stared upward. "John Chapman," he said, as if he didn't believe it. "I talked to him three days ago and he was as well as I was."

"Bo . . ." Elsa said.

Poulsen flipped the lines and the sled started, the runners creaking in the dry snow, breaking down through the drift as he swung around toward the school. "Goodbye!" Elsa shouted. "I'll be up to see you every chance I get. And please be careful, do what they say . . . !"

For just an instant, as the sled slid away and she saw the schoolhouse two blocks beyond in the middle of the white field, the symbol now of plague and death because it housed in its four square rooms dozens of sick men and women, Elsa was shaken by utter panic. Then the moment passed and she turned back to the house. Bo would be better there. The doctor was living there now, and there were nurses on duty day and night. She would have plenty to do trying to keep the boys safe, and taking care of Bo's whiskey.

For an hour she went about the house cleaning up all the leavings of the two men, throwing Bo's clothes in a tub of water and starting them to boil, hanging out all the blankets and quilts that had been over him and Ole, scalding the used dishes with triple doses of boiling water. Then she stood and looked at the stack of sacked whiskey in the corner, the keg on the kitchen chair with its bung up. That next, the sooner the better.

Altogether she made three trips, taking two cases at a time on Chet's sled, going boldly through the main street because she believed literally Bo's story of the emergency. She knocked on doors and was greeted suspiciously from inside, until she told her errand, when the doors came wide and eager hands reached for the ears of the sacks. "I'll have to have the money right now," she told them stolidly. "Bo's sick, but he told me not to leave anything without the money, because he borrowed the money to get it and has to pay it back right away."

Two of her customers paid at once. A third grumbled about the price. Elsa said, quite honestly, that she knew nothing about that except what Bo had told her. If the price wasn't all right, she would take it back. But Bill Patterson, who was doing the grumbling, didn't want it taken back. He went and found forty-eight dollars in every denomination down to pennies.

At the fourth house Jewel King wanted the whiskey but didn't have the money. The bank was closed, Chapman was dead, he couldn't pay till he could get into the bank again.

"I'm sorry," Elsa said. "Bo said not to leave it without the money. I can't."

"But good Lord, Elsa," King said. "We need that stuff. If Bo was here he wouldn't hold out. I'd give you the money in a minute if I could lay hands on it."

If it had been her own doing she would have let him have it. But she didn't want to do anything that Bo could find fault with. She hated this job, so she would do it impeccably. "I wish I could, Jewel," she said, "but Bo said not to."

"Well, let me have some of it," Jewel said. "I got enough money for a bottle or two. I got to have something around, with all these germs in the air."

"You come down," Elsa said. "Bo tipped over on the way in and and broke quite a few, and that left some loose bottles. I'll sell you all you want of those, or there's some bulk in a keg."

"Okay," he said. "I'll come down. Bo tipped over, you say? How'd he get back up?"

"I don't know. He wouldn't tell me."

King, scratching himself thoughtfully under the arm, laughed. "Old Bo," he said. "He's quite a boy."

"He brought a homesteader named Ole Pederson in with him," Elsa said. "He had the flu, and now Bo's got it."

King eased his weight onto the other foot. He obviously did not care to continue the conversation. Gregariousness had suddenly ceased to be pleasurable in Whitemud. "Yeah," he said. "Tough. Well . . ."

So Elsa pulled the case of bourbon back to the house, unloaded it, put the Irish on the sled, and went to the schoolhouse to see Bo. They wouldn't let her in. Visitors were not allowed. The best she could do was wait in the vestibule while Regina Orullian went to find O'Malley. When he came, he didn't have the money either. "If you want to leave it anyway," he said, "I can have a check for you tonight."

For just an instant, looking at his young, tired, sleepless-eyed face, she hesitated.

"Don't leave it if you don't want to," he said. "I can see why you might not. I might die, and you'd never be able to distill it out of me."

"I guess I'll take a chance," she said, and smiled at him.

The doctor ducked out of the storm door and carried in the sack. "I suppose you want to know how your husband is."

"I'd like to, yes."

"I wouldn't worry," O'Malley said. "He's too ornery to be hurt much. I tried putting packs on his hands and feet and he about tore the ward down. He'll be all right."

Elsa saw that he didn't like Bo. He didn't like him and yet he had a sneaking admiration for him. A lot of people reacted to him that way, they saw only his hard side . . .

"Well, thanks," she said. "Can I come back here every day and find out how he is?"

"Or call up," he said. "That's better." He looked at her speculatively. "How many of you at home now?"

"The two boys and I."

"If any of you get it," he said, "call up here right away. I can't do a thing unless I have everybody in one place. And if you hear of anyone else, call me, will you?"

"I will," she said. "And you're sure Bo isn't really very sick?"

"He's sick enough," O'Malley said, "but I think he'll be all right."

On the way back home again through the crusted drifts, she saw the sun break through the mist and shine for a few minutes thin and watery on the snow. She was glad O'Malley was there instead of old Doctor Barber. She remembered Barber, sag-cheeked, shaking-handed, riddled with dope or whatever it was he took. He must have been pretty far gone to drink denatured alcohol on a bet, the way he did. It occurred to her that everywhere she and Bo had lived there was somebody like Doctor Barber, lost and derelict and painful to see. Were they all over, she wondered, or was it just that Bo took them always to the fringes of civilization where the misfits and the drifters all congregated?

After lunch there was the problem of keeping the boys in the parlor while she served the continuous stream of people who came, some with milk pails, some with fruit jars, some furtive, some loud. The kitchen was headachy with the barroom smell of rye slopped from the keg. By suppertime she had taken in, from case goods and bulk, two hundred and sixty-five dollars. At eight o'clock that night she bundled up and walked to the schoolhouse, found that

Bo was sleeping and doing as well as could be expected, collected the sixty-five dollars from the doctor, and came home again. She put her afternoon's total of three hundred and thirty along with the six she had got from Poulsen in the morning, tucking it down in a box at the bottom of her bureau drawer. Tomorrow, if things went right, she would be shut of the whiskey job.

She knew the moment she woke that she was sick. Her bones ached, her head throbbed, her throat was inflamed and sore, and her tongue, when she stuck it out in front of the mirror, was coated with gray-green moss. For a minute, desperately, she tried to pretend it wasn't true. She was just tired; she hadn't slept well; she was coming on toward her time, and that always made her feel low and draggy. But she hadn't been up ten minutes before the staggering weakness in her legs made her sit down. She called for Chet and Bruce, raising her voice painfully over her sore throat, and in a few minutes Chet came racing downstairs. "Ma!" he said. "Brucie's got it! He threw up all over the bed!"

"Oh my Lord!" she said. Driving herself, she stood up and started for the stairs. "Call Doctor O'Malley," she said. "Tell him Brucie and Mommie have both got it. You'll have to hold the fort alone, son."

"Jeez!" Chet said. For a moment she thought he was going to run and cling to her legs as Bruce sometimes did. But he stood still, running his tongue around his upper lip. "I can do it," he said. "I can milk old Red and sell the whiskey and do everything."

"Sell the whiskey!" she said. "You don't know what you're talking about."

Within an hour she lay in the hay-filled box of Poulsen's sleigh, with Bruce, pinched and delirious, against her side. Poulsen was not driving the sled today, but a young man she did not know. He said his name was Vickers, and he had just got in from the south the night before. Why, he must be a sort of neighbor of ours, out on the farm, she thought. But she was too weak and tired, and Chet was standing beside the sleigh too consciously brave in his mackinaw. The devil could have been driving the team and she wouldn't have paid very much attention.

She made Chet promise to call up twice a day and report to the hospital how he was getting along. She asked Vickers to look in once in a while on his trips around. When they pulled away she couldn't even kiss Chet, or hug him, for fear of the death her lips might carry. She could only wave, sitting up weakly with her muttering younger son under the blankets beside her, and say, "Goodbye, Chet, goodbye. You're the man of the family now, you've got to hold the fort."

Too weak and hurried to do anything else, she had left the whiskey in plain sight in the kitchen. The bundle of money she carried in a knotted sock in her purse.

4

Until afternoon Chet stayed indoors. The silence of the house bothered him, and the thought of what if Mom and Pa and Brucie never came back at all lay big as a sob in his throat. On his back was the burden of being the man of the house, responsible for the fires, the stock, for getting his own meals and keeping the house clean. He accepted those duties solemnly. For a while he was attentive to the fires as though they were in danger of flickering out every ten minutes. He made the beds. He got the broom and stirred a dust in parlor and dining room.

As he was eating his second bowl of bread and milk for lunch, the young man named Vickers came back and said he needed some beds and bedding, so Chet helped him knock down both double beds and load them on the sleigh. He would sleep on the couch in the parlor. It was warmer there anyway, and it would be pretty nice to undress right by the fire and pop into bed without any cold old floor and stairs.

In the kitchen, making a list of things he had taken, Vickers saw the keg, the sacked bottles. "Your dad doesn't want to sell any of that, does he?" he said.

"Sure," Chet said. "That's what he got it for, to sell for flu medicine."

"What have you got?"

"Rye and bourbon," Chet said promptly. "There isn't much bourbon left, I guess." He rummaged. "Five bottles is all."

"How much?" Vickers said, and reached for his wallet.

"Four dollars a bottle," Chet said. He caught himself, shot a look at Vickers' face. If he got more than the regular price, they'd have to admit he had held the fort to a fare-thee-well. "Or is it four and a half?" he said. "I forget."

Vickers' face was expressionless. "Sure it isn't five? I wouldn't want to cheat you." Under his eyes Chet broke and fled into the other room. "I'll go look," he said. "I think there's a list."

He stood in the front hall a minute before he came back with his face business-like and his mind crafty. "Four-fifty," he said casually. "I thought prob'bly it was."

Vickers counted twenty-two dollars out of the wallet, dug in his pocket for fifty cents, and picked up the ripped sack. He stood by the door and looked at Chet and laughed. "What are you going to do with the extra two-fifty?" he said.

Chet's heart stopped. His face began to burn. "What two-fifty?"

"Never mind," Vickers said. "Have you got all you need to eat here?"

"I got crocks of milk," Chet said in relief. He grinned at Vickers and Vickers grinned back. "Ma baked bread the other day, and there's spuds. I can go out and shoot a rabbit if I need some meat."

"Oh," Vickers said. His eyebrows went up. "You're a hunter, are you?"

"I shot rabbits all last fall for Mrs. Rieger," Chet said. He tried to make it sound matter-of-fact. "She lent me the shotgun and shells. She had to have rabbits and prairie chicken and stuff because she's 'nemic."

"Mmm," Vickers said. "I guess you can take care of yourself. How old are you?"

"Twelve."

"That's old enough," said Vickers. "Well, Mervin, if you need anything you call the school and I'll see that you get it."

"My name isn't Mervin. It's Chet."

"Okay," Vickers said. "Don't get careless with the fires."

"What do you think I am?" Chet said in scorn. He raised his hand stiffly to Vickers and went back to his bread and milk, excited and triumphant. That two and a half would look pretty good. He wondered how Vickers knew he had been euchred. Because he changed the price, probably. Next time he'd know better than that. He took the money out of his pocket and counted it. Twenty-two fifty was a lot of dough. He'd show Mom and Pa whether he could hold the fort or not.

But holding the fort got tiresome. The house was too empty. Sitting in the parlor with a book he heard the walls tick and the floors creak as if under stealthy feet. He looked up every thirty seconds. Then he stood up, stretched his arms elaborately, yawned, and walked through the whole house, basement to attic, as if he were just strolling around. But his eyes were sharp, and he stepped back a little as he threw open the doors of closets and bedrooms. He whistled a little between his teeth.

Downstairs again, his suspicions laid but his boredom even greater, he remembered suddenly that he was the boss of the place. He could go where he liked and do what he pleased, as long as the cows got fed and milked and the house was warm. He thought of the two traps he had set at muskrat holes under the river bank.

The flu had kept him from visiting them. It might be a good idea to take the gun and go out on a little hunt.

"Well," he said in the middle of the parlor rug. "I guess I will."

For an hour and a half he prowled the brush with his father's shotgun. Over on the path toward Heathcliff's he shot a snowshoe rabbit, white and furry and big-footed, and lugged it triumphantly toward home. One of his traps yielded a stiffly-frozen muskrat, and the weight of his game made him proud as he came up the dugway swinging the rabbit by a foot, the muskrat by its plated tail.

Coming past the barn, he looked toward Van Dam's, then the other way, toward Chance's, hoping somebody would be out and see him. He whistled loudly, sang a little into the cold afternoon air, but the desertion of the whole street, the unbroken fields of snow where ordinarily there would be sled tracks and fox-and-geese paths, let a chill in on his pride. He came up the back steps soberly and opened the unlocked door.

The muskrat's slippery tail slid through his mittened hand and the frozen body thumped on the floor. Two men were in the kitchen. His chest tight with surprise and shock, Chet looked from one, standing by the whiskey keg, to the other, at the table with a cup before him. One he didn't know. The one at the table was Louis Treat, a halfbreed who hung out at the stable and sometimes worked a little for old man Purcell. All Chet knew of him was that he could braid horsehair ropes and used to sing a lot of dirty songs.

"Aha!" Louis Treat said. He smiled at Chet and made rubbing motions with his hands. "We 'ave stop to get warm. You 'ave been hunting?"

"Yuh," Chet said. He stood where he was, his eyes swinging to the other man by the keg. The man was looking at Louis.

"Ees nice rabbit there," Louis said. His bright black eyes went over the boy. Chet lifted the rabbit and looked at the drops of frozen blood like red beads on the fur. "Yuh," he said. He was thinking about what his father said. You could trust an Indian if he was your friend, and you could trust a white man if his pocket-book wasn't involved, and you could trust a Chink more than either, but you couldn't trust a halfbreed. He looked at the man by the keg and decided that he looked tough.

Louis' voice went on. "You 'ave mushrat, too, eh? You lake me to 'elp you peel thees mushrat?" His hand dipped under his sheep-skin and produced a long-bladed knife that snapped open with the pressure of his thumb on a button.

Chet stayed where he was. "No thanks," he said. "I can peel him."

Louis shrugged and put the knife away. Then he shook his

shoulders inside the sheepskin, drained the cup he had been drinking from, and turned to thump the bung hard into the keg. "Ees tam we go," he said. "We 'ave been told to breeng thees w'iskey to the school."

"Who told you?" Chet said. He felt his insides growing tighter and his mind setting like plaster of Paris. If Pa was here he would throw these robbers out in a minute and scatter them from here to Chance's. But Pa wasn't here. He dropped the rabbit on the floor beside the muskrat, watching Louis Treat. You couldn't trust a halfbreed as far as you could throw a bull by the tail.

"The doctor, O'Malley," Louis said. He nodded to his companion. "You tak that end."

The other man stooped to lay hold of the keg. Chet's breath had left him. He bit his lip, and then in one jump he was around the kitchen table, out of reach of them in the dining room door, and he had the shotgun pointed straight at their chests. Without taking his eyes from them he cocked both hammers, *click, click.*

Louis Treat swore. "Put down that gun, you fool!"

"No sir!" Chet said. "I won't put it down. You drop that keg and get out of here."

The two men looked at each other. Louis set his end gently back on the chair and the other man did the same. "We 'ave been sent," Louis said. "You do not see w'at I mean. The doctor . . ."

"Like hell!" Chet said. "If Doctor O'Malley had wanted that he'd have had Mr. Vickers get it this afternoon."

The second man ran his tongue over his teeth and spat on the floor. He looked at Louis. "Think he knows how to shoot that thing?"

Chet's chest expanded. The gun barrels trembled so that he braced them against the door frame. "I shot that rabbit, didn't I?" he said.

Louis Treat's teeth were bared in a thin smile. He shrugged. "You are a fool."

"And you're a thief!" Chet said. He covered the two carefully as they backed out, and when they were down the steps he slammed the door and bolted it. Still carrying the cocked gun, he raced for the front hall, made sure the night lock was on, and peeked out. Louis and his friend were walking side by side up the bank of the irrigation ditch, the stranger pulling an empty box sled, Louis talking, throwing his hands around.

Very slowly and carefully Chet uncocked the hammers. Ordinarily he would have unloaded the gun, but not now, not with thieves like those around. He hung the gun above the mantel over the .30-30, looked in the door of the stove, threw on some lignite, went to the window again to see if he could still see the two men. Then he looked down at his hands. They were shaking. So were his knees. He sat down suddenly on the couch, unable to stand.

The days of holding the fort were long days. There was no one to talk to, no one to go hunting with, and he wouldn't have dared go hunting anyway, after what had happened that first day. The only people he saw were those who came to buy whiskey. Once his school teacher, Miss Landis, came apologetically and furtively with a two-quart fruit jar. He charged her four dollars a quart for rye and watched her hurry away toward the school with the jar under her coat. The men who came generally sat a while in the kitchen and told him about people who had died or got sick. They brought occasional news about the war. People were betting it would be over by Christmas.

But after three days people stopped coming for whiskey, and then there was only the twice-a-day telephone call to the school. His father was pretty sick. Then a day or two later his father was better but Mom had had a relapse because they got so short of beds they had to put Brucie in with her.

He moped around the house, milked the cow night and morning and couldn't possibly drink all the milk, so that the crocks piled up in the cellarway, all of them staying miraculously sweet, until he told the schoolhouse nurse about all the milk he had and Doctor O'Malley sent down old Gundar Moe to get it for the sick people.

Sometimes he stood on the porch on sunny, cold mornings and watched Lars Poulsen's sled go out along the river toward the graveyard, and the thought that maybe Mom or Pa or Bruce might die and be buried out there on the knoll by the sandhills made him swallow and go back inside where he couldn't see how deserted the street looked, and where he couldn't see the sled and the steaming gray horses move out along the river. He prayed earnestly at night, with tears, that none of them would die. He resolved to be a son his parents could be proud of, and sat down at the piano determined to learn a piece letter-perfect before Mom came home. But the dry silence of the house weighed on him; he lay sometimes with his forehead on the keyboard, and listened to the sound of one monotonous note. It sounded different with his head down, and he could concentrate on how different it sounded so that he didn't get afraid.

Nights were worst. He lay awake on the couch and stared into the sleepy red eyes of the heater and heard noises that walked the house. The death watch ticked in the walls, and there were crosses in the lamp chimney when he lighted it to drive away the dark and the fear.

For a week he lived alone, eating rabbit and duck soup and milk and bread, counting the tedious hours, playing with the Erector set until he lost interest in it entirely. On the fifth day he decided to write a book. In an old atlas he found a tributary of the Amazon called the Tapájos, and wrote his title firmly across the top line of a school tablet: "The Curse of the Tapájos." All that afternoon he wrote enthusiastically. He created a handsome young explorer and a sinister halfbreed guide very like Louis Treat. He lived for hours in the steaming Amazonian jungles, and when he got tired of those and the snakes got a little too thick even for his taste, he let his explorer emerge into a wide grassy pampa and see in the distance, crowning a golden hill, the lost city for which he had been searching. Then suddenly the explorer clutched his breast, reeled and fell, mysteriously stricken, and the halfbreed guide, smiling a sinister smile, disappeared quietly into the jungle. The curse of the Tapájos, which struck everyone who had ever set out in search of that lost city, had struck again. But the young hero was not dead . . .

Chet chewed his pencil and looked up. It was going to be hard to figure out just how his hero escaped the curse, and was only stunned by it, not killed. He rose, thinking, and wandered over to the window. A sled came across the irrigation ditch bridge and pulled on up to the Chances'. Out of it got Mr. Chance and Mrs. Chance and Harvey and Ed Chance. They were well, then. People were starting to come home cured. He rushed to the telephone and called the hospital. No, Regina Orullian said. His family weren't well yet, but they were getting better. How was he doing? Did he need anything? No, Chet said. He didn't need anything.

He was disappointed, but not too much so. The sight of the Chances coming home gave him new spirit. He wasn't the only soul on the street any more. That night after milking he took a syrup pail full over to the Chances. They were all weak, all smiling, and Mrs. Chance cried every time she tried to speak. They were awfully grateful for the milk. He promised them that he would bring milk every day, and chop wood for them until they got strong. When he went home wearing a halo of big words that Mr. Chance, whom everybody called Dictionary, had laid upon him, he felt virtuous, kindly, charitable, like a knight helping people in distress. He wondered if it might not be a good idea to have his explorer run onto a group of people, or maybe just a girl, in distress, and rescue them or her from some awful fate, cannibals or head hunters or spider men or something.

On the afternoon of the tenth day he was over at Chance's. He had spent a good deal of time there the last day or two. His own house had got heavier and heavier to bear, lonesomer and lonesomer in its dead stillness. Besides, there wasn't much there to eat any more. So he took milk to the Chances, chopped their wood, sat for hours in their warm kitchen listening to talk about the schoolhouse and the Death Ward where they put people who were going to die. The Death Ward was the seventh grade room, his own room, and he and Ed Chance speculated on how it would feel to go back to school there where so many people had died—Mrs. Rieger, John Chapman, old Gypsy Davy from Poverty Flat, lots of others. Mrs. Chance, still so weak she could barely totter around, sat by the range and wiped the tears from her eyes, and when anyone spoke to her she smiled and shook her head and the tears ran down. She didn't seem unhappy about anything; she just couldn't help crying.

Mr. Chance said, solemnly, that there would be many familiar faces missing when this was over. The old town would never be the same. He wouldn't be surprised if an orphan or two had to be adopted by every family in town. He pulled his sagging cheeks and said to Chet, "I'll tell you what, son, you're fortunate yourself. Many times in that hospital I said to myself that those poor Mason boys were going to lose a loving father, certain as grass is green. I'd lie there, and the first thing I'd hear, some old and valued friend had passed in the Death Ward. I gave your father up when they moved him in . . ."

Chet's throat was suddenly dry as dust. "Pa isn't in there!" he said.

"Ira," Mrs. Chance said, and shook her head and smiled and wiped the tears away. "Now you've got the child all worked up."

"He isn't there now," Mr. Chance said. "I never hope to see again a spectacle as heartening as Bo Mason coming out of that Death Ward alive. Hands and feet frozen, double pneumonia—what a picture of fortitude that was! You should be proud, son."

"Is he all right now?" Chet said.

"Right as the rain," said Mr. Chance. "You needn't worry about your family, my boy. Take your father, I'd bet on him to live through anything. But then on the other hand you take a man like that George Valet. I dislike speaking of such things, but he couldn't even hang onto himself in bed. Those girls cleaned up his bed four times a day while he lay there red as a beet for shame, but did he improve? No." Mr. Chance closed his fist and made a decisive motion into the air. "A man like that, there's no *push* in him," he said. "Everything about him is as loose as his bowels."

"Ira!" Mrs. Chance said.

"I'll make you a bet," Mr. Chance said. "I'll bet you he doesn't live through this epidemic."

"I wouldn't bet on a person's life that way," she said. "And I wish you'd keep your language clean in front of the children."

"Ma," Harvey called from the next room, where he was lying down. "What's all the noise about?"

They stopped talking and listened. The church bell, far uptown, was ringing madly. Then the bell in the firehouse joined it. The heavy bellow of a shotgun, both barrels, rolled over the snowflats. A six-shooter went off, *bang bang bang bang bang bang,* and there was a sound of distant yelling.

"Well, what in Heaven's name," Mrs. Chance said. They were all at the window by then, trying to see.

"Here comes somebody!" Ed said. The figure of a boy was streaking across the flat. He hesitated as if undecided whether to go up by Van Dam's or down at this end of the street. Mr. Chance opened the door and shouted at him. The boy ran closer, shouting something unintelligible.

"What?" Mr. Chance yelled.

Chet recognized the boy now. Spot Orullian. He cupped his hands and yelled from the road as if unwilling to waste a moment's time.

"War's over!" he shouted, and wheeled and was gone up the street.

Mr. Chance closed the door slowly. Mrs. Chance looked at him, her lip jutted and trembled, her weak eyes ran over with tears, and she fell into his arms. The three boys, not quite sure how one acted when a war ended but knowing that it called for celebration, stood around uneasily shooting furtive grins at each other, staring at Mrs. Chance's shaking back.

"Now Uncle Joe can come home," Ed said. "That's what she's bawling about."

"I'll be back in a sec," Chet said. He bolted out the kitchen door, raced over to his own house, pulled the loaded shotgun from above the mantel, and burst into the yard. He blew the lid off the silence in their end of town and split his throat with a wild long yell. Ed and Harvey answered from the open windows of their house, and another shotgun *boom-boomed* from downtown.

Still carrying the gun, Chet went back to Chance's. He felt grown up, a householder, able to hold up his end of any community obligations. Mrs. Chance was still incoherent. Broken ejaculations of joy came out of her, and she put a big red circle with a crayon around the date on the calendar. "I don't ever want to forget what day it happened on," she said.

"Neither you nor anyone else is likely to," said Mr. Chance. "This day history has come to one of its great turning points." Chet looked at him, his mind clicking with an idea that brought his tongue out between his teeth.

"Mr. Chance," he said, "would you like a drink to celebrate?"

Mr. Chance looked startled, interrupted in a high thought. "I beg pardon?"

"Pa's got some whiskey left. He'd throw a party if he was home. Come on over."

"I don't think we should," Mrs. Chance said. She looked at her husband dubiously. "Your father might . . ."

"Oh, Mother," Mr. Chance said, and laid his arm across her back. "One bumper to honor the day. One toast to that thin red line of heroes. Chester here is carrying on his father's tradition like a man of honor." He bowed and shook Chet's hand. "We'd be delighted, Sir," he said, and they all laughed.

Nobody knew exactly how the party achieved the proportions it did. Mr. Chance suggested, after one drink, that it would be pleasant to have a neighbor or two, rescued from the terrors of the plague, come around and join in the thanksgiving, and Chet said sure, that was a keen idea. So Mr. Chance called Jewel King on the telephone, and when Jewel came he brought Chubby Klein with him, and a few minutes later three more men came to the door, looked in to see people gathered with glasses in their hands, and came in with alacrity. Within an hour there were eight men, three women, and the two Chance boys, besides Chet. Mr. Chance wouldn't let any of the boys have any whiskey, but Chet, acting as bartender, sneaked a cup of it into the dining room and all three took a sip and smacked their lips. Later, Harvey called Chet into the parlor and whispered. "Hey, I'm drunk. Look." He staggered, hiccoughed, caught himself, bowed low and apologized, staggered again. "Hic," he said. "Had a drop too much." Ed and Chet watched him, laughing secretly while loud voices rose in the kitchen.

Mr. Chance was proposing toasts every three minutes. "Gentlemen," he would say, "I give you those heroic laddies in khaki who looked undaunted into the eyes of death and saved this ga-lorious empiah from the clutches of the Hun."

"Yay!" the others said, banging cups on the table. "Give her the other barrel, Dictionary."

"I crave your indulgence for one moment," Mr. Chance said. "For one leetle moment, while I imbibe a few swallows of this delectable amber fluid."

The noise went up and up. Chet went among them stiff with pride at having done all this, at having men pat him on the back or shake his hand and tell him, "You're all right, kid, you're a chip off the old block. What's the word from the folks?" He guggled liquor out of the sloshing cask into a milk crock, and men dipped largely and frequently. About four o'clock two more families arrived and were greeted with roars. People bulged the big kitchen; their laughter rattled the window frames. Dictionary Chance suggested periodically that it might be an idea worth consideration that some liquid refreshments be decanted from the aperture in the receptacle.

The more liquid refreshments were decanted from the aperture in the receptacle, the louder and more eloquent Mr. Chance became. He dominated the kitchen like an evangelist. He swung and swayed and chanted, led a rendition of "God Save the King," thundered denunciations of the Beast of Berlin, thrust a large fist into the lapels of new arrivals and demanded news of the war, which they did not have. Within five minutes Mr. Chance and Jewel King were off in a corner holding a two-man chorus of "Johnny McGree McGraw," keeping their voices down, in the interest of decency, to a level that couldn't have been heard past Van Dam's.

He did not forget to be grateful, either. Twice during the afternoon he caught Chet up in a long arm and publicly blessed him, and about five o'clock, while Mrs. Chance pulled his sleeve and tried to catch his eye, he rose and cleared his throat and waited for silence. Chubby Klein and Jewel King booed and hissed, but he bore their insults with a reproving eye. "Siddown!" they said. "Speech!" said others. Mr. Chance spread his hands abroad and begged for silence, and finally they gave it to him, snickering.

"Ladees and gen'lemen," Mr. Chance said. "We have come together on this auspicious occasion. . . ."

"What's suspicious about it?" Chubby Klein said.

"On this auspicious occasion, to do honor to the gallant boys in Flanders' fields, to celebrate the passing of the twin blights of pestilence and war . . ."

"Siddown," said Jewel King.

". . . and last, but not least," said Mr. Chance, "we are gathered here to cement our friendship with the owners of this good and hospitable house, our old friend Bo Mason and his wife, a universally loved woman." He cleared his throat and looked around.

"And finally, my friends, our immediate host, the boy who in the absence of father, mother, and brother, kept the home fires burning and finally, out of the greatness of his heart and the knowledge of what his father would do under similar circumstances, opened his house and his keg to our pleasure. Ladees and gen'lemen, the Right Honorable Chester Mason, may he live to bung many a barrel!"

Embarrassed and grinning and not knowing quite what to do with so many faces laughing at him, so many hands hiking cups up in salute, Chet stood in the dining room door and tried to be casual, tried to hide the fact that he was proud and excited and had never had such a grown-up feeling in his life.

And while he stood there with their loud and raucous approbation beating against him, the back door opened and the utterly flabbergasted face of his father looked in.

There was a moment of complete silence. Voices dropped away to nothing, cups hung at lips. Then in a concerted rush they were helping Bo in, limping heavily on slippered feet, his hands bandaged, his face drawn and hollow-eyed and bony with sickness. After him came Elsa, half-carrying Bruce and staggering under his weight. Hands took Bruce away from her, set him on the oven door, led her to a chair. All three of them, hospital-pale, sat and looked around. Chet saw that his father did not look pleased. His jaw was set harshly.

"What the devil is this?" he said.

From the dining room door Chet squeaked, "The war's over!"

"I know the war's over," his father said. "But what's this?" He jerked a bandaged hand at the silent ring of people. Chet swallowed and looked at Dictionary Chance.

Dictionary was not unequal to the occasion, after his temporary shock. He came up to clap Bo on the back; he swung and shook Elsa's hand; he twinkled at the white-faced, big-eyed Bruce on the oven door.

"This, Sir," he boomed, "is a welcoming committee of your friends and neighbors, met here to rejoice over your escape from the terrible sickness which has swept away to untimely graves so many of our good friends, God rest their souls! On the invitation of your manly young son we are here not only to celebrate that escape from the plague, but the emancipation of the whole world from the greater plague of war." With the cup in his hand he bent from the waist and twinkled at Bo. "How's it feel to get back, old hoss?"

Bo grunted. He looked across at Elsa and laughed a short,

choppy laugh. The way his eyes came around and rested on Chet made Chet stop breathing, but his father's voice was hearty enough. "You got a snootful," he said. "Looks like you've all got a snootful."

"Sir," said Dictionary Chance, "I have not had such a delightful snootful since the misguided government of this province suspended the God-given right of its free people to purchase and ingest intoxicating beverages." He drained his cup and set it on the table. "Now neighbors," he said, "it is clear that the Masons are not yet completely recovered in their strength. I suggest that we do whatever small jobs our ingenuity and gratitude can suggest, and silently steal away."

"Yeah," they said. "Sure." They went in a body out to the sleigh and brought in the one bed that had been sent back, lugged it through the kitchen and set it up in the dining room, piled the mattress on it, swooped together bedding and sheets and left them for the women. Before the bed was made people began to shake hands and leave. Dictionary Chance, voluble to the last, stopped long enough to pour into Bo's ear the virtues of his first-born. "We have enjoyed your hospitality, extended through young Chester," he said. "If we may be of any service during your convalescence, please do not hesitate to call upon us. I am happy to say that, thanks in good part to the excellent medicinal waters I have imbibed at your house, our family is almost completely recovered and at your service."

Mrs. Chance said goodbye with a quick, pleading smile and led Dictionary away, and there was nothing for Chet to do but face the eyes that had been waiting for him all the time.

"All right," his father said. "Now will you tell me why in the name of Christ you invited that damned windbag and all the rest of the sponges over here to drink up my whiskey?"

Chet stood sullenly in the door. He had already given up any hope of explaining. Under his father's hot eyes he boiled sulkily. Here he had held the fort all alone, milked the cows and kept the house. Everybody else praised him and said he was doing a keen job. But you could depend on Pa to fly off the handle and spoil everything.

"The war was over," he said. "I asked them over to have a drink and celebrate."

His father's face and neck began to swell. "You asked them over! You asked them over. You said come right on over and drink all the whiskey in the house! Why God damn you . . . !"

"Bo," Elsa said quietly. Chet slid his eyes toward her long

enough to see the pain and sympathy in her face, but he didn't move. He set his mouth and faced his father, who was flapping his hands and looking upward in impotent rage. "Leave the house for ten days," he said. "Go away for as much as a week and by Jesus everything goes wrong. How long were they over here?"

"Since about two," Chet said. He met his father's hard look with one just as bitter, and his father started from his chair as if to thrash him, but his sore hands and feet put him back, wincing. Two hot angry tears started from Chet's eyes. He wished the old man wasn't all crippled. It would be just fine if he tried to whip him and couldn't make him say a word. He'd bite his tongue out before he'd make a sound, or say he was sorry, or anything.

"How much did they drink?"

"I don't know," Chet said. "Three crocks, I think."

His father's head shook back and forth. "Three crocks. At least a gallon. Twelve dollars' worth. Oh Christ, if you had the sense of a pissant . . ."

Laboriously, swearing with pain, he got up and hobbled to the keg. When he put down his bandaged hand and shook it his whole body stiffened. "I thought you only sold six gallons out of this," he said to Elsa.

Her glance fluttered toward Chet. "I don't know," she said. "I thought that was all . . . Now Bo, don't fly off the handle. We're lucky to be alive . . ."

"I sold some out of there," Chet said. "I've got the money in here." His body stiff, his mind full of self-righteous, gloating hatred, he went in and got the money from the jar. With it was the list itemizing each sale. He laid it all on the table.

"So you've been selling liquor," his father said. "I thought your mother told you to let that alone."

"People came wanting it. It was medicine, so I thought I ought to sell it to them."

His father laughed unpleasantly. "Probably sold it for a dollar a bottle," he said, and picked up the list.

Now! Chet said. He waited, his blood beginning to pound with triumph. His father's eye went down the list, stopped. "What's this twenty-two fifty?"

"That's five bottles of bourbon to Mr. Vickers."

"That should only be twenty."

"I know it," Chet said. "But I got twenty-two fifty." He met his father's eye and almost beat it down.

"I ought to whale you within an inch of your life," his father said. "You had no business selling anything. Now you spread my affairs all over town, you charge people too much and ruin good customers, you ask the whole damned town over here to drink up twelve dollars' worth of stuff. . . ."

"All right!" Chet shouted. "All right, I'll tell you something!" He batted at his eyes with his forearm, seeing his father's sick-thin face and seeing nothing else. "The day Ma and Brucie left, Louis Treat and another guy came in here and were going to steal the whole keg and I run 'em out with the shotgun." He stood with his fists balled, the tears blurry in his eyes, shouting at his father's stiff, gray, expressionless face. "I wish I'd let 'em take it!" he said, his face twisting. "I wish I'd never done a thing to stop 'em!"

His father's face was dissolving, running, melting, and the bandaged hands were coming up in the air, and then his father was laughing, flung back against the kitchen table and shouting with uncontrollable mirth. Chet looked startled, and then sneered. His father's hands pointed at him, his father's breath came wheezy with laughter from spent lungs. "Okay, kid," he said. "Okay, you're a man. Nobody's going to take it away from you. If you looked at Treat the way you just looked at me he's running yet, I'd bet on it."

Everything had dissolved so suddenly, the defiant stand he had made had produced such unlooked-for results, that Chet went grouchily into the parlor and sat by himself. After a minute his mother came in, her lips twitching with the beginning of a smile, and put her arms around him.

"Don't be mad at Pa," she said. "He didn't understand at first. He's proud of you, proud as he can be. So am I. You did just fine, Chet. It was more than a boy should have had to shoulder . . ."

"If he's so proud," Chet said, "why does he have to *laugh?*"

"Because you looked so fierce you struck him funny, I guess."

Chet scowled at the .30-30 and the shotgun hanging one on top of the other above the mantel. He shook his shoulders irritably inside his mother's quick tight squeeze. "Well, there's no call to laugh!" he said.

5

A week after their return from the hospital, Bo sat counting his money in the dining room. Elsa was already in bed; he could feel her watching him. Deliberately he counted out fifty dollars and pocketed the rest, almost six hundred dollars, a fine fat roll with a rubber band around it. He sat down on the edge of the bed and shook off his slippers.

"Coming to bed already?" Elsa said.

"Lot to do tomorrow."

"What?"

He slid his pants off one leg, pulling at the cuff. "Change the wheels to bobs, for one thing."

He knew she was lying there stiffly, accusing him with her eyes, but he pulled his shirt over his head and pretended not to know. Finally she said, "To go to Montana?"

"Yep."

She lay stiff and straight on her side of the bed as he got into his nightgown and stretched out. Her voice went flatly up toward the ceiling. "So it wasn't the epidemic. You're in the whiskey business."

"Look," Bo said. He put his arm around her but she didn't yield or turn her face. "I've still got six hundred, and it'll be over a week before they get the bank open again and I have to pay that note. I can take the wagon and bring back twice as much as I did before. Double my money again."

They lay in silence, with bitterness between them. Then Elsa said, "Fourteen years ago you were in the liquor business and you got out. Now you're back in it worse."

"What's wrong with the liquor business?" he said. "Almost anywhere it's perfectly legal. Just because this crackpot province passes a war measure . . ."

"Even where it's legal it isn't respectable," she said.

In exasperation he turned his back on her, turned over again just as abruptly to say, "You sold some a while ago. Did it burn your fingers? Did the money you got for it poison you? I suppose you think you and Chet are a cinch for hellfire because you both sold whiskey."

"It isn't hellfire that bothers me," she said. "I just want us to have a good solid place in the world where nobody can shame us with anything."

"That's sure ambitious," he said. "That shows a lot of imagination, that does. Any dirt farmer in the province can claim that, practically."

"But we can't," she said.

"Okay," he said. "Okay, I'll go down tomorrow and get the job of driving the honey-wagon. That's a nice solid place in the world. That's a steady job. And Heathcliff's dead, they'll need somebody."

"Bo," she said, "I'd rather see you doing that than what you're going to do."

"By God," he said, almost in wonder, "I believe you would." He turned away from her and settled himself to sleep. As long as he remained awake he did not feel her stir. When he woke in the morning he felt the antagonism still between them, but he went ahead anyway. And when he had returned with the load, and had peddled it in town and in all the little towns along the line, and had turned the whiskey into cash and paid back the note to the bank, he took off again with team and bobsled in January, and brought back enough to last through the rest of the winter.

Now the long closed winter, blizzard and cold snap and Chinook, delusive thaws in February and iron cold in March and heavy snow in April. Two line-riding cowpunchers from the Half-Diamond Bar froze to death on St. Patrick's day in a forty-below blizzard. Mrs. John Chapman, widowed by the flu, created a sensation by taking strychnine for the lost affections of Hank Freeze, the most prosperous farmer on the north bench. As soon as it was clear that Mrs. Chapman had taken an overdose and would recover, people had a good deal of fun with that. What could you expect of a guy named Freeze?

In formal meeting, the town council voted to collect money for a bronze plaque to be erected in the firehouse in honor of the four local boys who had died in the war and the eleven others who had served. The Reverend Charles Evans, successor to the Reverend John Morrison who had died of the flu, bought a half column of space in the Whitemud *Ledger* to deplore, more publicly than he could from his pulpit, the falling away of Sunday school and church attendance.

Early in April Howard Palmer, who had hung up a shingle reading "Barrister" two years before, stood up in church to denounce the wickedness of the town. He thundered, his head shook, his eyes went bloodshot with passion, foam gathered at the corners of his mouth. He called down hellfire on three sinful women, and named their names. He blasted the person who had brought liquor in in defiance of provincial law, and named his name. He took a passing swipe at Ed Anderson's billiard hell and the Pastime Movie Theater. When he had cracked his damnation blacksnake over most of the town's backs, he fell down between the pews in a fit, and that night, while Bo Mason was winning a pearl-handled jackknife for figure skating at the annual ice carnival, they carted the barrister off to Saskatoon to the bughouse, and that was a nine-days' wonder.

Until finally there came a time when the sun was up before most of the townspeople, and by the time breakfasts were over the eaves began to drip. They dripped all day, and after a day or so women emerged on front porches and swept out the accumulated rubbish of the winter. The nights froze hard, but before eight in the morning water was running again, and anyone walking below the bench hills was likely to break through the sodden crust and fill his shoes with icewater, and if he stood quietly and listened he could hear the streams under the snow. Thermometers stood at forty-five, ninety degrees above where they had stood a time or two during the winter. Dogs ran dirty-footed through the town, boys felt the misty, warming air on their faces and hated school. Because this was it: this was the real spring thaw. It might freeze every night, it might even snow again, but the weather had broken. The awakening was like a sunny morning after long rain, or light after long darkness, and the blood leaped to the sound of the spring freshets coming down the gullies from the hills.

After a week of thaw Bo went downtown and brought back the Ford from Bert Withers' garage, where he had left it to get a new radiator put on. Three days later, as soon as the sun had dried the roads a little, he was ready to go.

"Keep an eye on Daisy," he said to Elsa. "She'll throw her colt any time now. I asked Jim Enich to come around every other day or so."

"Are you going to be gone long?"

"I might be gone ten days."

"But why? With the car . . ."

"I'm going to peddle this in the other towns," he said. "The quicker I get rid of this the fatter the stake gets. I want to build up a good one before two or three other guys get the idea the roads are passable."

"Is there anything you want me to do?" she said.

He looked at her quickly. "Like what?"

"Like selling any stuff you've got left over."

"I thought you didn't want anything to do with it?"

"I didn't," she said. "But I'd rather be in it with you than have you going off on these trips without telling me anything. We always did things together, till now."

"Old Mama," he said, and put his arm around her. "Now you're playing ball."

An hour later he climbed into the Ford and drove out toward the bench, his tracks like parallel wriggling ditches in the thick gumbo mud.

For eleven months of the year the Whitemud River was a sleepy, slow, clear stream, looping in wide meanders between the bench hills, shallowing to brief rapids, deepening along the cutbanks in the bends. But for a week or two around the end of April it was a flood thirty feet deep, jammed with ice cakes and driftwood and the splintered timbers of bridges. It completely covered the willows across the channel from the Mason house, and what had been a wilderness of brush and scrub was a chocolate expanse of water, moving in places with terrible quiet speed, stalling at others into eddies and backwashes.

It began with the first sudden thaw, when every little drainage gully from the hills began pouring water down onto the river ice, and it kept on until the channel was gorged and overflowed by this new river on top of the old. In the sun, in the wet, exciting wind, groups of people lined the banks waiting for the breakup. Somebody reported that she was going below the dam; in ten minutes there was word that ice was backed twenty feet high behind the upper railroad bridge. By the time the townspeople arrived, a section gang working cautiously from a handcar was dropping dynamite into the moving, sliding, ponderous pressure of the pack. They might as well have dropped firecrackers.

After one look, some of the men went home for pikepoles. In a timberless country, those forty- and fifty-foot piles and those heavy hemlock timbers were worth fishing for.

Bruce, coming home from school at four, was told to take Daisy out and picket her for a couple of hours, give her a breath of air and some exercise. He led her out, rubbing down along her shoulder, working off some heavy winter hair. He wished she would hurry up and have her colt, so he could feed it and try to teach it tricks.

He led Daisy down into the northward loop of the river, drove in the picket pin, and snapped the chain into her halter ring. "Okay," he said. "You take a little stroll around and get a bite of grass and I'll come for you about dark." He slapped her haunch and rubbed her poll when she poked her head at him. She was so round with her colt that her legs spraddled.

Coming back, he heard the blasting out by the bridge, and saw the people moving that way. Harvey Chance was just starting to sprint down the muddy road. "Come on," he said, and jumped up and down waiting. "The bridge is going!"

Together they raced past Van Dam's, through the south pasture fence, out toward the abandoned oil derrick on the town side of the bridge. There were boys on the derrick's top, the bank was black with people, men with pikepoles were posted along the lower side.

"There she goes!" The crowd's voice rose, an enormous, exciting, soaring yell. Bruce and Harvey ducked in to the cutbank edge just in time to see the handcar scuttle off the bridge. The spindly structure was already buckling and kneeling above the white ice and brown water. Timber groaned. A cake of ice was hurled against the yielding piles of the upper side, snapped two of them off, and split in two, falling with a heavy double crash. The bridge buckled more, the right rail split loose from a half dozen ties and snapped straight, the left one was bent inexorably downward. From then on the measure of the bridge's yielding was that widening rift between the rails. The ice growled heavily upstream. A few cakes, released by the snapping of the two piles, slid through edgewise and splashed in the open water below.

There was another heaving, straining, wood-splitting, nail-and-spike-bending, ice-burdened groan from the bridge. The left hand rail broke loose and snapped almost upright, humming like a mighty tuning fork, and the crowd sighed, a noise like a sudden wind, as the ice mounted the upper piles and the whole toothpick structure bent over very slowly toward the river, held together momentarily against the seethe of edgewise, endwise, flatwise, twisting and righting and grinding and overflowing icepans and dirty floodwater. Then the whole middle section fell apart, went out in a spider-legged tangle of timbers. The townward side held except for three cabled-together piles that were gnawed off by the ice. But the excitement by then was gone from the bridge. The excitement was in the log fishing downriver. The whole crowd fled, even the impotent section gang, to help the men with pikepoles.

One man, hanging to a willow bush, his feet on the slippery edge of the rising water, leaned far out and hooked a pile with his pike-pole, hauled it closer, lost it to a driving ice cake and yelled to the next man downstream, who hooked it and snaked it halfway in, where a dozen hands laid hold and dragged it up the bank.

"God bless the C.P.R.!" somebody yelled. There was laughter and noise, more yells as someone else snaked in a pole. A detachment left for the next bend, racing the pounding icepans and the matchlike logs, to fish in less troubled water farther down.

They stayed for hours, virtually the whole town, men, women, children, and dogs. The bigger boys went along the cutbanks kicking great undermined blocks of earth into the river. Women went home at supper time and came back with coffee and sandwiches. Men split firewood and built up a bonfire. Every ten minutes the bridge would obligingly drop off another timber or group of timbers, and they were dragged out of the water and ice with a "Heave! Heave! Heave!" and yells of laughter. It was a picnic, a spontaneous spring overflowing. It was ten o'clock before Bruce and Chet and their mother walked home all together, arm in arm, singing.

Bruce went to bed late, drunk and exhausted with excitement. Through his sleep, a faint and disturbing titillation of his eardrums, he heard the noise, and when he stirred and woke in the morning he realized that he had not been dreaming it. The window, open clear to the top of the sash for the first time in months, let in a shivery draft of fresh damp air, and with it the faint yelping, far off.

Chet was already up and gone. When Bruce got dressed and went down into the kitchen the dogs were still yapping down in the bend.

"What's the matter with all the pooches?" he said. "Where's Spot?"

"He's out running with them," his mother said. "Probably they've got a porcupine treed or something. Dogs go crazy in the spring."

"It's dog days they go crazy."

"They go crazy in the spring, too," she said, and hummed a little as she set his breakfast out. "You'd better run out quick and feed the horses. I told Chet to, but he went right on by the barn as if he'd never seen it."

Bruce stood still in the middle of the kitchen. "Oh my gosh!" he said. "I left Daisy out all night!"

He saw from his mother's face that it might be serious. "Where?" she said.

"Down in the bend."

"Where those dogs are?"

"I think it was higher up," he said, but he was sick and afraid. In a minute they were both running. Bruce broke ahead, around Chance's shed, and searched the brown wet meadow at the head of the U. No sign of the mare where he had left her. He opened his mouth, half-turned, running, to shout at his mother coming behind him, and sprinted for the bottom of the bend.

As soon as he rounded the bay of brush fringing the cutbank behind Chance's he saw the mare, a brown spot against the gray brush, and on the ground beside her another smaller spot. There were six or eight dogs leaping around, barking, sitting in a circle. He saw his own dog and the Chapman's airedale.

Shouting, he pumped on. At a gravelly patch he stooped and clawed and straightened, still running, with a handful of small pebbles. In one pausing, spraddling, aiming motion, he let fly at the distant pack. The rocks fell far short, but the dogs drifted out in a widening circle, sat on their haunches and let out defiant short barks, each bark a sharp muscular contraction of their whole bodies. Bruce yelled and threw again, watching the colt at Daisy's

Such as into himself at last Eternity has changed him . . .

To give a purer sense to the words of the tribe . . .

White night of icicles and cruel snow . . .

A throw of the dice will never abolish chance.

There is only beauty, and beauty has only one perfect expression—Poetry.

Poetry is the expression, through human language reduced to its essential rhythm, of the mysterious meaning of aspects of existence; it thereby endows our stay on earth with authenticity and poses us our only spiritual task.

To *name* an object is to obliterate three-quarters of our pleasure in the poem, which consists in gradually divining it; to *suggest* it, that is the ideal. That is making the best possible use of the mystery which constitutes the symbol.

You don't make a poem with ideas, but with words.

To tell a painter that he ought to take nature as it is, is like telling a virtuoso that he may sit on the piano.

Hérédia was born in Cuba; Parnassian poet, noted for masterful sonnets.

A boundless sea where galleys were in flight.

They saw new stars emerging from the ocean
And rising toward an unknown sky.

Coppée, poet and playwright, enjoyed great popularity toward the end of the nineteenth century.

My story, your honors, will be short.
Here it is. The blacksmiths all went out on strike.

He was a little grocer in Montrouge,
And his dark shop with its red-painted shutters
Had a stale odor you smelled from the sidewalk.

Verlaine classed himself among the "accursed poets"—*Les Poètes Maudits* (title of his essays publ. 1884)—with Corbière, Rimbaud, Desbordes-Valmore, and Villiers de l'Isle-Adam, whose eventual fame he did much to promote. In the same book he says of himself that he had always suffered from his "rage to love," and that the story of his life was the story of "the disasters of his heart."

I often have this strange and moving dream
of an unknown woman whom I love and who loves me,
and who each time is neither quite the same
nor quite another, and who loves me and understands.

The long sobbings
of the violins
of autumn
wound my heart
with monotonous
languor.

Your soul is a choice landscape.

Weeping in my heart—
Rain falling on the city.

Voici des fruits, des fleurs, des feuilles et des branches
Et puis voici mon cœur qui ne bat que pour vous.

Id., Green

—Qu'as-tu fait, ô toi que voilà
    Pleurant sans cesse,
Dis, qu'as-tu fait, toi que voilà
    De ta jeunesse?

Sagesse, III, 6

De la musique avant toute chose,
Et pour cela préfère l'Impair.

• • •

Prends l'éloquence et tords lui son cou!

• • •

Et tout le reste est littérature.

Jadis et Naguère, L'art poétique

ANATOLE FRANCE

(1844–1924)

Le bon critique est celui qui raconte les aventures de son âme au milieu des chefs-d'œuvres. *La Vie littéraire (Préface)*

La faim et l'amour sont les deux axes du monde. L'humanité roule toute entière sur l'amour et la faim.

Id., III, George Sand

L'artiste doit aimer la vie et nous montrer qu'elle est belle. Sans lui nous en douterions. *Le Jardin d'Epicure*

L'Ironie et la Pitié sont deux bonnes conseillères; l'une, en souriant, nous rend la vie aimable; l'autre, qui pleure, nous là rend sacrée. *Id.*

Here are fruits, flowers, leaves, and branches,
And here is my heart which beats only for you.

What have you done—yes, you,
Weeping there ceaselessly;
Tell me, what have you—yes, you—
Done with your youth?

Music must be paramount:
Prefer an Uneven rhythm.

• • •

Take eloquence and wring its neck!

• • •

And all else is literature.

Anatole France, celebrated in his lifetime for his polished literary style and gentle irony, wrote novels, poems, critical essays; Nobel Prize for literature in 1921.

A good critic is one who tells the story of his mind's adventures among the masterpieces.

Hunger and love are the pivots on which the world turns. Mankind is entirely determined by love and hunger.

The artist should love life and show us that it is beautiful. Without him we might not find it so.

Irony and Pity are excellent counselors. With a smile, the former makes life pleasant; the latter, with its tears, makes it sacred.

La paix universelle se réalisera un jour non parce que les hommes deviendront meilleurs (il n'est pas permis de l'espérer); mais parce qu'un nouvel ordre de choses, une science nouvelle, de nouvelles nécessités économiques leur imposeront l'état pacifique. *Sur la pierre blanche*

J'aime la vérité. Je crois que l'humanité en a besoin; mais elle a bien plus grand besoin encore du mensonge qui la flatte, la console, lui donne des espérances infinies. Sans le mensonge, elle périrait de désespoir et d'ennui. *La Vie en fleur, Postface*

Le poireau, c'est l'asperge du pauvre. *Crainquebille*

...la majestueuse égalité des lois, qui interdit au riche comme au pauvre de coucher sous les ponts, de mendier dans les rues et de voler du pain. *Le Lys rouge*

Aimer la guerre parce qu'elle fait des héros, c'est aimer le croup, parce que des médecins et des infirmières sont morts en voulant sauver un enfant. *Dernières Pages inédites*

TRISTAN CORBIÈRE
(1845–1875)

Tu ne me veux pas en rêve?
–Tu m'auras en cauchemar!
Les Amours jaunes (1873), Elixir d'amour

Qu'ils se payent des républiques,
Hommes libres!–carcan au cou–
Qu'ils peuplent leurs nids domestiques! . . .
–Moi je suis le maigre coucou. *Id., Paria*

L'idéal à moi: c'est un songe
Creux; mon horizon–l'imprévu–
Et le mal du pays me ronge . . .
Du pays que je n'ai pas vu. *Ibid.*

World peace will become a reality one day, not because men have become better (that is more than we can hope for), but because a new order of things, a new science, and new economic necessities will require the state of peace.

I love truth. I believe humanity has need of it. However, what it has even greater need of is a lie to flatter it, console it, and give it infinite hope. Without lies, humanity would perish of despair and boredom.

The leek is the poor man's asparagus.

The law, in its majestic equality, forbids the rich as well as the poor to sleep under bridges, to beg in the streets, and to steal bread.

To love war because it produces heroes, is to love the croup because doctors and nurses died of it trying to save a child.

Corbière, an original poet, one of Verlaine's "discoveries": "His verse lives, laughs, weeps very little, jeers very well, and jokes even better. He is bitter and salty like his beloved ocean" (Verlaine).

You don't want me as a dream?
—Then you'll have me as a nightmare!

Let them treat themselves to republics,
Free men!—with yokes around their necks—
Let them fill their domestic nests! . . .
—I am the lean cuckoo.

My own ideal is a hollow dream,
My horizon the unforeseen,
And I am homesick,
Homesick for a land I have not seen.

ISIDORE DUCASSE, COMTE DE LAUTRÉAMONT

(1846–1870)

Vieil Océan, ta forme harmonieusement sphérique, qui réjouit la face grave de la géométrie, ne me rappelle que trop les petits yeux de l'homme, pareils à ceux du sanglier pour la petitesse et à ceux des oiseaux de nuit pour la perfection circulaire du contour. . . . *Les Chants de Maldoror, I*

O pou, ô ta prunelle recroquevillée. . . . Saleté, reine des empires, conserve aux yeux de ma haine le spectacle de l'accroissement insensible des muscles de ta progéniture affamée. . . . *Id., II*

Beau . . . comme la rencontre fortuite sur une table de dissection d'une machine à coudre et d'un parapluie. *Id., VI*

Le doute est un hommage rendu à l'espoir. Ce n'est pas un hommage volontaire. L'espoir ne consentirait pas à n'être qu'un hommage. *Poésies*

Si la morale de Cléopâtre eût été moins courte, la face du monde aurait changé. Son nez n'en serait pas devenu plus long.
Poésies, II

La poésie doit être faite par tous. Non par un. Pauvre Hugo!
Id.

LÉON BLOY

(1846–1917)

La douleur est l'auxiliaire de la création.
Pages de Léon Bloy, choisies par Raïssa Maritain (1951)

Lautréamont, born in Montevideo, came to Paris in 1867; claimed by the Surrealists as one of their forerunners.

Old Ocean, your harmoniously spherical form, which rejoices the solemn face of geometry, reminds me only too much of man's little eyes, by their littleness like those of the boar, and by the circular perfection of their outline like those of the night birds. . . .

O louse, O the tiny twisted pupil of your eye. . . . Filth, queen of empires, preserve in the eyes of my hatred the spectacle of your starving offspring's imperceptibly growing muscles. . . .

Beautiful . . . as the chance encounter on a dissecting table of a sewing machine and an umbrella.

Doubt is a tribute paid to hope. It is not a voluntary tribute. Hope would never consent to being no more than a tribute.

If Cleopatra's morality had been less short, the face of the world would have been altered. Her nose would not thereby have grown longer.

Poetry ought to be composed by everyone. Not by one. Poor Hugo!

Léon Bloy wrote novels and religious and polemical essays.

Suffering is an auxiliary of creation.

La sentimentalité, c'est d'avoir compassion des bourreaux de Jésus-Christ. Pauvres gens si mal payés pour tant de fatigue!

Id., Pensées détachées

Quand on demande à Dieu la souffrance, on est toujours sûr d'être exaucé. *Id.*

Le temps est un chien qui ne mord que les pauvres. *Journal*

Je me suis demandé souvent quelle pouvait être la différence entre la *charité* de tant de chrétiens et la méchanceté des démons.

Le sang du pauvre

GUY DE MAUPASSANT

(1850–1893)

Quand on a le physique d'un emploi, on en a l'âme. *Mont-Oriol*

Causer, qu'est cela? Mystère! C'est l'art de ne jamais paraître ennuyeux, de savoir tout dire avec intérêt, de plaire avec n'importe quoi, de séduire avec rien du tout.
Comment définir ce vif effleurement des choses par les mots, ce jeu de raquette avec des paroles souples, cette espèce de sourire léger des idées que doit être la causerie? *Sur l'eau*

L'histoire, cette vieille dame exaltée et menteuse. *Id.*

Une femme a toujours, en vérité, la situation qu'elle impose par l'illusion qu'elle sait produire. *Notre Cœur*

PAUL BOURGET

(1852–1935)

Il faut vivre comme on pense, sans quoi l'on finira par penser comme on a vécu. *Le Démon du midi. Conclusion*

Sentimentality is feeling sorry for Christ's executioners. Poor men, they worked so hard and were so poorly paid!

When you ask God to send you trials, you may be sure your prayer will be granted.

Time is a dog who bites only the poor.

Just what might the difference be, I have often wondered, between the so-called charity of many Christians and the wickedness of demons?

Maupassant, novelist and short-story writer; highly praised by Anatole France for his limpid prose.

A man who looks a part has the soul of that part.

What is conversation really? . . . It is the art of never seeming a bore, the ability to say everything in an interesting way, to make a trifle sound pleasant, and nothing at all perfectly charming. How are we to define this swift verbal skimming over of things, this batting of words back and forth like balls over a net, this graceful intellectual game that conversation should be?

History, that excitable and lying old lady.

A woman's actual position is always the one she imposes by means of the illusion she creates.

Bourget wrote novels and important critical essays.

We had better live as we think, otherwise we shall end up by thinking as we have lived.

La pensée est à la littérature ce que la lumière est à la peinture.
La Physiologie de l'amour moderne (1890)

Un amour qui a passé la jalousie est comme un joli visage qui a passé par la petite vérole: il est toujours un peu grêlé. *Id.*

Il n'y a qu'une manière d'être heureux par le cœur: c'est de ne pas en avoir. *Id.*

Ce qui prouve que l'expérience ne sert à rien, c'est que la fin de nos anciennes amours ne nous dégoûte pas d'en commencer d'autres. *Id.*

ARTHUR RIMBAUD

(1854–1891)

Et j'ai vu quelquefois ce que l'homme a cru voir.
Poésies, Le Bateau ivre (1871)

Je regrette l'Europe aux anciens parapets! *Ibid.*

J'ai vu des archipels sidéraux! et des îles
Dont les cieux délirants sont ouverts au vogueur:
—Est-ce en ces nuits sans fonds que tu dors et t'exiles,
Million d'oiseaux d'or, ô future vigueur? *Ibid.*

A noir, E blanc, I rouge, U vert, O bleu: voyelles,
Je dirai quelque jour vos naissances latentes. *Id., Voyelles*

Oisive jeunesse
A tout asservie,
Par délicatesse
J'ai perdu ma vie.
Ah! Que le temps vienne
Où les cœurs s'éprennent!

Chanson de la plus haute tour (1872)

Ideas are to literature what light is to painting.

Love that survives jealousy is like a pretty face after smallpox: a bit pockmarked forever after.

There is only one way of being happy by the heart: namely, to have none.

The best proof that experience is useless is that the end of one love does not disgust us from beginning another.

> Rimbaud produced all his poetic work before the age of twenty when he abandoned writing to become trader in Abyssinia. Crucial influence in modern poetry.

I've sometimes seen what men have only dreamed of seeing.

I long for Europe of the ancient parapets!

I've seen sidereal archipelagoes! and isles
Where raving skies are opened to the sailor:
—Is it in these depthless nights that you sleep, exiled,
A million golden birds, O future Vigor?

Black A, white E, red I, green U, blue O: vowels,
Someday I shall recount your latent births.

Idle youth
To everything enslaved,
Out of delicacy
I have wasted my life.
Ah, would the time come
When hearts fall in love!

Elle est retrouvée.
Quoi? L'Eternité.
C'est la mer allée
Avec le soleil. *L'Éternité (1872)*

Science avec patience,
Le supplice est sûr. *Ibid.*

O saisons, ô châteaux,
Quelle âme est sans défauts? *Bonheur*

J'ai fait la magique étude
Du bonheur que nul n'élude. *Ibid.*

Un soir, j'ai assis la beauté sur mes genoux.—Et je l'ai trouvée amère.—Et je l'ai injuriée. *Une Saison en enfer (1873)*

J'ai horreur de tous les métiers. Maîtres et ouvriers, tous paysans, ignobles. La main à plume vaut la main à charrue.
Id., Le Mauvais Sang

Je dis qu'il faut être *voyant*, se faire *voyant*.
Le poète se fait *voyant* par un long, immense et raisonné *dérèglement* de *tous les sens* . . . il a besoin de toute la foi, de toute la force surhumaine . . . il devient entre tous le grand malade, le grand criminel, le grand maudit— et le suprême Savant!— Car il arrive à l'*inconnu*! *Lettre à Paul Demeny, 15 mai 1871*

Le poète est vraiment voleur de feu. *Ibid.*

Baudelaire est le premier voyant, roi des poètes, *un vrai Dieu*. Encore a-t-il vécu dans un milieu trop artiste; et la forme si vantée en lui est mesquine. Les inventions d'inconnu réclament des formes nouvelles. *Ibid.*

It is found again.
What? Eternity.
It is the sea
Gone with the sun.

Science with patience:
Martyrdom is sure.

O seasons, O châteaus,
What soul has no flaws?

I have pursued the magic study
Of happiness, which no one can evade.

One night I seated Beauty in my lap.—And I found her bitter-tasting.—And I called her bad names.

I loathe all trades. Master workmen, workmen, all peasants—unspeakable. The hand that holds the pen is worth no more than that which holds the plow.

I say one must be a *seer*, make oneself a *seer*.
The Poet makes himself a *seer* by an immense, lengthy, deliberate *derangement* of all his *senses* . . . he has need of all his faith, all his superhuman strength . . . he becomes of all men the sickest, the most criminal, the most accursed—and the supreme Scientist!—For he attains the *unknown*.

The poet is truly a thief of fire.

Baudelaire was the first seer, king of poets, a *true God*. Even so, he lived in too artistic a milieu; his so highly praised form is shoddy. Ventures into the unknown cry out for new forms.

ÉMILE VERHAEREN

(1855–1916)

Avec ses suçoirs noirs et ses rouges haleines,
Hallucinant et attirant les gens des plaines,
C'est la ville que le jour plombe et la nuit éclaire,
La ville en plâtre, en stuc, en bois, en marbre, en fer, en or,
Tentaculaire!

Les Campagnes hallucinées, Le Départ

Rien n'est plus beau, malgré l'angoisse et le tourment,
Que la bataille avec l'énigme et les ténèbres.

Les Forces tumultueuses, Les Cultes

EDMOND HARAUCOURT

(1856–1941)

Partir, c'est mourir un peu;
C'est mourir à ce qu'on aime.
On laisse un peu de soi-même
En toute heure et dans tout lieu.

Choix de poésies (1891). Rondel de l'Adieu

REMY DE GOURMONT

(1858–1915)

La beauté est une logique qui est perçue comme un plaisir.

Culture des idées

Quand on réussit à opposer au géant Ennui l'armée des nains Plaisirs, le géant étouffe les nains en quelques gestes et reprend sa pose lassée. *Promenades philosophiques, III*

Verhaeren, poet and dramatist, was the leading Belgian Symbolist.

This thing with sucking black mouths and scarlet breath,
Hallucinating, luring the people of the plains,
Is the city, leaden by day and lit up by night,
The city in plaster, stucco, wood, marble, iron, gold—
The Tentacular city!

There is nothing nobler, despite the anguish and the torment,
Than to battle against mystery and darkness.

Haraucourt, poet and dramatist.

To leave is to die a little,
To die to what we love.
We leave behind a bit of ourselves
Wherever we have been.

Gourmont, Symbolist poet, novelist, critic.

Beauty is a logic that we perceive as a pleasure.

When we succeed in setting against the giant called Boredom the army of dwarfs called Pleasures, the giant strangles the dwarfs with almost no effort, and resumes his blasé pose.

L'homme est un animal arrivé, voilà tout.

Promenades philosophiques

Un imbécile ne s'ennuie jamais; il se contemple. *Id.*

Les malades sont toujours optimistes. Peut-être que l'optimisme lui-même est une maladie. *Id.*

La pensée fait mal aux reins. On ne peut à la fois porter des fardeaux et des idées. *Id.*

La pudeur sexuelle est un progrès sur l'exhibitionnisme des singes. *Id.*

Le citoyen est une variété de l'homme; variété dégénérée ou primitive, il est à l'homme ce que le chat de gouttière est au chat sauvage. *Epilogues. Paradoxes sur le citoyen*

Il est à peu près évident que ceux qui soutiennent la peine de mort ont plus d'affinités avec les assassins que ceux qui la combattent. *Pensées inédites*

ALFRED CAPUS

(1858–1922)

Les imbéciles ont toujours été exploités et c'est justice. Le jour où ils cesseraient de l'être, ils triompheraient, et le monde serait perdu. *Mariage bourgeois, IV, 6*

Les meilleurs souvenirs sont ceux que l'on a oubliés.

Notes et pensées (in *L'Esprit d'A.C.*, 1926)

Combien de gens ne se brouillent que parce qu'ils ont des amis communs? *Id.*

Aujourd'hui ceux qui ont de la noblesse d'âme sont sans énergie et ceux qui ont de la volonté sont sans scrupules. *Id.*

Man is merely a *successful* animal.

A blockhead is never bored: he always has himself to think about.

Sick people are invariably optimistic. Optimism itself may be a sickness.

Thinking is hard work. You can't simultaneously carry burdens and have ideas.

Sexual modesty marks some advance over the exhibitionism of monkeys.

The citizen is one variety of mankind. Whether a primitive or a degenerate variety, he is in human terms what the alley cat is to the wild cat.

It is well-nigh obvious that those who are in favor of the death penalty have more affinities with murderers than those who oppose it.

Capus, journalist, author of successful comedies.

Fools have always been exploited, and that's as it should be. The day they ceased being exploited, they would triumph, and the world would be wrecked.

The best memories are those we have forgotten.

How many people quarrel simply because they have mutual friends!

Today those who have noble aspirations lack all energy, and those who go after what they want lack all scruples.

On ne doit se résigner qu'au bonheur. *Id.*

Ce n'est pas la peine de te répéter chaque jour que tu es mortel: tu le verras bien. *Id.*

Epouser une femme qu'on aime et qui vous aime, c'est parier avec elle à qui cessera le premier d'aimer. *Id.*

On peut obtenir la justice pour les autres, jamais pour soi. *Id.*

On aimerait à savoir si c'est la littérature qui corrompt les mœurs ou les mœurs au contraire qui corrompent la littérature. *Id.*

Il y a des femmes qui n'aiment pas faire souffrir plusieurs hommes à la fois et qui préfèrent s'appliquer à un seul: ce sont les femmes fidèles. *Id.*

HENRI BERGSON

(1859–1941)

Celles-là seules de nos idées qui nous appartiennent le moins sont adéquatement exprimables par le mot.
Essai sur les données immédiates de la conscience (1889)

Nous sommes libres quand nos actes émanent de notre personnalité entière, quand ils l'expriment, quand ils ont avec elle cette indéfinissable ressemblance qu'on trouve parfois entre l'œuvre et l'artiste. *Id.*

Ce qu'on appelle ordinairement un *fait*, ce n'est pas la réalité telle qu'elle apparaîtrait à une intuition immédiate, mais une adaptation du réel aux intérêts de la pratique et aux exigences de la vie sociale. *Matière et Mémoire (1896)*

Explorer l'inconscient, travailler dans le sous-sol de l'esprit avec des méthodes spécialement appropriées, telle sera la tâche principale du siècle qui s'ouvre. *Le Rêve (1901)*

Happiness is the only thing one should ever be resigned to.

It's no use reminding yourself daily that you are mortal: it will be brought home to you soon enough.

To marry a woman you love and who loves you is to lay a bet with her as to which of you will fall out of love first.

It is possible to get justice done to others, never to oneself.

It would be nice to know whether it is literature that is corrupting morality or whether it is morality that is corrupting literature.

There are women who do not like to cause suffering to many men at a time, and who prefer to concentrate on one man: these are the faithful women.

Bergson, philosopher whose theories of time and intuition considerably influenced writers and artists; Nobel Prize for literature, 1927.

Only those ideas that are least truly ours can be adequately expressed in words.

We are free when our actions emanate from our total personality, when they express it, when they resemble it in the indefinable way a work of art sometimes seems to us to resemble its maker.

What is commonly called "a fact" is not reality as it would appear to direct intuition, but an adaptation of reality to practical interests and to demands of life in society.

The major task of the twentieth century will be to explore the unconscious, to investigate the subsoil of the mind by specially devised methods.

Originellement, nous ne pensons que pour agir. C'est dans le moule de l'action que notre intelligence a été coulée. La spéculation est un luxe, tandis que l'action est une nécessité.

L'Évolution créatrice (1707)

L'intelligence est caractérisée par une incompréhension naturelle de la vie. *Id.*

La création continue d'imprévisibles nouveautés . . . semble se poursuivre dans l'univers. Pour ma part, je crois l'expérimenter à chaque instant. *Le Possible et le Réel (1930)*

L'univers . . . est une machine à faire des dieux. . . .

Les deux sources de la morale et de la religion (1932)

Les termes qui désignent le temps sont empruntés à la langue de l'espace. Quand nous évoquons le temps, c'est l'espace qui répond à l'appel. *La Pensée et le Mouvant (1935)*

JULES LAFORGUE

(1860–1887)

Automne, automne, adieux de l'Adieu,

. . .

Est-il de vrais yeux?
Nulle ne songe à m'aimer un peu.

Les Complaintes (1883), Complainte de l'automne monotone

Jupes de quinze ans, aurores de femmes,
Qui veut, enfin, du palais de mon âme?

Id., Complainte du pauvre Chevalier-Errant

Ah! que la vie est quotidienne . . .
Et du plus vrai qu'on se souvienne
Comme on fut piètre et sans génie.

Id., Complainte sur certains ennuis

At its origins, thinking served only action. It is in the mold of action that our intelligence was cast. Speculation is a luxury, whereas action is a necessity.

Intelligence is characterized by a natural inability to understand life.

A process of continuous creation of the new and unforeseeable seems to be taking place in the universe. For my part, I think I experience it at every moment.

The universe is a machine for making gods.

The terms denoting time are borrowed from the language of space. When we summon time, it is space that answers.

Jules Laforgue, born in Montevideo, was a Symbolist poet, one of the first to use *vers libre;* influenced T. S. Eliot.

Autumn, autumn, good-bys of the Good-by,

. . .

Are there eyes that tell the truth?
No woman thinks of loving me a little.

Fifteen-year-old nymphs, dawn of womanhood,
Who will at last enter the palace of my soul?

Ah, Life is so banal!
Deep down we know
How paltry we were, how devoid of genius.

GEORGES COURTELINE

(1860–1929)

Un des plus clairs effets de la présence d'un enfant dans le ménage est de rendre complètement idiots de braves parents qui, sans lui, n'eussent peut-être été que de simples imbéciles.

La Philosophie de Georges Courteline

Peut-être est-on fondé à reprocher au bon Dieu d'avoir fait les hommes mauvais mais il faut le louer sans réserve d'avoir placé en contrepoids à leur méchanceté probable leur extraordinaire bêtise qui, elle, ne fait aucun doute. *Id.*

Qu'est l'orgueil d'un Leverrier, voyant apparaître au jour dit et à la place désignée, en l'immensité des espaces, l'astre annoncé depuis vingt ans, comparé à la gloire d'une brute qui a trouvé plus bête qu'elle? *Id.*

Il est évidemment bien dur de ne plus être aimé quand on aime, mais cela n'est pas comparable à l'être encore quand on n'aime plus. *Id.*

Passer pour un idiot aux yeux d'un imbécile est une volupté de fin gourmet. *Id.*

Il vaut mieux gâcher sa jeunesse que de n'en faire rien du tout. *Id.*

MAURICE MAETERLINCK

(1862–1949)

Si j'étais Dieu, j'aurais pitié du cœur des hommes.

Pelléas et Mélisande

On se trompe toujours lorsqu'on ne ferme pas les yeux pour pardonner ou pour mieux regarder en soi-même. *Id.*

Courteline, humorist, satirist, author of short stories, sketches, comedies.

One of the most unmistakable effects of a child's presence in the household is that the worthy parents turn into complete idiots. Without the child, they might have been mere imbeciles.

We may be justified in criticizing God for having made men wicked, but we should praise Him unreservedly for having counterbalanced their presumable wickedness by extraordinary stupidity. Nothing "presumable" about that.

The pride of a Leverrier at the appearance, in the immensity of space, on the right day and at the right place, of the star he foretold twenty years earlier is as nothing compared to the elation of a brute who has just found someone stupider than himself.

It is of course quite painful to be loved no longer when one is still in love, but that is incomparably less painful than being loved still when one has fallen out of love.

To be taken for an idiot by an imbecile is as exquisite a delight as any the most refined gourmet knows.

It is better to waste one's youth than to do nothing with it at all.

Maeterlinck, Belgian Symbolist poet, essayist, dramatist, Nobel Prize, 1911.

If I were God, I should be merciful to the human heart.

It is always a mistake not to close our eyes, whether to forgive or to look more closely into ourselves.

Seigneur, j'ai fait ce que j'ai pu! Est-ce ma faute si vous n'avez pas parlé plus clairement? Je n'ai cherché qu'à comprendre.
L'autre monde

MAURICE BARRÈS

(1862–1923)

Amusons-nous aux moyens sans souci du but. Faisons des rêves chaque matin, et avec une extrême énergie, mais sachons qu'ils n'aboutiront pas. Soyons ardents et sceptiques.
Un Homme libre, Préface

Mon indulgence, faite de compréhension, doit s'étendre jusqu'à ma propre faiblesse. *Id.*

Le réaliste trie les réalités, choisit l'immonde et dit: "Les abeilles, les lys, les soleils ont des taches." *Mes Cahiers, XII*

L'homme politique est un équilibriste. Il s'équilibre en disant le contraire de ce qu'il fait. *Id.*

JULES RENARD

(1864–1910)

La clarté est la politesse de l'homme de lettres. *Journal*

Pour arriver, il faut mettre de l'eau dans son vin, jusqu'à ce qu'il n'y ait plus de vin. *Id.*

On est si heureux de donner un conseil à un autre qu'il peut arriver, après tout, qu'on le lui donne dans son intérêt. *Id.*

La vie est courte, mais l'ennui l'allonge. Aucune vie n'est assez courte pour que l'ennui n'y trouve pas sa place. *Id.*

Lord, I did what I could! Is it my fault Thou didst not speak more clearly? I tried my best to understand.

Barrès, novelist, essayist, politician; began as an individualist aesthete exalting the "*culte du moi,*" later developed into an extreme nationalist.

Let us enjoy the means without worrying about the end. Let us dream daily, and with extreme energy, but always keeping in mind that our dreams will come to nothing. Let us be ardent and skeptical.

My indulgence, based on understanding, must extend to my own weakness.

The realist sorts out realities, selects the filth, and says, "The bees, the lilies, the suns have spots."

The politician is an acrobat. He keeps his balance by saying the opposite of what he does.

Jules Renard, known as the author of *Poil de Carotte;* his *Journal* is a revealing document, replete with his characteristic wry humor.

Clarity is the politeness of the man of letters.

To succeed, you must add water to your wine, until there is no more wine.

We are so happy to give advice that occasionally our advice is even disinterested.

Life is short, but boredom lengthens it. No life is short enough to leave no room for boredom.

Il y a des gens si ennuyeux qu'ils vous font perdre une journée en cinq minutes. *Id.*

Il ne suffit pas d'être heureux: il faut encore que les autres ne le soient pas. *Id.*

L'espérance, c'est sortir par un beau soleil et rentrer sous la pluie. *Id.*

Je sais enfin ce qui distingue l'homme de la bête: ce sont les ennuis d'argent. *Id.*

Dieu nous jette aux yeux de la poudre d'étoiles. Qu'y a-t-il derrière elles? Rien. *Id.*

Il y a des moments où tout réussit: il ne faut pas s'effrayer, ça passe. *Id.*

Je ne suis pas sincère, et je ne le suis pas, même au moment où je dis que je ne le suis pas. *Id.*

On ne comprend pas plus la vie à quarante ans qu'à vingt, mais on le sait et on l'avoue. *Id.*

Dieu. "Aux petits oiseaux il donne la pâture," et il les laisse, ensuite, l'hiver, crever de faim. *Id.*

ROMAIN ROLLAND
(1866–1944)

Je hais l'idéalisme couard, qui détourne les yeux des misères de la vie et des faiblesses de l'âme. Il faut le dire à un peuple sensible aux illusions décevantes des paroles sonores: le mensonge héroïque est une lâcheté. Il n'y a qu'un héroïsme au monde: c'est de voir le monde tel qu'il est, et de l'aimer.
Vie de Michel-Ange

Some people are so boring that they make you waste an entire day in five minutes.

It is not enough to be happy; it is necessary, in addition, that others not be.

What hope is: the weather is fine when you start out, but it rains on the way back.

I know at last what distinguishes man from animals: financial worries.

God throws star dust in our eyes. What is behind the stars? Nothing.

There are moments when everything goes as you wish; don't be frightened, it won't last.

I am not sincere, even when I am saying that I am not sincere.

We don't understand life any better at forty than at twenty, but we know it and admit it.

God. "The heavenly Father feedeth the fowls of the air"—and in winter He letteth them starve to death.

Romain Rolland, novelist, playwright, essayist; Nobel Prize for literature in 1916; his best-known work is his novel in many volumes, *Jean-Christophe;* prominent pacifist.

I hate the cowardly kind of idealism, the kind that turns its eyes away from life's miseries and the weakness of the spirit. This must be said to a nation prone to fall for the deceptive illusions of sonorous words: the heroic lie is an act of cowardice. There is only one kind of heroism in the world: this is to see the world as it is, and to love it.

On ne vit pas pour être heureux. . . . Souffre. Meurs. Mais sois ce que tu dois être: un Homme. *Jean-Christophe*

Par toute son éducation, par tout ce qu'il voit et entend autour de lui, l'enfant absorbe une telle somme de mensonges et de sottises, mélangées à des vérités essentielles, que le premier devoir de l'adolescent qui veut être un homme sain est de tout dégorger. *Id.*

Un héros c'est celui qui fait ce qu'il peut. Les autres ne le font pas. *Id.*

Tout homme qui est un vrai homme doit apprendre à rester seul au milieu de tous, à penser seul pour tous— et au besoin contre tous. *Clérambault*

TRISTAN BERNARD
(1866–1947)

Les hommes sont toujours sincères. Ils changent de sincérité, voilà tout. *Ce que l'on dit aux femmes*

Quand on n'est pas assez fortuné pour se payer le bonheur, il ne faut pas s'en approcher trop et le regarder. . . . Non, non, ne regardons pas les étalages. *Le Danseur inconnu*

A certains maris il ne suffit pas de n'être pas trompés par leur femme. Ils veulent avoir toute la gloire de ne pas l'être et courir tous les risques possibles.
Mémoires d'un jeune homme rangé (1899)

We do not live to be happy. . . . Suffer. Die. But be what you should be: a Man.

As a result of all his education, of all he sees and hears around him, the child absorbs such an amount of lies and stupidities, mingled with essential truths, that the first duty of the adolescent who wants to be a healthy man is to disgorge everything.

A hero is one who does what he can. The others don't.

Every man who is truly a man must learn to be alone in the midst of all others, and if need be against all others.

Tristan Bernard, noted raconteur, humorist, author of successful comedies, and a novel, *Mémoires d'un jeune homme rangé.*

People are always sincere. They change sincerities, that's all.

When you are not rich enough to buy happiness, you must not come too close to watch it. . . . No, don't indulge in window-shopping.

Not to be betrayed by his wife is not enough for a certain type of husband. He takes pride in her fidelity and at the same time exposes her to every possible temptation.

MARCEL SCHWOB

(1867–1905)

Toute pensée qui dure est contradiction. Tout amour qui dure est haine. Toute sincérité qui dure est mensonge. Toute justice qui dure est injustice. Tout bonheur qui dure est malheur.
Le Livre de Monelle (1894)

PAUL-JEAN TOULET

(1867–1920)

On a dit de la beauté que c'était une promesse de bonheur. On n'a pas dit qu'elle fût tenue. *Les Trois Impostures*

D'aimer son mari, c'est un fournisseur que l'on paie. Mais son amant, c'est comme donner aux pauvres. *Id.*

La fièvre, à ce que l'on dit, nous délivre des puces, et l'infortune de nos amis. *Id.*

Passe que l'amour porte des épines: il est une fleur. Mais quoi? l'amitié? Ce n'est qu'un légume. *Id.*

L'amour est comme ces hôtels meublés dont tout le luxe est au vestibule. *Le Carnet de Monsieur du Paur, homme public*

L'exactitude de la femme désirée n'est pas un plaisir proportionné aux souffrances que cause son retard. *Id.*

Schwob, Symbolist essayist and critic.

Every thought that endures is contradictory. Every love that endures is hatred. Every sincerity that endures is a lie. Every justice that endures is injustice. Every happiness that endures is unhappiness.

P.-J. Toulet, poet (author of *Contrerimes*) and novelist.

It was said of beauty that it is a promise of happiness. It was not said that the promise is kept.

A woman who loves her husband is merely paying her bills. A woman who loves her lover gives alms to the poor.

Fever, it is said, frees us from fleas; misfortune frees us from our friends.

Love has its thorns: all right, it is a flower. But friendship? Friendship is a vegetable.

Love is like those second-rate hotels where all the luxury is in the lobby.

Punctuality on the part of a woman we desire is not a pleasure commensurable with the pain she causes us when she is late.

EDMOND ROSTAND

(1868–1918)

O Soleil! toi sans qui les choses
Ne seraient que ce qu'elles sont.
Chantecler, I, 2 (Ode au Soleil)

Et si de tous les chants mon chant est le plus fier,
C'est que je chante clair afin qu'il fasse clair! *Id., II, 3*

C'est la nuit qu'il est beau de croire à la lumière. *Ibid.*

ANDRÉ SUARÈS

(1868–1948)

L'hérésie est la vie de la religion. C'est la foi qui fait les hérétiques. Dans une religion morte, il n'y a plus d'hérésies. *Péguy*

Comme on fait la guerre avec le sang des autres, on fait fortune avec l'argent d'autrui. *Voici l'homme*

La morale est l'hygiène des niais, et désormais, l'hygiène est la morale de toutes les turpitudes. *Id.*

L'art du clown va bien au-delà de ce qu'on pense. Il n'est ni tragique ni comique. Il est le miroir comique de la tragédie et le miroir tragique de la comédie. *Remarques, Essai sur le clown*

Rostand, poet and dramatist.

O Sun, thou but for whom things
Would be no more than what they are.

And if my song is of all songs the proudest,
Why, I sing so piercingly that there may be light!

It is at night that faith in light is sublime.

André Suarès, essayist and critic.

Heresy is the lifeblood of religions. It is faith that begets heretics. There are no heresies in a dead religion.

Just as war is waged with the blood of others, so fortunes are made with other people's money.

Morality is the hygiene of the simple minded, and eventually hygiene becomes the moral justification of every sort of turpitude.

The art of the clown goes well beyond what people generally suppose. It is neither tragic nor comic. It is a comic mirror of tragedy and a tragic mirror of comedy.

ALAIN (ÉMILE CHARTIER)

(1868–1951)

Le plus difficile au monde est de dire en y pensant ce que tout le monde dit sans y penser. *Histoire de mes pensées*

Une idée que j'ai, il faut que je la nie; c'est une manière de l'essayer. . . . Je suis bien sûr qu'à secouer ainsi l'arbre de la connaissance, les bons fruits seront sauvés, et les mauvais jetés à l'inutile. *Id.*

Penser, c'est dire non. *Le citoyen contre les pouvoirs.*

L'âme, c'est ce qui refuse le corps. Par exemple ce qui refuse de fuir quand le corps tremble, ce qui refuse de frapper quand le corps s'irrite, ce qui refuse de boire quand le corps a soif. *Définitions*

On prouve tout ce qu'on veut, et la vraie difficulté est de savoir ce qu'on veut prouver. *Système des beaux-arts*

Le mauvais goût n'est peut-être que la passion d'orner pour orner. *Id.*

Le doute n'est pas au-dessous du savoir mais au-dessus. *Libres-propos*

Rien de plus dangereux qu'une idée, quand on n'a qu'une idée. *Id.*

PAUL CLAUDEL

(1868–1955)

Ma vie à moi, cette chose qu'aucune femme n'épouse, qu'aucune mère ne berce, qu'aucun contrat n'engage ... *Tête d'or (1890)*

Alain, teacher of philosophy, author of numerous essays and aphorisms on philosophy, the arts, etc.

The hardest thing in the world is to say, thinking it, what everybody says without thinking.

When I have an idea, I feel the need to deny it: it is one way of testing it. . . . I am persuaded that if the tree of knowledge were shaken in this way, the good fruit would be saved, the bad fruit discarded.

To think is to say No.

The soul is that which refuses to comply with the body. For instance, that which refuses to run away when the body shivers in dread, that which refuses to strike when the body is angry, that which refuses to drink when the body is thirsty.

We prove what we want to prove; the real difficulty lies in knowing what we want to prove.

Bad taste may be merely a passion to decorate for the sake of decorating.

Doubt is not a stage below knowledge, but a stage above it.

Nothing is more dangerous than an idea, when that is the only idea we have.

Claudel, poet, essayist, best known for his lyrical dramas.

My own life, that thing which no woman marries, no mother cradles, no contract commits.

Tu n'expliques rien, ô poète, mais toutes choses par toi deviennent explicables. *La Ville*

Ouvrez les yeux! Le monde est encore intact; il est vierge comme au premier jour, frais comme le lait! *Art poétique (1907)*

Toute créature est, par cela même que créée, créatrice. *Id.*

O mon âme! le poème n'est point fait de ces lettres que je plante comme des clous, mais du blanc qui reste sur le papier.
Cinq Grandes Odes (1910). Les Muses

D'un bout de votre création jusqu'à l'autre,
Il ne cesse point continuité, non plus que de l'âme au corps.
Ibid.

Les mots que j'emploie,
Ce sont les mots de tous les jours, et ce ne sont point les mêmes!
Vous ne trouverez point de rimes dans mes vers ni aucun sortilège. Ce sont vos phrases mêmes. . . .
Id., La muse qui est la grâce

Notre résurrection n'est pas tout entière dans le futur, elle est aussi en nous, elle commence, elle a déjà commencé.
Correspondance avec André Gide (1899–1926)

Quand l'homme essaie d'imaginer le Paradis sur terre, ça fait tout de suite un Enfer très convenable.
Conversations dans le Loir-et-Cher (1929)

Le temps, tout le consume et l'amour seul l'emploie.
L'Oiseau noir dans le soleil levant

You explain nothing, O poet, but thanks to you all things become explicable.

Open your eyes! The world is still intact; it is as pristine as it was on the first day, as fresh as milk!

Every creature, by the very fact of having been created, is creative.

O my soul! the poem is not made up of these letters I set down as though driving nails, but of the blank space that is left on the paper.

From end to end of Thy creation,
There is no break in continuity, no more than between body and soul.

The words I use
Are everyday words, and yet they are not at all the same!
You will not find rhymes in my verse, nor wizardry.
They are your very own expressions. . . .

Our resurrection does not wholly lie in the future; it is also within us, it is starting now, it has already started.

When man tries to imagine Paradise on earth, the immediate result is a very respectable Hell.

Time: all things consume it, love alone makes use of it.

ANDRÉ GIDE
(1869–1951)

Nous avons bâti sur le sable
Des cathédrales impérissables. *Paludes (1895)*

Que mon livre t'enseigne à t'intéresser plus à toi qu'à lui-même —puis à tout le reste plus qu'à toi.
Les Nourritures terrestres (1897)

Familles! je vous hais! Foyers clos; portes refermées; possessions jalouses du bonheur. *Id.*

Le péché, c'est ce qui obscurcit l'âme.
La Symphonie pastorale (1919)

Les actions les plus décisives de notre vie . . . sont le plus souvent des actions inconsidérées. *Les Faux Monnayeurs (1925)*

Il est bon de suivre sa pente, pourvu que ce soit en montant. *Id.*

Mon bonheur est d'augmenter celui des autres. J'ai besoin du bonheur de tous pour être heureux.
Les Nouvelles Nourritures (1935)

Connais-toi toi-même. Maxime aussi pernicieuse que laide. Quiconque s'observe arrête son développement. La chenille qui chercherait à se bien connaître ne deviendrait jamais papillon. *Id.*

L'art commence à la résistance; à la résistance vaincue. Aucun chef-d'œuvre humain, qui ne soit laborieusement obtenu.
Poétique

Pour paraître affecté, il n'est qu'à chercher à être sincère.
Journal, 27 juillet 1922

Le bonheur de l'homme n'est pas dans la liberté, mais dans l'acceptation d'un devoir. *Id., 8 février 1932*

C'est avec de beaux sentiments qu'on fait de la mauvaise littérature. *Lettre à François Mauriac, 1928*

Gide, novelist, critic, dramatist: Nobel Prize for literature, 1947.

We have built imperishable
Cathedrals on sand.

May my book teach you to be concerned more with yourself than with it—and then with everything more than with yourself.

Families, I hate you! Shut-in lives, closed doors, jealous protectors of happiness.

Sin is whatever obscures the soul.

The most crucial actions of our life . . . are most often unconsidered ones.

It is good to follow one's own bent, so long as it leads upward.

My happiness lies in increasing the happiness of others. I need the happiness of all to be happy myself.

Know thyself. A maxim as pernicious as it is ugly. Whoever studies himself arrests his own development. A caterpillar that set out really "to know itself" would never become a butterfly.

Art begins with resistance—at the point where resistance is overcome. There is no masterpiece by man that has not been achieved laboriously.

To seem affected, all you have to do is try to be sincere.

Man's happiness does not lie in freedom, but in the acceptance of a duty.

It is with noble sentiments that bad literature gets written.

MARCEL PROUST

(1871–1922)

La réalité ne se forme que dans la mémoire, les fleurs qu'on me montre aujourd'hui pour la première fois ne me semblent pas de vraies fleurs. *Du Côté de chez Swann, I, 2*

Non seulement on ne retient pas tout de suite les œuvres vraiment rares, mais même au sein de chacune des ces œuvres-là ce sont les parties les moins précieuses qu'on perçoit d'abord. Moins décevants que la vie, ces grands chef-d'œuvres ne commencent pas par nous donner que ce qu'elles ont de meilleur.
A l'ombre des jeunes filles en fleur, I

Nous sommes tous obligés pour rendre la réalité supportable d'entretenir en nous quelques petites folies. *Id.*

Toute action de l'esprit est aisée si elle n'est pas soumise au réel.
Sodome et Gomorrhe, II, 1

On a dit que la beauté est une promesse de bonheur. Inversément, la possibilité du plaisir peut être un commencement de beauté. *La Prisonnière*

L'adultère introduit l'esprit dans la lettre que bien souvent le mariage eût laissée morte. *Id.*

Le plagiat humain auquel il est le plus difficile d'échapper, c'est le plagiat de soi même. *Albertine disparue, I*

La reconnaissance en soi-même, par le lecteur, de ce que dit ce livre, est la preuve de sa vérité. *Le Temps retrouvé, II*

Le temps qui change les êtres ne modifie pas l'image que nous avons gardée d'eux. *Id.*

Il vaut mieux rêver sa vie que la vivre, encore que la vivre ce soit encore la rêver. *Les Plaisirs et les Jours*

Proust is recognized as one of the greatest novelists of our century.

Reality takes shape only in memory: the flowers I am shown today for the first time do not seem true flowers to me.

Not only do we not take in the truly rare works all at once, but even within each such work it is the least valuable parts that we perceive first. Less deceptive than life, the great masterpieces do not give us their best at first meeting.

All of us must indulge in a few small follies if we are to make reality bearable.

Every mental operation is easy so long as it is not controlled by reality.

It has been said that beauty is a promise of happiness. Conversely, the possibility of pleasure can be a beginning of beauty.

Adultery introduces spirit into what might otherwise have been the dead letter of marriage.

The human plagiarism hardest to avoid is self-plagiarism.

The reader's recognition within himself of what is said in this book is proof of its truth.

Though time changes people, it does not alter the image we have kept of them.

It is better to dream one's life than to live it, even though to live it is also to dream it.

PAUL VALÉRY

(1871–1945)

Génie! ô longue impatience . . .

Charmes (1922), Ébauche d'un serpent

La mer, la mer toujours recommencée! *Id., le cimetière marin*

O récompense après une pensée
Qu'un long regard sur le calme des dieux! *Ibid.*

Le temps scintille et le songe est savoir. *Ibid.*

. . . rendre la lumière
Suppose d'ombre une morne moitié. *Ibid.*

Patience, patience,
Patience dans l'azur!
Chaque atome de silence
Est la chance d'un fruit mûr. *Id., Palme*

La bêtise n'est pas mon fort. *Monsieur Teste*

Monsieur Teste, d'ailleurs, pense que l'amour consiste à être bête ensemble. *Id.*

La plupart des hommes ont de la poésie une idée si vague que ce vague même de leur idée est pour eux la définition de la poésie. *Littérature (1930)*

La poésie n'est que la littérature réduite à l'essentiel de son principe actif. On l'a purgée des idoles de toute espèce et des illusions réalistes; de l'équivoque possible entre le langage de la "vérité" et le langage de la "création". *Ibid.*

Nous autres, civilisations, nous savons maintenant que nous sommes mortelles. *Variété I. La Crise de l'esprit*

Paul Valéry, poet, essayist, aphorist. "Valéry's conversation puts me into a frightful dilemma: either I must find ridiculous what he says, or I must find ridiculous what I do" (Gide).

Genius! O long impatience . . .

The sea, the sea that ever starts anew!

O what a reward after a thought
Is a long glance at the calm of the gods!

Time sparkles and the dream is knowledge.

. . . the rendering of light
Entails a gloomy moiety of shadow.

Patience, patience,
Patience in the azure!
Every atom of silence
Is a chance for a ripe fruit.

Stupidity is not my strong suit.

Monsieur Teste, however, thinks that love consists in being stupid together.

Most people have so vague an idea of poetry that their vagueness on this score serves as their definition of poetry.

Poetry is simply literature reduced to the essence of its active principle. It is literature purged of all idols, of all realistic illusions, of every conceivable equivocation between the language of "truth" and the language of "creation."

Speaking for civilizations, we know today that we are mortal.

L'Histoire est la science des choses qui ne se répètent pas.

Variété, IV

Le silence éternel de ces espaces infinis m'effraie (Pascal, *Pensées*, 206). Cette phrase, dont la force de ce qu'elle veut imprimer aux âmes et la magnificence de sa forme ont fait une des paroles les plus fameuses qui aient jamais été articulées, est un *Poème*, et point du tout une *Pensée.* Car *Eternel* et *Infini* sont des symboles de non-pensée. Leur valeur est tout affective. Ils n'agissent que sur une certaine sensibilité. Ils provoquent la sensation particulière de l'impuissance d'imaginer. *Variété*

Je n'aime pas trop les musées. Il y en a beaucoup d'admirables, il n'en est point de délicieux. *Pièces sur l'art (1934)*

Le moi est haïssable . . . mais il s'agit de celui des autres.

Mélanges

Choses rares ou choses belles
Ici savamment assemblées
Instruisent l'œil à regarder
Comme jamais encore vues
Toutes choses qui sont au monde.

Inscription, Musée de L'Homme (1937)

Une femme intelligente est une femme avec laquelle on peut être aussi bête que l'on veut.

Mauvaises pensées et autres (1941)

Qu'est-ce qu'un sot?—Peut-être ce n'est qu'un esprit peu exigeant, qui se contente de peu. Un sot serait-il un sage? *Id.*

Le peintre ne doit pas faire ce qu'il voit, mais ce qui sera vu. *Id.*

Dieu a tout fait de rien. Mais le rien perce. *Id.*

Chaque pensée est une exception à une règle générale qui est de ne pas penser. *Id.*

History is the science of things that do not repeat themselves.

"The eternal silence of those infinite spaces frightens me" (Pascal, *Pensées,* 206). This sentence, so vigorous in its imprint upon our minds and so magnificent in its form that it has become one of the most famous ever uttered, is a *Poem,* not at all a *Thought.* For "eternal" and "infinite" are symbols of non-thought. The value of these terms is entirely emotional. Their appeal is wholly to a certain sensibility. They provoke the specific sensation of incapacity to imagine things.

I don't much care for museums. There are many admirable ones, but no delightful ones.

The self is hateful . . . that is, any except our own.

Things rare, things beautiful
Here artfully assembled
Teach the eye to look upon
As though for the first time
All the things the world contains.

An intelligent woman is a woman with whom we can be as stupid as we like.

What is a fool?—Perhaps simply an undemanding mind, which is satisfied with little. Could it be that a fool is really wise?

The painter should not paint what he sees, but what will be seen.

God made everything out of nothing. But the nothingness shows through.

Every thought is an exception to this general rule: people don't think.

Tentation ou les réponses d'Adam

Ut eritis sicut Dei . . .
—Je n'y tiens pas le moins du monde, cher Serpent.
. . . bonum malumque scientes.
—J'aimerais mieux savoir autre chose. *Id.*

Ne dites jamais: *Aime-moi.* Cela ne sert de rien. Toutefois Dieu le dit. *Id.*

La femme est ennemie de l'esprit, soit qu'elle donne, soit qu'elle refuse l'amour.—Ennemie naturelle et nécessaire; et même le meilleur ennemi de l'esprit.—Le meilleur ennemi est celui qui fait créer les plus subtils et les plus sages moyens de défense ou de l'attaque. *Id.*

Les bons souvenirs sont des bijoux perdus. *Id.*

Louange de l'hypocrite.
L'hypocrite ne peut pas être aussi entièrement méchant ou mauvais que le sincère. *Id.*

Dieu créa l'homme et ne le trouvant pas assez seul, il lui donna une compagne pour lui faire mieux sentir sa solitude.
Tel quel (1943)

L'objet de la psychologie est de nous donner une idée tout autre des choses que nous connaissons le mieux. *Id.*

La politique est l'art d'empêcher les gens de se mêler de ce qui les regarde. *Id.*

Le poème—cette hésitation prolongée entre le son et les sens. *Id.*

Le martyr: j'aime mieux mourir que . . . réfléchir. *Id.*

Ye shall be as gods . . .
—Nothing could interest me less, dear Serpent.
. . . *knowing good and evil.*
—I'd rather know something else.

Never say, "Love me." It is of no use. And yet God says it.

Woman is an enemy of the spirit, whether she gives or withholds love. A natural and necessary enemy, the spirit's best enemy, really. One's best enemy forces you to invent ever subtler, wiser means of attack and defense.

Good memories are lost jewels.

In praise of the hypocrite: The hypocrite cannot be as wholly vicious or unkind as the sincere man.

God created man, and, finding him not sufficiently alone, gave him a female companion to make him feel his solitude more keenly.

The purpose of psychology is to give us an entirely different idea of the things we know best.

Politics is the art of preventing people from busying themselves with what is their own business.

The poem—this protracted hesitation between sound and sense.

The martyr: I'd rather die than . . . reconsider.

ALFRED JARRY

(1873–1907)

Quant à l'action, elle se passe en Pologne, c'est-à-dire nulle part.
Ubu Roi (1896), Introduction

Mère Ubu, tu es bien laide aujourd'hui. Est-ce parce que nous avons du monde? *Id.*

Avec ce système, j'aurai vite fait fortune, alors je tuerai tout le monde et je m'en irai. *Id.*

S'apercevoir que sa mère est vierge.
—*Les 36 situations dramatiques*
trente-septième *situation.*
L'Amour absolu (1899), Ch. III, épigraphe

L'indiscipline aveugle et de tous les instants fait la force principale des hommes libres. *Ubu enchaîné (1900)*

CHARLES PÉGUY

(1873–1914)

C'est embêtant, dit Dieu. Quand il n'y aura plus ces Français,
Il y a des choses que je fais, il n'y aura plus personne pour les
comprendre. *Les Sept contre Paris*

Heureux ceux qui sont morts, car ils sont retournés
Dans la première argile et la première terre.
Heureux ceux qui sont morts dans une juste guerre.
Heureux les épis mûrs et les blés moissonnés.
Les Tapisseries (1914), Eve

Jarry, poet and humorist who tried to live like his own fantastic characters; the hero of his satirical farce, *Ubu Roi,* has become the prototype of the petty tyrant.

As for the action, it is laid in Poland, that is to say, nowhere.

Mother Ubu, you're very ugly today. Is it because you have company?

This way I'll get rich quick, and then I'll kill off everybody and clear out of here.

The thirty-seventh dramatic situation:
To become aware that one's mother is a virgin.
[*Refers to Georges Polti's* Thirty-Six Dramatic Situations]

Blind indiscipline, always and everywhere, is the main strength of free men.

Péguy, mystical poet and polemical writer; killed in the battle of the Marne.

It's a nuisance, God said. When the Frenchmen are gone,
No one will be left to understand certain things I do.

Happy those who are dead, for they have returned
To the original dust and the primal earth.
Happy those who died in a just war,
Happy the ripe ears of grain and wheat in sheaves.

Voici la nudité, le reste est vêtement . . .
Voici la pauvreté, le reste est ornement.

Présentation de la Beauce

Une capitulation est essentiellement une opération par laquelle on se met à expliquer au lieu d'agir.

Les Cahiers de la quinzaine, 1905

Quand il s'agit d'histoire ancienne, on ne peut pas faire d'histoire parce qu'on manque de références. Quand il s'agit d'histoire moderne, on ne peut pas faire d'histoire, parce qu'on regorge de références. *Clio*

Homère est nouveau ce matin, et rien n'est peut-être aussi vieux que le journal d'aujourd'hui.

Note sur M. Bergson et la philosophie bergsonienne (1914)

Une grande philosophie n'est point une philosophie sans reproche. C'est une philosophie sans peur . . .
Une grande philosophie n'est pas celle qui prononce des jugements définitifs, qui installe une vérité définitive. C'est celle qui introduit une inquiétude, qui ouvre un ébranlement. *Id.*

Il y a des idées qui sont toutes faites pendant qu'on les fait, avant qu'on les fasse. *Id.*

SIDONIE-GABRIELLE COLETTE
(1873–1954)

Sens qui savent goûter un parfum sur la langue, palper une couleur et voir, fine comme un cheveu, fine comme une herbe, la ligne d'un chant imaginaire. *La Maison de Claudine*

Ces plaisirs qu'on nomme, à la légère, physiques... *Mélanges*

Connaître ce qui lui était caché, c'est la griserie, l'honneur et la perte de l'homme. *Id.*

Here is true nakedness, the rest is dressing up . . .
Here is true poverty, the rest is adornment.

Surrender is essentially an operation by means of which we set about explaining instead of acting.

In the case of ancient history, we cannot write history for lack of source materials. In the case of modern history, we cannot write history because we have too great an abundance of source materials.

Homer is new and fresh this morning, while there is nothing, perhaps, as old and tired as today's newspaper.

A great philosophy is not a flawless philosophy, but a fearless philosophy . . . A great philosophy is not one that utters definitive judgments, that lays down some definitive truth. It is one that introduces restlessness, that stirs things up.

There are ideas that are ready-made even while they are just being worked out, even before they have been worked out.

Colette, novelist noted for her sensuous prose and subtle psychological analyses of childhood.

Senses capable of tasting a fragrance on the tongue, of feeling a color at the fingertips, and of seeing, thin as a hair, thin as a blade of grass, the line of an imaginary song.

Those pleasures so lightly called physical . . .

Knowledge of the hidden is man's intoxication, honor, and ruin.

MAX JACOB
(1876–1944)

Le poète cache sous l'expression de la joie le désespoir de n'en avoir pas trouvé la réalité. *La Défense de Tartufe*

Il se peut qu'un rêve étrange
Vous ait occupée ce soir,
Vous avez cru voir un ange
Et c'était votre miroir. *Le laboratoire central*

Terre où pourrit le péché et l'erreur,
terre où la vie dure quelques heures,
te quitter est la seule envie
que me laissent mes terreurs. *Fond de l'eau. Méditation*

La grande affaire est de vivre, de vivre par l'imagination et la poitrine, d'inventer, de savoir, de jouer. L'art es un jeu. Tant pis pour celui qui s'en fait un devoir. *Conseils à un jeune poète*

C'est au moment où l'on triche pour le beau que l'on est artiste. *Art poétique*

Qui a compris une fois le vrai beau a gâté pour l'avenir toutes ses joies artistiques. *Id.*

Ce qu'on appelle une œuvre sincère, est celle qui est douée d'assez de force pour donner de la réalité à une illusion. *Id.*

Une personnalité n'est qu'une erreur persistante. *Id.*

La poésie moderne ou le dessous des cartes. *Id.*

Max Jacob, poet and novelist, of Jewish origin; became Catholic after seeing the Virgin in a vision; died in a German concentration camp.

The poet's expression of joy conceals his despair at not having found the reality of joy.

A strange dream perhaps
Has haunted you tonight:
You thought you saw an angel,
It was your mirror only.

Earth where sin and error rot,
earth where life endures a short time,
to quit you is the only desire
that terrors leave me.

The important thing is to live, to live by your imagination and your lungs, to invent, to know, to play. Art is a game. So much the worse for those who turn it into a piece of homework.

When you get to the point where you cheat for the sake of beauty, you're an artist.

He who has once grasped true beauty, spoils all his future artistic joys.

What is called a sincere work is one that is endowed with enough strength to give reality to an illusion.

Personality is merely a persistent error.

Modern poetry: the more-than-meets-the-eye.

APOLLINAIRE (GUILLAUME KOSTROWITZKY)

(1880–1918)

A la fin tu es las de ce monde ancien
Bergère ô tour Eiffel le troupeau des ponts bêle ce matin
Tu en as assez de vivre dans l'antiquité grecque et romaine
Alcools (1913), Zone

Vienne la nuit sonne l'heure
Les jours s'en vont je demeure *Id., Le Pont Mirabeau*

Je connais gens de toutes sortes
Ils n'égalent pas leur destin *Id., Marizibill*

Perdre
Mais perdre vraiment
Pour laisser place à la trouvaille
Perdre
La vie pour trouver la Victoire *Calligrammes, Toujours*

Nous voulons vous donner de vastes et d'étranges domaines
Où le mystère en fleurs s'offre à qui veut les cueillir
Il y a là des feux nouveaux de couleurs jamais vues
Mille phantasmes impondérables
Auxquels il faut donner de la réalité *Id., La jolie rousse*

Pitié pour nous qui combattons toujours aux frontières
De l'illimité et de l'avenir *Ibid.*

Et toi mon cœur pourquoi bats-tu
Comme un guetteur mélancolique
J'observe la nuit et la mort *Le Guetteur mélancolique*

Apollinaire, poet, author of stories and essays, friend of Picasso, Braque, etc. Inventor of the word "Surrealism." "A gypsy Villon" (Marcel Arland).

In the end you are weary of this world so old
Shepherdess O Eiffel Tower the flock of bridges is bleating this morning
You've had enough of living amid Greek and Roman monuments

Night comes the hour sounds
The days go by I endure

I know people of every sort
They don't measure up to their fates

To lose
But really to lose
To make room for the chance discovery
To lose
Life so as to find Victory

We want to give you vast and strange domains
Where the flowers of mystery await whoever cares to pluck them
Where there are new fires colors never seen before
A myriad imponderable phantasms
Clamoring to be endowed with reality

Pity us who have always to fight on the frontiers
Of the unlimited of the future

And you my heart why do you pound
Like some melancholy watchman
I am looking into night and death

JEAN GIRAUDOUX

(1882–1944)

Il n'est de parfait en ce bas monde que les calamités. En ce qu'elles détruisent et en ce qu'elles épargnent, elles font toujours une œuvre raffinée et définitive. *Littérature*

Le plagiat est la base de toutes les littératures, excepté de la première, qui d'ailleurs est inconnue. *Siegfried et le Limousin*

La principale difficulté avec les femmes honnêtes n'est pas de les séduire, c'est de les amener dans un endroit clos. Leur vertu est faite de portes entr'ouvertes. *Amphitryon 38*

Les femmes fidèles sont toutes les mêmes, elles ne pensent qu'à leur fidélité, jamais à leur mari. *Id.*

Les gens ont pitié des autres dans la mesure où ils auraient pitié d'eux-mêmes. Le malheur ou la laideur sont des miroirs qu'ils ne supportent pas. *La Guerre de Troie n'aura pas lieu*

GEORGES BERNANOS

(1888–1948)

La bêtise féminine est déjà bien irritante, la bêtise cléricale l'est plus encore que la bêtise féminine dont elle semble parfois le mystérieux surgeon. *Le journal d'un curé de campagne*

L'enfer, Madame, c'est de ne plus aimer. *Ibid.*

Les démocraties ne peuvent pas plus se passer d'être hypocrites que les dictatures d'être cyniques. *Nous autres Français*

Giraudoux, novelist, playwright; chief of French propaganda in 1939–40.

Nothing here below is as perfect as calamities. In what they destroy and in what they spare, they are always the last word in refinement and completeness.

Plagiarism is the basis of all literatures, except the first one, which is, however, unknown.

The main problem with honest women is not how to seduce them, but how to take them to a private place. Their virtue hinges on half-open doors.

Faithful women are all alike, they think only of their fidelity, never of their husbands.

People pity others to the extent that they would pity themselves. Misfortune and ugliness are mirrors they cannot bear.

Bernanos, novelist and polemical writer.

Feminine stupidity is annoying enough, but clerical stupidity is even more annoying than feminine stupidity whose mysterious offshoot it sometimes seems to be.

Hell, Madame, is to love no longer.

Democracies cannot dispense with hypocrisy any more than dictatorships can with cynicism.

Les plus dangereux de nos calculs sont ceux que nous appelons des illusions. *Le Dialogue des Carmélites*

L'optimisme est une fausse espérance à l'usage des lâches et des imbéciles.
L'espérance est une vertu, *virtus*, une détermination héroïque de l'âme.
La plus haute forme de l'espérance, c'est le désespoir surmonté.
La liberté pour quoi faire

LOUIS-FERDINAND CÉLINE (L. F. DESTOUCHES)

(1894–1960)

Celui qui parle de l'avenir est un coquin. C'est l'actuel qui compte. Invoquer sa postérité, c'est faire un discours aux asticots.
Voyage au bout de la nuit (1932)

Engraisser les sillons du laboureur anonyme, c'est le véritable avenir du véritable soldat. Ce monde n'est, je vous l'assure, qu'une immense entreprise à se foutre du monde. *Id.*

Trahir, qu'on dit, c'est vite dit. Faut encore saisir l'occasion. C'est comme d'ouvrir une fenêtre dans une prison. Trahir, tout le monde en a envie, mais c'est rare qu'on puisse. *Id.*

Les Anglais, c'est drôle quand même comme dégaîne, c'est mi-curé, mi-garçonnet. *Mort à crédit (1935)*

Dès que dans l'existence ça va un tout petit peu mieux, on ne pense plus qu'aux saloperies. *Id.*

PAUL ÉLUARD

(1895–1952)

Je fis un feu
L'azur m'ayant abandonné. *Pour vivre ici (1918)*

The most dangerous of our calculations are those we call illusions.

Optimism is a false hope made for fools and cowards. Hope is a virtue, *virtus,* a heroic resolve of the soul. The highest form of hope is despair overcome.

Céline, novelist noted for his free use of colloquial language.

Those who talk about the future are scoundrels. It is the present that matters. To invoke one's posterity is to make a speech to maggots.

The real future of the real soldier is to fertilize the soil of the anonymous tiller. I assure you, this world is nothing but a vast attempt to swindle.

Treason, that's easier said than done. You still have to know how to seize the opportunity. It's like opening a window in a prison. Everybody wants to betray, but you can do it only rarely.

The English are certainly peculiar—half-clergyman, half-little-boy.

The moment things begin to look up a bit in life, one thinks only of obscenities.

Eluard who began as a Surrealist is considered one of the leading modern French poets.

I made a fire
The blue sky having deserted me.

Ta bouche aux lèvres d'or n'est pas en moi pour rire.
Capitale de la douleur (1926)

Je suis né pour te connaître
Pour te nommer
Liberté. *Poésie et vérité (1942), Liberté*

Le poète est celui qui inspire bien plus que celui qui est inspiré.
L'Évidence poétique (1936)

RAYMOND RADIGUET

(1903–1923)

La saveur du premier baiser m'avait déçu comme un fruit que l'on goûte pour la première fois. Ce n'est pas dans la nouveauté, c'est dans l'habitude que nous trouvons les plus grands plaisirs.
Le Diable au corps (1923)

C'est lorsqu'un mal entre en nous que nous nous croyons en danger. Dès qu'il sera installé, nous pourrons faire bon ménage avec lui, voire même ne pas soupçonner sa présence.
Le Bal du comte d'Orgel (1924)

Les manoeuvres inconscientes d'une âme pure sont encore plus singulières que les combinaisons du vice. *Id.*

SIMONE WEIL

(1909–1943)

Dieu ne peut être présent dans la création que sous forme de l'absence. *La Pesanteur et la Grâce (1947)*

L'attachement est fabricateur d'illusions, et quiconque veut le réel doit être détaché. *Id.*

Your golden-lipped mouth is not in mine to laugh.

I was born to know you
To give you your name
Freedom.

The poet is much more the inspirer than the one who is inspired.

Radiguet died at the age of twenty having written two outstanding novels.

The taste of the first kiss disappointed me like a fruit tasted for the first time. It is not in novelty, it is in habit that we find the greatest pleasures.

It is only at our first contact with evil that we feel threatened. Once it has made itself at home within us, we are able to get along with it, indeed, we may not suspect its presence.

The unconscious maneuvers of a naïve soul are even more astonishing than the complicated schemes of vice.

Simone Weil wrote essays on religion and philosophy.

God can be present in creation only in the form of absence.

Attachment is the great fabricator of illusions; reality can be attained only by someone who is detached.

La chair est dangereuse pour autant qu'elle se refuse à aimer Dieu, mais aussi pour autant qu'elle se mêle indiscrètement de l'aimer. *Id.*

La pureté est le pouvoir de contempler la souillure. *Id.*

Seul l'être humain a une destinée éternelle. Les collectivités humaines n'en ont pas. Aussi n'y a-t-il pas à leur égard d'obligations directes qui soient éternelles. Seul est éternel le devoir envers l'être humain comme tel. *L'Enracinement (1949)*

La culture est un instrument manié par les professeurs pour fabriquer des professeurs qui, à leur tour, fabriqueront des professeurs. *Id.*

ALBERT CAMUS
(1913–1960)

Je veux que tout me soit expliqué ou rien. Et la raison est impuissante devant ce cri du cœur. . . . L'absurde naît de cette confrontation entre l'appel humain et le silence déraisonnable du monde. *Le Mythe de Sisyphe (1942)*

L'absurde est la notion essentielle et la première vérité. *Id.*

Peut-on être un saint sans Dieu: c'est le seul problème concret que je connaisse aujourd'hui. *La Peste (1947)*

La vérité, comme la lumière, aveugle. Le mensonge, au contraire, est un beau crépuscule qui met chaque objet en valeur. *La Chute (1956)*

The flesh is dangerous to the extent that it refuses to love God, but also to the extent that it involves itself indiscreetly in the love of Him.

Purity is the ability to contemplate defilement.

Only the individual human being has an eternal destiny. Human collectivities do not have one. Nor are our direct obligations to them eternal. Only our duty to the human being as such is eternal.

Culture is an implement professors wield to turn out more professors, who will then turn out more professors.

Camus, born in Algeria, wrote novels, essays, and plays. Nobel Prize, 1957.

I want everything to be explained to me or nothing. And reason is helpless before this cry from the heart. . . . The absurd springs from this confrontation between the human call and the world's unreasonable silence.

The absurd is the essential concept and the first truth.

Is it possible to be a saint when there is no God? This is the only concrete problem I know today.

Truth, like light, is dazzling. By contrast, untruth is a beautiful sunset that enhances everything.

INDEX OF AUTHORS

INDEX OF FIRST LINES, FRENCH

INDEX OF FIRST LINES, ENGLISH